Rosie Hendry lives by the sea in Norfolk with her husband and two children. She is the author of the East End Angels series, uplifting and heart-warming sagas that follow the lives and loves of Winnie, Frankie and Bella, who all work for the London Auxiliary Ambulance Service (LAAS) during the Blitz. Listening to her father's tales of life during the Second World War sparked Rosie's interest in this period and she loves researching further, searching out gems of real life events which inspire her writing.

Keep up to date with Rosie by following her on Twitter, becoming her friend on Facebook or visiting her website:

@hendry_rosie
rosie.hendry.94
www.rosiehendry.com

Also by this author

The East End Angels
Secrets of the East End Angels
Christmas with the East End Angels

Rosie HENDRY

Victory for the East End Angels

sphere

SPHERE

First published in Great Britain in 2019 by Sphere

3 5 7 9 10 8 6 4

A CIP catalogue record for this book
is available from the British Library.

ISBN 978-0-7515-7569-9

Typeset in Bembo by M Rules
Printed and bound in Great Britain by
Clays Ltd, Elcograf S.p.A.

Papers used by Sphere are from well-managed forests
and other responsible sources.

MIX
Paper from
responsible sources
FSC® C104740

Sphere
An imprint of
Little, Brown Book Group
Carmelite House
50 Victoria Embankment
London EC4Y 0DZ

An Hachette UK Company
www.hachette.co.uk

www.littlebrown.co.uk

For Tom,
with love.

Chapter One

February, 1944

'Ready?' Bella glanced across at Frankie who was sitting beside her in the ambulance cab, her friend's face shadowy under the brim of her steel helmet, while the white letter 'A' painted on the front stood out in the pale, ghostly moonlight cast down by the full bombers' moon streaming in through the windscreen.

'Yes.' Frankie nodded. 'Let's go.'

Bella put the ambulance into gear and pulled away, carefully steering it through the narrow archway that led out of Station 75 and onto the Minories, then, turning right, they headed towards the Tower of London which stood blackly silhouetted against the red glow of burning buildings across the far side of the River Thames. Following a familiar route, Bella drove them further into the East End towards the incident that they'd been sent to.

'Blimey, that was close!' Frankie yelped, as a loud

1

explosion in a neighbouring street made them both jump in surprise.

'We don't want anything closer than that, thank you very much.' Bella aimed her words upwards, looking at the sky which was criss-crossed with searchlights trying to catch enemy planes in their probing beams. The drone of the bombers' unsynchronised engines flying overhead, the sound of which always made Bella's blood run cold, kept on and on, like a backing soundtrack to the destruction that was being rained down on London yet again.

After the huge, devastating raid in May 1941 that had ended the Blitz, there hadn't been any big bombing raids and Londoners had once more grown accustomed to spending the whole night sleeping in their own beds instead of having to flee to the shelters when the air-raid sirens started to wail. The ambulance crews of Station 75 had become used to quieter shifts, but all that had changed last month when the bombers had once more turned their sights on London, and they'd been coming back regularly ever since. People had started to call it the mini Blitz, and how long it would go on for was anyone's guess. Bella hoped it wouldn't live up to the ferocity of the first one, which had mercilessly pounded London for months on end, leaving so many dead and injured, and changing the city landscape for ever.

'I don't think they can 'ear you,' Frankie said.

'I know, but it makes me feel better.' Bella slowed as she reached the junction and turned left, bumping the ambulance slowly across some fire hoses that snaked across the street to where firemen were tackling a blaze in a shop, probably started by one of the many incendiary bombs that had been raining down.

Finally arriving at the incident they'd been sent to, she saw that there'd been a direct hit on one house, hollowing it out of the row, like a missing tooth, and causing several neighbouring houses to crumple in on themselves, spilling rubble out across the road. Bella pulled the ambulance over to the side of the road where the waiting ARP man signalled for her to stop. Winding down her window she called out to him, 'What have you got for us?'

'Three casualties pulled out so far, all alive, but there's more in there. I ain't so sure about them yet, they're still trying to dig them out but it ain't helped by them buggers still dropping bombs on us.' He winced as another loud crump filled the air from a few streets away.

'We'll load up who you've got to start with,' Bella said.

He nodded and touched the rim of his steel helmet. 'Right you are then.'

Bella turned to Frankie. 'Here we go again.'

Outside, they slipped into a well-rehearsed routine, taking stretchers out of the back of the ambulance and hurrying over to the casualties, ready to quickly assess them; their job was to provide basic first aid and get them to hospital where they could be properly treated. Always, they had to make sure their patient was as comfortable, warm and secure as they could make them.

'Hello, I'm Bella.' She knelt beside an old woman who was coated in a thick layer of grey dust making her look like a ghost. She was shivering, despite the blanket draped over her, not surprisingly as it was a cold night.

Bella felt cold herself, despite wearing her greatcoat, scarf and gloves.

'Herbert, my 'usband, 'ave they found him yet?' the old woman asked, her voice croaky with dust.

'I'm not sure, but the rescue workers are searching right now,' Bella reassured her. 'What's your name?'

'Joyce, Joyce Stephens.'

'Well, Joyce, I just need to check you over to see if you've broken anything, and we'll get you in the ambulance tucked up with some hot-water bottles to warm you up. Do you hurt anywhere?'

'Me ankle.'

Bella gently felt her ankle and could tell that it was broken. She felt along the rest of her limbs but apart from scratches, bruises and the broken ankle Joyce had come out of the bombed house relatively unscathed.

'Right, I'm going to sort your ankle out, so it will be more comfortable while we get you to hospital, all right?'

Bella took some bandages and splints out of her bag and carefully arranged and secured them around Joyce's ankle. 'There you are, that should keep it from moving around.' She took a label out of her bag and started to fill in the details ready for the hospital to use – Joyce's name and address, time of incident and type of injury – then she secured it to a button on the older woman's cardigan. 'That's so they know who you are and what you've been up to.'

'Thank you, ducks,' Joyce said.

After Frankie helped her move Joyce onto a stretcher, Bella swapped the blanket over for one of the Ambulance

Service blankets and then secured the straps around her to stop her falling off when they moved her. 'Right, you're all tucked in and ready to go in the ambulance as soon as my crew mate's ready.' She looked over to where Frankie was attending to another casualty, going through the same routine, checking, treating and labelling ready for the hospital.

'You nearly done, Frankie?' Bella called over to her.

Frankie looked up and nodded.

'You'll 'ave a look for my Herbert, won't yer?' Joyce asked, pulling her hand out from under the blanket and grabbing hold of Bella's arm.

'Of course I will, we'll just get you safely into the ambulance and then I'll ask.' Bella looked up at the ARP man who'd just come over from where the rescue workers were digging out more casualties and must have heard what Joyce had said. He looked at Bella and gave the slightest shake of his head, the meaning painfully clear – they'd now found Joyce's husband, but the outcome wasn't good, he was dead.

Bella nodded at him and swallowed hard. She couldn't tell her, now was not the time or place.

'Ready?' Frankie said, coming over. 'Shall we take this lady first?' She smiled at Joyce.

Bella nodded and went to the head of the stretcher and took hold of the handles. 'On the count of three – one, two, three.' Together she and Frankie carried Joyce into the ambulance, where she tucked some hot-water bottles in beside her to warm her up.

After they'd loaded in three other casualties and while

5

Frankie made the final preparations in the back of the ambulance before they left, Bella hurried over to the ARP man to check that she'd got the right message. 'Did they find Joyce's husband?'

He nodded. 'Yes, poor fella's gone, nothing any of us can do for him now.' He nodded to where some bodies lay, shrouded in blankets; Joyce's husband clearly hadn't been the only one killed here tonight.

Bella shook her head. 'Poor Joyce.'

'They'd been married for nearly fifty years,' the ARP man said. 'They was goin' to have a celebration in the Blue Flag next week, my missus and me were goin'.' He sighed and shrugged. 'You'd better get her to hospital, they'll look after her and I'll go and see her in the mornin', tell her what happened.'

Back at the ambulance Bella checked in the back where Frankie would stay with the casualties on the journey to hospital. 'Ready to go?' Bella asked.

Frankie nodded. 'We're all set.'

'See you at the London.' Bella closed the back doors and went around to the cab, climbed in, started the engine and pulled away gently, doing her best to make the journey as smooth as she could, aware that every bump and jolt could cause pain to the casualties. She was constantly on the lookout for any craters or rubble scattered across the road, that might jerk the ambulance, and that, combined with sticking to the strict sixteen miles per hour top speed that ambulances were allowed to travel, helped to make it a comfortable journey for their patients.

As she drove, Bella couldn't stop her mind from thinking

about Joyce and how she'd feel when she found out about her husband's death after fifty years together – the poor woman would be devasted. Her life would never be the same again. Bella bit her bottom lip, aware of how that felt; she hadn't been married to someone for fifty years, not even engaged, but she'd loved James dearly and when he'd been killed on that foggy Armistice Day in 1942 when London had been shrouded in a thick, dank fog, knocked over by a bus he didn't see until it was too late . . . She knew how it felt to suddenly lose someone you loved. How much it hurt. And went on hurting. That was something Bella never wanted to experience again; she wasn't ever going to put herself in a position where that might happen again. They say it is better to have loved and lost than never to have loved at all, she thought. Yes, perhaps, but she'd done just that and bore the scar and wasn't planning on repeating it – a career was a better, safer path for her to take and she was already well on the way to it now she was selling more of her writing to magazines.

'Are we nearly there?' Frankie's voice coming through the grille at the back of the cab brought Bella's mind back to the present.

'Another five minutes.' And then they'd hand over their casualties and go back to Station 75. Poor Joyce would have her broken ankle fixed, Bella thought, but the broken heart she'd get when she heard about her husband wouldn't be so easily mended.

Chapter Two

Winnie stroked Trixie's butter-soft ears while the little dog slept on her lap. She'd curled herself up and seemed oblivious to the sounds of the air raid going on outside Station 75's air-raid shelter. She loved the way Trixie could go to sleep no matter what was happening. It was surprising that she could after what had happened to her – being buried in a raid under the rubble of a bombed-out house in which her previous owner had perished – but she seemed to have forgotten it and was now happily living with Winnie and being an unofficial part of Station 75's crew. Winnie wished she could switch off and go to sleep like her dog, it would make sitting here waiting so much easier.

'Are you all right?' Rose whispered. She was sitting next to Winnie and had been engrossed in a book since they'd come in here.

Winnie nodded. 'I'm still not used to these raids.' She

spoke softly so that only Rose could hear her. 'I'm afraid I'd got rather used to the quieter shifts that we'd been having.' She shrugged. 'But I'm sure I'll get used to air raids again if they carry on long enough.'

She glanced up and saw that Station Officer Steele was looking at her, the older woman raising her eyebrows at her questioningly. Being Deputy Station Officer, Winnie knew that it wouldn't do for her to show her discomfort, so she smiled back at the boss as if she were feeling perfectly at ease while bombers flew overhead and there was the distinct possibility of being sent out at any moment to an incident in the middle of tonight's raid.

The arrival of the mini Blitz had come as a shock to them all, but they had no option other than to do as they'd done during the first Blitz and get on with the job. Glancing around at the other crew members who were sitting along the benches that lined the inside of Station 75's shelter, she could see everyone was occupying themselves while they waited for a call-out: some people were reading, others playing a rowdy game of cards, a few, like Trixie, even trying to snatch a bit of sleep despite the noise of the bombers and crump of falling bombs.

The sudden jangling of the telephone made everyone stop and stare at Station Officer Steele as she snatched up the receiver and listened intently to the message. She grabbed a chit of paper and quickly began writing down the details of the call-out. Winnie knew everyone would be thinking the same question: who would be sent out to attend the incident?

'Winnie, Rose,' Station Officer Steele said without looking up as she finished writing up the chit.

Winnie looked at Rose as they stood up in unison, and the younger girl nodded back at her and smiled, knowing the routine well. Tucking Trixie, who'd been woken up by the telephone, under her arm, Winnie made for the door of the shelter, going out first to get the ambulance started as the drivers always did while Rose, who worked as the attendant, got the chit and found out where they needed to go.

Outside, the drone of the planes was even more ominous and when she glanced up into the moonlit sky, Winnie saw their black silhouettes passing over the pale face of the full moon; it sent a shiver down her spine. Trixie whined, and Winnie hugged her tightly.

'It's all right, Trix.' She stroked the little dog's head as she hurried over to the garages where the ambulances stood prepared and ready to go.

By the time Rose came out, Winnie had started the ambulance, pulled out of the garage into the courtyard and was ready to leave.

'Any clue what the incident is?' Winnie asked as she drove along, her hands clasped tightly around the steering wheel.

'Of course not,' Rose replied. 'You know that there never is on the chit, only the address to go to.'

'I know, but I'm trying to keep my mind busy wondering, that's all.' Winnie winced as another loud boom from the ack-ack guns reverberated through the streets from the nearest gun emplacement. She wondered if they

10

ever actually hit an enemy plane, but she supposed at least the sound of them blasting off made the people cowering under the falling bombs feel that something was being done to protect them.

Without the coming incident to ponder over, Winnie's mind reverted to the safety of her favourite thoughts, those about her husband, Mac. He had been a conscientious objector who'd come to work at Station 75 as an ambulance driver back in 1940, and during the last Blitz he'd often been out to incidents with her. She'd loved being out with him, even with bombs raining down, but after the bombing had stopped he'd wanted to do more and had left to join bomb disposal. Winnie had hated him working there, fearing every day that he'd get blown up by one of the UXBs that it was his job to dig up, but thankfully he hadn't and last year she'd been so relieved when he'd left bomb disposal – moving on as there was less bombing and so fewer UXBs to deal with – and volunteered to join the Parachute Field Ambulance. The only problem with his new unit was that it would mean he'd be parachuting into enemy territory when the invasion of Hitler's Fortress Europe began. When that happened, she'd be exchanging one worry about him for another. Winnie sighed, she'd be worrying about Mac until this damn war was over and when that would be nobody could tell. It couldn't come quick enough for her.

When they reached the incident, there was an unusual sense of panic and worry in the air: an underground shelter had caved in from the force of an explosion and when some rescue workers had gone in to bring out the

11

casualties the structure had collapsed, trapping them inside as well. The rescuers left on the outside were now frantically digging to get out their own people as well as those originally trapped in the shelter.

'Let's hope they're still alive in there,' an ARP warden said as Winnie and Rose pulled a stretcher out of the back of the ambulance ready to receive the first casualty.

Winnie nodded; it was bad enough innocent people getting hurt by the bombs, especially when they were in a shelter that was supposed to protect them, but when those that had gone in to rescue them had, in turn, been hurt or worse, it seemed doubly tragic. There was nothing they could do but wait and hope.

It couldn't have been more than a few minutes and yet felt much longer before the shout went up from one of the rescue workers. News quickly spread that the trapped rescue workers were alive and had been digging their way out from the inside. A short while later the first of the casualties were brought out and Winnie and Rose jumped into action.

The young woman whom Winnie was treating was unconscious, so she had to write an X for her name on the label she filled in for the hospital, hoping they would find out who she was when she came round, if she came round. At least she had made it this far; some of the others who'd been in the shelter hadn't been so lucky and they were being brought out and covered with blankets, ready to be picked up by the mortuary van later.

In the end there were only two survivors from those originally in the shelter when it was damaged, and when they were loaded into the back of the ambulance, Rose stayed with them, keeping a close eye on them for the journey to hospital. Winnie closed the back doors and climbed back into the cab with Trixie who'd been waiting for her. The little dog came over, wagging her tail ecstatically, and Winnie allowed herself a quick hug, resting her head on Trixie's to regain a bit of happiness before she had to drive to the London Hospital where she hoped the doctors and nurses could save the young woman and the little girl that Rose had treated. Putting Trixie over on to the passenger seat she took a deep breath and started the engine – this was her job and she would do it the best she could because these people were relying on her and she wasn't going to let them down.

Chapter Three

Bicycling home a little after nine o'clock the next morning having just finished her twenty-four-hour shift at Station 75, Frankie's thoughts were focused on what she always worried about when she headed home after a raid – would her home in Matlock Street, Stepney, still be standing? As she and Rose pedalled along side by side, they could see evidence of the night's bombing: windows with the glass blown in; collapsed and crumpled buildings spilling rubble across pavements; bits of shrapnel pitted into the road; and the acrid tang of smoke in the air from fires that were still burning.

Turning into Matlock Street she sighed with relief at the sight of all the houses in the terrace still standing and in one piece. So far, the street had been extremely lucky, with minimal damage, just some broken slates and fire damage to one house from an incendiary bomb during the Blitz. No one had died or been injured or lost their home.

'Mornin', ducks!' Josie called to them, as she stopped sweeping the pavement outside her home at number 5, her breath pluming in the cold air. 'We made it through another raid.'

'Frankie! Rose!' Flora, Josie's two-year-old daughter, dropped her own little brush at the sight of them and rushed over, her arms outstretched, ready for a hug.

Frankie braked and jumped off her bicycle, bending down and scooping Flora up into her arms and hugging her warmly. She had a special bond with the little girl, having been there when she was born, and had enjoyed watching her grow up into a delightful character.

'Rose's turn, now.' Flora wriggled to be put down and as soon as her feet touched the ground she flung herself at Rose who hugged her back with equal enthusiasm. She, like Frankie, had been there when Flora had been born and the two of them had also developed a warm and loving relationship.

'Now that's what I call a fine greetin',' Josie said, watching the proceedings with a smile on her face and one hand on her ample hip.

'It's a lovely way to be welcomed home,' Rose said, hitching Flora onto her hip while she balanced her bicycle against the other.

'Just what we needed this mornin'.' Frankie tucked a stray wisp of her auburn hair behind her ear. 'It was rough out there last night again.'

Josie shook her head. 'There was plenty of lumps and thumps of bombs goin' off, made our Anderson shiver and shake at times. Mind you, Flora slept right the way

15

through it. Do you think it's goin' to go on as long as the last Blitz? I 'ope not.'

Frankie shrugged. 'I wish I knew. We'll just 'ave to wait and see.'

'Any news from your young man?' Josie asked.

Frankie shook her head. 'Not for several weeks now. He did warn me in his letters not to be disappointed if I don't 'ear from him for a bit as he might be moving around a lot and it's difficult for letters to get through . . . but I can't 'elp worrying when I don't hear anything.'

Frankie's fiancé, Alastair, was now working as a doctor in Egypt as part of the Royal Army Medical Corps and she hadn't seen him since he'd been shipped out in September 1942 which seemed like a lifetime ago now. His letters had become a lifeline for her, a fragile connection between them which she desperately missed when they failed to arrive regularly.

'Perhaps there'll be a letter in the post for you today,' Josie said. She reached out her arms to take Flora from Rose. 'Come on, you, we need to go shoppin' or the butcher will have run out of meat by the time we get there.'

Frankie looked at Rose. 'We need to go shoppin' as well, the cupboard's getting bare. We might see you there later on, Josie.'

Josie laughed. 'I'll see you in the queue then.'

As soon as she opened the door of number 25 Matlock Street, Frankie knew that Ivy, her step-grandmother, was at home – the wireless was playing in the kitchen and she could smell fresh toast. Instantly, Frankie felt herself tensing, preparing for a battle with the vile woman. Glancing

16

at Rose she could see that she, too, wasn't as relaxed as she had been just moments ago when they'd been chatting to Josie. The presence of Ivy in the house always put them both on edge but thankfully their twenty-four-hour pattern of shift work meant that they didn't see very much of the older woman. Ivy had been milder over the past months, Frankie's threat to throw her out after she'd been so vile to Rose did seem to have had some effect on her, but she hadn't miraculously become kind, or even pleasant, and now tried to avoid them as much as they avoided her. When they did happen to be in the same room, Ivy said very little and in fact Frankie wasn't sure of the last time she'd heard her speak to Rose. It made for an odd, cold atmosphere when they were all together but that was preferable to Ivy's vindictive, spiteful comments that she used to throw out at Frankie or anyone else whom she felt deserved it. Ivy clearly wanted to stay living here as it was comfortable and easy for her, allowing her to live her life the way she pleased outside her work at Cohen's clothing factory, and she made no effort to hide the fact that she spent most of her wages on buying luxuries like make-up which were hard to come by these days.

Walking into the kitchen Frankie saw that Ivy was in her usual place, sitting in the armchair, her feet propped up on a stool, and a plate of toast balanced on her lap while she flicked through the latest *Picture Post* magazine that she so loved. She didn't even glance up at them, keeping her face looking down so only her peroxide-blonde hair, done up in its fancy style like that of her favourite film stars, was visible; she just carried on munching on her toast which,

Frankie noticed, was thickly spread with butter and jam, far more generously than the rationing would normally allow. Ivy had obviously been spending her wages on black-market food again. Frankie wasn't going to bother arguing with her about it; if she carried on doing it there was a good chance that she'd be caught and in trouble with the police, possibly put in prison. Now that would be good, Frankie thought, before quickly remonstrating with herself for thinking such a thing, because she knew her grandfather would have been mortified to know how low his wife had stooped.

'Cup of tea?' Rose asked, picking up the kettle and filling it up at the sink.

'Please,' Frankie said. 'Actually, why don't I make it while you go and feed the hens?'

'All right.' Rose handed her the kettle and went out through the scullery to the back door to see to their small flock of chickens that they kept at the bottom of the garden.

Frankie put the kettle on to boil, aware of what she'd just instinctively done, sending Rose out rather than leaving her on her own in the kitchen with Ivy. Although Ivy had avoided any arguments with Rose, Frankie still didn't trust her to not make some unpleasant jibe at her if they were alone together and she felt very protective of Rose, who'd become more like a younger sister than a work colleague and lodger in her home. Rose had had enough to deal with in her life already, having had to leave her family behind in Austria when she was sent to safety by her parents on the Kindertransport before the start of the war.

18

While the kettle boiled Frankie cut some slices of her and Rose's loaf of bread and put it under the grill to toast. They'd had some breakfast at the end of their shift, but she was feeling hungry after their busy night and knew that she would need to catch up on some sleep before they went out shopping later.

Looking in the larder for their butter ration she saw that only a small bit was left – the amount they were allowed didn't go very far but looking at the dish in which Ivy kept hers she didn't have the same problem, she still had plenty left and it was far more than one person's weekly ration. It had to be black-market butter and for that reason alone Frankie would never ask Ivy if she could spare some for them – she would say no anyway. The thought of eating something that was illegally bought would make the food stick in Frankie's throat when so many people were doing all they could to help with the war effort, going without and making do and mending, but not Ivy. She wasn't depriving herself of anything and that was utterly typical of the self-centred woman that Frankie had as a step-grandmother.

Chapter Four

Turning into Bedford Place with Trixie trotting along at her heels, Winnie was desperate for a hot cup of tea to warm herself up after their long walk in Regent's Park. Hurrying up the steps of Connie's grand Georgian town-house she let herself in the front door and saw that her godmother was in the hall talking on the telephone.

'Ah! Here she is.' Connie spoke into the receiver, beckoning Winnie to hurry over to her. 'Goodbye then, Mac, lovely to talk to you.' She handed Winnie the receiver, smiling broadly before going downstairs to the basement kitchen.

'Mac? Is everything all right?' Winnie pulled off her gloves and woollen beret.

'That's what I've rung to ask *you*.' Mac's familiar voice, with its distinctive warm Gloucestershire accent that she loved so much, came down the line, filling her with longing to see him again. 'I heard that there'd been more bombing on London and was worried about you, needed to check that you're all right.'

'I'm absolutely fine, a bit tired but nothing a decent night's sleep won't fix if the bombers will keep away long enough so that we can stay in our beds all night, or not have to go out to incidents if I'm on shift.'

'Connie said you had a busy shift last night.'

'Rather. Busy shifts with lots of call-outs are taking some adjusting to, but we managed last time and I'm sure we'll get used to it again if it goes on for long enough. What about you, are you all right?'

'I'm a bit bruised. I landed awkwardly on today's jump, the wind caught my parachute just as I was coming in to land and swung me around, so I landed on my backside instead of my feet,' Mac said.

'Are you sure you're not hurt, no bones broken?'

Mac laughed. 'Only my pride because I thought I'd got over those type of landings.'

The thought of her husband throwing himself out of an aeroplane wasn't something that Winnie liked to think about too much, but it was all part of the job when you were in the Field Ambulance Parachute unit and Mac had explained how it all worked to try and stop her worrying about him. At least he didn't ever have to fall through the air like some flightless bird after jumping out of the plane, desperately hoping his parachute would open when he pulled the ripcord, Winnie thought, because thankfully they used static-line parachutes which opened automatically as soon as they left the aircraft. When the time came for Mac to be parachuted into France he'd also have to take a large bag of medical supplies and a stretcher with him. His job now was much more physically demanding of him than his role at Station 75 used to be – as well as jumping out of planes he often had to complete route marches with heavy kit to practise for what he might have to do once the Allied invasion began.

'Any news about some leave?' Winnie asked, ever hopeful that Mac would be given some time off and be allowed to come home. She missed him desperately and since they'd been married they had only managed snatched days here and there together.

'Not at the moment, they're keeping us busy, but I hope they'll give us some leave before . . . ' Mac didn't need to finish what he was saying as they both knew what was coming and the role that he'd have to play in it. Winnie just hoped the army would send him back to her before they sent him to face the enemy in occupied France.

'I hope . . . ' Mac began but stopped. Winnie could hear another man's voice in the background but not what he was saying. 'Look, I'm going to have to go now, we're due on the parade ground again. I hope there's no raid tonight and you can catch up on your sleep.'

'So do I,' Winnie said. 'We're going to the pictures and doing a collection for the Red Cross prisoner of war parcels appeal after the film. It's *Jane Eyre* and I'd rather like to see it right the way through to the end.'

'Enjoy yourself, goodbye, Winnie.'

'Goodbye, I—' Winnie stopped, Mac had gone. Replacing the telephone receiver in its cradle she felt a warm glow of happiness at the unexpected chance of talking to her husband but the awful feeling that it wasn't enough crept in at the edges and left her wanting more. They never had enough time to talk or be together and wouldn't until this war was over because their life together was dependent on the whims of the army. She bent down and scooped Trixie up, who had been patiently sitting beside her, hugging her tightly against her greatcoat. She knew she should be grateful to have any personal contact with Mac, because for so many wives the only communication they had with their husbands was by flimsy letters, often weeks after they were written, and they may not have seen their husbands for months or even years. Compared with that she was lucky, and she needed to remember that.

Chapter Five

'This is it,' Bella whispered to Frankie who was sitting next to her in the packed picture house.

Frankie squeezed Bella's arm in response, both of them looking forwards to where the beam of light sliced through the fog of cigarette smoke like a lighthouse through mist, projecting the opening images of *Until the Day* on to the large screen at the front of the picture house.

They'd already watched the most recent film from the Ministry of Information – *Naples is a Battlefield* – which had shown the devastated city which had now been liberated by the Allies, who were helping to get it up and running again, and now it was the turn of the Red Cross's *Until the Day* charity appeal film which was showing to help raise funds to send parcels out to prisoners of war. Bella, Frankie, Winnie and Rose, each dressed in their Ambulance Service uniforms, would be rattling the tins at the end of the show to collect donations.

Bella had been helping pack prisoner of war parcels for the Red Cross since her brother had been taken prisoner in 1941. She'd wanted to do something to help and knew from Walter's letters how important the parcels were to the men, in some cases making the difference between life and death as they helped to supplement the meagre food rations POWs were fed in the camps. She'd jumped at the chance to help collect money at the pictures and had easily persuaded her friends to help too.

The film started off with the parents of an airman posted to Egypt, eagerly listening to the wireless on Christmas morning in the hope of hearing his voice on one of the recorded messages made by members of the services to family back home. Bella took hold of Frankie's hand, aware of how the film must be touching her with Alastair in Egypt. She, like many people in the audience, had loved ones serving overseas and could relate to the couple on the screen waiting in hope to hear their son. But this was a film designed to raise money and the fate of the son in the film quickly took a turn for the worse as his parents received a telegram that same Christmas morning to say that he was missing in action -- there would be no message from him on the wireless.

The next scene showed his parents having heard the good news a while later, that their son was alive and now a prisoner of war, and in the way of all caring parents, they wanted to do all they could for him. The parents visited a Red Cross office and found out exactly where their son was being held and were shown one of the food parcels that prisoners were sent every week, the contents – which Bella was so familiar with, having packed hundreds of them over the past few years – giving the audience a good idea of exactly what their money would be spent on.

The woman manning the Red Cross office went on to explain the shocking numbers of just how many British POWs were being held – nearly 150,000 in Europe – and that the Red Cross were spending £12,000 a day on sending out parcels, books and equipment to help them get through and survive their captivity. Bella could feel those astonishing figures having a sobering effect on the audience; no doubt many of them knew somebody who was a POW but to know collectively just how many there were, and how much it cost to keep sending out parcels, was staggering.

Finally, the father looked straight towards the camera, seemingly out of the screen and directly to the audience, saying he was sure they would gladly help and now was their chance as there'd be a collection box going round.

The very last shot of the film emphasised the importance of the POW parcels, showing a quote from a POW's letter in large text across the screen. Bella read it knowing how true it was, and if any of the audience were in any doubt of the value of the Red Cross parcels this should show them how vital they were: *If it was not for the Red X parcels many of us would* never *see Blighty again.*

The audience sat in silence for a few moments after the Red Cross appeal film finished, the message hopefully sinking in, while the projectionist readied the main feature.

Winnie leaned forward in her seat on the other side of Frankie. 'If that doesn't get people to put their hands in their pockets afterwards, then nothing will,' she said in a voice loud enough for nearly the whole picture house to hear. 'It could happen to anyone's son, husband, father or brother.'

Bella smiled at her friend who was the perfect ally to have with her, she wasn't shy about getting the point across. 'I hope so.'

'We'll be rattling our tins,' Frankie added.

Flickering on the screen announced the beginning of the feature film, and Bella settled back into her seat, ready to enjoy watching Orson Welles and Joan Fontaine as Mr Rochester and Jane Eyre.

As the film credits began to roll at the end of the film, Bella felt the familiar sense of having to pull herself back to reality; it was always the sign that she'd really enjoyed it and that it had swept her away from her everyday life for a while. This film had pulled her in more than usual as it was based on one of her favourite books, a story that she'd read so many times over the years, and seeing it brought to life had been a joy.

'Come on, Bella.' Frankie got up from her seat. 'We need to get in place to take the collection.'

The collection – of course, that was what they were there for, to collect money for the Red Cross. Bella picked up her collection tin from where she'd put it by her feet and got up from her seat at the end of the aisle, with Frankie, Winnie and Rose following. They made their way to the exit; she and Frankie would go around to the door at the other exit while Winnie and Rose would wait with the collection tins at this one. Hurrying around to the other door they were in place by the time the audience started to filter out.

'Give your donations to help send more POW parcels 'ere,' Frankie said, rattling her collection tin as the audience passed by.

Bella was pleased to see that the film had obviously touched people as most of them gave some money as they passed by and her collection tin quickly grew much heavier with coins.

'My son's a POW,' one woman said as she put some coins in Bella's tin. 'I had no idea it cost so much every day to keep those parcels going. I know how important they are to him.'

'My brother's a POW, too,' Bella said.

The woman smiled sympathetically. 'We won't settle until they're home again, eh?'

Bella nodded. 'In the meantime, it's the parcels that help keep them going.'

After Bella had handed in the collection tins to the manager of the picture house to be put in the safe ready for someone from the Red Cross to collect tomorrow, they all headed to a nearby café for tea and toast.

'That Red Cross film nearly had me in tears,' Winnie said, reaching for a piece of toast from the plate the waitress had put in the middle of the table.

'It was meant to pull at your 'eartstrings,' Frankie said. 'That bit at the start when they were waiting to hear

28

messages on the wireless from servicemen in Egypt ... '
She stopped and shrugged.

'Made you think of Alastair?' Bella touched Frankie's arm.

Her friend nodded and took a sip of tea.

'The main thing is that it made people put their hands
in their pockets,' Winnie said. 'We must have collected
quite a bit and if they're showing that film in all picture
houses it's going to bring in a lot of money to the Red
Cross.' She smiled. 'I rather enjoyed shaking my collection
tin at the audience as they came out.'

Rose laughed. 'You embarrassed that man who walked
past without giving a donation.'

'He said he'd forgotten, but at least he gave some
money, he'd have walked off and not given a penny if I
hadn't called after him,' Winnie said.

'You want to watch out, the Red Cross will be ropin'
you in to collect after all the films if you're going to get
everyone to give,' Frankie said. 'No one would dare say
no to you when you're in full flow ....' She stopped as the
familiar sound of the air-raid siren began its plaintive wail
over the London roof tops. 'Not again!'

'Come on, grab a piece of toast,' Winnie said, taking
another piece herself. 'We need to get to the nearest shelter.'

Joining the throng of people flooding down into the
nearest Underground station, Bella felt sick and had to fight
the urge to turn around and run back out into the street.
She hated going down into the depths of the Underground
at the best of times and, with the air-raid siren still wailing
and the imminent arrival of enemy bombers, the packed

station was making her heart race and she struggled to keep calm.

Reaching the platform, Winnie led them to some space at the far end, picking her way through the people that were already setting up with their blankets and bags ready to spend another night sheltering underground. Bella trailed behind the others and was glad when she finally sat down next to Frankie and leaned back against the cool tiled wall of the station, her legs feeling as if the bones had been removed and replaced with jelly.

'My toast is stony cold now,' Winnie said, before taking a bite. 'Tastes all right though. Do you remember the last time we spent the night in the Underground?'

'I hope no one's going to 'ave a baby down here tonight,' Frankie said. 'We haven't got Alastair here to deliver one.'

'What happened?' Rose asked.

'We were out dancin' at the Lyceum during the last Blitz when the air-raid siren went off and we had to shelter in Aldwych Underground station,' Frankie explained. 'And while we were down there a woman went into labour and Alastair delivered the baby with the rest of us holding up blankets to give her some privacy.'

'The mother-to-be nearly squeezed your hand off, Frankie, as I recall,' Winnie said. 'You had the job of assisting Alastair while the rest of us held the blankets. It was rather lovely being there when a new life came into the world, even if it was in the middle of an air raid. Do you remember how everyone cheered and clapped when the new-born baby started to cry?'

30

'And 'ow the stationmaster brought us all a cup of tea,' Frankie added.

Bella listened as they told Rose about that night which had been a mixture of emotions from the discomfort and fear of being underground in the raid to the wonder of a new baby being born. Unfortunately, that hadn't been her only experience of Underground stations during air raids; by comparison that night had ended well but the other time she'd had to go to an Underground station during a raid had been horrific. During the last Blitz she and Frankie had been called to Bank station which had received a direct hit, killing and injuring many people, most of whom were there seeking shelter in a place that they'd thought was safe but had turned out to be anything but. Some had been killed while they slept on the stilled escalators, the blast from the bomb, which had hit the booking office, hurtling down the enclosed tunnels right to the platform where people had been blown onto the rails.

'Bella? Are you all right?' Frankie's voice brought Bella back to the present.

Bella looked at her friend who was looking at her, her blue eyes filled with concern. 'I ... I don't like being down here, reminds me of what happened at Bank station.'

Frankie nodded and linked her arm through Bella's. 'That was a bad night and not something you'll forget in a 'urry, but that was exceptional and if you think of all the other nights that people have sheltered in the Underground, for the majority of the time it's been safe, better than being out on the streets like we usually are if we're on shift and called out.'

'I know, but I just don't like being down here so far underground . . . It makes me feel trapped.' Bella wrung her hands together, doing her best to ignore the crumps and thumps that echoed through the ground from falling bombs, and the gentle patter of dust that fell like dirty snow from the ceiling of the tunnel.

'Bella, do you remember . . .' Winnie started but was silenced by a look from Frankie. She got up and came over to where Bella was sitting and crouched down in front of her. 'You're awfully pale, are you feeling ill?'

'She's just feelin' a bit uncomfortable down 'ere, that's all,' Frankie said. 'Bella ain't very fond of Underground stations in air raids 'cos she ain't had the best experiences in them.'

Winnie nodded, her face serious as she took hold of Bella's hand. 'I know, Bella, but we'll be all right and we'll get out of here just as soon as we can. Hopefully this raid won't go on for long and then we can all go back to Connie's house for the rest of the night.' She smiled brightly. 'So, I've been wondering what we're all going to do when this war is finally over,' she said, changing the subject. 'Frankie, are you planning on going back to the garment factory?'

'Not if I can 'elp it,' Frankie said. 'I ain't sure what I'll do but one thing's for sure: I'll be making a home for Stanley to come back to, and Alastair. I suppose he'll go back to working at the London, but as for me . . .' She shrugged. 'After working for the Ambulance Service I don't want to sit sewin' clothes all day again, I'll need to find something else.'

Bella listened as her friends talked, knowing full well what Winnie was doing; her friend was distracting her, doing her best to make being down here more bearable and take her mind off what was going on.

'What about you, Bella?' Winnie asked.

'Well I'm not going back to my old job either,' she said.

'What did you do before?' Rose asked.

'I was a housemaid here in London, and I hated it,' Bella said.

Rose looked surprised. 'I always thought you were a teacher or something like that, you're so clever, Bella.'

Bella shrugged. 'I wanted to be a teacher but after my father died I had to leave school and get a job. Working as a maid gave me a job and a home of sorts. The only good thing about it was I could read any of the books in the house library, which was more than any of the people I worked for ever did.'

'So, what do you want to do next?' Winnie asked. 'Or should I make a guess.' She smiled. 'You'd like to carry on with your writing, you're doing so well with it now, and if you could write full-time imagine what you could achieve.'

Bella's face grew warm. 'Well, I'd love to write full time, but I'll have to wait and see. What about you, Winnie, you've been asking us, now it's your turn.'

Winnie laughed. 'I want Mac to come home so that we can live a normal married life, just that, and it would make me happier than anything else.' She paused for a moment before going on, 'Of course, I'm sure I'll have to find something else to do, you know me, but what it might be I don't know yet. Nothing with lots of rules and regulations though, you know how much I hate them.'

'And there speaks the Deputy Station Officer of Station 75!' Frankie said. 'The woman who has strained and bent the rules more than the rest of us crew members put together.'

They all started to laugh, and a pink bloom spread across Winnie's peachy complexion.

'What about you, Rose?' Bella asked.

'I need to find my parents,' Rose said, her blue eyes filling with tears, 'and then I will see.'

Frankie put her arm around Rose's shoulder. 'We all hope you'll find them and be able to be a family again.'

Bella nodded and smiled at Rose who had become like a younger sister to them all since she'd come to work at Station 75. It was heart-breaking to see her so worried about her parents. She'd had no word from them for a long time and had no idea where they were now. The poor girl lived in hope that they would once again be reunited when the war finally was over.

Chapter Six

Winnie had just fallen into a light doze when the steady wail of the all-clear jolted her awake. Glancing at her watch she saw that it was only half past one in the morning. She stretched her back, which was aching after leaning against the cold tiles lining the platform walls, and looked around her. Bella was sitting upright, wide-awake, her arms wrapped around herself, and it was obvious from the dark smudges under her eyes that she hadn't slept a wink, while Frankie, who was sitting next to her, and Rose were both asleep, their heads resting against each other, Frankie's auburn hair contrasting with Rose's brown hair colouring. They weren't the only ones who'd managed to fall asleep – looking further along the platform there were many huddled forms lying down or propped up against the wall, all sleeping, probably used to having to spend their nights down here – but Winnie wanted her own comfortable bed and with several hours of the night still to go, she'd much sooner go home and get some proper sleep rather than trying to snatch any more down here.

'Shall we go home?' Winnie whispered to Bella.

Bella nodded and quickly stood up, clearly wanting to get out of there as soon as possible.

After gently shaking Frankie and Rose awake, Winnie got up and stretched some more. 'We'll all go back and get a bit more shut-eye at Connie's, it'll be a lot more comfortable there,' she whispered, rubbing her aching back. 'We've got to be at work at nine and I need some more sleep before then.'

Winnie picked her way across the platform, carefully stepping over the sleeping forms with Bella and bleary-eyed Frankie and Rose following.

Back at Connie's house, Winnie organised a place for Frankie and Rose to sleep in one of the spare rooms and everyone quickly took themselves off to bed, glad of a chance to lie down properly and get some proper sleep before they had to report for their shift at Station 75 later that morning.

Connie was already in the kitchen, with Bella, Frankie and Rose sitting around the table eating porridge, when Winnie went downstairs a little after eight. Trixie, who had, as usual, slept in Winnie's room, was delighted to see everyone and threw herself at Bella, Frankie, Rose and Connie in turn, her tail wagging so hard that her whole body swung from side to side.

'Good morning,' Connie said cheerfully as she poured out a cup of tea from the bone china teapot and put it in front of Winnie as she sat down at the table. Trixie plonked herself by her side, having completed her greetings, and leaned against her mistress's legs.

'Mornin', Winnie, thought we were goin' to have to come and wake you up,' Frankie said, smiling at her.

'I could still do with a few hours' more sleep,' Winnie said, running her hand through her honey-blonde hair which hung loose around her shoulders as she hadn't yet put it into its usual rolled style that she wore at work.

'We all could.' Bella scooped up the last of the porridge from her bowl. 'I just hope we don't get a raid tonight, so we can catch up on a bit of sleep later.'

'Would you like some porridge?' Connie asked Winnie.

'Yes, please. Were you all right here last night, Connie?'

'Absolutely, I was a lot more comfortable than all of you in the Underground.' Connie always sheltered in the large cupboard under the stairs during air raids, which they'd made comfortable with a mattress. 'I had a rather surprising telephone call before the siren went off, heard some wonderful news.'

Winnie looked at her godmother who clearly was bursting to share the news. 'What is it?'

Connie handed Winnie a bowl of porridge and sat down at the table opposite her. 'Well, it was Harry, he telephoned to tell me that he's going to be a father! He and Meredith are expecting their first child in August,' she said happily. 'He's quite over the moon about it.'

Winnie was lost for words for a moment – her brother was going to be a father. After all he'd been through, having been badly burned when his Spitfire was shot down during the Battle of Britain, this was a wonderful thing to happen for him, he would make a wonderful father. 'That's marvellous. James would have been delighted. He'd have made a smashing uncle. Is Meredith well?'

'She's blooming, apparently, and Harry's fussing around her like an old mother hen, so she told me when she came onto the telephone.' Connie poured herself a cup of tea. 'And it means of course that you will become an aunt.'

'An aunt who'll no doubt lead her niece or nephew into mischief,' Bella said.

Winnie laughed. 'Isn't that what aunts are supposed to do? Rather like godmothers.' She looked at Connie who raised her eyebrows back at her.

'I don't know what you mean,' Connie said, feigning innocence.

'You have done far more interesting and exciting things with me and my brothers than our parents ever did,' Winnie said. 'I'm sure Harry and Meredith will be much better parents than ours were to us. I know Meredith would never leave her child for someone else to look after, like ours did.'

'Who looked after you?' Rose asked.

'We had an ayah, darling Sita, who was much more of a mother to us than our own.' Winnie paused for a moment, remembering how much love Sita had shown them and how much it had hurt to leave her behind when Winnie had left India and been sent to boarding school in England. She still missed the loving Indian woman very much and wrote to her often.

'I'm sure you're right.' Connie offered the teapot round

for more cups of tea. 'Perhaps your parents will enjoy being grandparents much more than they did parents.'

Winnie laughed. 'I very much doubt that, the only thing my mother would be interested in is bossing Harry and Meredith around to do things the way she thinks they should be done. Luckily, my brother and his wife have minds of their own and aren't afraid to follow what they believe is right. They'll most definitely look after their child the way they want to, and it will certainly be a whole lot better than my mother's way.'

Chapter Seven

Station Officer Violet Steele stood by the common room window of Station 75 looking down at the activity in the courtyard below. Crew members were busy making the daily checks on their ambulances, topping up oil and water, measuring tyre pressure and cleaning the vehicles until they were spotless, or at least as clean as they could get the battle-scarred ambulances to be – most of them bore dents from where they'd been caught by falling rubble or from where bits of shrapnel had landed on them, embedding into the vehicle's bodywork.

'You all right, boss?' Sparky came over and stood beside her.

She glanced at him and shook her head. 'I'm worried, Sparky. The crews are looking tired and strained.'

'Well that ain't surprising, is it? Not with the bleedin' Jerries bombing us again.' Sparky folded his arms across the front of his navy overalls. 'I'd got used to spending the whole night asleep in my bed but now we're either runnin' for the shelter and not getting much sleep in there or laying there awake waiting for the siren to go off. And if you do drop off, you'll be woken up by the Moaning Minnie starting to wail.'

Station Officer Steele sighed. 'Do you think it will go on as long as the last Blitz?'

Sparky shrugged. 'I bleedin' hope not! I just wish they'd get on with the invasion and go and sort Hitler out. 'im and his army have done more than enough damage to this country and wherever they've turned their greedy sights.'

'I don't think Churchill's going to order an invasion until the weather's better.' She looked out the window at the grey sky, where the clouds hung low and heavy, and were being buffeted along by a strong wind. 'Hopefully in the summer, when the weather should make it easier to land forces and the soldiers won't have to battle through mud and freezing weather. It was bad enough in the Great War, and they were only battling over small distances – this time our army will have a lot further to go.'

'I suppose you're right but let's 'ope we don't keep getting bombed right up until then,' Sparky said, before leaving the lookout post and going back down to the courtyard to carry on working on his own ambulance.

Station Officer Steele watched the crews for a few more minutes, hoping that there wouldn't be another air raid again tonight and that they could catch up on some precious sleep. With London being once more at the mercy of the bombers it made her glad that her sister and two nieces had gone to live with her parents down in Devon. They'd considered staying in London with her, but she'd persuaded them to move out to the safety of the countryside, knowing that the bombers could and probably would come back at any time. Her sister and her two girls had already been through enough, having escaped from Singapore when the Japanese invaded, fleeing to South Africa, then boarding a ship to bring them back to England, only to have it torpedoed and sunk by a German submarine. They'd been lucky to survive and had spent some time in a camp in North Africa before finally coming home on Christmas Eve of 1942, which was the best present that she'd ever had. It had been a horribly worrying time not knowing where they were and what had happened to them. At least with them now safely in Devon she didn't have to worry about them, and she could focus her attention fully on running Station 75 and the well-being of her crews. With the bombing and sleep deprivation clearly beginning to take its toll she needed to keep a close eye on them and do what she could to keep up their spirits in any way she could, and she knew what might be just the ticket to help.

Leaving her lookout spot, she headed for the kitchen where Mrs Connelly, Station 75's cook, was busy preparing their midday meal helped by Hooky, who used to work as Winnie's attendant but now worked in the kitchen.

'Mrs Connelly.' Station Officer Steele smiled at the older woman who was busy rolling out pastry to put on top of the pie she was making, her grey curls bobbing about as she worked. 'I have a favour to ask of you: would you be able to make some carrot buns for the crew to have on their tea break this afternoon, please?'

The cook stopped rolling and looked at her. 'If I've got enough carrots, I will. They went down a treat last time I made them, as I recall.'

She nodded, remembering how pleased the crew had been to have the carrot buns which were surprisingly sweet considering the lack of sugar in them. 'Yes, they were extremely popular and had to be divided up fairly so that everybody had their equal share. And I'm sure they'll be delighted to have some more. I think we could all do with a treat with this bombing going on again, don't you? Thank you, Mrs Connelly, I appreciate it very much and I'm sure so will everybody else.'

Chapter Eight

Frankie smudged the pencil shading with her finger, blending it carefully until she was satisfied with how it looked, then she added a few more strokes until she was happy with her drawing of Trixie who lay curled up fast asleep on one of the armchairs in Station 75's common room. It was afternoon break but the common room was quiet for once. Winnie and Rose had gone out to do their weekly voluntary work at the American Eagle club and Bella had gone to the post office to send off her latest story to a magazine.

The ringing of the telephone in Station Officer Steele's office made Frankie jump and woke Trixie up. She stroked the little dog's ears, straining to listen to the boss's voice as she answered, trying to work out if it was a call-out to an incident or not. There hadn't been an air raid, but sometimes they were sent to take patients to hospital if the other Ambulance Service was busy, but as far as she could make out from what the boss said it didn't seem like it.

'Frankie!' Station Officer Steele called as she hurried out of her office and, standing in the doorway, beckoned her. 'Come quick, there's someone who wants to speak to you.'

Frankie hurried to the office. Who would be ringing her? Was Stanley ill? 'Is it Stanley, is he all right?'

Station Officer Steele just smiled at her, her brown eyes warm behind her owlish horn-rimmed glasses, and nodded to the telephone receiver which lay waiting on her desk. 'Go on, pick it up and find out.' And without saying any more she left the office, closing the door shut behind her.

With her heart banging in her chest, Frankie picked up the receiver. 'Hello?'

'Frankie, it's me!'

She knew that voice instantly with its beautiful Scottish accent – it was Alastair.

'Alastair! Are you all right?'

He laughed, the rich sound coming down the wires. 'Absolutely. I'm back, my ship's just docked in Clydeside, in Scotland, and I'll be seeing you soon.'

'You're in Scotland, but how? I thought you were still in Egypt.'

'Not any more, I've been sent home for a while and I want to make good that promise I made to you before I left, remember? I want us to be married when I come down to London. That's if you still want to.'

Frankie laughed. 'Of course I do. When will you be 'ere?'

45

'Since I'm in Scotland I'm going to see my mother for a few days and then I'll come down to London.' Frankie could hear some other voices in the background. 'Look, I'll have to go, there's a big queue for the telephone, lots of the men who came off my ship want to ring someone. I can't wait to see you again, Frankie. I'll be in touch and let you know when I'll arrive in London. Goodbye.'

'Goodbye,' Frankie said. 'I . . . ' But the line went dead, he was gone.

She slowly replaced the telephone receiver, feeling a maelstrom of emotions: shock, elation and excitement. Alastair was home! And she'd see him in a matter of days. Her worry over not hearing from him for weeks had instantly evaporated with the knowledge that he was safe and well, and on top of that he wanted to make good on the promise he'd made her before they left. They were getting married, and soon!

The door of the office opened, and Station Officer Steele looked in. 'Everything all right?'

Frankie nodded and smiled. 'Alastair's coming 'ome! And he wants us to get married.' Saying it out loud to someone made it even more real.

'That's marvellous.' The boss walked across the room and put her arm around Frankie. 'I'm so pleased, I know you've been worried about him. So are you going to get married then?'

'Yes, we've got the chance and I'm goin' to grab it. I'd thought I wouldn't see him again until the war was over but now . . . ' Her voice wavered, her throat thickening with emotion.

46

'It's wonderful news and I'm very happy for you. When is he arriving?'

'In a few days and then we can get married. It will 'ave to be a rushed wedding, nothing fancy, as long as we can be married that's all that matters.'

'Well I'll do everything I can to help you, and I'm sure the others will too,' Station Officer Steele said. 'You can use my wedding dress if you like. It will need altering a bit, of course, like it was for Winnie, but you might have other ideas, so I won't be offended if you don't want it.'

Frankie looked at her boss. 'I'd love to wear it, thank you. It's a beautiful dress and I'd be honoured to get married in it.'

The older woman beamed at her. 'That's one thing settled then. Where will you get married?'

'My local church where my grandparents were married, and where I was christened, that's if the parson will allow it – we'd 'ave to get a special licence as there wouldn't be time for the usual banns to be read, but that ain't nothing unusual these days.'

'We'd better start a list.' Station Officer Steele sat down at her desk and picked up a pen and paper and started to write.

Frankie sat down in the chair beside the desk, marvelling at how things could change in a matter of minutes. Just moments ago she'd been drawing Winnie's little dog and now here she was, thinking about what needed to be done to get married!

*

'Married!' Winnie stared at Frankie for a few moments before throwing her arms around her; she was closely followed by Bella and Rose whose equally stunned faces were now smiling broadly, her friends clearly delighted at the news.

'When?' Bella said, loosening her hold on Frankie and stepping back to look at her. 'And where?'

Frankie told them all about what she and the boss had talked about and what needed to be done. 'I was 'oping you three would be my bridesmaids.'

'Absolutely, try and stop us,' Winnie said. 'Bella, you could wear the silk dress you wore for my wedding and I could wear the one Frankie wore, and Rose, I've got just the perfect dress for you, too.'

'I don't know if I should, you've both known Frankie so much longer than me,' Rose said.

'That don't matter,' Frankie said. 'You're like a sister to me and I truly would like you to be my bridesmaid as well.'

Rose's face flushed prettily, and she smiled. 'Then I would be very happy, thank you, Frankie, I am honoured that you asked me.'

'Well,' Winnie said, her hands on her hips, 'we've got a wedding to arrange and look forward to – this is going to be fun.'

Frankie smiled at her dear friends. She couldn't imagine getting married without them by her side.

Chapter Nine

Bella couldn't sleep. She lay on one of the mattresses on the floor of the women's rest room at Station 75. Around her she could hear the soft, rhythmic breathing of other sleeping crew members who were taking advantage of the air-raid-free night to catch up on some sleep. She was tired, the lack of sleep from spending half last night in the Underground made her body feel heavy and sluggish and yet her mind wouldn't rest and allow her to drop off, it kept thinking about her brother Walter, wondering where he was and if he was still alive.

It was no good lying there going over and over the same questions which she had no answer to, she decided. If she got up she could do some writing – at least thinking about characters and their stories would help distract her own thoughts. Bella got up and quietly tiptoed her way between the mattresses, glad of the sliver of light coming in from under the door which safely guided her past her sleeping colleagues.

After making herself a cup of tea in the common room's kitchen area, she settled down at the table and picked up her pencil and started to write in her notebook, losing herself in her latest story which she'd set in the countryside where she'd grown up.

As always, when she was engrossed in her writing, she was unaware of the passage of time and it was only when she stopped to take a sip of tea and found that it had gone stone-cold that she realised how long she'd been working. Looking back at what she'd written, she saw that she'd filled up several pages of her notebook. She'd need to type it up on Connie's typewriter before it was ready to send off to *The People's Friend* magazine to whom she'd sold many stories and articles over the past year.

'Would you like another cup, only hot this time?' Station Officer Steele asked from her office doorway. She always stayed in there, or within hearing distance of the telephone, right through the night just in case it rang, never seeming to tire or needing to lie down and sleep like the rest of the crew did if there were no incidents to go out to.

'Yes, thank you, I got distracted and forgot to drink it.' Bella passed the cup to the boss.

'Sounds like a good story then. I'll be back in a moment with a fresh cup.'

Sitting down at the table opposite her a short while later, with fresh cups of hot tea for them both, Station Officer Steele fixed her shrewd brown eyes on Bella's face. 'Couldn't you sleep? Only you look like you could do with some, if you don't mind me saying so.'

She shook her head. 'My mind wouldn't rest, it kept thinking the same things over and over, trying to work out an answer when there isn't one to be had, not yet anyway, and maybe never.' She shrugged and took a sip of tea, enjoying the warmth of the hot liquid as it went down.

'Sounds like you're worrying about something you can't fix. Is there anything I can do to help?' the boss probed gently.

Bella sighed. 'I wish there was but there's nothing any of us can do until we hear from Walter himself or from the War Office that something has happened to him, but it doesn't stop my mind from going over and over where he might be and what he could be doing. If he's alive even.' She hadn't heard anything from him since the Italians surrendered last year.

Station Officer Steele leaned across the table and patted Bella's arm. 'Rather like what I went through worrying about my sister when Singapore fell.' She shook her head. 'This blasted war is hard on so many counts – not just for the men and women serving but also for those who are left behind worrying about them and not being able to do anything about it. You just have to keep yourself busy as that helps take your mind off your worries for a while. You're busy enough, Bella, what with your shifts here, writing, and volunteering at the POW parcel packing centre on your days off.'

'I like being busy.' Bella took a sip of tea. 'At least Frankie's worries are over for the moment, it's wonderful that she and Alastair are going to get married. She was

51

absolutely glowing with happiness this afternoon; she deserves it after all that's happened to her.'

'Absolutely, and her happiness rubs off on the rest of us, too. It's going to be wonderful to have a wedding for one of my crew again. Winnie and Mac's was such a lovely day.'

Bella smiled at the memory of her dear friend's wedding day, and soon another friend would marry. 'She's asked Winnie, Rose and me to be bridesmaids which will be fun. I'm making a habit of that role, always the bridesmaid and never the bride.'

'Oh, you don't know that, you're young and there's still plenty of time to meet the perfect man for you to marry,' Station Officer Steele said.

'I've already met him.' Bella's eyes were stinging with sudden tears. 'And I lost him. James was the perfect man for me and no one could ever replace him.' She paused for a moment to compose herself. 'I'm not interested in looking for someone who would always be second best to him.'

The boss frowned, her brown eyes concerned behind her owlish glasses. 'Believe me, I do understand how you feel. I lost my fiancé in the Great War, as you know. He was the perfect man for me but I never dismissed the idea of perhaps finding someone else that I might love and want to marry, but my generation lost so many men the chances of that happening were slim.' She shrugged. 'It hasn't happened, yet, and probably never will now, but I'm happy with my life. Being married isn't everything – better to be single than married to someone who makes your life a misery.'

'It's not just finding someone else, there's always the danger that if you do come to love them that you might lose them again. I don't want to experience that hurt ever again.' Bella twisted her cup around in her hands. 'I still miss James, so very much.'

Station Officer Steele nodded sympathetically. 'Of course you do, and part of you always will, but James wouldn't want you to forgo love if the chance came along again, would he?'

Bella shrugged. 'We never discussed it.'

'You didn't need to, he was a good, kind and very caring man who adored you. He would want you to be happy however that came about, remember that.' She smiled at Bella. 'He would be immensely proud of the way you've carried on and thrilled with the success you've achieved with your writing; you haven't given up even though it was hard.'

Bella nodded, unable to say anything because her throat was aching with emotion and she couldn't trust herself not to cry.

Chapter Ten

Alastair's train was late. Frankie kept glancing up at the huge clock as she paced up and down inside King's Cross station, but its hands seemed to have slowed down and were inching around the clock face so slowly while she anxiously waited for the Edinburgh train which he should be on. Late trains were nothing unusual these days, she told herself, but it didn't help when she was so desperate to see him. She hadn't seen him for over a year and a half and she felt every one of these added extra minutes.

Trying to distract herself, she thought about all that had happened since he'd telephoned Station 75 three days ago to tell her he was home. She'd been busy making arrangements for their wedding: they'd be married by special licence in two days' time at St Dunstan's church, Stepney – where her grandparents had been married and where she'd been christened – and the reception would be held at a pie and mash shop which Alastair had specifically requested and she'd loved the idea of too. The alterations to Station Officer Steele's wedding dress were almost finished, Josie was helping her to do them, and Winnie, Bella and Rose's dresses were all organised and fitted. Now all she needed was the bridegroom.

Frankie's stomach felt as if it were filled with thousands of fluttering butterflies when at last the Edinburgh train pulled up at the platform forty minutes late and with a great shooshing of steam and tang of coal. She watched eagerly as the carriage doors opened and passengers began to spill out, many of them servicemen and women in the khaki, black or air force blue of the different service uniforms. Scanning the faces, she spotted Alastair before he saw her, her heart leaping in her chest at the sight of him.

'Alastair!' she shouted, waving her arms above her head, catching the attention of not just him but many of the other passengers who smiled as she started to run towards him, pushing her way through the crowded platform. He dropped his kitbag and opened his arms wide to capture her and as Frankie flew into them she couldn't help the tears of relief and joy that rolled down her face.

Alastair hugged her tightly and they stood wrapped in each other's arms, oblivious to the passengers skirting round them, many of them smiling at the joyful reunion. When they eventually loosened their hold of each other and stepped back to drink in each other's face, Frankie thought he looked different, there were faint lines fanning out from the corners of his beautiful blue eyes which didn't used to be there, and his face was tanned, unlike most of the people around whose faces were pale and pasty after the long British winter, but he was still her gorgeous Alastair and it was hard to believe that he was actually here – that this wasn't just a dream. Frankie smiled broadly at him, touching his face. 'I can 'ardly believe you're really here, I've been waiting for this moment so long.'

'Me too.' Alastair's eyes held hers for a few moments before he kissed her passionately which earned them several wolf whistles from passing servicemen.

Laughing when they came up for air, they linked hands and headed towards the exit of the busy station.

'I'm starving, let's go and get something to eat,' Alastair said.

Settled at one of the tables in a British Restaurant a short while later, Frankie watched as he tucked in to a plate of shepherd's pie and cabbage. 'You look like you needed that.'

He nodded while he chewed, his mouth full. 'There was no food on the train and it was a long time since breakfast.' He smiled. 'I need something like this to help keep me warm, I've got used to the heat in Egypt. England feels a lot colder than it used to after being there.'

Frankie laughed. 'You come from Scotland where it's often colder than 'ere, you've gone soft.'

He raised his eyebrows and smiled as he took another mouthful of food.

'I thought you'd be sent to Italy, I never expected you to be sent home.' Frankie speared a piece of her own cabbage and popped it in her mouth.

'I would have been, but I had to spend a bit of time in hospital.'

Frankie nearly choked on her mouthful. 'What? When? Why? You never said in your letters.'

Alastair shrugged. 'I didn't want to worry you, and it was only for a couple of weeks. I had a gippy tummy – a touch of dysentery – and it got bad enough to put me in hospital.' He reached across and took hold of her hand. 'I'm perfectly all right now but I lost my field unit and ended up working at the hospital where I was a patient for a bit once I was better. My old unit had gone, been sent on to Italy, so I missed being posted with them otherwise I'd have been there now instead of sitting here with you.' He smiled. 'So, I'm glad I was ill because it's brought me home and we can get married.'

'I was worried when I didn't 'ear from you for a while. I know you did say that can happen sometimes if you're on the move, but I couldn't help it.' Frankie squeezed his hand. 'Are you working with a new unit now?'

He nodded. 'Yes, after a spell working at the hospital I was sent to join a casualty clearing station out in the desert again and now things have quietened down out there they decided to send us all home for a bit.'

'What will happen to you now, will you be posted to a military 'ospital here?' Frankie said.

'I doubt it, but I'll hopefully be in England for a while yet.' Alastair finished the last of his first course and reached for his pudding of apple crumble and custard. 'But I expect I'll be sent abroad again. I've got to go because I need to see this through to the end, Frankie. I'm staying in the RAMC until we've beaten them, I couldn't pull out now even if they'd let me.' He sighed. 'After what I've seen, I need to do my bit to finish this off.'

She couldn't help wishing that his time serving overseas was over, but she knew that in reality an experienced doctor like him would be needed when the invasion began, and it was highly likely that he'd be sent to France. She was lucky to have him come home at all; if it hadn't been for his illness he'd be in Italy right now with little hope of coming home until the war was over, whenever that might be. If there was one thing that this horrible war had taught her, it was that you had to grab at every chance of happiness that came your way and not worry too much about what was coming next.

'Then we need to make the most of it while you are here.' She smiled at him. 'I've arranged for you to stay at Winnie's house until the wedding, now you ain't got your room at the doctors' residences at the London any more, and it wouldn't be right for you to stay at mine, so we thought it was the best place for you for a couple of nights. And after that we'll be on our honeymoon. Are you going to tell me where we're going?'

'No. Otherwise it won't be a surprise, will it?' He put down his spoon and rummaged in his large kitbag, taking out something wrapped in brown paper and handing it to her. 'I bought this for you in Cairo, thought you could perhaps make something nice to wear with it.'

Frankie took the package and carefully unwrapped it, gasping in delight when she saw what was inside. She ran her fingers over the beautiful teal-coloured silk which shimmered in the light and from which an exotic smell of spices and perfume rose up. 'It's so beautiful, thank you. Thank you so much.'

'I thought the colour would suit you and I know how good you are at dressmaking. When I saw it in the market I knew it was perfect for you.'

Frankie got up and went around to his side of the table and threw her arms around him, hugging him tightly. 'I love you, Alastair Munro, and having you come home again is the best thing that's happened to me in a long while.'

Chapter Eleven

Bella sat perched on the arm of Winnie's chair only half listening to Station Officer Steele's morning briefing, her thoughts instead drifting to Frankie who'd been given the day off by the boss to prepare for her wedding tomorrow. It felt odd not to have her here as they'd worked so closely together since her friend had joined Station 75. Loud groans and mutterings brought Bella's attention back to the present and she looked around at her fellow crew members who didn't look very happy.

'Eating sandwiches for just one day isn't going to kill you!' Station Officer Steele said, a hint of impatience in her voice. 'You've all become rather spoiled with hot meals since we switched to twenty-four-hour shifts and got our own station cook.'

'What's going on?' Bella whispered to Winnie.

'The gas was cut off by last night's raid,' Winnie

explained, keeping her voice low. 'So, there'll be no hot meals made for us today – just sandwiches.'

Station Officer Steele tapped a teaspoon loudly against her mug of tea, bringing the common room into silence once more. 'That is quite enough! We have faced far greater challenges during this war and I expect you all to get on with your work without any more fuss. I—' She stopped as Mrs Connelly, Station 75's cook, came bustling into the common room, her face flushed under her grey curls.

'There ain't no need for sandwiches after all, I've had an idea that'll work. I can cook outside! If we get a fire going out in the courtyard I can rig up a tripod over it and hang a cooking pot from it and have other pots standing in the embers as well.' She smiled at the crew. 'Old Hitler's not goin' to stop us from having a hot dinner if I can help it!'

'What are you goin' to burn on the fire?' Sparky said. 'We ain't got much coal ration to spare.'

Mrs Connelly put one hand on her hip. 'There ain't no need for coal if some of you can go out and collect some wood from nearby bomb sites for me – there's plenty of that just lying around. It's perfect for burning on a campfire.'

Station Officer Steele beamed at Mrs Connelly. 'That's a marvellous idea, it'll be rather like the Girl Guides. Sparky, would you and Paterson and a couple of other volunteers go out and collect some wood for the fire?'

Sparky nodded. 'There's plenty of wood further along the Minories where that building got bombed the other week, we'll go there.'

'Excellent,' the boss said. 'In the meantime, the rest of us will get on with our jobs and work up an appetite for Mrs Connelly's dinner.'

'I feel like a bit of a change so I'm going to volunteer to go and collect some wood, do you want to come as well?' Bella asked Winnie as the crew started to disperse to do their usual morning jobs preparing the ambulances.

'Not me,' Winnie said. 'I'd rather work on your and Frankie's ambulance as well as mine, if you don't mind.'

'I'll come with you,' Rose said, standing up from where she'd been sitting on the other arm of Winnie's chair.

Bella smiled at her. 'Good, let's go and volunteer our services to Sparky then.'

The bomb site further down the Minories was proving to be a rich source of firewood: the wheelbarrow which they'd brought with them from Station 75 soon became piled high with pieces of wood that they'd scavenged out of the ruins of the building.

Bella was enjoying doing something different rather than the usual checking of ambulances that they did at the start of every shift. Lifting and carrying the wood was warm work and she and Rose had both discarded their coats, hanging them up on an old pipe that was protruding out of the ruins.

'How was Frankie this morning?' Bella asked, her breath pluming in the cold air as she and Rose worked together to pull out a large chunk of wood from under some rubble, dislodging powdery brick dust that swirled up and settled on their trouser legs.

'I think she's a bit nervous, but excited, too.' Rose smiled. 'It's a big day for her tomorrow.'

'I'm glad Alastair's been sent home so they've got a chance to get married, we all need a bit of joy right now and their wedding is going to be lovely.' Together they tugged at the wood, which finally came free, then they carried it over to the heaped wheelbarrow.

'That's enough on there or we'll never be able to shift it,' Sparky said. 'I'll take this back to the station and come back for some more. I won't be long.' He left, pushing the heavy barrow, whistling cheerfully as he went.

'I heard some good news yesterday,' Rose said as they resumed their search for firewood. 'I had a letter from my uncle telling me that my American cousins are shipping out any day now and will be coming to England, and hopefully I'll get to meet them. Perhaps they might even come and stay at the American Eagle club here in London. I've told them about volunteering there in my letters.'

'It'll be exciting to meet them for the first time; they're your family and yet you've never met.'

Rose nodded. 'But at least I'll be able to see them, unlike the rest of my family.' She paused, a look of pain shadowing her face.

Bella put her hand on Rose's shoulder. 'But you'll be able to see them again one day when all this war is over. Just keep thinking of that and in the meantime enjoy whatever life throws at you, like Frankie's wedding tomorrow, and like when you finally get to meet your cousins.' She could only imagine the heartache that poor

Rose was going through having not heard from her parents in so long and not knowing what had happened to them under the Nazis' brutal regime.

'Come on, we need to find some more firewood or Sparky will be back and be complaining that we've been slacking,' Rose said, nodding to where Paterson was already piling up some wood ready for when the wheelbarrow came back.

Chapter Twelve

Frankie threw a handful of corn into the chicken run and watched the hens fussing and clucking as they pecked at it, shouldering each other out of the way in case there was something better to be had. Watching them always amused her, their antics helping to soothe her if she was feeling out of sorts, like she was this morning. With only one day left to go before the wedding all the preparations were in place, there was just the final fitting of her wedding dress to do with Josie this morning and then everything would be ready. The only other thing left to do was to ask Ivy if she'd made up her mind if she was coming or not. She might as well go and get it over with. She threw the last of the corn into the run, and went inside to face her step-grandmother, feeling as if she was about to put a stick into a wasps' nest.

Ivy was sitting at the kitchen table eating her breakfast of two generous rashers of bacon and a slice of fried bread.

She glanced up at Frankie and without saying anything returned her attention to her plate.

Frankie pulled out a chair and sat down at the table opposite her. 'Ivy, have you made up your mind about the wedding, whether you're comin' tomorrow or not?' She'd asked her two days ago as soon as the church was organised, but the older woman had just shrugged and not given her an answer, only now she needed to know who was coming or not so there'd be enough pies and mash to go around at the reception.

Ivy slowly chewed on her mouthful making Frankie wait for her reply, and then looked at her, her icy-blue eyes cold. 'Why on earth would I want to come and see *you* get married? I ain't havin' time off work and losin' money over you.' Her words dripped scorn.

Frankie felt as if she'd just been slapped in the face by the vile woman's poisonous attitude, she didn't even *want* her to come, but her contemptuous, uncaring jibe still stung. It would have cost Ivy nothing to just say no, there'd been no need for her to say what she had, but that was her step-grandmother all over and she really shouldn't have been surprised by her answer and was annoyed with herself that she let it affect her.

Frankie nodded and stood up. 'Well, don't say I didn't ask you.'

Ivy didn't say anything, just returned her attention to her breakfast and carried on eating.

Walking up the street to Josie's house a little while later, Frankie had managed to shrug off Ivy's nasty response. She was glad she wasn't coming as the foul woman would only have spoilt what was going to be a special day – she hadn't intended asking her at all and it was only because Josie had persuaded her that she should out of respect to the memory of her grandfather that she had.

Opening the front door of number 5 Matlock Street, Frankie called out, 'Only me, Josie,' as she went in.

'I'm in 'ere,' Josie's voice called from the front room.

Frankie went in the room that her friend kept for best, high days and holidays, where the furniture was polished to a gleam and where Josie had set up her sewing equipment to do the alterations on the wedding dress. Seeing it hanging on a coat-hanger from the picture rail, a shiver of anticipation trickled down her spine; she still found it hard to believe that she'd be wearing it for real tomorrow when she would become Alastair's wife. Beside it hung the new dress that Josie had helped her make out of the teal-coloured silk that Alastair had brought her. It had been a rush to finish it, as well as complete the wedding dress alterations, but with both of them working on it they had managed to create a stunning outfit which she would wear when they left for their honeymoon.

Flora jumped up at the sight of her, abandoning her dolls' tea set which she'd been playing with on the floor, and threw herself at Frankie who scooped her up into her arms.

'Hello, Flora.' Frankie hugged her tightly. 'I've finally got Ivy's answer, Josie.'

'Well, is she coming or not?' Josie asked.

'No!' Frankie smiled broadly. 'She said that she ain't

taking time off work and losin' money to come and see me get married. And I'm glad.'

'That woman ...' Josie shook her head, pursing her lips in disgust. 'Well at least she won't be there making a bad atmosphere. It's for the best, but you did the right thing, ducks, in asking her.' Josie tutted. 'Your grandad would've been appalled with her, though.' She paused and then smiled at her. 'The important thing is you'll have your mum there, and young Stanley to give you away as well, it'll be lovely to see him here again.'

Frankie's mother had been delighted to hear that she was getting married and was making the journey down from Suffolk to attend, and to meet Alastair for the first time. Having her mother there – who she hadn't known was alive for most of her life and only discovered the truth after her grandfather had been killed in 1941 – meant a lot to Frankie, she only wished her grandparents could be there too. On top of that, Stanley was returning to Stepney for the day to give her away. He'd insisted on coming as he was the only male member of her family left and their grandad would have wanted him to do it. Frankie was delighted he'd be coming but had insisted that he should go home again that night before any bombers might come back – she wasn't going to risk him getting caught and hurt, or worse, in an air raid.

'And Eve's coming, too.' Frankie was looking forward to seeing her youngest sister again, they'd developed a good relationship through their weekly letters.

'What about the oldest one, Lizzie?' Josie asked.

Frankie pulled a face. 'She wouldn't come even if I

asked her, so I didn't bother. I ain't heard from her or seen her since I went to her balloon site with Bella to interview the crew for one of her newspaper articles, and that's well over a year ago now. Lizzie made it quite clear then that she didn't want anything to do with me.'

Josie frowned. 'The girl's a fool. She should be glad to have a sister in London and take the chance to get to know you.'

She shrugged. 'I ain't bothered, Josie. The way she behaved to me wasn't very appealing and I don't need any more difficult people in my life, Ivy is quite enough!'

Josie laughed. 'I see your point. Right, let's get this dress finished, we just need to check the hem and then I can sew it up properly.' She smiled at Frankie. 'You're goin' to look a picture in it. Your Alastair's goin' to think he's the luckiest man on earth to be marrying you, and he'd be right!'

Chapter Thirteen

Frankie stood in the kitchen of 25 Matlock Street not quite believing what was happening: here she was, wearing her wedding dress, about to leave to go to the church to get married, her mother was with her and Stanley back home too. It all felt rather dreamlike, so many things that had never seemed possible coming together here and now.

'You look beautiful,' her mother said, adjusting Frankie's veil so that it fell evenly at the front. 'I'm so glad I'm here today, I never thought I would be after what I did.'

Frankie smiled at her. 'I'm glad too, though it does feel odd to have you here in the house, it's like the first time for me. I ain't got no memory of when you were here before when I was a baby. Is it strange being back here after all this time?'

Her mother nodded, looking around at the kitchen. 'There's lots still the same as when I was last here – the same clock on the mantelpiece, pictures on the walls, I keep expecting your gran and grandad to walk in.' She sighed. 'They would have been so proud of you today, and your father.'

'Did you marry him at St Dunstan's?'

'No, we were married in France, at a little church near the hospital where I worked. Some of my fellow VAD nurses came and his soldier pals too.' Her mother smiled, looking thoughtful. 'It was lovely, and we had a brief honeymoon at the coast before we both had to go back to the war, and then a few months later I realised I was expecting you and had to leave my job and your father suggested I go home to live here to wait for him to return when the war was over ...' She shrugged. 'But by then he'd been killed – I'm so glad that he got to see you on his last leave.'

'Did you ...?' Frankie began but stopped as Stanley came in from the back garden where he'd been to look at the chickens. 'Is everything all right out there?'

'Yes, the hens are fine, plenty of water and gobbling down the food I threw them,' Stanley said. 'The garden's a lot smaller than I remember it.'

'And you're a lot taller than you were when you were last here.' Frankie looked up at him as he was now several inches taller than her. 'That puts a new perspective on things, plus you're used to the space of the countryside now. Are you ready to walk me up the aisle, then?'

Stanley nodded. 'Is it time to go?'

Frankie glanced at the clock on the mantelpiece. 'A couple more minutes and then we'll leave, I don't want to be late.'

Most of the neighbours, whom she'd known for years,

71

were standing out in the street waiting to see her off as Frankie, her mother and Stanley left for St Dunstan's.

'Good luck to you, ducks,' one called.

'Your fella's a lucky man,' another said.

Frankie smiled at them all. 'Thank you.'

The walk to St Dunstan's didn't take long and luckily the weather was dry although cold, but with a blue sky making the day bright and cheerful, it was perfect for a winter wedding.

Winnie, Bella and Rose were waiting for them outside the church with the parson, having left a little before them from Matlock Street. The three of them looked lovely in their pre-war silk dresses, the colours complementing their complexions perfectly: Winnie in blue, Bella wearing wine-red and Rose in emerald green.

'Here she is!' Winnie said. 'You haven't changed your mind then?' She winked at Frankie. 'Though there was never any doubt of that, you and Alastair are made for each other.'

Frankie smiled at her friend. Now she was here, a whole host of butterflies were looping the loop inside her stomach and although Winnie was right about her and Alastair, she was still nervous.

'All set?' the parson said.

'Absolutely.' Frankie put her arm through Stanley's, the young man standing up proud, looking so smart in his shirt and tie and jacket.

Her mother patted her arm and went into the church with the parson while the others got in position behind her and Stanley, ready to proceed down the aisle.

'Remember, it's not a race, take it slowly, Stanley,' Winnie advised him. 'Give everyone a chance to see how beautiful Frankie looks.'

'Winnie!' Bella said. 'Stanley knows what to do, don't you?'

Stanley nodded, looking worried at his responsibility. 'I'll do my best.'

'I know you will.' Frankie smiled at him. 'I'm glad you're doing this for me. I—' The first bars of the wedding march boomed out from the church organ and the congregation stood up. 'Time to go then.' She glanced back at her friends who were beaming at her encouragingly and then stepped forwards and in through the church doors, her eyes fixing on the familiar and dearly loved figure of Alastair who stood at the front waiting for her. He turned to look at her before she reached him, smiling at her, his eyes full of love, and she returned the look knowing with absolute certainty that he was the man she wanted to be with the rest of her life.

The inside of the windows of the pie and mash shop were steamed up and there was much lively chatter and laughing going on as everyone tucked in to plates of piping hot food. Frankie sat next to her new husband and was blissfully happy.

'That was delicious. I sometimes dreamt about a plate of pie and mash when I was in Egypt, really fancied one as a change from army rations and sand.' Alastair speared his final forkful of pie and chewed with a look of pleasure on his face, then placed his knife and fork down on his cleared plate. 'What?' he asked, noticing she was watching him intently. 'Are you all right?' He took hold of her left hand where the golden wedding ring he'd given her shone brightly against her pale skin.

Frankie nodded, smiling at him. 'I'm absolutely fine, very happy. You know I don't think there are many doctors wanting their wedding reception held in a pie and mash shop.'

'Then they're missing out. This,' he waved his hand at his plate, 'is one of the delightful things that you've introduced me to, Frankie. I never knew what I was missing until you took me to have my first plate of pie and mash.' He gently touched her cheek. 'I'm very happy to be married to you. I—'

'Aye, aye, you two, save all that lovey-dovey stuff for your honeymoon,' Sparky said coming up behind them. 'The boss wants you over there when you can tear yourselves away from each other.' He laughed. 'She's got something for you.'

Alastair looked at her questioningly and Frankie shrugged, she had no idea what it was about, so the pair of them got up and went over to where Station Officer Steele was waiting behind the shop counter next to the owner.

Seeing them approach she tapped a spoon loudly against her cup, making everyone fall silent and turn to look their way.

'Ladies and gentlemen, I'm sure that I speak on behalf of everyone here when I say what a great pleasure it's been to see Frankie and Alastair marry and to share in their obvious joy at being together, and to wish them both a very

74

long and happy marriage.' The room erupted into clapping and cheering with a few loud whistles added to the mix. Waiting for the cacophony to settle down, she then went on, 'On behalf of everyone at Station 75 I would like to present . . . ' she paused for a moment as the owner of the pie and mash shop put a cake on the counter, 'this cake, which our station cook, Mrs Connelly, has baked for you, with rations contributed by crew members.' She tapped the white cardboard cover which from a distance looked like a perfectly iced wedding cake. 'I'm afraid we couldn't run to actually icing it, rations being what they are, but the cake underneath promises to be quite delicious. So, Dr and Mrs Munro . . . ' which elicited more cheering and clapping, 'if you'd like to do the honour of cutting your wedding cake.'

Station Officer Steele carefully removed the cardboard mock-icing cover to reveal a large sponge cake, with a filling of ruby-red jam running through the middle. She handed Frankie a large knife to cut it with.

'Ready?' Frankie asked her new husband, smiling at him as he put his hands over hers, and together they pushed the knife down through the light and fluffy sponge.

'Did you know about this?' Alastair whispered to Frankie.

'No, not a thing.'

While the owner of the shop carefully sliced the cake up into thin portions so that everybody would have a piece, Frankie and Alastair turned to face all their friends and family.

'Thank you, everyone, for being here with us today,'

Alastair said. 'It's not every day I get to marry a beautiful woman like Frankie, and I'm very glad that she waited for me to finally come home.' Frankie's cheeks grew warm. 'Thank you all for giving up your precious rations to bake our wedding cake. My wife and I,' his eyes met hers as he said this, 'very much appreciate it.'

The room erupted into clapping and cheering again, and Frankie looked around at all those present, smiling happily at them – her neighbour Josie, her family and friends from Station 75, each one of them played an important role in her life and having them here with her on this special day made it even better – she would remember this day for the rest of her life.

Station Officer Violet Steele wiped away the tears with her neatly ironed handkerchief with one hand whilst waving with the other, as she watched the taxi carrying Frankie and Alastair away to begin their honeymoon drive down the street until it turned at the end and then vanished from sight.

'Didn't she look a picture, that dress we made from the silk Alastair brought 'ome really suits her. The colour's a perfect match for her auburn hair,' Josie said, wiping the tears from her own eyes. 'Her gran and grandad would 'ave been so proud of her today.'

'They make a lovely couple,' Station Officer Steele said.

Josie nodded and sniffed, pulling herself together. 'Right, I don't know about you, but I'm parched and could do with a good cup of tea and a sit down. How about comin' back to my house in Matlock Street for a brew?'

Violet looked around at the rest of the wedding guests who looked like they would be carrying on the celebrations for a little while yet. The pie and mash shop had closed for other customers for the afternoon and so they could stay there for a while longer enjoying themselves, but the idea of a quiet cup of tea and the chance to sit down was most appealing.

'Yes, thank you, I'd like that very much. I've never been to Matlock Street before and it will be nice to visit and see where Frankie and Rose live.'

'Well you're most welcome.' Josie picked up little Flora who was looking tired, her thumb firmly fixed in her mouth, as she laid her head on her mother's shoulder, her eyes starting to flicker with sleep. 'Come on, this one will soon be asleep, so I can lay her down and we can put our own feet up for a while.'

As they walked down Matlock Street a few minutes later, Josie pointed out, 'That's Frankie's house, number twenty-five. I'm at number five.'

The street of terraced houses was like so many in the East End but had been fortunate not to have been reduced to rubble. Station Officer Steele knew how fond of it Frankie was, and how she'd battled to hang on to her home despite having to live with the unpleasant Ivy.

With little Flora laid down to sleep, Josie bustled around her kitchen and quickly made a pot of tea and produced a packet of biscuits for them to share, spreading some out on a plate.

They sat in armchairs either side of the fireplace in the kitchen. Violet Steele sank back into the chair, a cup of tea cradled in her hands, and relaxed for the first time today.

'You look like you needed that as much as I did,' Josie said, holding her own cup of tea. 'Weddings are lovely, but they don't 'alf take it out of you emotionally, especially when you think so much of the person getting married.'

Violet nodded in agreement. 'I can see that you're very fond of Frankie, as well. She's such a lovely young woman and very easy to grow to care about. I think with all that's happened to her, losing her grandfather the way she did and finding out about her mother, well, it's no wonder we've both taken her under our wings.'

'And don't forget 'aving to put up with Ivy!' Josie took a sip of tea. 'I could swing for that woman, I really could, 'er not coming to the weddin' was downright rude after all Frankie's put up with from her. Gawd knows what her grandfather would have said at the woman's behaviour, he'd be turning in his grave if he 'ad one.'

'I think it was probably for the best that she didn't come. From what I've heard of her she may well have put a damper on such a lovely occasion; better that she kept away than spoil it for Frankie.' Violet Steele took a biscuit from the plate.

'Ivy's more interested in steppin' out with a spiv these days who can keep her in stockings and lipstick – it's a right come-down from being married to a police sergeant.' Josie pulled a face. 'I ain't sure if Frankie knows about him, she ain't said anything and I've not mentioned it to her – I'm not sure if I should or not.'

'What does your instinct tell you?'

Josie frowned. 'Not to, she'll find out soon enough if

she has to, Ivy's no fool, she won't have 'im there when Frankie's at home. In the meantime, I'm keeping an eye on Ivy. Who knows, perhaps she'll marry him and move out, leave Frankie in peace.' She sighed. 'Anyway, while she's got people like you and me looking out for her, she'll be all right.'

'A toast, then.' Station Officer Steele held up her cup. 'To Frankie and Alastair, and all the people who look out for them.'

'Hear, hear.' Josie chinked her cup against Violet's and smiled warmly. 'Tell me about runnin' an ambulance station, then, what's it really like?'

'How long have you got? I could go on about it for hours.'

Josie looked at the teapot. 'We've got as long as the tea keeps comin' and it's a big pot. We can drink it dry and you can tell me about how Station 75 works.'

Violet Steele smiled, she liked Josie immensely and was going to enjoy telling her tales of Station 75. 'Well, first of all ...'

Chapter Fourteen

Pedalling away from Liverpool Street Station where she'd just said goodbye to Alastair, Frankie decided to head for Station 75 rather than return straight home to Matlock Street. She and Alastair had returned from a blissfully happy week's honeymoon this morning and he'd had to leave straight away to return to his unit which, for the moment, was stationed near Cambridge. Now, after a week of being together, Frankie felt his absence badly and didn't want to be on her own.

Saying goodbye to him had been difficult and she'd had to keep telling herself that at least he was only going as far as Cambridgeshire this time and not thousands of miles away to Egypt. There'd be chances to see each other, at least until he was posted elsewhere. She needed to focus on the positive but it was hard to wave off the man she loved with all her heart, knowing that their times together would always be limited and at the whim of the army until the war was over.

Turning off the Minories, and riding in under the archway into Station 75, her bicycle wheels bumping over the cobbles, she knew she'd done the right thing coming back here rather than going straight home. Seeing the familiar sight of her fellow crew members busy doing the daily checks and preparation of the ambulances was just what she needed.

'Aye, aye, look who's back ... Mrs Munro!' Sparky shouted having spotted her as she dismounted and leaned her bicycle against the garage wall. 'Welcome back.'

'Frankie!' Winnie yelled from where she was balanced on top of a ladder cleaning the back of her and Rose's ambulance. She quickly climbed down and rushed over to her, folding her in a warm embrace, closely followed by Bella, Rose and Trixie who'd been sleeping on the ambulance cab and was woken up by the noise.

'It's good to see you.' Bella gave Frankie a hug. 'Welcome back.'

'I've missed you,' Rose said. 'Did you have a lovely time?'

Frankie smiled. 'It was wonderful.' She sighed. 'I've just seen Alastair off at Liverpool Street station, he ...'

'Come on.' Winnie put her arm through Frankie's. 'You need some tea. I'll go and put the kettle on. Bella and Rose, come and join us.'

Frankie didn't protest and allowed Winnie to march her up to the common room.

'I know how it feels, so sit yourself down and I'll make the tea.'

Frankie did as she was told and sat down on the battered old sofa and looked around at the familiar common room with its mish-mash of furniture and evidence of the crew members who served there: their books, knitting and sewing, Sparky's newspaper collection. It felt like being wrapped in a warm, comforting blanket, which she needed right now.

'There, drink that up.' Winnie placed a mug of tea on the table beside the sofa and sat down beside her. 'It's utterly horrible waving them off, isn't it? There's not much I can say that will help you, just to keep yourself busy.'

Frankie smiled at her friend. 'It's such a bump coming back to reality after our honeymoon, goin' from bliss to waving him off . . .'

'Is there any tea for us?' Bella said as she and Rose came in.

'Over by the sink.' Winnie nodded to where she'd left their drinks in the kitchen area. 'So where did you go? We've all been wondering.'

'The New Forest, a colleague of Alastair's has a cottage there which he loaned us. It was lovely, right in the middle of nowhere – a world away from London.' Frankie sighed, remembering the cosy cottage where the short winter days hadn't mattered as they were too wrapped up in each other to notice, snuggling up in front of the big fire enjoying being together. 'It was bliss.'

'Over too soon?' Bella said.

She nodded. 'The war pulled us back, but for a little while at least we could forget about it.'

'Your wedding was lovely,' Rose said. 'Station Officer Steele hit it off with Josie. She went back to her house

82

after you'd left, for tea and a chat. Josie said they had a great time talking.'

Frankie smiled at the thought of Josie and the boss hitting it off, two people who were unlikely to have ever crossed paths if it hadn't been for the war bringing them together. Rather like her and Alastair, who she'd met when she was on a call-out to casualties in a bombed-out Anderson shelter and he'd been the doctor attending to help the little boy trapped inside. 'Where is she?'

'At a meeting at headquarters. She'll be pleased to see you back,' Winnie said. 'Station 75 hasn't been the same without you, Frankie. We've all missed you.'

'Thank you. If I can't be with Alastair then I'd rather be with all of you than anyone else.' Frankie smiled at her friends. 'You lot won't let me get all maudlin, will you?'

'Certainly not!' Bella said. 'We don't let Winnie and now we shan't let you either.'

Frankie laughed, glad that her friends were straight-talking and that she could rely on them to see her through when times were tough, just as she did for them.

Chapter Fifteen

Frankie and Rose hurried along Matlock Street, taking care to avoid the puddles, as they were eager to get home out of the cold April rain which was soaking into their coats making them shiver. They'd been shopping, the pair of them working as a team and going to separate shops to save time, otherwise it took twice as long for one person to do the job with all the queuing. Opening the door of number 25 they went inside and quickly peeled off their coats, giving them a brisk shake outside before hanging them on the pegs to dry.

'I ain't going out—' Frankie began but stopped at the sound of a man's voice coming from the kitchen, followed by Ivy's throaty laugh.

Rose had heard it too, her eyes meeting Frankie's. 'Who's that?' she whispered.

Frankie shrugged, memories of the last time she'd come home and found Ivy entertaining an American GI flooding back to her. Was her step-grandmother up to her old tricks again? Who had she got in there this time and what had she been doing?

'Let's go and find out.' She picked up the shopping basket and went down the hall, Rose following behind. Pausing by the door, Frankie could hear the man's voice more clearly, her stomach knotting as she heard his American accent. Blasted Ivy, the woman couldn't be trusted . . . She took a deep breath and prepared for battle then opened the door and marched in.

The American GI, who'd been sitting at the table, immediately jumped to his feet looking startled, but at the sight of Rose standing beside Frankie, his face broke into a wide smile. 'Erika!' He rushed over to her and took hold of her hand in both of his. 'Gee, it's good to meet you at last.'

His use of Rose's real name shocked Frankie but she quickly realised that this was no GI picked up in some pub by Ivy, but one of Rose's cousins who were now serving at American airbases somewhere in East Anglia.

'John!' Rose's face was flushed with delight. She'd never met him before, only seen photographs sent by her uncle from America. 'I'm sorry, I didn't know you were coming otherwise I'd have been here to meet you.'

'It's no problem, I didn't know I was getting a forty-eight-hour pass until yesterday. Ivy here has been looking after me.' He grinned at Ivy, who gave the handsome young man one of her rare smiles.

'I'll leave you to it.' Ivy got up from her chair and headed for the door. 'I've got some shopping to do of me own.'

'Thank you, ma'am, for looking after me while I waited, I sure appreciated it,' John said.

Frankie stepped to one side to allow her step-grandmother to pass but the woman blanked her, not saying anything or even looking at her.

'This is Frankie, who I work with at Station 75,' Rose introduced her.

'Good to meet you, Frankie, I've heard lots about you in Erika's letters.' He held out his hand to her.

She shook his hand. 'All good, I hope.'

'Absolutely, my cousin thinks the world of you,' John said.

'The feeling is mutual.' Frankie smiled at Rose. 'I'll put the kettle on and we can have some tea.'

When they were all settled at the table, with the brown earthenware teapot brewing the tea, Frankie could see the resemblance between the two cousins: both had brown hair and the same blue eyes, although John was a great deal taller than Rose.

'So where are you staying?' Frankie asked as she poured out three cups of tea.

'At the American Eagle club, it comes highly recommended.' He grinned at Rose. 'I wasn't sure if you'd be on duty there. I asked and they said you only volunteer there on Wednesday afternoons.'

Rose nodded. 'They'll look after you well. What do you want to do while you're in London?'

'Well, I was kinda hoping you might want to come out and show me around, that's if you don't have to work or need to do something else. I know I'm springing this on you.'

'You're lucky it's my day off, so we could go and see the sights?' Rose smiled. 'It'll be fun.'

'How about you, would you like to join us, Frankie?' John asked. 'You'd be most welcome.'

'Thank you, but no, I've got some things I need to see to here.' Frankie took a sip of her tea.

'So, what do you think of England, then?' Rose asked.

John put down his teacup. 'It sure is different from New York. The villages around the base are tiny and there's so many things that are odd to us and take some getting used to. You know every GI is given a book to help us understand things better. I have to keep reminding myself to ride my bike on the left-hand side of the road when we go to the village pub.' He smiled. 'But it sure is beautiful and quaint. I'll get used to it by the time the war's over, however long that is.'

'I thought you got to go home after your tour of duty,' Frankie said.

'That's only for the fly boys, the airmen – after they do so many missions they can go home; the rest of us ground-based crew are here for the duration,' John explained.

Frankie knew from Rose that John worked in the control tower on his base, while his older brother was a pilot. She hoped he was lucky enough to survive his missions and get the chance to go home, because so many didn't.

'I've brought something.' John reached down to a bag on the floor beside his chair. 'I hope you can both make good use of these.' He pulled out some cans of peaches, Spam, bars of Hershey's chocolate and four pairs of stockings.

Frankie stared at them for a moment. 'They ain't from the black market, are they?'

'No, they're from our PX stores on base; us Americans aren't so rationed as you guys. I thought you would appreciate them.'

'We certainly do, thank you very much, it's very kind of you.' Frankie picked up a pair of the stockings. 'These are like gold dust, we won't have to use the gravy browning now, Rose.'

John frowned. 'Gravy browning?'

Rose laughed. 'When stockings are in short supply, some girls resort to painting their legs with a solution of gravy browning to make it look like they're wearing stockings when they're not.'

'And draw a line up the back of their legs for the seam,' Frankie added.

'In that case I'm sure glad to provide you with the real thing.' John smiled. 'You can keep the gravy browning for your cooking instead.'

Chapter Sixteen

'This must be like the equivalent of a child waiting outside a sweet shop for your little dog,' said the woman who was standing behind Winnie in the queue snaking down the pavement from the butcher's shop.

Winnie smiled at her. 'You're absolutely right, she's always on the lookout for a bone, if the butcher's got any going spare, but she's very good, she always waits outside for me.'

Trixie, sensing that they were talking about her, got up from where she was sitting beside Winnie's basket and wagged her tail at the woman who responded by stroking her soft, golden ears.

'She's a lovely little thing.'

'She's not just a pretty dog,' Winnie said. 'She's a working dog, comes to work with me at the ambulance station and has saved people's lives, sniffing them out where they've been buried in the rubble of their bombed houses.'

'Then she thoroughly deserves any bone she gets from the butcher, I hope he has one for her today.'

Trixie, who'd been enjoying the attention from the woman, suddenly changed her composure from relaxed to full alert, her attention drawn to something further down the street, and before Winnie could do anything let out a short, sharp bark and tore off, dodging around the various queues outside the parade of shops.

'Trixie!' Winnie shouted, abandoning her basket and place in the queue and tearing off after her. 'Trixie, come back here.'

But the little dog ignored her, and Winnie had only gone a short way down the street when she came to an abrupt halt as she recognised a familiar figure striding towards her with Trixie in his arms.

'Mac!' Winnie stood staring at him for a few seconds, seemingly rooted to the spot in shock, but quickly recovered herself and ran towards him, throwing her arms around him. Pulling back, she smiled happily at him, drinking in his handsome face, her eyes meeting his beautiful dark blue ones. 'Trixie sensed you were coming.'

Mac smiled at her, stroking her cheek tenderly. 'She's a clever girl, but we've always known that. It's so good to see you, Winnie.'

She nodded, her throat suddenly clogged with emotion. She was delighted to see him, but she knew what sudden returns from the army like this heralded – embarkation leave. Mac was being sent away soon, although he could probably never admit it, especially because of where he would be going. The thought of what he would be facing when he did return to his unit made her stomach writhe ... She took a deep breath and gave herself a mental shake – for however long Mac was here she mustn't let what was to come in the weeks and months ahead spoil it, now was the time for some stiff upper lip and making the most of each day, every single moment with him, without worrying about what the future held.

'Come on, let's get you home.' Winnie linked her arm through Mac's and they started to walk back along the street.

As they neared the butcher shop the woman to whom she'd been talking called out to her. 'You've left your basket, and I've kept your place in the queue.'

'Thank you, but I'll forget about the shopping for now,' Winnie said, picking up the basket. 'My husband's just come home.'

'Wait,' Mac said. 'Let's get the shopping. I'd like to do some normal things for once, it'll make a nice change from army routines, and if we don't do the shopping what can we have for our tea?'

'All right, but queueing up for rations isn't very exciting,' Winnie said as she took up her place in the butcher shop queue again with him beside her.

'As long as I'm with you, that's all that matters,' Mac said. His comment earned him a lot of admiring looks from other women standing in the queue, but Winnie didn't notice as she only had eyes for her husband.

Winnie turned on to her side, enjoying the sight of Mac sleeping in her bed. It was late afternoon and with the house to themselves, Connie out at some Red Cross meeting and Bella doing her voluntary work packing POW parcels, they'd taken advantage and spent a delightful afternoon of lovemaking, making up for the months apart they'd had to endure. Now Mac was sleeping peacefully, while Winnie had only dropped off for a short while, spooned in his arms, but she'd woken up with a start, her mind starting to race with questions that she knew she'd have to ask him before she'd allow herself to settle and enjoy what time they had together. Try as she might to block out what was to come, her patience was limited, and she preferred to be forewarned because, as the saying went, she was then forearmed.

She reached out and softly traced Mac's face with the tip of her finger, travelling along his jawline and then over to his lips. Her touch made him stir and he opened his eyes and looked at her, before breaking into a wide smile and pulling her to him and kissing her gently.

'I dream about waking up with you,' he said as he hooked a strand of her honey-blonde hair behind her ear.

'So do I. I wish I could wake up with you every morning.'

Mac's eyes held hers. 'One day, we will.'

He wrapped his arms around her and held her tight.

Winnie laid her head on his chest and listened to his heart beating, its rhythm strong and regular. 'Can I ask you something?'

'Of course. I might not be able to tell you the answer though.'

'You know what I'm going to say, don't you?'

'I have a very good idea. I know you well, Winnie.'

'Indeed you do, so tell me — are you on embarkation leave, and if you are then when are you going? And where exactly?' Now it was May, and with the weather gradually improving, Winnie, like the rest of the country, was expecting the long-awaited invasion to happen sometime soon. Mac's unexpected leave tied in with that theory.

Mac laughed. 'You know I can't tell you that and I honestly don't know, that's all I can say. You know how it is, and the job I signed up for and what it involves, so when the time comes I'll have to do it.'

Winnie rolled off his chest back on to her side, propping her head up on one elbow to look at him. 'Well I had to ask, didn't I, and you've told me enough to tell me but without actually saying anything that would get you in trouble with the army.' She paused for a moment, reaching out to grab hold of his hand. 'When you do parachute in, will you at least take a gun with you? Please.' They'd talked about this before several times: Mac's refusal to bear arms of any kind because of his conscientious objector beliefs scared her; he'd be going into enemy territory with no means of defending himself while facing enemy troops who most certainly did have weapons and wouldn't hesitate to use them.

Mac squeezed her hand. 'You know the answer to that one as well. I haven't changed my mind, Winnie. When I go in, I'm going as a medic not a fighting soldier. That's what I believe is right for me.'

Winnie's throat ached, and her eyes stung with tears. Part of her wanted to shout at him for being so obstinate and ridiculous that he wouldn't even carry a small pistol, but another part of her admired his convictions and strong beliefs that he wasn't prepared to carry weapons at all because he simply believed that he could not kill another human under any circumstances.

She nodded and did her best to smile at him. 'I understand, but I had to ask and it's only because I love you so much and want to keep you safe.'

'I know, and I promise you I won't take stupid risks, I have every intention of coming home to you so that we can enjoy waking up next to each other for the rest of our lives.'

Chapter Seventeen

'It was lovely.' Rose smiled at Frankie as they walked along the street, enjoying the fine June evening after the smoky darkness inside the pictures. 'It whisked me away for a while.'

Frankie put her arm through Rose's, her stride matching her friend's. They'd just been to see the musical comedy film *Higher and Higher* on their night off. 'I know just what you mean, it felt like a whole different world from wartime London.'

Turning the corner at the end of the road, three soldiers walking abreast across the width of the pavement almost bumped into them, just managing to swerve out of their way at the last moment but making Frankie and Rose jump.

'I beg your pardon, ladies,' the tallest one said, swaying slightly and giving off a strong smell of beer. 'Are you all right?'

'We're fine.' Frankie smiled at them. 'Honestly, no 'arm done.'

'Let us buy you a drink to apologise,' the soldier said.

'There's no need, and we're on duty in the morning so we need to have a clear head,' Frankie said.

The soldier laughed, his two friends joining in. 'We're not worrying about tomorrow, we're just enjoying today, aren't we, lads?' He leaned closer to her, his beery breath strong as he whispered, 'We shouldn't even be out here, we should be back with the others in West Ham football stadium, but we got out.' He smiled broadly and put his finger to his lips and made an exaggerated shhing motion. 'They're trying to round us all up again, but they'll have trouble getting us while there's still some beer to be had – we're just off to another pub.' He looked at his friends who nodded in agreement. 'Can you point us in the right direction then, if you're sure about not coming with us?'

'Look out!' One of the other soldiers grabbed the arm of the one who'd been talking to them and pointed down the street back towards the picture house where two policemen were walking in their direction. 'About turn, lads.'

The three of them turned and hurried off as best they could back the way they'd come in a bid to preserve their freedom for a little while longer. Watching them go, Frankie felt sorry for them. They, like thousands of other troops, had arrived in London over the past few days and were now corralled together in places like West Ham football stadium or camped out on Wanstead Flats, according to Sparky who knew all the goings-on around here better than anyone, and were waiting, poised for whatever was soon to come. Everyone had seen the troops arriving, military vehicles filling the streets, merging with the London traffic, and now waited expectantly, knowing something was up but not quite what or exactly when, only that it must be soon. It was no wonder that the soldiers had wanted to escape and enjoy themselves while they still could because who knew what they'd be facing, and it was likely that not all of them would be coming back.

'Do you think they'll go back to the stadium?' Rose asked as they crossed over the road and headed back towards Matlock Street.

'I expect so; if they really wanted to go AWOL the last thing they'd do is wander around the East End drinking in pubs – they'd get themselves as far away from here as possible. They're just out enjoying themselves, making the most of it while they can and will either get picked up by military police or constables or end up falling asleep in a pub and be found that way. Good luck to them.'

Frankie's thoughts went to Alastair, as they so often did. Was he somewhere nearby waiting with his unit? There was no way of knowing and frustratingly, even if he was just a short distance away, perhaps camped out on Wanstead Flats even, there was no possibility of seeing him. He could be near but yet untouchable as far as the army was concerned – they paid no heed to the wants of their soldiers and their wives, the army and its needs always came first. Frankie wished it was different, she'd only managed to see him once since their honeymoon and she would so dearly love to see him before he went.

Chapter Eighteen

Winnie couldn't sleep. She didn't know what was wrong, but her gut feeling told her that something wasn't right, she felt unsettled and anxious, her mind refused to be still and let sleep claim her. Trixie, who slept on a blanket on the floor beside Winnie's bed, didn't have her mistress's problem and had soon dropped off to sleep not long after they'd come up to bed a little after ten o'clock, and had been snuffling gently in her sleep, probably dreaming of chasing squirrels in the park.

Winnie was pondering over whether to get up and make some cocoa in the hope that it would help her finally settle down when Trixie woke with a start, leapt out of her bed and dashed over to the window, pushing her way through the heavy velvet curtains and scrabbling at the blackout beyond.

'Trixie, whatever's the matter?' Winnie threw off her covers and hurried over to see what was upsetting her.

'Come on, it's all right, come back to bed, we're on shift in the morning and need to get some sleep.' She bent down to pick up Trixie but to her surprise she growled at her, something that she'd rarely ever done before, and continued to scrape at the blackout curtain, desperate to get to the other side of it.

'What on earth has got into you?' Winnie pulled the blackout curtains aside and Trixie immediately calmed down, her golden fur looking strangely grey in the pale moonlight shining down from the full moon hanging like a light over London. It was then that Winnie heard the noise, the unmistakable sound of planes getting closer by the moment. Trixie must have heard them coming long before her. A wave of panic hit her: there'd been no air-raid siren to warn them of bombers, but then she realised that these planes weren't making the noise that she'd come to dread from hearing it so often during the Blitz, the voom, voom sound made by the enemies' unsynchronised engines, these planes were singing a far sweeter thrum – they must be Allied planes, the RAF's, or American Army Air Force's.

Peering up into the sky, she could see squadrons of planes going over, their black shapes silhouetted against the moonlight where the clouds parted. There were hundreds of them and they were all heading southwards. Winnie's heart skipped a beat. Was this the invasion they'd all been waiting for, had it finally begun? And if it had, then Mac would be up there somewhere, on his way to parachute into enemy territory. She suddenly felt sick. Trixie, sensing her mistress's despair, turned her attention away from the planes and nudged at Winnie's hand, trying to bring her comfort. She bent down and scooped the little dog up into her arms, burying her face in her soft fur.

A soft knocking made her turn as the door opened and Bella's face peeped around. 'Oh, you're awake.' She came into the room and hurried over to the window looking up at the sky. 'Did the planes wake you?'

'No, not me, I couldn't get to sleep, but they woke Trixie. What time is it?'

'Just after midnight,' Bella said, peering up at the swarm of planes still going over. 'This must mean the invasion has begun.'

Winnie nodded, chewing on her bottom lip. 'And Mac must be up there somewhere . . .' Her voice caught, and she had to swallow a sob down before it burst out. She took a moment to gather herself. 'I feel so hopeless down here, there's nothing I can do to protect him from what he's about to face, I . . .'

Bella put her arm around Winnie's shoulders. 'I know, it's hard to think of what they're going into . . . all we can do is wait and hope.' She paused, her eyes drawn to the planes again. 'If it's any help, those men up there are going with all the hopes, fears and prayers of their families and people of this country behind them.'

Winnie leaned her head on Bella's and the two of them stood in the window watching as the planes went over, wishing with all their hearts that wherever they were heading in enemy territory, they would make it through and be able to come home to their families one day.

*

100

It was a wonder that any work at all had been done at Station 75 that morning as every crew member was full of talk about the waves of planes that had gone over in the middle of the night, most having heard or seen the armada. Added to which there'd been an announcement on the eight o'clock news that morning, that the Allies had given advance warning of aerial attack for coastal areas of Hitler's Fortress Europe, and that targets to be bombed would be warned to evacuate by leaflets dropped from Allied planes, and people advised to make for open country well away from target towns – they all knew that the invasion had begun for sure.

The announcement on the wireless that the attack had begun was both a relief and a worry, Winnie thought. Finally, after years of waiting since the retreat at Dunkirk, the Allies were striking back at the occupied countries, but with Mac being part of it, it felt bittersweet. Winnie imagined the people living in those areas by the French coast panicking, and their scramble to get to safety, but perhaps they would be glad that at last the occupying enemy might be ousted.

'Winnie, do you realise you've spent at least the last ten minutes cleaning that one windowpane?' Frankie asked.

Her friend's voice brought her attention back to what she should be doing. 'Oh, I didn't realise, I was just thinking.' She shrugged.

Frankie smiled sympathetically and took the rag out of Winnie's hand and dropped it in the bucket of soapy water. 'Come on, it's nearly midday and everyone's gathering to hear the news, we don't want to miss it.' She put her arm through Winnie's and marched her up to the common room which was noisy with chatter as everyone was giving their opinion and thoughts about the attack and were eager to know what was going on. Many of them had family or friends who would be involved with the invasion and were naturally worried and anxious for any snippet of information.

'Shhhh, you lot!' Sparky said, turning on the wireless set to give it time to warm up before the news started.

Bella was sitting on the sofa next to Rose and the two of them budged up to make room for Winnie and Frankie.

Station Officer Steele appeared in the doorway of her office just as the clock hands moved round to twelve and the room fell silent as the wireless crackled into life and the BBC Home Service announcer introduced a special bulletin.

The atmosphere of the common room was electric as the words 'D-Day has come. Early this morning the Allies began the assault . . .' were read out. Winnie closed her eyes and concentrated hard on every word that the newsreader said as he talked about how the Allied armies were landing along the northern coast of France and how General Montgomery was in command of them. As he read out Eisenhower's words – 'Your task will not be an easy one. Your enemy is well-trained, well-equipped and battle hardened. He will fight savagely . . .' – it made her stomach clench at the thought of what Mac would be facing. He wasn't there to fight, but to help the injured, but that offered no guarantee of his safety in the heat of battle. Hearing that paratroops had landed and met with stiff fighting was almost too much to bear and it was only with the most difficulty that she stayed where she was instead of rushing out of the room. She clasped her hands tightly together as if she were holding on to her self-control in her grasp.

A warm hand touched hers and she opened her eyes to see Bella looking closely at her as the common room erupted into noisy chatter at the end of the broadcast.

'Come on.' Bella pulled her up to standing and led her to the women's rest room where the quietness seemed all the more pronounced after the noise of the common room. 'Right, sit yourself down and take some slow, steady breaths. Frankie's gone to make some sweet tea for you.'

'I'm fine, there's no need to fuss.'

'Just do as you're told for once and sit down.' Bella pushed her towards a pile of mattresses. 'Sit.'

'All right, all right, but really, there's no need.' Winnie sat down.

'Looking at your face, which has gone the colour of Mrs Connelly's dumplings, I'd say you're in shock and upset, and it's not surprising after hearing that. No doubt many wives and mothers and sisters are feeling the same if their menfolk are involved in the invasion.' Bella looked at her sympathetically. 'So just take a few minutes to let the news sink in.'

The door opened, and Trixie came scurrying in, throwing herself into Winnie's arms, and she hugged the little dog to her, glad of her solid warmth.

'Tea up.' Frankie followed behind with a tray of steaming cups. 'The boss said you were to have some sugar in your tea, so that's yours on the left.' She nodded at the cup at one end of the tray.

Winnie took the cup of tea and cradled her fingers around it, glad of the warmth as her hands had gone cold. 'Thank you.'

'Well it's a lot more peaceful in here,' Frankie said. 'There's a right debate going on out there about how the Allies will get on.' She raised her eyebrows. 'You know Sparky, he's revelling in it and no doubt we'll be getting day-by-day accounts as soon as he gets his newspapers.'

Winnie did her best to smile, she knew her friends were trying their best to protect and support her but there was nothing any of them could do or say which was anything other than surface comfort. All she could do now was hope along with thousands of others as they waited for news of their loved ones going into battle. They had to trust that those in charge of the invasion knew what they were doing, although they often hadn't in the Great War, but this time the fighting was on a whole different scale.

Chapter Nineteen

Frankie watched two-year-old Sylvia pile wooden bricks on top of each other, thinking how innocent and care-free the little girl was, she had no idea of the momentous happenings that were going on today. She might have a father who at this moment was battling his way onto French soil but she was completely oblivious to it, unlike the adults at the nursery who unsurprisingly seemed a bit distracted today. She'd been glad to escape from Station 75 to do her voluntary work here at the nursery, as she'd been doing every week since they moved on to the new twenty-four-hour shift system. It was a welcome distraction from what was happening. The invasion was all anyone wanted to talk about at work, crew members mulling over what was happening, topping up their knowledge by listening avidly to every wireless news bulletin they could, debating over what might be happening. It was a vitally important turning point of the war, but Frankie's take on it invariably focused on Alastair and where he was among it all and that made for worrying thoughts. He wouldn't have gone over in the first wave like Winnie's Mac had – who'd be with the fighting soldiers who'd be battling to get a foothold – but nevertheless he would be heading that way, and very soon, if he hadn't gone already.

Sylvia carefully placed the last brick on top of the stack and paused her hand just inches from it then grinned at Frankie before knocking it over, her giggles ringing out as the bricks tumbled down. Frankie laughed with her, unable to resist her infectious, delightful laughter – spending time playing with the little girl was proving to be a much-needed tonic.

Her two hours at the nursery passed quickly and as Frankie wheeled her bicycle out of the gate to head back to Station 75 she had to halt to avoid running into a woman hurrying along the pavement pushing a pram.

The woman stopped at the sight of Frankie. 'If you're planning on goin' that way,' she nodded her head back the way she'd come from, 'you ain't going to get anywhere in a hurry. The roads are jammed with army trucks all heading down to the ports, they're jam-packed, the medical ones 'ave even got beds strapped on the side.'

Frankie's stomach knotted. Medical trucks – was Alastair among them? 'How'd you know they're medical ones?'

''Cos of the red cross on the truck doors, of course.' The woman sighed. 'They'll be needin' as many of them as they can with our boys going in to fight.' The baby started to wake up, making grizzling sounds which the woman responded to by rocking the pram to and fro. 'I'd better get going, she's due for a feed soon and I want to get 'ome before she starts to cry.' She smiled at Frankie and hurried off.

So if the medical trucks were heading for the port, Alastair could well be among them, but she had no idea where he'd be leaving from – it could be just down the road or from any other port in the country. Frankie chewed her bottom lip; she should be returning to Station 75, they were only allowed two hours away to do voluntary work . . . but if there was a chance to see him, however small . . . It was calling to her, niggling at her, because even a tiny chance was better than none and with the prospect of not knowing when she might see him again she had to grab whatever opportunity came her way. She climbed onto her bike and pushed off, pedalling fast in the opposite direction to Station 75, grateful that the nursery was in Stepney and not far from the docks.

It didn't take her long to reach the convoy heading towards West India docks. The army vehicles were going slow, almost bumper to bumper as they packed the streets leading down to the dockyard. People out shopping stood watching them, waving and cheering at the men as they passed by. Frankie realised it was going be impossible to get through on her bicycle and dismounted, looking around for a good place to leave it. Spotting an alleyway leading to the back of a butcher's she pushed it down there and leaned it against the wall before hurrying into the shop, glad of her uniform to avoid being told off by the queue of East End housewives who were waiting their turn to get their rations.

'Is it all right if I leave my bike in your alleyway?' she asked the butcher who was wrapping up some meat in paper. 'It's an emergency of sorts.'

He looked up at her. 'Course it is, ducks.'

'Thanks.' She hurried out of the door and ran along the line of army trucks looking for medical ones.

'You coming with us, darlin'?' a soldier shouted out from the back of a packed lorry.

She shook her head and smiled at him as she ran past. There was a definite sense of purpose and excitement in the air: this was what the country had been waiting for, what these men had been training for, and now D-Day was here, they were finally on their way.

Further along the column of trucks she spotted the familiar Red Cross symbol painted on the doors of several lorries, each of them packed to the gunwales with equipment and, like the woman had told her, with beds strapped onto their sides and tents piled onto the canvas tops with men hanging on at the back as best they could. She hurried along to reach them and stopped at the cab of the first one, peering in at the four men sitting inside, but none of them were Alastair, and none in the two medical trucks in front either. Bitter disappointment welled up in her, she knew it had only been a tiny chance, but even so she desperately hoped that it might come true.

'You lookin' for someone?' The driver of the last truck leaned out his window looking down at her.

'My husband, Alastair Munro, he's a doctor with one of the casualty clearin' station units, but I don't know if he's shipping out from here, I just took a chance ...' She shrugged.

'There's more medical trucks further down the convoy,' the driver said, nodding his head towards the docks. 'We ain't the only ones. Hope you find him.'

'Thanks.' Frankie felt a flame of hope ignite inside her again and hurried on, looking for more medical trucks. She spotted two not far from the gates of the West India docks and ran towards them; they were stationary now but could be waved through any moment.

The first one, like all the others, was packed with equipment and men, either squeezed in the cab or in the back, but none of them were her husband. This was turning into a wild goose chase, Frankie thought as she approached the last truck, the white circle with its red cross in the centre standing out brightly against the khaki paintwork on the cab doors, but at least she'd tried, and no doubt Alastair would laugh about her chasing army trucks when she told him about it in a letter. She peered inside the cab window quickly, ready to turn away, when a familiar warm Scottish voice called out to her. 'Frankie!' It was Alastair, he was there! She stared at him for a few moments, lost for words and not quite believing her eyes. He quickly clambered out of the cab and hurried round and threw his arms around her, as the other men in the cab cheered at them and several of the others clinging on at the back wolf-whistled.

'What are you doing here?' he asked stepping back and

looking at her, his hands on her shoulders, his vivid blue eyes meeting hers. 'It's so good to see you.'

'I heard there were medical trucks goin' down to the port and I had to come, just in case you were 'ere and . . .' She smiled at him. 'And you are!'

'I couldn't tell you, you know that, I wanted to, so much. It was hard to be so close to you and not be able to see you. I—'

'Sorry to interrupt you two lovebirds,' the driver of Alastair's truck said, leaning out of the cab window, 'only it looks like we'll be off in a moment.'

Frankie looked around and saw that the line of trucks beyond the gateway into West India docks had moved further in, making a gap for these ones to follow, and standing guarding the gates were the Port of London police who were stopping anyone else from going in; she would have to stay out here once Alastair's truck passed inside.

'All right, I'll be with you in a moment, if you drive in I'll catch you up,' Alastair said. He put his arm around Frankie's shoulders and guided her across to the side of the road. 'We haven't got long. I'm really glad you came looking for me, Frankie, I'll treasure this time.'

'Do you know where you're going?' Frankie asked.

Alastair smiled at her. 'You know I can't tell you that, but you'll have heard the announcements on the wireless, I'm sure.'

She nodded. 'You will be careful, won't you?'

'I will, it's pointless me telling you not to worry but I'm not going there to fight, I won't be on the front line.'

'I know but I still . . .' She paused as the driver of

110

Alastair's truck started the engine and drove in through the dock gates, her heart quickening as their time together drained away fast, like sand in a timer.

Alastair glanced at the truck and turned back to her. 'I'm going to have to go.' He looked deep into her eyes. 'Look after yourself, Frankie. I'll be counting the days until I come back to you.' He pulled her into his arms and kissed her tenderly. 'I love you.'

Frankie's throat was painful with emotion, she nodded. 'I love you, too. Take care of yourself and write to me.'

'I promise.' He pulled her into a fierce hug and swiftly kissed her again and then with a last look turned and hurried in through the dock gates to join his truck, pausing to wave at her before he climbed inside.

Frankie stayed where she was, watching until his truck vanished from sight, lost within the maze of the dock warehouses as it made its way down to the ships waiting at the jetty. Only then did she turn and retrace her steps, wiping away the tears that rolled down her cheeks.

Chapter Twenty

Bella hurried along the pavement, dodging around puddles as rain pitter-pattered loudly on her umbrella. So much for it being summertime, she thought, it was bad enough for people in England, but how much worse must it be for the Allied troops who were battling their way across northern France, the persistent rain undoubtedly turning the land to mud, making travelling more difficult, let alone fighting.

Turning into the doorway of the building where the Red Cross prisoner of war parcels were packed, she paused, collapsing her umbrella and giving it a good shake before going inside, where the level of noise surprised her. The volunteers who packed the parcels often talked, but it was usually a low-level hum with the wireless playing in the background, but today the volume of chatter was turned up, with many conversations going on as people filled the boxes to be sent out.

She didn't have to listen to know what they were talking about because the whole country seemed to be fixated on what was happening with the invasion into Hitler's Fortress Europe. It was just the same at Station 75 where newspaper articles were devoured and discussed at length and news bulletins on the wireless listened to with great concentration.

After hanging up her coat to dry she made her way over to the packing tables and found a space next to Maud, an older woman whom she'd met there and who'd become a friend.

'Hello, Maud, how are you?' Bella took one of the prepared empty boxes, with the goods ready to be packed already put on its lid by another volunteer, and started work, expertly fitting in the different-shaped boxes and tins.

'Oh, Bella, I was hoping you'd be in today, I've got something to show you.' Maud bent down to rummage in her basket which she'd stowed beneath the table and pulled out a copy of *The Prisoner of War* magazine that was published by the Red Cross and St John war organisation every month and sent to POWs' next of kin. It was full of information about anything to do with the imprisoned men, from photos of them at the camps to useful articles for their families. Maud flicked through the magazine until she came to the page she wanted and held it out for Bella to see. 'This is yours, isn't it?'

Bella looked at the article on the packing of POW parcels. It was her work, she'd written it based on what they did here, thinking it would be helpful to families to know the process behind the parcels that were sent to their loved ones held in camps. 'Yes, did you like it?'

Maud smiled at her. 'It's marvellous, you've told it just as it is and if I didn't know about it already through working here, then I know I'd be glad to read it and understand more.'

'Good, that's what I hoped it would do. Most people who have someone in the camps don't know what goes on behind the scenes here, so I thought it would help. They've asked me to write another article about the next of kin parcel centre, hoping if people understand exactly how it works it might stop them trying to put contraband items in their parcels – they'll only be removed and won't be sent out.'

'I'll look out for it then.' Maud put her magazine back in her basket and returned to packing her box, expertly tucking pieces of shredded paper into the gaps between the tins and packets to stop them moving around in transit. 'I read your story in *The People's Friend* last week, it was very good – you are clever, Bella, such a good writer.'

Bella's cheeks grew warm. 'Well I love doing it, and it's a good diversion. Working on a story or article takes my mind off things, makes me forget my worries for a while.'

Maud touched Bella's arm. 'Have you heard anything about your brother?'

She shook her head. 'No, there's been no more news, the army doesn't know where he is. He wasn't taken to a German camp and was last seen at an Italian one before they surrendered, and after that we just don't know what happened to him or where he is now.' She shrugged. 'Not

114

knowing is hard, but it's what so many people are going through now, waiting and hoping – my friends are desperate to hear from their husbands who went over to France on D-Day, they haven't heard anything since.'

'It's a worrying time. I'm glad that at least I know where my son is – being in a POW camp isn't wonderful but at least he's out of the fighting and for that I'm grateful.'

'And he gets one of these parcels regularly.' Bella smiled at her friend. 'Come on, we'd better get to work, there are prisoners relying on us.'

Maud laughed and started work packing her box again. 'I hope your friends hear from their husbands soon.'

Bella fitted a tin of butter neatly into a gap in the box. 'So do I. They are doing their best to be patient but as every day goes by I can see them getting more and more anxious.'

Chapter Twenty-one

Frankie lay on her side staring out of her bedroom window at the stars twinkling down on London. They must be looking down on Alastair, wherever he is, she thought. Was he watching them too? Since the invasion had begun she'd often woken up in the middle of the night, like she had again tonight, and had taken to pulling the blackout blind down so that she could lie on her bed and look up at the night sky.

The past week since D-Day, when she'd watched Alastair going in through the dockyard gates on his way to France, had been a maelstrom of emotions. She'd listened avidly to every news report on the wireless and scoured through newspaper items to learn everything she could about the Allies' advance in northern France. She looked for anything that might give her a clue and help her know where Alastair could be and what he might be facing, because there'd been no word from him since he'd gone with the invading troops.

Frankie wasn't the only one who was preoccupied with the events in France: many crew members were following it closely as well. Winnie, who, like her, was worrying about her husband, and others like Sparky who'd started cutting out the map the *Daily Herald* printed on its front page every day showing the Allies' advance, pinning them up on the noticeboard in the common room like some general with his battle plans.

She sighed. It was a little past four in the morning and she was due at Station 75 at nine o'clock for a twenty-four-hour shift. She needed to stop thinking so much and get some rest, so with a last look up at the stars she closed her eyes and willed herself to go back to sleep.

Waves of sleep were slowly beginning to creep up on her when a strange sound, getting louder and nearer, startled Frankie awake. Was it an aeroplane? If it was, then it sounded like it was in trouble, its engines more like a noisy motorbike without a silencer than the usual steady thrum beat that she'd heard so often.

Getting out of bed she went over to the window and gasped when she saw a plane coming in towards her with a flame burning out of its tail, and making a buzzing sound like an angry wasp. It had just passed over when the flame suddenly stuttered and went out and she lost sight of it against the dark sky. She'd just climbed into bed and lain down again when a loud explosion echoed out across the East End rooftops. Leaping up, she hurried over to the window and peered out but couldn't see anything. Did the plane crash? Was it a German bomber that had got through undetected and dropped its bombs?

There'd been no air-raid siren, no warning, whatever it was had arrived unexpectedly and must have caused the explosion.

There was nothing she could do about it, so once more Frankie went back to bed and hoped that sleep would soon come.

Sparky was in full flow later that morning when Frankie arrived at Station 75. He was sitting in one of the armchairs with many of the crew members gathered around him listening to what he was saying. Spotting Frankie and Rose walking into the common room he stopped and called out to them, 'Did you hear it?'

'What?' Frankie asked, going over to where he sat.

'That sound in the night, did you hear it? About a quarter past four it was, woke me and my missus up, thought it was a plane in trouble at first, but it weren't that.'

'Yes, I heard it, too. Whatever it was 'ad a flame coming out the back, but it went out and then a few seconds later there was an explosion. Did the plane come down?'

'It came down all right,' Sparky said, shaking his head. 'But it weren't no plane in trouble, it hit the railway bridge on Grove Road, blocked the main line out to East Anglia and demolished a house, people killed and all.' He paused for a moment. 'It was a robot rocket.'

'How d'you know?' another crew member asked.

''Cos I've been there to have a look. It ain't far from my house and I've been talking to the rescue services who were there, some good pals of mine. They could see it weren't a plane or a bomb, this was somethin' different – a new weapon that can come over here all on its own, don't need a pilot to fly it.'

Everyone was silent for a moment as they absorbed the idea of Hitler's new weapon. Frankie shivered, the idea of a robot rocket seemed far more sinister, cold and calculating than a bomber flown by a human being.

'It'll be on the news on the wireless,' Paterson said.

Sparky shook his head. 'I doubt it. The rescue fellas I know said the government will keep quiet about this for the meantime, just you wait and see.'

'But they'll have to tell us,' Frankie said. 'You can't hide something like that fallin' out of the sky and blowing things up.'

'Perhaps there won't be any more,' Rose said.

Several of the crew members looked at each other, clearly hoping the same thing. They'd all seen enough of what explosions could do and the fear of a new type of weapon bringing more destruction and death to London wasn't something any of them wanted.

'If old Hitler's gone to all the trouble of making a new robot rocket he ain't goin' to not use it, is he?' Sparky said. 'I have a feeling we'll be seeing more of these in the days and months to come, so if you hear them coming – and you're not goin' to miss them because of the sound they make – then take cover.'

Frankie hoped that Sparky was wrong, but in her heart she knew what he said made sense. Just when it looked like the war might finally be turning in their favour now the invasion was under way, this arrival of a robot rocket showed London would be under attack once more.

Chapter Twenty-two

Station Officer Steele studied the newspaper that Sparky had just brought in to her office, placing it down on her desk in front of her with a flourish.

'See, the government has finally admitted it – only took them three days and more rockets falling to be honest about what was going on, but you can hardly hide the damn things now they've fallen out the sky on to innocent people.' Sparky pointed at the article on the front page of today's *Daily Herald* paper. 'I told you Hitler'd started sendin' over robot rockets.'

She read through the article which quoted the statement made by the Home Secretary, Herbert Morrison, last night, which talked about the pilotless aircraft now targeting London and the south-east of England, beside which an official spotting guide to the rockets had been printed, showing what they looked like from all angles, and even a photograph of the flare produced by them lighting up the night sky.

'Can you gather the crew together in the common room for me, please, Sparky? And can I hold on to this paper for a little while?'

'Course you can. I'll go rally the troops and let you know when everyone's ready.'

When Sparky had gone, she reread the article, taking in the advice about what should be done if one of these rockets headed your way, knowing it was her duty to make sure that all her crew were as prepared as they could be if they had to face one of these insidious new weapons. She'd hoped that with the Allies now pushing back the enemy in France, the war had turned a corner and people on the home front were much safer now, but the arrival of these rockets had brought a new, sinister danger.

It didn't take long for Sparky to assemble all the crew members on duty in the common room and when Station Officer Steele went in to speak to them she took the *Daily Herald* newspaper with her.

'You will no doubt be aware that the government have finally admitted that we *are* being targeted by these pilotless, robot rockets, which doesn't come as a surprise to us. Sparky was quite right about having seen the very first one a few days ago.'

'They weren't goin' to be able to keep it quiet with them fallin' out the sky,' one of the crew said.

'Exactly.' Station Officer Steele held up Sparky's newspaper so that all the crew could see the front page. 'For those of you who haven't seen one yet, this is what they look like.' She pointed to the diagrams on the front. 'Or at night you'll just see a flare in the sky and, of course, will be able to hear them. The important thing is to know what to do if you do see one. Remember, as long as the engine is running the rocket will keep flying but when the engine cuts out and the flame vanishes from its tail then it's going to dive down to the ground and explode some five to fifteen seconds later.' She paused for a moment while the crew muttered amongst themselves. 'The official advice is to take refuge from the blast.'

'Will there be any warning that these rockets are on their way?' Winnie asked.

'Apparently the usual siren will be given whether enemy planes are pilotless ones or not, so if the siren goes while you are here on duty you need to follow the usual procedure and get to the shelter as quickly as you can,' she said. 'The important thing is that we now understand how these things operate: as long as the engine keeps running it will fly over, it's when it cuts out that we need to worry. Obviously with these things now being fired at us we are likely to be much busier with call-outs again.'

'I'll stick the spotters' guide to these rockets up on the noticeboard, shall I?' Sparky said.

'Good idea.' She handed him back his newspaper. 'Right, back to work, everybody, and if the siren goes . . . get to the shelter and make sure you're wearing your steel helmets.'

Chapter Twenty-three

Bella had just bumped her bicycle down the steps to the basement of Connie's house, with Winnie and Trixie following on close behind, when the door leading into the house was thrown open by Connie.

'I've been looking out for you. Bella, you've had a phone call from your mother.' Connie beamed at her. 'It's the most marvellous news – your brother's come home! Walter's alive and well and arrived back at her house late last night. She telephoned here an hour ago to let you know.'

Bella stared at her as the news slowly sank in.

'That's utterly marvellous!' Winnie threw her arm around Bella's shoulders and hugged her. 'You must go and see him.'

Bella nodded, her eyes blurring with tears. Her brother was alive and had come home, she could hardly believe it. She'd tried hard to keep hopeful that he was still alive somewhere, but it was hard sometimes, especially as more and more months passed since they'd last heard from him. 'Is he all right?'

'Yes, apart from being very skinny so your mother says. She has plans to fatten him up while he's there,' Connie said.

'I must go to see him.' Bella had just under twenty-four hours until she needed to be back on duty at Station 75, so there was time to get to Buckinghamshire and back again. She could even stay the night and get the early train back to London in the morning.

Connie took hold of Bella's bicycle from her. 'I'll take this, you go inside and get yourself ready; you should be able to get there easily by midday, with luck and a train that doesn't get delayed.'

'Thank you.' Bella hurried inside to quickly pack some overnight things into a bag and get some money. She decided to just have a quick wash and go still wearing her uniform rather than waste time changing into something else. She wanted to get there as soon as possible, she'd waited long enough to see her brother again and she wasn't going to delay it for a moment longer than was necessary.

Walking up the driveway to Linden House later that morning after a thankfully uninterrupted train journey out from Euston station to Little Claydon, Bella's stomach was fluttering, like a thousand moths around a lamp post, with a heady mixture of excitement and nerves at the prospect of seeing her brother again for the first time in over three and a half years since he was posted abroad to North Africa. They'd sent letters, and latterly parcels when he was in a POW camp in Italy, but they weren't the same as seeing somebody, talking to them face to face and being able to read their expressions and the emotions in their eyes. Her mind was filled with so many questions, they'd whirled around her head as she'd sat in the train, playing out different scenarios of what could have happened to him since he'd been in the prison camp.

Going around to the back of the house, a delicious smell of freshly baked bread met her as she opened the kitchen door and saw her mother turning a hot loaf out of its tin to cool next to others on the scrubbed pine table.

'Hello,' Bella said, hurrying over to kiss her mother and throwing her arms around her, squeezing her tight. 'I came as soon as I got the news.'

'We've been expecting you. Connie telephoned after you'd left to say you were on your way.' Her mother stepped back and looked at her. 'You look very smart in your uniform.'

Bella smiled. 'I came straight here after I got home from work, didn't want to waste time getting changed. So where is he then?'

'Asleep. He arrived here very late last night and is exhausted.'

'Where's he been all this time?' Bella asked.

Her mother smiled at her. 'It's quite a story but I'll let him tell you it, it's his to tell, not mine. I'm just glad he's home again.'

Bella was itching to know more but she knew her mother wouldn't budge, and it wasn't fair to badger her,

125

she'd just have to wait until Walter woke up. 'Is it all right if I stay tonight and get the early train back to London in the morning?'

'Of course it is. It's a rare treat for me to have both my children here with me.'

It wasn't until early afternoon when Walter finally got up and appeared down in the kitchen, where Bella was chopping up carrots to help her mother prepare the evening meal, coming in with his dark brown hair sticking up from sleep. Bella's first reaction was how thin he was, immediately followed by dropping her knife onto the table and rushing over and throwing her arms around him.

'There you are, sleepyhead. I come all the way from London to see you and you're fast asleep!' She loosened her grip and stepped back, looking up at him as he was much taller than she was. 'It's good to see you.'

Walter beamed down at her. 'And you.'

Bella laughed. 'So where have you been all this time? What happened to you?'

'Let the lad have something to eat first, then he can tell you what happened,' their mother said, putting a plate of bread thickly spread with butter and jam down on the table and motioning for Walter to sit down. 'I'll fry you some eggs in a minute.'

'Thanks.' Walter sat down and began to tuck in, his eyes closing in appreciation of the taste of the food as he chewed. Wherever he'd been, thought Bella, food had obviously been in short supply.

'Right, I'd better tell you where I've been before you

burst.' Walter grinned at her as he wiped up the last bits of egg yolk with a piece of bread and then popped it into his mouth.

'Go on then, I'm all ears.'

'Where do you think I've been?' Walter teased.

Bella threw up her hands in exasperation. 'I don't know. The last time we heard from you, you were in the POW camp in Italy, but after the Italians capitulated we heard nothing. So where did you go?'

Her brother sat back in his chair. 'I've been in Italy ever since, on the run and helping the Italian partisans fight the Germans.'

Bella stared at him for a few moments and then looked across the kitchen to their mother who was frying onions at the kitchen range, all the while watching them and listening to what was being said. Her eyes met Bella's and she nodded, clearly having already heard this but listening again.

'How did that happen? You were supposed to be in the POW camp.'

Walter shrugged. 'I was, but when the Italians surrendered, the guards all cleared off and we were supposed to stay there because the Allies had landed in southern Italy and it was only a matter of time before they reached us, but me and some pals didn't like the idea of hanging around with the Nazis still in the war, they could come in and we'd be there like sitting ducks.' He paused for a moment. 'So, we ran for it and hid up in the hills. We used to go out on working parties from the camp, helping the locals in the fields, and we'd got to know some

127

of them – they were good people, and we picked up a bit of the language as well. It was just as well we did run off because the Nazis soon arrived and shipped the men that had stayed in the camp off to God knows where. We weren't the only ones on the run, there were plenty of POWs on the loose. We moved at night and scrounged food out of the fields and many Italians helped us, some of them risking their lives when the Germans arrived. Anyway, we found an area with plenty of good hide-aways, we stayed in a cave up in the hills and eventually we met some Italian partisans and helped them make life difficult for the Nazis.' He grinned.

Bella had spent a lot of time over the past year wondering where her brother was and what he was doing, though she'd never expected him to have been hiding out in caves and fighting with partisans, but she was glad that he hadn't stayed in the camp and been taken by the Germans. 'What did you do?'

'Blow up bridges, ambush patrols, anything that would hinder the Nazis and get rid of them.' Walter's face was shadowed for a moment and then he smiled at her, but she noticed it didn't quite reach his eyes. She could see that what he'd told her didn't fully convey the serious-ness of what he'd been doing and all the terrible danger he'd been in.

'What would have happened if they'd caught you?'

'They'd have shot me, like they did the crew of the American bomber who bailed out before their plane crashed – they hid in an old shed at the top of a mountain, but the Nazi SS found them and shot them.'

Bella's eyes filled with tears. 'They should have been taken as prisoners of war.'

Walter nodded. 'I know, but tell that to the SS,' he said bitterly. 'But don't worry, I reported the bastards when I went for Allied Screening before they repatriated me.' He paused for a moment, looking far away. 'It was a wonderful sight when we saw the British Army finally arrive where we were – I knew I could come home then.'

'What's going to happen next?' Bella asked.

'He's going to rest and get plenty of decent food inside him,' their mother said putting a cup of tea in front of each of them.

Walter laughed. 'I'm still in the army, Mum, I'm going to have to report for duty when they tell me, though at least I'll have a couple of weeks off before then.'

Bella frowned. 'But where will they send you? Not into France, I hope? You've done enough, surely?'

'My fate is in the army's hands, but I wouldn't say no to a nice Blighty posting.' Walter took a sip of tea. 'Enough talk of the army, tell me what you've been up to, sis, you look smart in your uniform, it suits you.'

Chapter Twenty-four

'Top secret!' Winnie stared at Station Officer Steele who'd summoned her, Bella, Frankie and Rose to her office shortly after they'd finished eating their evening meal. 'And why us?'

The boss looked at them, her shrewd brown eyes twinkling behind her horn-rimmed glasses. 'Because I think you'll do a jolly good job – that's why I've chosen you four to do this task. You're a good team and I know that I can rely on you not to let Station 75 down.'

'So, what is it you want us to do?' Winnie asked impatiently.

'You're to join a convoy made up of ambulances from different stations which will travel out to an unnamed destination in the country. That's all I am permitted to tell you,' the boss said.

'What will we be doing there?' Frankie asked. 'Do you know?'

'Of course I do, but I have been ordered not to say any more – just that you are to meet at the rendezvous point here,' she pointed to the large street map of London which was pinned on her office wall, 'from there you will travel in convoy to the designated place out in the countryside. You'll find out more when you get there. I really can't tell you any more other than this is a very important job.'

Winnie glanced at her friends who all looked as curious as she felt, but it was clear that the boss wasn't going to tell them any more than she already had, and the only way that they would find out what was going on was as they did it. 'What time do we need to leave?'

'The rendezvous is for twenty-two hundred hours, so it would be wise to leave here by twenty-one hundred hours to make sure you don't miss it. I've been told the convoy will not wait beyond the appointed time,' Station Officer Steele said. 'So that gives you a little over an hour to get yourselves ready. Make sure you wear some warm clothes as it's cold out there tonight and do not, I repeat, do *not*, say anything to any other crew members about this job, understand?' They all nodded. 'Jolly good, I know you won't let me down.'

Winnie was glad when it was finally time to leave because it had been hard not to say a word to each other about what they were going to do. She'd felt like she'd burst with all the questions about what the job might be whizzing around her head, though she'd thankfully managed to keep silent about it.

Climbing into the ambulance cab next to Rose, she

was finally able to say what she wanted. 'What do you think this is all about? I've been racking my brains trying to work out what it might be. Why would they send ambulances on a top-secret convoy? Presumably we must be going to get patients of some sort, but who are they and from where?'

Rose laughed as she settled Trixie on her lap. 'I bet your imagination has been running wild since the boss told us she was sending us on a top-secret job.'

'Of course it has.' She put the ambulance into gear and followed Frankie and Bella as they drove under the archway and out onto the road. 'I've come up with several different scenarios of what we might be going to – what do you think?'

'Well it must be to collect patients otherwise what's the point of sending ambulances, but who they are I don't know, and why such secrecy either, we'll just have to wait and see.'

They arrived at the rendezvous point in good time and as they waited more and more ambulances arrived to join in the convoy. Bang on the dot of 22:00 hours they moved off, following a lead army car, and travelled southwards out through the suburbs of London, the houses all in darkness in the blackout and just the faint beams from their covered headlights lighting the way.

'Look!' Rose grabbed Winnie's arm, pointing up into the sky where they could see the flickering lights of two robot rockets flying fast through the darkness towards London. The sight of them made her shiver, knowing that as soon as that bright flame went out the rocket would dive and explode on some unsuspecting victims.

'I hope wherever they come down people will have had a chance to get to a shelter,' Winnie said.

They saw several more rockets flying northwards before the convoy reached its destination at midnight, which turned out to be Epsom Downs station.

'Looks like we're meeting a train,' Winnie said as she parked the ambulance next to Frankie and Bella's.

When all the ambulance crews had gathered on the station platform, their faces looking ghostly grey in the light of the waning moon, the army officer who was in charge and had travelled in the car at the head of the convoy shouted, 'Can I have your attention, please? You're here to meet casualties from D-Day and will be taking them back to London hospitals for further treatment. You all need to stay on the platform until the train gets in – what time that will be I can't say. The important thing is that we are here waiting and the ambulances ready, now all we have to do is wait for the train.' Without waiting for any questions he turned and walked off with the station master, leaving the ambulance crews muttering amongst themselves at the news.

D-Day casualties – the words spun around in Winnie's head. Could Mac be among them? He'd gone over on D-Day, parachuting in with his unit, and she'd heard nothing since he'd landed in France, not a word. She had no idea if he was still alive, injured ... or worse.

She touched the last letter she'd had from him, that she'd taken to carrying around everywhere with her and which was safe inside her tunic pocket. He'd written it to her before D-Day, explaining that it would be posted after he'd been mobilised. He had been full of optimism for what he was about to do, and told her how much he loved her and intended coming home to her. Carrying it with her felt like she had a small part of him with her, a connection, however fleeting and distant, and right now she was desperate for any sense of Mac that she could get.

'Winnie?' Bella touched her arm. 'Are you all right?'

'Mac could be one of them coming here tonight ... I wouldn't know.' She felt sick at the thought.

'You don't know that,' Bella said softly.

'I know,' Winnie snapped and then sighed. 'I'm sorry, Bella, I'm worried. He could be injured or dead and they haven't told me yet.'

'I know, but Mac will do everything he can to come back to you, you know that, and if by any chance he is coming here then he will be delighted to see you.'

Winnie nodded. 'You're right, I'm just being an utter misery because I'm worried about him. I'm not the only one who's got a husband out there.' She looked over to where Frankie was talking to Rose; she knew that her friend was worried about Alastair, too.

'Well, whoever arrives on the train, they'll be glad to be back home,' Bella said. 'We'll need to be cheerful for them like when we met the ambulance train at Liverpool Street station that time.'

'That was the day the boss went out to meet them,' Winnie said. 'She left me in charge at the station, surprising us all. Let's hope the train gets here soon, it's so cold.'

She, like many of the other ambulance crews, was

wearing her greatcoat, glad of its bulk on this bitterly cold night. It might be almost midsummer, but it felt more like winter, and with nowhere to shelter on the platform it was hard to keep warm. 'Come on, I need to move around a bit to warm up.' Winnie linked her arm in Bella's and she was grateful to feel the benefit of her body warming up a bit as they strode up and down the length of the platform several times.

When the train still hadn't arrived by four a.m., Winnie wasn't the only one who was tired, cold and hungry, and there was a definite sense of spirits starting to flag and energy sapping after the initial sense of readiness had worn off. Crews sat huddled together along the platform trying to keep warm, some of them even managing to fall asleep. The unexpected arrival of some WVS ladies bearing trays of beef sandwiches and cups of tea was a wonderful surprise and was greeted with an appreciative cheer from the ambulance crews.

With a sandwich inside her and her fingers warmed from cradling her cup of tea, Winnie felt much better and when the train finally came steaming into the platform a short while later, as the sky began to lighten with the approach of dawn, she was determined to find out if Mac was on the train.

As the army orderlies began to unload the casualties, placing the men on stretchers along the length of the platform, Winnie walked up and down, anxiously searching for Mac. With each unfamiliar face she wasn't sure if she was glad it wasn't him or wished it was, and that he was home and out of it. But none of them were Mac, just other

135

women's husbands or mother's sons who'd been injured; some so badly that they'd never be sent back to fight again.

'Come on, Winnie, we need to get our casualties.' Rose hurried over to her, nodding to where other ambulance crews were busy collecting the men on stretchers and carrying them off to their waiting ambulances.

'I know, I just needed to check, that's all, but he's not here.'

As they loaded the fourth man into the back of their ambulance a short while later, Winnie realised that she suddenly had a golden opportunity to find out what was going on out there, and perhaps even get word of Mac – only she needed help to do it.

'Rose, can you check the straps are secure on the stretchers? I just need to speak to Bella and Frankie quickly before we leave.'

'Yes of course,' Rose said.

Winnie jumped out of the back of their ambulance and hurried to where her friends were about to close the back doors of their ambulance, ready to leave.

'Wait! Would one of you please swap places with me on the way back? I want to ride in the back so I can talk to the men, and Rose can't drive our ambulance.'

'Why do you want to do that?' Bella asked, leaning out of the back of her ambulance.

'I might be able to find out something about Mac, he might have treated one of them. I might not get another chance like this.'

Bella glanced at Frankie, who shrugged her shoulders. 'All right then, I'll drive for you, if Rose will come and be attendant in our ambulance, if that's all right with you, Frankie?'

'All right, but we need to get going, these men need to get to hospital.'

Winnie beamed at them. 'Thank you, thank you, both, you are the best of friends.'

Frankie laughed. 'Ain't we just!'

It felt odd to Winnie being shut in the back of the ambulance, unable to see out and only knowing they were moving from the motion of the vehicle.

'Are you all warm enough?' Winnie asked. Each man had some hot-water bottles tucked in under his blankets, but they weren't as warm as they would normally be as it was hours since they'd been topped up what with waiting so long for the train.

'Being back in Blighty warms my heart,' the soldier on one of the top stretchers said. 'After where we've been that's the best medicine, believe you me.'

'Too bleeding right!' one of the other soldiers added.

'Was it bad out there?' Winnie asked. 'We hear about it on the wireless and read reports in the newspapers, but I suspect they don't tell us everything.'

'I bet they don't. Let's just say the Jerries didn't give in easily,' the soldier on the top bunk said. 'Getting up the beach was bleeding hard.'

One of the other soldiers scoffed. 'That's one way to put it.' He looked at Winnie. 'Best you don't know, love. All that matters is we're home now and hope those poor blighters left out there survive.'

137

Winnie felt sick and she must have looked it because the soldier suddenly looked worried. 'Didn't mean to upset you, love. Our men will sort Hitler out all right, don't you worry.'

'I'm not upset,' she said. 'I'm worried about my husband, he's out there. He's in the Field Ambulance Parachute, went in on D-Day. Did any of you see him, did he treat any of you? His name's Mac. I haven't heard anything from him.'

'Sorry, love,' the soldier said. 'To be honest I didn't take much notice of the medic who helped me, I was in a lot of pain. Whoever it was did a good job and saved my leg. Any of you others meet a medic called Mac?'

All the other soldiers shook their heads. 'You don't think of asking someone's name at the time.'

'Well, I'm glad you got help, whoever it was.'

'Just because you ain't heard from him yet don't mean that he's been hurt or anything. Writing letters home ain't easy when there's so much happening. He'll write soon as he can, I'm sure.'

Winnie nodded. She had to be content with that for now because there was nothing else she could do but wait and hope.

Chapter Twenty-five

'Look!' Frankie leaned forwards in the passenger seat of their ambulance and pointed up into the sky, as Bella negotiated their way across Ludgate Circus and into Fleet Street.

Bella glanced up through the windscreen and could see the telltale sign of a doodlebug's strike – a pall of smoke – which still hung in the air having hardly dispersed in the still summer day. They'd unfortunately become all too familiar with these new weapons of Hitler's – the so-called V1 vengeance rockets whose nickname of 'doodlebug' belied its vicious capabilities – which had been raining down on London, and rapidly increased the number of incidents Station 75 now had to deal with. All they knew about this afternoon's one was that it had struck in Aldwych, and must have caused a huge number of casualties as they'd been called in to help in an area that wasn't part of their usual patch.

'It's marking the spot, all right.' Bella checked in her wing mirror to see that Winnie and Rose were still following close behind. 'I dread to think what we'll find, Aldwych's such a busy area.'

Her fears proved true as when they arrived a few minutes later, the devastation was plain to see. The doodlebug had exploded in the middle of Aldwych's semi-circular street between Kingsway, the BBC's Bush House and the Air Ministry, gouging a deep hole in the road, and the blast had scythed down the street destroying everything in its path.

Parking as close as was safe, they each grabbed a stretcher out of the back and made their way towards the injured. Bella had seen a lot of bomb damage in her time working in the Ambulance Service, but this was one of the worst she'd seen. Bright red double-decker buses, such a common sight around London, had been ripped apart, one of them with its roof peeled back as if it had been cut open by a giant tin opener; others had their bodywork ripped to pieces along with their passengers. Trees that would have been flush with green leaves a short while ago had had them stripped bare and now were hung with pieces of human flesh; while the ground crunched underfoot, littered with broken glass blown out from the hundreds of windows overlooking the area that now gaped darkly, like empty eye sockets.

Civil defence workers already on the scene had started the grim task of sorting the living from the dead and there was a sea of stretchers lined up with victims on them that would never move again.

'Over here.' A policeman beckoned to them where two injured women lay on the ground.

Glad of something to focus on, Bella hurried over with Frankie.

'Hello, I'm Bella, what's your name?' she asked, kneeling down by the young woman whose clothes were in shreds and whose exposed skin was peppered with the type of small grazes caused by flying glass.

'Alice.' Her voice was husky from the dust. 'I was waiting at the post office.'

'Can you tell me if you hurt anywhere?'

'My head, my side.'

'All right, I'm just going to check your legs and arms for any breaks and then we'll get you on a stretcher and off to hospital.' She quickly checked for breaks, aware that Frankie was busy doing the same thing with the other woman who lay nearby. Luckily for this woman she didn't appear to have any bones broken but her injuries might be less obvious and hidden inside her.

Frankie helped her lift Alice on to the stretcher where Bella covered her with a blanket, quickly filling in a label and attaching it to a button on what remained of the young woman's jacket. Bella was just waiting for Frankie to be ready to help her carry Alice to the ambulance when a man's voice made her look round.

'I help you?' The voice belonged to a tall man, dressed in RAF uniform, with striking cornflower-blue eyes and who she noticed had 'Poland' embroidered on a shoulder flash at the top of his sleeve – that explained his accent. 'I help you lift, will be quicker.'

Bella glanced at Frankie who was busy splinting her own casualty's legs together and wouldn't be ready for a few minutes yet. She nodded and smiled at him. 'Thank you, yes, I'd appreciate your help. There are so many casualties here . . . we need to get them to hospital as quickly as we can.'

The man clicked his heels together and gave a little bow before he went to the far end of the stretcher ready to lift. Between them they transferred Alice to the ambulance and returned to where Frankie was now ready to take her own casualty. The Polish airman then helped Frankie, leaving Bella free to attend to an unconscious man who had a nasty-looking wound on his head, blood running down and soaking his white shirt.

'That was a big help, pity we don't get someone to do that all the time,' Frankie said when she returned with another stretcher. 'He's gone off 'elping carry more casualties. See?'

Bella glanced up from where she was preparing a dressing for the man's head wound and saw that the Polish airman was assisting another ambulance crew to transfer a patient to their ambulance. 'He'll be kept busy here, that's for sure.'

Bella was surprised but glad when he returned to help her with the man.

'You're being a huge support, you know,' Bella said to his back as they carried the man between them. 'Not having to wait for your crew mate to give me a lift really saves time and I couldn't help noticing what you're doing helping other crews.'

'I'm glad to help,' he called back over his shoulder. 'This is very bad, so many hurt and killed.'

'One of the worst doodlebug attacks I've seen so far.'

After they'd loaded the stretcher into the back of the Station 75 ambulance, he went back to help Frankie with her patient while Bella did the final preparations for the man, who still remained unconscious, tucking a hot-water bottle in under the blanket to keep him warm.

With four casualties in the back, and Frankie staying in there to watch over them on the drive to St Bart's, the nearest hospital, Bella closed the back doors and turned to the Polish airman and smiled. 'Thank you for your help, we both really appreciate it. These casualties will get to hospital all the quicker because of you.'

The officer smiled at her. 'I hope they can be made better again.' He clicked his heels and gave a little bow. 'Drive safely.'

'I always do,' Bella said over her shoulder as she hurried round to the driver's door. 'Thanks again.'

As she drove away she thought about the new airman. The fact that he was a Polish officer explained the unusual manners, the bowing and clicking of heels which she rather liked. Whoever he was, his help was making a difference today; getting casualties to hospital that bit faster sometimes made the difference between life and death.

After delivering the first four casualties to St Bart's they returned to Aldwych for more and she saw that the Polish airman was still there and had been commandeered into helping carry stretchers into the army lorries which were also being used to take survivors to hospital. He didn't have a chance to come over to help them again, but he did nod his head and smile at Bella as he passed nearby, carrying a stretcher with a soldier.

Chapter Twenty-six

Frankie stirred a spoonful of precious sugar into her tea – she needed it after the shift they'd just done. Taking it outside to the garden she sat down on the back step in the June sunshine but, despite its warmth and the heat of the cup cradled in her hands, she still felt chilled to the bone. She'd been to so many incidents since she'd joined the Ambulance Service, and seen things that nobody would ever want to see, but yesterday's call-out to Aldwych had left her badly shaken. The blasted doodlebug rockets were worse in many ways than when the bombers droned overhead – at least then most people were in the shelters – but these weapons arrived at any time of day and night, hurting and killing people who were just going about their everyday lives. One moment they were doing their jobs or walking down the street, the next the doodlebug came diving down on them and ... *boom*.

'Here she is.' Rose's voice startled Frankie and she

looked up to see her and Josie standing in the doorway. Rose had Flora in her arms, the little girl's arms hooked around her friend's neck.

'Mornin', ducks,' Josie said. 'Mind if I join yer?'

Frankie shook her head and beckoned Josie to sit beside her. 'There's tea in the pot. Rose, pour a cup for you and Josie, will you, please?'

'You all right?' Josie asked. 'Only you look a bit peaky today.'

Frankie shrugged. 'We had a bad call-out yesterday, doodlebug exploded in Aldwych ... A lot of people were killed and injured. They weren't doing anyone any harm, just going about their lives and then ... ' She shook her head.

'I've come to ask your advice, but I think I know now what you'll say.' Josie paused to take a cup of tea that Rose had just brought out to her. 'Thanks, ducks.' She waited for a moment, watching Rose lead Flora down the far end of the garden to look at the hens, and once they were out of earshot she went on, 'I've been thinking about them blasted doodlebugs and the way they come over. They ain't like the bombers and I'm worried about my children. There's talk of evacuating them again and I think I've got to send them for their own safety. I don't want to but if the worst happened ...'

Frankie put her hand on Josie's arm. 'After what I've seen I wouldn't hesitate to send them out of harm's way.'

Josie nodded. 'That's what me head says, even though the heart's crying at the thought of doing it but you know what you're talking about, you've seen the havoc and injuries them blasted things can cause ... so I'll do the right thing.'

'I wish this 'orrible war was done,' Frankie said. 'We just think we're getting somewhere and then it goes and gets even worse. So, do what you have to do to protect your children, Josie. A few months of them away in the countryside is better than the alternative of what might 'appen to them if they stay here.'

Chapter Twenty-seven

July's warm weather had brought perfect growing conditions for the vegetables and fruits planted on Station 75's allotment, but it was also ideal for the weeds, too, Bella thought as she pinched out a tiny fat hen plant that was fighting for space with a small beetroot seedling. She, Winnie and Frankie had come down to the allotment this afternoon to do some weeding which Bella was enjoying, being outside in the summer sunshine, doing a therapeutic sort of task while being able to chat with her friends – it felt perfect.

'Mac hasn't told me where he is,' Winnie said. 'At least if I knew that I'd be able to look it up on a map.'

'You know they can't say where they are, Winnie, and if they did it would only get blacked out by the censor.' Frankie leaned back on her heels. 'I know it's frustrating not knowin', but you've got to stop torturing yourself about it or it'll drive you crazy.'

Bella looked at her two friends who were both in the same boat with their husbands somewhere in France. Luckily, they'd both now heard from them since they went over with the invasion, the letters arriving just a few days ago, much to their delight. At least her worry about her brother was over for the moment; he was still staying with their mother but was due to return to the army to a new unit next week, but where he'd be sent to then she didn't know. She hoped it would be somewhere in England, thinking he'd already done his fair share of fighting. Though whether the army would take that into consideration or not she didn't know, but it was no use worrying about it now, she would have to cross that bridge if she came to it.

'I know that!' Winnie said. 'But it won't stop me wanting to know, I'm nosy.' She threw a plucked weed over at Frankie who quickly retaliated, the two of them launching into a full-scale weed fight.

'Hey, you two, we're supposed to be pulling up weeds, not throwing them around,' Bella said, sternly.

The pair of them stopped for a moment and grinned at each other, then with a nod of agreement both launched a barrage of plucked weeds at Bella. She had no choice but to defend herself and joined in the fight, which ended quickly as the three of them were giggling so much that they rolled over onto their backs, laughing up at the blue sky which was dappled with fluffy clouds, while Trixie cavorted around them barking loudly.

'That was fun,' Winnie said a few minutes later.

'We'll have to clear up the mess, though.' Bella stared

up at the clouds which drifted slowly over the city, tempering the heat of the sun when they passed in front of it.

'We will, don't worry,' Frankie said. 'But not just yet, let's lie 'ere for a bit longer.'

They fell into silence, and with the warmth of the day, Bella's eyelids grew heavy and she felt herself slowly beginning to drift towards sleep but was hauled back by Trixie suddenly barking. Opening her eyes, and shielding them against the sun, she saw that the little dog had run off to greet a tall figure walking towards them who stopped and patted her for a moment before heading their way again. Had Station Officer Steele sent someone to fetch them?

'Looks like we got a visitor.' Frankie sat up beside her and then nudged Bella in the arm. 'It's him!'

'Who?' Winnie said.

'The Polish airman who helped us at Aldwych,' Frankie whispered. 'What's he doing here? And why's he carrying a bunch of flowers?'

Bella and Winnie sat up in unison and the three of them watched as the airman approached with Trixie skipping along at his heels, clearly happy to see him.

'Good afternoon.' The airman took off his RAF cap, smoothing down his dark brown hair, and bowed stiffly from the waist, clicking his heels as he did so.

'Good afternoon.' Winnie stood up. 'Can we help you?'

Frankie got up as well, pulling Bella with her.

'I went to your ambulance station, number 75, and they said that you,' his eyes met Bella's, 'were here. Remember we met at Aldwych.'

Bella nodded. 'Yes, you were very kind and helped me and Frankie.'

'We don't usually get visits from people who help us at incidents,' Winnie said. 'So, what brings you here?'

'Winnie!' Frankie said. 'You'll have to excuse our friend, she's rather direct at times.'

The Polish airman smiled. 'Is good to be direct, I think, so I will be. My name is Stefan Kaminski and you please tell me your names.'

'I'm Winnie, this is Frankie, and Bella,' Winnie said, pointing first to Frankie and then to Bella.

'Then I would like to ask you, Bella, if you would do me the pleasure of coming to a dance with me?' His striking cornflower-blue eyes fixed on her face as he held out the bunch of flowers to her, with a small bow.

Bella's cheeks grew warm and she ignored the nudge in her arms from both Winnie and Frankie who stood either side of her. She was lost for words for a few moments, completely taken aback by his invitation.

'Bella would love to—' Winnie began.

Her friend's words spurred her into action. 'I'm sorry but I don't think that's a good idea,' Bella said, steeling herself against the look of disappointment on Stefan's face.

'Why ever not?' Winnie said. 'It would do you good to go out dancing.'

'No!' Bella said. 'But thank you for asking.' She wanted to turn round and run back to Station 75, but before she could leave Winnie took the bunch of flowers from Stefan and thrust them into her hands.

'All right, if you don't want to go dancing, how about going for a cup of tea with Stefan now? There's a little café just around the corner, perfect for a cuppa,' Winnie suggested. 'Frankie and I can finish up here.'

'A cup of tea together would be good,' Stefan agreed.

Bella considered for a moment, looking down at the bunch of summer flowers which were beautiful, the scent of the fragrant sweet peas amongst them perfuming the air. It would be churlish and rude to refuse to at least have a cup of tea with him since he'd gone to all the trouble to come here, brought her flowers and had helped them at Aldwych. 'All right, a cup of tea, thank you.'

'Excellent, we'll see you back at Station 75 in a while then,' Winnie said. 'Don't hurry back.'

'We're goin' to take a long time to get this finished if you carry on at the rate you're going,' Frankie said.

Winnie tore her eyes away from the retreating backs of Bella and Stefan as they walked back past the Tower of London towards the little café. She was delighted that her friend had attracted the attention of a handsome airman – Bella had shut herself off from any chance of love for long enough. 'I'll catch up in a minute, don't worry.'

Frankie sat back on her heels on her side of the vegetable bed. 'Do you think Bella's done the right thing?'

'Absolutely. She's mourned for James quite long enough, it's time she had some fun again, some love from a good man in her life again.'

'How do we know if Stefan *is* a good man? I'd hate to see Bella get hurt again.'

'I think he is for several reasons. Firstly, he was there helping at Aldwych, it wasn't very pleasant and plenty of people would have gone the other way rather than help and have to see what was there; and secondly, Trixie likes him. She's a wonderful judge of character, aren't you?' She stroked Trixie's ears as the little dog had heard her name mentioned and come over to her mistress for some attention.

'But ain't Polish airmen supposed to be rather ... dashing and cavalier and have a reputation from their love of enjoyin' the company of many different women? Their manners alone make them stand out from British fellas.'

'Well he has got lovely manners,' Winnie laughed. 'I love all that bowing and clicking of heels, and bringing Bella a bunch of flowers was lovely. I know some Polish pilots have the reputation of wooing many women, I remember Harry telling me that some of the pilots in his squadron used to pretend to be Polish because they got so much female attention. Not surprising since they seem to be better at courting women than British chaps are. He also spoke very highly of the Poles in his squadron, said they were grand chaps, very courageous, brave as lions and terrifically good pilots.' She smiled at Frankie. 'Don't worry, I have every intention of keeping a close eye on Bella. I won't let anybody hurt her, regardless of whether they click heels and bow.'

'Well I suppose it's only a cup of tea they've gone to

'ave, so let's not jump the gun on this, although it would be lovely for Bella to fall in love with a decent fella, she's missed James badly.'

'I know, she's buried herself away in her writing for far too long, but perhaps now it's time for her to find some love again, and why not with the handsome Stefan?'

Chapter Twenty-eight

Bella wasn't in the habit of going to cafés, or anywhere else for that matter, with men she knew nothing about and it felt odd and awkward to be sitting here opposite Stefan who had been nothing but considerate, kind and polite since he'd arrived at the allotment.

'Cheers.' Stefan held up his cup of tea in salute to her. 'And thank you for coming here with me, I must seem very . . .' He paused, searching for the right word, 'bold to arrive and ask you go to dance. I not do this before but . . .' He looked down at the table for a few moments, fiddling with a teaspoon on his saucer, before looking up and meeting her eyes. 'I think about you a lot since I see you at Aldwych last week, there's something about you that . . .' He shrugged and smiled at her, his cornflower-blue eyes crinkling at the corners.

Bella's cheeks grew warm again, she wasn't used to this sort of attention so she fixed her eyes on his wings badge on the front of his tunic for a moment, noticing how different it was from the British RAF pilots' which she'd seen on Winnie's brother Harry's uniform. This one was in the form of an eagle with drooping wings carrying what looked like a wreath. She looked up at him, meeting his eyes. 'How did you know where to find me?'

'I see the number on your ambulance – Station 75. I find out where it is and come and find you there, but they say you not there but at allotment.'

'Who told you where to find me?'

'I don't know, he sit by the garage reading newspaper.'

'Did he have brown hair and a cigarette tucked behind his ear?' Bella asked.

Stefan nodded.

'That was Sparky then. Did he quiz you about why you wanted to find me?'

'Yes.' He smiled. 'But don't worry, I not say.'

'Good, or I'd never hear the end of it. Sparky's an excellent crew member, but he loves a good gossip.' Bella took a sip of tea, thinking she rather liked the way Stefan had dealt with Sparky. 'Thank you for your help at Aldwych, it helped us to get the casualties to hospital that bit quicker, we don't often get assistance from other people.'

'I glad to help, was bad place for a witch to land, so many people around.'

Bella frowned. 'A witch?'

He smiled at her. 'Is what we call doodlebugs. We do best to shoot them down before they get to London.'

'What do you fly?' Bella asked.

156

'A Spitfire.' He smiled again. 'I love it, is marvellous machine.'

'Winnie's brother used to fly a Spitfire till he got hit during the Battle of Britain. He was badly burnt and bailed out into the sea. He was lucky to survive.'

A shadow passed across Stefan's face.

Bella put a hand to her mouth. 'I'm sorry, I shouldn't have said that.'

Stefan's eyes met hers. 'Is fine, is what happens sometimes, I lost good friends. Your friend's brother was lucky, many are not.' He paused for a moment, sombre-faced, before smiling again. 'So, we must enjoy life for them and us. Tell me, Bella, you always live in London?'

'No, I grew up in the countryside. My father was a gardener on a big estate and I only came to London after he died because I needed a job, so I came to work as a housemaid. I'd wanted to be a teacher, but I had to find work and somewhere to live and . . .' She shrugged. 'A home of sorts went with the job, but I hated it and when the war started I was very glad to leave and join the Ambulance Service.'

Stefan nodded sympathetically. 'After war you become a teacher, live your dream, yes?'

Bella smiled. 'I have another dream now, and I've already started to fulfil it and if I can I want to carry on and do more after the war. I love it very much and it feels the right thing for me to do.'

'What is it?'

'I love to write and want to earn my living as a writer. I've already sold stories to magazines and had articles in newspapers, and I'd like to write novels as well.'

157

'I wish you great success.'

'What about you?' Bella asked. 'Did you grow up in a city or the countryside?'

'In Warsaw, my father has shop and I go to work with him but then I see aeroplane . . . ' he shrugged, 'then I want to be a pilot. I get a place to train and become fighter pilot in 1939 and then the Nazis came.' The shadow passed over his face again as he tapped his fingers on the table, before sighing and looking at Bella and shrugging. 'We fight hard, but their planes better . . . faster, and they had more than us, we outnumbered . . . we had no planes to replace the ones shot down. It was bad, we have fighting spirit but no chance against so many.'

'What happened?'

'We escape over border to Romania and was put in internment camp, but I not wait to see what happen next. I want to fight not wait. I escape and go to France with other pilots, then come to England and join RAF.'

'From what I hear Polish pilots have made a huge con-tribution to defending the country,' Bella said.

Stefan shrugged. 'We fight to stop the Nazis and to go home again one day to what is left. They destroy so much of my beautiful country.' He fell silent for a moment and shook his head. 'We should talk about happy things. Bella, what do you write about, why do you write? Do you feel you must, in here?' He put his hand over his heart.

Bella stared at him for a moment. She had never been asked that before, certainly not how her writing made her feel. There was something different about Stefan compared with all the British men she'd known. He had a passion about him, he wasn't frightened of talking about how something made him feel or to think of emotions in others. She rather liked it.

By the time they'd finished their tea and ordered another cup, and drunk that, too, Bella was surprised to see that they'd been in the café for well over an hour and it was time that she was getting back to Station 75 before the boss was on the warpath.

'I'm going to have to go back to work. Thank you for the tea, it's been lovely talking to you.' She started to get up and Stefan immediately hurried round to pull out her chair for her.

'Can I walk you back?'

She nodded. 'All right, thank you.'

Arriving at the entrance to Station 75, Bella turned to Stefan. 'I'll say goodbye here, thank you for walking me back.'

'My pleasure. Can I see you again, for cup of tea?' Stefan asked.

To her surprise, Bella's mind instantly said yes, she'd enjoyed spending time with him and what harm would it do to meet again sometime? 'I'd like that.'

Stefan took hold of her hand and kissed it, then clicked his heels and bowed. 'Goodbye, Bella, I look forward seeing you again.'

She smiled at him. 'Goodbye then.' As she walked through the archway into Station 75 she could feel him watching her but resisted the sudden urge to turn around and wave back at him.

'There she is!' Winnie's voice shrieked out of the

common room window above the garages and Bella looked up to see her friend waving at her; she'd clearly been watching out for her return.

Bella laughed, she knew that she was about to be grilled – Winnie would want to know everything that had gone on, and in particular what she thought of Stefan. So, what did she think of him? She had to admit she rather liked him and would be happy to see him again, although she wasn't going to let on to Winnie. It would be rather fun to let her stew for a while, especially after she'd been so adamant about her accepting Stefan's invitation earlier.

Chapter Twenty-nine

Frankie loved being sent out to do this job, it made a welcome break from the usual routine work at Station 75 and gave her a chance to get out and about without an incident to attend to, as well as seeing how other ambulance stations were run. This one, Station 101 on White Horse Lane in Stepney, was situated in the Trafalgar School and ambulances now stood in the playground where children used to play.

'There you are.' The Station Officer handed her a pile of completed pay sheets which it was her job to collect from all the stations in their sector this morning and then deliver them all together to the pay office. 'Who's next on your list to collect?'

'Just Station 114 on Rifle Street in Poplar,' Frankie said. 'I've been working outwards from the nearest to the furthest, it's a lovely day to be out and about.'

'Indeed it is. If you came back here later no doubt you'd

see my crew making the most of it sitting out in deckchairs soaking up the sun.'

Frankie laughed. 'We do that too, it's nice to sit down and 'ave a rest once the ambulances are ready to go. Right, I'd better be off, thanks for these.'

Back in the car she set off for Station 114, driving past St Dunstan's church where she and Alastair had been married. Memories of that day came flooding back to her, making the hollow feeling of missing her husband ache even more inside. It was so hard not being able to see him, talk to him, hold him, just having to wait for precious letters to arrive, and working twenty-four-hour shifts didn't help either because if a letter arrived on the day she was working then she wouldn't get it until she returned home the next morning ... If a letter from him arrived today she wouldn't get it till tomorrow ... there could be one lying on the doormat waiting for her right now. Frankie smiled; she was only a street away from home, she could drop by and check. Turning the car left at the junction she headed for Matlock Street, taking a short diversion on the way to Poplar.

No one in Matlock Street owned a car so Frankie's arrival in one of Station 75's cars didn't go unnoticed. Parking outside number 25 she climbed out and waved to several of her neighbours who were out chatting in the street and enjoying the sunshine. As she opened the front door, Frankie closed her eyes and made a silent wish that there would be a letter for her on the doormat, but when she opened them she was disappointed, the only envelope that lay there was for Rose, all the way from her uncle in America. There was nothing from Alastair again. She picked up Rose's letter and put it in her pocket to give her friend later, doing her best to stamp down the swell of disappointment inside her.

She was about to leave when a sudden burst of laughter came from the kitchen, the familiar throaty laugh of Ivy combined with a deeper one – a man's. A flicker of anger sparked in Frankie. Who had she brought home this time? Was it another hapless GI who'd succumbed to her dubious charms?

Frankie hurried down the hall and without stopping to think burst into the kitchen where Ivy stood with her back to her, her arms wrapped around a man. But it was an Englishman, and one who Frankie knew – a local spiv, Micky Chandler. She stared at them, thinking Ivy had sunk to new depths: she'd gone from being married to a well-respected policeman to being involved with a spiv who, if rumour had it right, had wriggled his way out of National Service by paying for a dodgy doctor's certificate to get him out on medical grounds.

Ivy spun around and glared at her. 'What are you doing 'ere?' she sneered. 'You should be at work.'

'I am, and I'm workin' out this way so called in to see if there was any post. Caught you out, have I?'

'Ladies, ladies.' Micky raised his hands. 'There ain't no need to argue.' He smiled at Frankie, but his nicotine-stained teeth had more the look of a shark than a friendly greeting. 'I was just payin' my friend Ivy here a visit.'

Frankie rolled her eyes. 'And then some, by the look of it. It's your life, Ivy, but I don't think your late 'usband would be very happy about this.' She turned to go.

'Well he shouldn't 'ave bleedin' well got himself killed then, should he!' Ivy spat. 'I'm only 'aving a bit of fun, there's no harm in that.'

'That's right, we're just having fun,' Micky echoed. 'You've got to enjoy today because you don't know if you'll 'ave a tomorrow with this war on.' He reached into his suit pocket and pulled out a packet of nylons and held them out to Frankie. 'Here, 'ave these.'

Frankie stared at them for a few moments, taken aback by the man's gall. 'I'll stick to paintin' legs with gravy browning, thanks very much.'

'Well I'll 'ave them.' Ivy snatched them out of Mickey's hand and laughed. 'I ain't going to look a gift horse in the mouth.'

Anger flooded through Frankie and she turned and left them, banging the front door loudly as she went out, gulping in lungsful of air, glad of the warmth of the sunny day outside after the sickening revelation in the kitchen. Ivy was clearly happily involved with the slimy, cheating world of Micky Chandler and his black-market deals.

She climbed back into the car and sat for a few moments drumming her fingers on the steering wheel, trying to calm herself down. A knocking on the door window made her jump.

'Cooee, what you doing 'ere?' Josie called.

Frankie opened the driver's door. 'Hello, Josie, I'm out collectin' the pay sheets for our sector and thought I'd call in and see if there's any post for me ...' She shrugged. 'But there ain't.'

164

Josie narrowed her eyes. 'And . . . You look a bit peaky, ducks. If you ain't got a letter from Alastair today it don't mean anything, you know, the post from France ain't exactly regular. He'll write when he can because that fella loves you and will do everything he can to come back to you, just you wait and see.'

'I know, I just miss 'im and worry about him.' She paused for a moment. 'I had a shock in there, Ivy's got a visitor . . . That spiv, Micky Chandler, and they were looking very cosy.' Her friend looked uncomfortable and avoided Frankie's eyes. 'Do you know anything about this, Josie?'

Josie nodded. 'She's been 'anging around with him for a few months. I've seen them together walkin' down the street when you're on shift—'

'Why the hell didn't you tell me?' Frankie interrupted her. 'You're supposed to be my friend.'

'I *am* your friend.' Josie reached out and touched Frankie's shoulder. 'And that's why I didn't tell you. You've got enough on your plate workin' and worrying about Alastair without getting into more fights with Ivy over who she chooses to spend her time with. She's a bleedin' fool, if you ask me.' She paused for a moment. 'You know, even if I did tell her to stop seeing Chandler she wouldn't, so I've saved me breath. What would you 'ave done if I told you?'

Frankie bit her bottom lip and shrugged. 'I know what I'd like to do – chuck her out. I'll 'ave to tell her to stop seeing him, try and make 'er realise how upset Grandad would've been with her.'

'Save your breath, ducks. She wouldn't take a blind bit of notice of what you say, and it'll only cause more rows and upset in the 'ouse. Least it's been fairly calm lately with her, and until now she's had the sense to hide it from you, it was only you coming 'ome unexpected that's let the cat out of the bag.'

'It explains a lot, the extra butter and eggs and other black-market stuff.'

'Look, I know it ain't right and she's gone from one extreme to the other, from your grandad to Chandler, but look on the bright side: maybe she'll marry 'im and leave, that would be good, wouldn't it?'

Frankie nodded. 'Let's hope she does then, and the sooner the better. Josie, just promise me that you'll tell me anythin' else she gets up to, please. I'd rather know what's going on than stumble in on something like I did just now.'

'All right, ducks, I promise, but I only did it because I thought it was for the best for you. Your grandad asked me to look out for you and that's all I was doing.'

'I know.' She smiled at Josie. 'I don't know what I'd 'ave done without you here in Matlock Street. Since Grandad died you've been a treasure, you really 'ave.'

Josie laughed. 'Get away with you, you'll be makin' me blush.'

'Now, are you all right? Have you heard from the children?' Frankie asked. Josie's children, including little Flora, had been evacuated at the start of the week along with many others because of the new threat posed by the doodlebugs.

'I 'ad a letter yesterday, they've been lucky, and all kept together, fallen on their feet billeted in a big 'ouse in the

166

countryside.' Josie smiled but it didn't quite reach her eyes. Sending her children away to safety hadn't been easy for her, but she'd done it to keep them safe. 'It's so quiet in the 'ouse without them, though . . . Why don't you and Rose pop round for a cuppa tomorrow when you're at home?'

'We will do. I'd better get going, I'm due at Station 114 on Rifle Street next.' She started the engine and put the car into gear. 'See you tomorrow then.'

As she drove out of Matlock Street, the car juddering over the cobbles, Frankie was glad that she'd decided to go home to check for the post. She didn't like what she'd found but with Ivy it was always better to know what was going on than not know the whole story. The vile woman had sunk to even lower depths than before but if her hooking up with Chandler led to her marrying him and leaving Matlock Street for ever then that would be a good thing.

Chapter Thirty

Winnie knew there was something wrong as soon as she walked into the kitchen and saw Connie's face. Her carefree, happy mood from her long walk in Regent's Park with Trixie, enjoying the warmth of the summer's day, evaporated as her eyes were somehow instinctively drawn to the buff-coloured envelope lying on the kitchen table – a telegram. Trixie, sensing the sudden change of her mistress's mood, whined and jumped up, resting her small paws on Winnie's leg. She leaned down and patted the little dog's head, glad of a few moments' normality.

'It might not be what you think,' Connie said, rushing over to Winnie and putting her arm around her.

She picked up the telegram, her hands shaking as she checked the name and address on the front: it was for her. She looked at Connie, feeling like a young girl again, wishing that her godmother could fix things, make her feel better, because she feared that whatever was inside the envelope was going to alter her life, and possibly in a way that she would never, ever want it to be.

'Do you want me to open it for you?' Connie asked, gently.

Winnie shook her head. Taking a deep breath, she tore the envelope open and took out the single sheet of folded paper, closing her eyes for a moment to brace herself for what it may contain, then she opened them and read the words, her eyes skittering over them, not wanting to believe the news they carried.

DEEPLY REGRET TO INFORM YOU THAT YOUR HUSBAND
576329 PVT MCARTNEY MISSING IN ACTION FROM
OPERATIONS 4TH JULY.

'Mac's missing in action,' she managed to say before her legs buckled, her bones seeming to have turned to jelly. Connie grabbed hold of her and steered her towards a chair which she gratefully slumped down on, leaning her head forwards in her hands. Mac was missing. What did that really mean? Was he missing and dead, but not yet found? Missing and injured but not found? Or missing and being held prisoner somewhere? She had no answers to these questions.

A cold wet nose butted at her hand and she sat up. Trixie immediately jumped onto her lap and leaned against her, her liquid brown eyes watching Winnie's face closely. She wrapped her arm around the little dog, glad of her solid, comforting presence.

'Here, drink this.' Connie put a glass of brandy on the table in front of her. 'It'll help.'

She grabbed hold of it and took a sip, the fiery liquid warming her as it went down, its flame-like heat easing the icy chill that had settled in her stomach after reading those terrible words.

Connie kneeled down beside her and took hold of one of Winnie's hands. 'I know it says missing, but that doesn't mean what you're thinking. He could just have got separated from his unit, it doesn't mean that he's dead, Winnie. Don't go crossing bridges until you have to, keep hoping, you must keep doing that.'

She looked into her godmother's blue eyes, which were bright with tears. She'd suffered the loss of her fiancé in the Great War and knew too well the pain of losing someone you loved in wartime.

'Where is he then?' Her voice broke and she started to cry, silent tears to begin with but then the momentum of sobs took over, and she felt Connie's arms wrap around her and heard Trixie whining at her mistress's distress.

'Winnie.' Bella's voice filtered through to her, pulling her back from the heavy drifting feeling as she dozed. She felt a soft, warm hand brush her forehead and opened her eyes to see her friend anxiously peering at her, while Trixie lay on the edge of the bed watching her every move.

Bella sat down on the side of her bed. 'Connie told me about the telegram.' She took hold of Winnie's hand which lay on top of a blanket. Connie must have come in and draped one over her when she'd fallen asleep on her bed after she'd come up to her room to be alone. 'You mustn't give up hope, not while there's still a chance. Promise me you won't, Winnie.'

'But it's so hard not to think the worst.' Winnie sighed. 'Of course I want him to be found alive and well, more than anything, but what if he isn't?'

'Now look here.' Bella put her hand on her hip. 'You don't know that and until you're told otherwise you need to keep on hoping. You've always talked about showing some stiff upper lip when times get tough, well that's now and you need to do just that. Mac would want you to keep going and not crumble, you've got a job to do and with doodlebugs being fired at us every day you're very much needed at Station 75. You've got to get a grip!' Bella's cheeks were flushed pink by the time she'd finished.

Winnie stared at her friend in shock. She'd never spoken to her like that before, and it was quite a revelation to see her friend so emboldened. She couldn't help smiling.

Bella frowned. 'What are you smiling for?'

'You, you gave me a jolly good telling-off there. And I probably deserved it.' She shrugged. 'I know what you say is right, but it feels impossible to keep my chin up, my upper lip stiff.' She did her best to smile, again. 'But I'm going to have to, aren't I?'

'Yes, because if you don't the not knowing will eat away at you and you can't let that happen, Winnie, not when you've got an important job to do with casualties' lives depending on you doing it well. There's no telling how long it will be before you get any news about what's

171

happened to Mac. So, in the meantime, you must keep on going, even when it feels so hard to do just that. Right?'

Winnie nodded. 'Keep reminding me please, Bella. Will you?'

'Of course I will, we'll all do everything we can to help you. Connie's been on the telephone to your father at the War Office to see if he can find out anything more and he said he'll do his best. It's useful having him in the right place.'

Winnie sighed, grateful that her father was prepared to help. Unlike her mother, he hadn't shown direct dislike or rudeness to Mac, in fact they hadn't actually met properly, not even at their wedding as her parents had sat at the back and then slipped away before she could introduce him to her new husband. He'd always been a distant father, leaving dealing with the children to his wife and generally went along with her ways, preferring a quiet life, but in this case he was obviously prepared to do what he could for her.

'And in the meantime, I need to keep hoping, yes?' Winnie said, mentally applying some of that hope towards her father discovering more about what had happened.

Bella smiled at her. 'You're learning fast. Now come on, you should come downstairs and help peel some potatoes – that will help keep you occupied. I managed to get some rabbit from the butcher's this afternoon so it's rabbit stew tonight.'

172

Chapter Thirty-one

'This arrived for you in this morning's post.' Station Officer Steele handed Bella an envelope with her first name and the address of Station 75 written on the front in bold handwriting.

Bella stopped sweeping out the back of the ambulance and took it from the boss, frowning, as she stared at the unfamiliar writing, wondering who had written to her here. Anyone she usually had letters from knew her home address and sent them there. 'Thank you.'

'You look rather surprised, if you don't mind me saying so,' Station Officer Steele said. 'I hope it's not bad news.'

'Only one way to find out,' Frankie said, appearing at the back of the ambulance from where she'd been polishing the wing mirrors during the regular morning preparations on their vehicle. 'Open it.'

'Or perhaps you'd rather wait and do it when you're on your own,' the boss said.

Bella shook her head. 'No, it's all right. I'll do it now

and see who it's from.' She opened the envelope and took out a single sheet of paper and looked at the name signed at the bottom – it was from Stefan. Immediately her cheeks grew warm and she was aware of her friend's and the boss's gaze on her.

'Who's it from then?' Frankie asked.

'Stefan.'

Station Officer Steele raised her eyebrows. 'Ah, the Polish pilot.'

'What does he say?' Frankie leaned forward to try and get a look but Bella quickly snatched the letter out of the way so she couldn't read it.

'I haven't read it myself yet.' She sat on the back of the ambulance and began to read.

Dear Bella,

Would please you do me great honour of accompany me to dance on Saturday evening? I very much like to take you I enjoy to be with you on Tuesday.

If you say yes, please telephone the officers' mess at West Malling 359 and ask speak to me.

I hope you say yes.

Yours,

Stefan

'Well?' Frankie said. 'What does it say?'

'He's asked me to go to a dance with him on Saturday night,' she said. 'But I can't go.'

'Why ever not?' the boss said. 'I had the impression you rather liked him.' It hadn't taken long for word to get around

174

Station 75 that Bella had had a cup of tea with a handsome Polish pilot, who had sought her out and gone to find her at the allotment. Station Officer Steele had been very interested in what had happened and had quizzed Bella about him and their visit to the café earlier in the week, always looking out for her crew members in a motherly fashion.

'I do, we got on very well and I enjoyed spending time with him, but it wouldn't be right to go out to a dance while Winnie's so worried about Mac. She's doing reasonably well but needs our support.'

'I appreciate your sentiment, Bella, but I think it's totally wrong in this case,' the boss said. 'Winnie's a grown woman and yes, she is very anxious about her husband's disappearance, but it doesn't mean that you shouldn't go out and enjoy yourself. I doubt very much that Winnie would want you to say no because of her.'

'You should go,' Frankie agreed. 'Ask Winnie when she gets back, I bet she'll tell you to go as well.' She grinned. 'She was delighted when Stefan turned up at the allotment the other day, so there's no way she'll tell you to turn him down.'

Bella nodded. 'All right, I'll go but only if Winnie doesn't mind. I'll ask her when she gets back from the incident with Rose.'

'And then you can telephone Stefan's aerodrome from my office and accept his invitation.' Station Officer Steele beamed at her. 'It will do you good to go out dancing.'

Bella caught Frankie's eye and her friend winked at her. 'Why do I get the feeling that I'm outnumbered here?'

'Because we want you to be happy and enjoy yourself,' Frankie said.

Chapter Thirty-two

The air-raid siren began to wail across the rooftops of London, its rising and falling like some frightened beast, making the crew of Station 75 once again abandon what they were doing and run for the shelter.

'Here we go again! Another bleedin' doodlebug!' Sparky shouted, looking up into the sky, shielding his eyes with his hand against the glare of the July sunshine.

'Come on, Sparky, you know the routine.' Frankie dropped her rag into the pail of soapy water, grabbed her steel helmet from where she'd left it on the front seat of the ambulance and put it on. 'Don't stand there lookin' because if it's heading our way we need to get to the shelter.' She caught hold of Sparky's arm and pulled him along with her, following the rest of the crew across the courtyard to the brick-built shelter which they were in and out of, some days, like yo-yos.

'Right, that's everybody now in here,' Station Officer

Steele said, ticking off their names on her list of crew members on duty, as Frankie closed the door behind her and Sparky.

Coming in from the bright light outside, it took a few moments for her eyes to adjust to the dimmer light of the shelter, which was packed with crew.

'Over here, Frankie,' Rose called to her. 'I saved you a seat.'

'Thanks.' She sat down next to Rose and leaned back against the brick wall, glad of the cooler temperature inside, out of the glare of the sun.

'Do you think we'll be long in here?' Rose asked.

Frankie shrugged. 'Who knows, it—' She stopped as the all too familiar sound of a doodlebug's engine, getting louder by the moment, could be heard. Other crew members fell silent, the atmosphere in the shelter changing as if everyone was willing the 'phut-phut' noise of the engine to keep on going, at least just enough to get past them, as it got louder and nearer. The sudden cut-out of the rocket's engine seemed to draw all the air out of the shelter and Frankie was sure that hers wasn't the only heart that had started to beat harder and faster as she began to count inside her head. Every second that passed meant the rocket was nearer to exploding, but how near it was as it began its deadly descent towards the ground, they had no idea.

'Brace yourselves!' Station Officer Steele shouted, and as one, everyone curled themselves up as best they could. Rose reached out and grabbed hold of Frankie's hand as a loud explosion rocked the ground somewhere close by, sending dust pattering down onto their steel helmets from the ceiling.

'Is everybody all right, anybody hurt?' The boss's voice rang out loud and clear through the dusty atmosphere of the shelter.

Frankie sat up, aware that she was shaking, and from the feel of Rose's hand in hers, she wasn't the only one.

'No,' many of the crew called out, looking around at each other, checking everyone was unhurt.

Frankie noticed that Rose also had tight hold of Bella's hand, on the other side of her, and Winnie, who was on the far side of Bella, was cuddling Trixie tightly in her arms. All three of them were looking as shaken as Frankie felt.

'That was bleedin' close!' Sparky said. 'Do you want me to go out and have a look first, boss, see what the damage is?'

'I'll come with you. The rest of you stay here until we get back,' Station Officer Steele instructed before she and Sparky hurried outside. The moment they left, the remaining crew erupted into discussion about what had happened, where the doodlebug could have landed.

'Are you all right?' Frankie asked Rose.

Rose nodded. 'It was a bit of a shock. Where do you think it hit?'

'It can't be far away.' Frankie hoped that Station 75 hadn't suffered any damage. So far, they'd been extremely lucky, any incendiaries that had fallen during the Blitz had been quickly put out and even when an unexploded bomb had landed in the courtyard, it had been successfully dug up and defused with no damage done other than a large hole, which was easily filled in and the cobbles redone.

'Wish they'd hurry up and get back,' Winnie said stroking Trixie's head. 'Sitting in here not knowing what's going on isn't fun.'

It was only a matter of minutes, though it seemed much longer, before Station Officer Steele returned. 'Paterson, you go straight out, Sparky's waiting to go in your ambulance.' She waited until Sparky's attendant had gone before addressing the rest of the crew. 'The rocket came down just the other side of the railway line, a short way up the Minories from us. Several buildings have been destroyed and we need to send out some more ambulances.' She paused for a moment, grabbing hold of the back of her chair where she always sat beside the telephone waiting for call-outs. 'We have been extremely lucky, it missed us by a matter of tens of yards, and the fact that Station 75 is enclosed within the courtyard has saved us from the effects of the blast. Our first actions now are to attend to the injured, so, Frankie and Rose, Winnie and Bella, you take your ambulances out onto the Minories ready for any casualties, I don't know how many there will be, and we haven't officially been asked, but since we're the nearest station it's common sense to send ambulances from here. As for the rest of you, I'll organise some of you to go out and help too, keeping some crews here on standby as well.'

Frankie, Rose, Winnie and Bella got up and hurried out to the ambulances.

'The boss looks pretty shaken up,' Winnie said, carrying Trixie in her arms.

'She ain't the only one,' Frankie said. 'If that doodle-bug's engine had cut out a mere fraction of a second earlier it would have plummeted down right on top of us.'

'Don't say that.' Bella pulled a face.

Frankie put her arm through Bella's. 'It's true though; there but for the grace of God go I. So, come on, girls, let's go and do our job and help those who haven't been so lucky as us today – at least it won't take us long to get there.'

Chapter Thirty-three

As soon as Winnie opened the front door of Connie's house, Trixie rushed in, her claws clattering on the black and white tiles on the floor, before she suddenly halted, her nose held high as she sniffed and then growled low in her throat.

'What . . .' Winnie began as she stepped inside but paused as the familiar scent of Chanel No. 5 hit her, making her stomach instantly knot. Her mother was here. She turned to go out again, silently beckoning Trixie over to her with her hand, but before she could slip out of the front door and escape, the sitting room door opened and Connie came out, a warning look on her face, and all hope of running away vanished.

'Hello,' she said loudly, before mouthing silently, 'your mother's here to see you.' She indicated with a flick of her eyes towards the sitting room, where her visitor was waiting.

Winnie pulled a face, she had no desire to see her. 'What does she want?' she whispered.

Connie shrugged, and leaned close to her, speaking softly into her ear. 'She hasn't said, we've just been talking about Harry's new baby.' Winnie's brother's wife, Meredith, had given birth to their first son last week.

'Right, I just need to go and powder my nose and I'll be right down,' she said loudly, playing for time. She needed to prepare herself for battle because, from past experience, going back right to when she was a little girl, time spent with her mother was rarely pleasant, and certainly over the past few years had been downright awful. Why she'd arrived today, Winnie didn't know, but she wasn't optimistic about her visit because her mother never came to see her without some hidden agenda and right now, with her worry about Mac being at the forefront of her mind, she definitely wasn't in the mood to deal with any of her mother's nonsense.

'All right, I'll go and make some more tea, it will be ready by the time you come down.' Connie spoke in a loud voice, laying a hand on Winnie's arm and squeezing it sympathetically. 'Don't be long, better to get it over and done with as she's already been waiting for over an hour,' she finished whispering into Winnie's ear.

Upstairs, Winnie stretched out her reprieve to ten minutes, her mind going over different scenarios of why her mother had arrived, none of them good. The only way that she could get her mother to leave was to go down and face her. Picking up Trixie and tucking her under her arm she slowly went downstairs, her legs feeling like they were filling up with lead with each step she took.

'Ah, there you are, at last.' Her mother glanced at her

watch as Winnie entered the room. 'I've been waiting here since two o'clock and I have a train to catch, Margot.' The use of her real name jarred, as no one else but her parents used it now. She preferred to use her Station 75 nickname which suited her much better. Her mother proffered up her cheek to be kissed and Winnie dutifully approached and although she felt more like slapping it, her upbringing dictated that she peck briefly on the powdered skin, taking care to hold her breath as she did so to avoid inhaling an extra strong dose of Chanel No. 5. It was her mother's signature perfume and a whiff of it had the ability to whisk her back to her childhood and the memory of one of many reprimands that her mother had given her.

'I didn't know you were coming.' Winnie sat down on the sofa beside Connie, settling Trixie on her lap. The dog was glaring at her mother, a strange sight to see from such a normally sweet-natured animal, but she had witnessed her mistress's distress at the hands of her mother in the past and clearly remembered it and was now in full protection mode.

'Some tea?' Connie picked up the teapot, ready to pour her a cup.

She smiled at her godmother, glad that she was here. 'Yes, please.'

'I'll come straight to the point then, since I've a train to catch.' Her mother touched the string of pearls at her neck. 'Your father has made enquiries about . . . your husband's disappearance.' Winnie curled her hands into fists, squeezing them tightly; her mother couldn't even bring herself to say Mac's name, and if she wasn't so desperate to hear the results of her father's search then she'd have happily walked out of here right now, letting all the rules of polite society that she'd been brought up in go to hell. 'But I'm afraid he's drawn a complete blank, there's no more information to be had, not surprising with the amount of men out there and the fighting that's going on – the disappearance of one man is rather insignificant in the grand scheme of things.'

'Not to me it isn't!' Winnie snapped. 'He's my husband and I love him, and I want to know what's happened to him.'

Connie put her hand on Winnie's arm. 'It doesn't mean that he's not still alive though, it's just that no more word has come through yet.'

Winnie nodded and smiled gratefully at her godmother and picked up her teacup to take a welcome sip. The unaccustomed sweetness hit her straight away – Connie had put some of their precious sugar ration in it for the shock of finding her mother there.

'Well, the fact remains that he's still missing in action and so in that case I think you really should prepare yourself for the worst,' her mother said. 'Better to not expect good news than hold on to foolish hope.' She fixed her pale, icy-blue eyes on Winnie. 'If indeed you are widowed it doesn't mean that you can never marry again; in fact, you might find somebody far more suitable—'

'Cynthia!' Connie glared at Winnie's mother. 'Your daughter *does not* need to hear that sort of advice now, or indeed ever. I am shocked and frankly extremely disappointed that you could even think such thoughts.'

'I'm not,' Winnie said, recovering her voice after being left speechless at her mother's cold and callous words. 'I am never giving up hope that Mac will be found alive and well.' She stood up, with Trixie in her arms. 'My dog has got more compassion than you have, Mother. Don't bother calling again unless you have something pleasant to say for once.'

Flashing a look of apology at Connie, Winnie stalked out of the room and up the stairs to the privacy of her bedroom, her heart pounding and her blood thrumming around her body with anger and astonishment at the sheer cold-heartedness of her mother. She'd disapproved of Mac from the first time she'd seen him, when they were presented with their George Medals at Buckingham Palace, and had discovered that he was a conscientious objector, so when Winnie agreed to marry him it had been no surprise that her mother had been so against it – and clearly the passage of time had done nothing to change her opinion. The fact that Winnie loved him, and that he was a good, honourable man, did nothing to sway her mother's bigoted view and for her to come here and suggest that if . . . hot, stinging tears filled her eyes . . . if Mac didn't come back then she'd be free to marry someone her mother considered more socially suitable was utterly, utterly despicable.

Slumping down on her bed, she put Trixie down beside her and picked up the photograph frame with the picture of her and Mac together that she so loved, tracing his dear face with the tip of her finger. 'Please come back to me, Mac, wherever you are.'

Chapter Thirty-four

'I can stay at home, if you'd rather I didn't go.' Bella was watching Winnie's reflection in the dressing table mirror, where her friend was putting the finishing touches to her hair for her.

Winnie put a hand on her hip. 'Absolutely not! You have the chance to go out dancing with a dashing airman and there's no reason for you not to go. Especially if you have the crazy idea that I need to be mollycoddled and protected because Mac is missing.' Winnie's grey eyes met Bella's in the mirror. 'You going dancing isn't going to have the slightest effect on when I hear about Mac, and I suspect you might be feeling rather nervous about tonight and part of you would be quite happy to wriggle out of it.'

Bella's cheeks grew warm. 'All right, I admit I *am* nervous but honestly, Winnie, if you want me to stay with you, I will, I don't mind.'

'But I would, and so would Stefan.' Winnie rolled her

eyes. 'For goodness' sake, Bella, you *are* going to the ball. Now, turn around, Cinderella, so I can see what make-up you need.'

Bella swivelled around on the stool so that she was facing her friend and submitted to Winnie's expert hand, closing her eyes as lipstick, powder and mascara were applied, her friend having put herself in charge of preparing her for her evening out, doing her hair and make-up and giving her one of her pre-war silk dresses to wear, which was a rich emerald colour and swished delightfully and smoothly as she walked.

'Now keep your eyes shut until I tell you.' Winnie put her hands on Bella's shoulders and turned her back to face the mirror. 'Now you can look.'

Bella stared at herself, taken aback by the effect of the make-up that Winnie had applied. It was much more vibrant than she'd ever use herself, with pillar-box red lipstick accentuating the curved shape of her mouth.

'Well? What do you think?' Winnie asked. 'I think you look beautiful, Stefan's going to be bowled over when he sees you. Pillar-box red really suits you, with your gorgeous dark-brown hair and creamy skin, probably a lot better than me, actually.'

'I look ... well, different, more confident ... it gives me a bit more courage, I think. Thank you.' Bella turned and looked at her, smiling. 'Don't stop wearing pillar-box red though, will you, Winnie? It suits your personality more than mine.'

The ring of the doorbell echoed in the hall downstairs and Bella's stomach knotted. 'That must be him.'

She reached out and grasped Winnie's arm. 'Am I doing the right thing going out with him, Winnie? Having a cup of tea was one thing but this feels much more ...' She shrugged.

'Do you like him?' Winnie asked, seriously.

She nodded. 'Yes, I do.'

Winnie beamed at her. 'Well then, what are you waiting for?'

Stefan was waiting in the sitting room with Connie when they went downstairs, and as soon as she and Winnie went into the room he stood up and bowed from the waist, clicking his heels. 'Good evening.' His eyes settled on Bella, smiling warmly at her as he came over and took hold of her hand and kissed it. 'You look beautiful, Bella.'

'Doesn't she just!' Winnie said before Bella could say anything.

'Hello, Stefan.' Bella's cheeks flushed at the unaccustomed compliment and the fact that he was still holding her hand.

'That dress really suits you,' Connie said. 'It's the perfect colour for your complexion and hair, and I must say that lipstick really sets it off beautifully.'

'Where are you going?' Winnie asked.

'To the Covent Garden Opera House. I hear the dances very good and I love to dance. Will be good evening.' He smiled at Bella, finally letting go of her hand and offering her his arm. 'You are ready?'

She nodded and slipped her hand through his arm.

*

Bella had never been inside the Covent Garden Opera House before. She'd passed it many times but never ventured inside until now; the grand building had been converted into a dance hall for the duration of the war and had become a popular destination, with dances held every afternoon and evening most days.

'It's beautiful.' She looked around her, amazed at the stunning building with its three horseshoe-shaped tiers of balconies overlooking the dance floor, and the ornate spoke-patterned roof high overhead. The dance floor was thronged with couples moving in time to the music which was being performed by Ivy Benson's female swing band.

Stefan smiled at her and took hold of her hand. 'May I have pleasure of this dance?'

'Don't say I didn't warn you about my two left feet, I'm a terrible dancer.' She'd already cautioned him about her lack of dancing ability when she'd telephoned to accept his invitation, giving him plenty of chance to change his mind about taking her dancing, but he'd been adamant that he still wanted to.

'Just follow me, you will be fine.' He led her onto the dance floor and put his arm around her waist as she put her hand on his shoulder. 'Do not think too much, relax, listen to music, let it . . . ' he paused to search for the right words, 'sweep you away.' He smiled warmly at her and they began to dance.

It wasn't the music that did the sweeping away, Bella thought a short while later, it was most definitely Stefan. He was an excellent dancer and led her around the dance floor with such grace; after treading on his toes a few times

189

she found herself gradually improving and, by following his lead, actually began to enjoy dancing – something that had always evaded her before. James had had two left feet like her, and their attempts at dancing together had never worked well. The sudden thought of James startled her and for a moment she faltered on the edge of tears but recovered herself because he'd want her to be out enjoying life. He'd been gone for a year and a half now and it was time to let go. She would never, ever forget him and what they had but she shouldn't let his loss stop her from enjoying her life now.

'Bella, are you all right?' Stefan's face was concerned, he'd obviously sensed her hesitation.

She nodded and smiled at him. 'Yes, I'm fine and glad I'm here with you.'

'As am I, with you, Bella.'

By the end of the dance, which finished at midnight, she'd danced more than she had for the rest of her life added together and had finally broken the belief that she couldn't do it, because tonight, with Stefan's expert guidance, she had danced and had enjoyed it very much. She'd discovered the delight of letting herself go, feeling the rhythm of the music and the thrill of dancing with someone who enjoyed it too, and, even better, who she was growing to like very much.

Walking back to Connie's house through the blacked-out London streets, with the milky light of a full moon shining down on them, Bella felt happy and relaxed. The evening that she'd been so unsure about had been a delight and when they reached Connie's house and Stefan stopped on the steps leading up to the front door, taking both of her hands in his, she didn't want the evening to end.

'I would like see you again?' Stefan asked.

'I'd like that.' Bella smiled at him.

He lifted one of her hands and kissed it. 'It is good, makes me very happy to see you again. Thank you for delightful evening.' He bowed from the waist and clicked his heels.

'Thank you, I've never enjoyed a dance so much before.'

He smiled and nodded. 'We go again, I think. Now I say goodnight.' Once again, he kissed her hand and then with a last look turned and left. She saw him stop and look back at her when he got to the end of the street because she was still watching him.

Bella had gone inside and just closed the front door behind her when Trixie came bounding down the stairs, skittering across the tiled floor, her claws clicking as she ran and her tail wagging rapidly from side to side in greeting. She bent down to greet the little dog, 'Hello Trix,' then she looked up to see Winnie not far behind, tying the belt of her silk dressing gown around her waist as she hurried towards her.

'Well?' Winnie smiled at her. 'How did you get on? You certainly looked like you were happy when you got back.' She sighed. 'I love how he kisses your hand, it's so romantic.'

'How ...' Bella frowned. 'Were you watching from your bedroom window?'

Winnie looked uncomfortable. 'Not really ... I was just looking out for you coming back and I saw him kiss your

191

hand and bow, I wasn't spying on you, just looking out for you, making sure you were all right.' She put her hand on Bella's arm. 'I don't want you to get hurt, that's all.'

'But you're the one that pushed me into going for a cup of tea with him in the first place. I said no, remember?' Bella paused for a moment and then smiled at her friend. 'I'm glad you did though, I've had a marvellous time, and do you know, I can actually dance after all.' She laughed. 'My two left feet are cured, thanks to Stefan – he's a wonderful dancer. Not sure I could do it on my own but with him leading, all I have to do is follow and it feels like I'm floating around to the music.'

Winnie threw her arms around Bella and squeezed her tight. 'I'm delighted that Stefan found you, you deserve to have a lovely man courting you. So, when are you next seeing him? You are going to, aren't you?'

'Sometime, I'm not sure when yet. Stefan asked me if I would and I said yes.' Bella linked her arm through Winnie's. 'Come on, we need to get some sleep, we've got to be at Station 75 by nine o'clock in the morning.' Though whether she'd get much sleep before then, Bella wasn't sure because her mind was full of the delight of dancing with Stefan and would probably be replaying it over and over well into the small hours.

Chapter Thirty-five

It was a beautiful early September morning, the air gently warm yet with a hint of mellowness and a promise of autumn that always arrived at this time of year. Winnie was checking the level of the oil in her ambulance, listening as she worked to Sparky, who was in full flow reading out the newspaper headlines from today's *Daily Herald* which he'd spread out on the bonnet of his and Paterson's ambulance. He was in a jubilant mood as Allied troops had entered Holland last night and having crossed the country's border the armies were that bit nearer their ultimate goal of reaching Hitler in Berlin. Since the invasion Sparky had become something of an expert, following the Allies' progress, and often read articles out to the crew while they worked on the ambulances.

'I bet the Dutch were pleased to see them,' Paterson said as he cleaned their ambulance's windscreen.

'Unlike the Jerries!' someone else shouted out, making the others laugh.

'Let me finish,' Sparky said. He carried on reading but suddenly stopped mid-sentence. 'Bloody hell!'

Winnie looked up at Sparky who was staring at something behind her, back towards the archway leading out onto the road, his mouth an O of surprise, and he wasn't the only one looking that way. 'What's the matter . . .' she began before quickly turning around to look for herself. Who she saw walking straight towards her made her heart trip up, skipping a beat. Frozen to the spot for a few moments, she couldn't quite believe what she was seeing, but as he came nearer there was no doubt that this was real, she wasn't dreaming, Mac was alive and he was here.

Dropping the oil dipstick on the floor, she flew across the courtyard towards him and he caught her in his arms. She hung on to him tightly, resting her head on his chest and breathing in the wonderful familiar smell of Mac. When she eventually loosened her grip, Mac smiled, his eyes meeting hers before he bent down and thoroughly kissed her, making up for all the time and worry since they'd last been together. Winnie was vaguely aware of the cheering, clapping and whistling from the other crew members and the yelps of delight from Trixie – she'd been asleep on the driver's seat of the ambulance, and must have been woken up by all the noise. She'd rushed over to greet Mac, too, and was dancing around his legs with joy.

'Where have you been? They told me you were missing in action,' Winnie asked when they came up for air.

'Didn't they tell you?' Mac frowned. 'I've been a prisoner of war.'

Winnie stared at him for a few moments. 'A prisoner of war, but why didn't they tell me? How . . . '

Mac didn't get a chance to explain before he was swamped with crew members, patting him on the back, shaking his hand and welcoming him home. Even Station Officer Steele, who had heard all the commotion up in her office and come down to see what was going on, had thrown her arms around him and kissed his cheek.

'Are you all right, Winnie?' Frankie asked, coming over and slipping her arm through Winnie's as they watched Mac surrounded by his former colleagues, all of whom thought very highly of him and had been devastated when they'd heard he was missing.

She turned to her friend and smiled. 'Yes, absolutely and completely fine. I'm shocked but very, very happy. I can hardly believe he's here – this isn't just a dream, is it?'

Frankie laughed. 'No, it's definitely real. Mac really has come home – I'm so happy for you.'

Tears suddenly smarted Winnie's eyes and she swallowed against the hard lump that had lodged itself in her throat. 'I was so scared he'd never come back.' Her voice wavered.

Frankie put her head against Winnie's. 'I know, but he has.'

Up in the common room a short while later, Winnie perched on the arm of the chair where Mac was sitting. He'd been plied with a cup of tea and one of Mrs Connelly's carrot buns still warm from the oven, and many of the crew had taken their break early and were sitting around him and, like her, anxious to hear what had happened to him.

'So, 'ow'd you come to be taken prisoner then?' Sparky asked, leaning forward on his chair, elbows on his knees and chin cupped in his hands.

'Give the man a chance to have his tea and something to eat first,' Station Officer Steele said.

'It's all right, boss,' Mac said. 'I'd better tell you what happened, or we run the danger of my lovely wife exploding with impatience.' He looked up at Winnie and winked at her. 'I was taken prisoner about a week after we went in – I'd been sent out to pick up some wounded and met a German patrol who duly took me prisoner and sent me to one of their POW hospitals in Rennes to work there since I was a medic. It was in an old girls' boarding school and that's where I've been for the past two months, until the Americans liberated us.'

'Did they treat you well?' Winnie asked.

Mac nodded. 'It wasn't luxurious, but we were a lot better off than some. There were other Field Ambulance orderlies there, and some of our doctors who'd also been captured. It was our job to help the French nurses look after the injured POWs; the nurses were good to us, smuggling in more food to keep us going.'

'Did you try to escape?' Sparky asked.

'No, the hospital was guarded and besides, we were doing the job we were supposed to be doing, helping look after our own men. We knew it was only a matter of time before we'd be liberated, so we stayed put and got on with the job and waited.'

196

'What happened to the Germans?' Paterson asked.

'They pulled out just before the Americans arrived and took any non-medical POWs with them. I don't know what happened to them after they were taken, but at least they left us there to look after the wounded.' Mac took a sip of tea.

'What happens now?' Frankie asked.

Mac took hold of Winnie's hand. 'Because I've done two months as a POW I'm entitled to some rest and recuperation leave.'

Winnie smiled at him. 'You're home for a while?'

Mac nodded.

'Well, I'm sure that I speak on behalf of everyone at Station 75 when I say how delighted we all are that you're safe and home again, Mac,' Station Officer Steele said. 'So, when you're ready, take your wife home. Winnie, you are granted a couple of days' leave.' She looked directly at Winnie, her eyes warm behind her horn-rimmed glasses. 'And that's an order!'

Winnie wasn't going to argue, she'd been given her husband back and she intended spending every precious moment she could with him. 'Thank you.'

Chapter Thirty-six

Bella and Stefan stood in the middle of Westminster Bridge, leaning on the parapet looking across the River Thames which was sparkling with diamonds of light in the afternoon sunshine.

'I love the old buildings,' Stefan said, nodding at the Houses of Parliament. 'So much history.'

'It's a miracle they're still standing after all the bombs that have been dropped on London,' Bella said. 'I hope none of those horrible doodlebugs fall on it.'

'We do our best to stop witches,' Stefan said. 'I got one today before it reach London.'

Bella turned to face him. 'Did you shoot it down?'

He shook his head and smiled. 'No, I tipped it, the witch changed course and went into the sea.'

'You tipped it?'

'Like this, see, this my Spitfire.' He held up his right hand, spreading out his thumb and little finger wide to represent the plane's wings. 'This the witch.' He held up his left hand to represent the doodlebug with his thumb and finger slightly splayed. 'I do this.' He demonstrated his Spitfire flying in until it was just below the doodlebug, then he suddenly swerved his plane so that his wing clipped the doodlebug's wing, tipping it at a different angle and sending the rocket flying off in another direction.

'Isn't it dangerous doing that?'

He grinned. 'Is fun, a challenge.'

Bella shook her head. 'You are crazy. Are all Polish pilots like you?'

Stefan shrugged and took hold of her hand in his. 'We like to fly and do our job. Other pilots tip witches off course too, I not first one to do this, we learn it from Tadeusz.'

The more time that Bella spent with Stefan the more she grew to like him. He was unlike any other man that she'd known before, his passion for what he did shone out and his sincerity was very appealing. They'd seen each other a couple of times since they'd been out dancing, snatching a few hours together when he was able to get away from West Malling aerodrome and into London, and like this afternoon when he'd turned up at Connie's house hoping to spend some time with her. Always he was perfectly mannered and courteous, and they either went out to a Lyons Corner House or, like now, went out for a walk, enjoying the fine weather.

'Is England very different to Poland?' Bella asked.

'Yes. Was hard when first came here, the planes are back to front in England, to open throttle here – you push.' He demonstrated the action with his free hand. 'In Polish planes, you pull. And height is in feet not metres and speed in miles not kilometres. RAF has different rules about how you make your bed!' He shook his head and shrugged. 'And the overboiled cabbage and . . . ' He frowned. 'Custard, what is it?'

Bella laughed. 'You don't have custard in Poland?'

'No! Definitely not.' His eyes met hers. 'But I get used to it and dream of good Polish food.'

'Shall we walk?' Bella asked. They headed across the bridge towards the Houses of Parliament, hand in hand. 'You're very patriotic, I think, aren't you?'

'We love our country,' Stefan said. 'We grow up to love it. In past Poland split and ruled by others – Russia, Germany and Austro-Hungary, was not right but at end of Great War we declared independent and finally free. When we children we taught to love our country and know to do everything we can to keep it free. That is why we fight the Nazis, we come here to help British fight because we want our country free again. I look forward very much to when war over and I go home.'

Bella pulled on his hand to stop him walking and looked into his eyes. 'I am sorry that the Nazis invaded Poland and took over again. I understand how terrible that must be for you all after your history of being ruled by others. To get your freedom and have it snatched away again a little over twenty years later is dreadful.'

Stefan's eyes brightened with tears. 'Thank you, Bella. Is hard to have my country invaded again. We must fight on, keep fighting till we win.'

Bella put her arms around him and hugged him tightly. She could imagine how terrible it was to be invaded. Britain had felt the threat after Dunkirk and what would it have been like if the Germans had come? Seeing enemy troops marching down the streets, new rules and regulations brought in to suit the conquering forces, the sense of powerlessness when the stronger enemy defeated and took over. It was the stuff of nightmares but had become reality in Poland and so many other countries. Britain had been lucky, no invasion had come, but poor Poland was now suffering under the Nazi rule and any who opposed it would have been dealt with.

'Is not all bad,' Stefan said. Bella loosened her grip and looked up at him. 'I meet you here in London. That is very good.' He kissed her, tenderly.

A sudden loud explosion rang out across the London rooftops, making them jump. They immediately looked around, searching the sky for any telltale signs, but couldn't see anything, their view limited by the tall buildings around them.

'What was that?' Bella asked. 'I didn't hear a doodlebug coming in, did you?'

'No.' He narrowed his eyes. 'Was something big.'

Bella remembered the last time she'd heard an unexpected explosion, well before the advent of the doodlebugs, when an unexploded bomb had blown up one fine June evening in Gurney Street, killing many innocent people. Had something like that happened again today? She shivered.

'Are you all right, Bella?'

She nodded. 'Just remembering another time when

something like this happened when I was on duty.' She briefly told him about the incident at Gurney Street.

Stefan held out his hand. 'Come on, we go and have tea, yes?'

'Yes, please.' She smiled at him. 'Tea always helps us British feel better, you're learning our ways.'

'Is because I like to be with you, Bella.'

She took his hand. 'And I with you, too.'

Chapter Thirty-seven

'Saying goodbye at stations is becoming something of a habit of ours,' Mac said, folding Winnie into his arms.

She leaned her head against his chest, hearing his heart thumping as fast as hers was, betraying his true feelings despite his joking words; their parting was traumatic for both of them. After a blissful couple of weeks together it was hard to say goodbye again, especially knowing that Mac would be sent abroad again, his skills much needed as the fighting continued. She hadn't forgotten, and never would, the fear of losing him, the dreadful heart-chilling arrival of a telegram, and now with Mac going back there was every chance that something might happen to him again, and he might not be so lucky next time. Swallowing hard, fighting back tears, she clung even harder to him.

The guard shouted from the far end of the platform, their precious seconds left together were fast ticking down.

'Winnie, I need to get on board.' Mac gently loosened

her arms and, hooking his finger under her chin, brought her gaze up to meet his. 'I don't want to leave, but I have to. I love you and promise with all my heart that I'll do everything in my power to come back to you.'

She looked into his beautiful dark blue eyes and nodded, not daring to speak herself.

'You look after yourself too. All right?'

She nodded again.

He kissed her tenderly and then grabbed his kitbag, slung it over his shoulder and climbed on board just as the guard passed by them, nodding at them. Mac slammed the carriage door shut and leaned out of the open window.

'I love you, Mac. Look after yourself.' Winnie squeezed her hands into fists, willing herself not to cry. She did her best to smile and send him away with that last cheerful face.

'Always, I promise.' Mac reached out and grabbed her hand as the train started to move, making her trot along beside it, but all too soon she had to let go and stood watching the train snake its way out of the station, putting her hand to her lips and kissing the skin that he had last touched.

'Come home to me, Mac,' she whispered with tears streaming down her cheeks as the train finally disappeared from sight.

Chapter Thirty-eight

'Look at this, I never expected to find this in the letter.' Frankie handed Bella the delicate lace that had arrived in yesterday's post for her — sent by Alastair all the way from Belgium. They were sitting in the quiet common room having a break after giving their ambulance a thorough cleaning.

'It's beautiful.' Bella stroked the delicate white lace with her fingertips, tracing the intricate pattern. 'Where'd he get this?'

'From a lace shop in Brussels, so he said in his letter. He went into the city after it had been liberated and thought I might like some. And I do like it, it's lovely.' She smiled. 'He said the streets were lined with happy people and they were so delighted to see the British army they were givin' them flowers and wanting to take them for a celebratory drink — it sounded like quite a party.'

Bella nodded. 'Can you imagine what it feels like to be

liberated after being occupied by the Nazis for so long? The sense of freedom again must have been wonderful.'

'Thank God we never had to go through that.' Frankie remembered how the country had felt like it was hanging on by its fingertips with the threat of invasion hanging over it back in the early years of the war, but thankfully the enemy had never actually put its invasion plans into action. 'I'm glad he gets to have some fun for a bit sometimes, it's difficult and exhausting workin' at a casualty clearing station.'

'It must be hard having to keep moving everything on all the time as well, following on behind the front line as it advances.' Bella handed her back the piece of lace. 'Imagine if we had to up sticks and move Station 75 and all the equipment every so often, having to pack everything up, move it and unpack again.'

Frankie tucked the lace safely back inside the envelope that Alastair had sent it in. 'I know, but he quite likes seeing different places and as our troops push further into enemy territory he'll get a chance to visit other towns.'

'Have you decided what you're going to use the lace for?' Bella asked.

'I thought I'd . . . ' Frankie began but stopped as Sparky came into the common room with a thunderous look on his face. 'What's the matter with you?'

Sparky threw himself down in the armchair opposite the sofa where they were sitting. 'I just went to get me paper and saw one of the Fire Service fellas I know, and he told me the bleedin' Nazis are firing a new type of rocket at us now. As if the bleeding doodlebugs ain't enough to have rainin' down on us night and day, we've now got another sort, only these blighters are a lot worse.'

'There's been nothing on the wireless or in the papers about it. Are you sure, Sparky?' Bella said.

Sparky threw up his hands. 'Of course I am. Just because we ain't been *told* about them don't mean they aren't falling on us. Ain't you heard the loud explosions?'

Bella nodded. 'Yes, the first one was when I was out with Stefan last week.'

'And there's been more since. The government have been blamin' them on gas leaks but from what the Fire Service fella told me they are rockets.' Sparky scowled. 'They've started calling 'em flying gas pipes, and these ones don't come with any warnin' like the doodlebugs, there ain't no sound of an engine and then the wait for it to cut out and hope that it don't land on you – these new ones don't give a warning, the first thing you know about is when they blow up.'

Frankie's stomach clenched. The doodlebugs were bad enough – at least you stood some chance – but a new rocket with no warning was a whole new level of danger. 'Why ain't the government said anything?'

'They probably don't want to cause panic until they're sure about what's goin' on,' Sparky said, drumming his fingers on the arm of the chair. 'Remember they didn't admit to the doodlebugs straight away either.'

'What can we do?' Bella asked.

Sparky shook his head. 'Not a bleedin' thing! If one of these lands where we are we'll be goners and won't know anything about it!'

Frankie looked at Bella, whose face had gone milky white. 'Well let's just 'ope our luck holds out then. At least when the bombers came we knew about it. They were bad enough, but the enemy have upped their game and looks like we're defenceless to do anything about it.'

Sparky stood up. 'That just about sums it up. Never thought I'd prefer the bombers!' He marched off, no doubt to tell other crew members about what he'd discovered.

'Are you all right, Bella?' Frankie asked.

Bella shrugged. 'Why do humans create such horrible things to kill and maim others with?'

Frankie put her arm around her friend's shoulders. 'I know, it ain't right but it's war and it's what they do to try and win. Let's 'ope our troops get to Berlin soon and this whole horrible mess will be over.'

Chapter Thirty-nine

Winnie loved soaking in the bath after coming home from a twenty-four-hour shift. She might have only been allowed a meagre four inches of hot water, but she made the most of them, staying in until it was almost cold, and her fingers and toes were as wrinkled as prunes.

'Are you nearly done in there?' Bella knocked on the door. 'Only I'm going to start cooking our lunch, my mother's sent some eggs for us, do you want some?'

'Yes please, I'm getting out now.' Winnie pulled the plug and stood up, grabbing a towel to dry herself.

'All right, I'll expect you downstairs in ten minutes then.'

Winnie quickly dried herself and started to get dressed, pulling on some clean underwear – silk knickers and a brassiere – but when she tried to do it up, her brassiere seemed to have shrunk, it didn't fit properly at the front. She struggled to do it up, hurting her breasts which for some strange reason were feeling very tender and sore. Perhaps she was due for her monthly, she thought, doing up the buttons on her blue silk blouse, but her fingers stilled when she realised she couldn't remember the last time she'd had her monthly. They weren't always particularly regular, but thinking back it was before Mac came home, at least two months ago. He was now with a new unit and had been sent back out to help with the Allied advance again. Since then she'd had nothing. Winnie gasped, her heart thumping hard – could she really be pregnant?

The idea settled like a lead weight in her stomach. She didn't want a baby, not now, maybe not ever. She wasn't sure if she was even the right sort of person to be a mother; her own hadn't exactly been the best example to learn from, had she? And even if she did want a child, now was most definitely not the right time – she had a job that she loved, Mac was away in the army and the world was in the middle of a hideous war. It was completely and utterly not the time or place to be bringing a child into.

Hold on, she reined in her runaway thoughts as she slumped down on the wicker chair beside the bath, she was jumping to conclusions here. She had no proof she was expecting, she was probably just due her monthly, that was all. It was silly letting her imagination run wild on her. In the meantime, she was more concerned with having some lunch as she was suddenly ravenously hungry.

'You're just in time,' Bella said, scooping the eggs out of the pan of boiling water and popping them into waiting egg cups. 'Five-minute eggs, perfect timing so the yolks are still runny for dipping soldiers in.' She carried the plates with already cut bread and marge soldiers and the boiled eggs over to the table.

'Thank you.' Winnie sat down at the table where Trixie settled by her side, on the lookout for any titbits of food that might come her way. 'How many eggs did your mother send this time?'

'A dozen, and all of them arrived without a single crack in them.' Bella hit the top of her egg with a spoon to crack the shell.

Winnie had been amazed the first time Bella's mother had sent them a parcel of fresh eggs, each one carefully wrapped in cloth and packed into an old toffee tin which had been shipped overnight by train and arrived perfectly safely the next morning. It was such a treat to have precious eggs sent to them from the countryside, they were so much nicer than the ghastly powdered egg they got on the ration.

Winnie began to break into her egg to reach the golden yolk that she loved to dip bread soldiers in, but a sudden wave of nausea hit her, and she dropped her spoon with a clatter. Putting her hand over her mouth she leapt up, rushing to the bathroom, closely followed by Trixie, where she was sick.

'Winnie? Are you all right?' Bella tapped on the door. 'Are you ill?'

She stood up from where she'd been sitting on the bathroom floor, her arm around her little dog who'd leaned against her as if to comfort her while her stomach settled, and opened the door.

'I'm all right, just suddenly came over sick, that's all.' Winnie shrugged. 'I'm all right now.'

Bella felt Winnie's forehead. 'You haven't got a temperature. Were you feeling ill before? You seemed fine earlier.'

'I was, it was just the smell of the egg, I think, it set me off.' Winnie did her best to smile. 'To be honest I feel hungry again now. I fancy some toast and some of Connie's honey, that would settle my stomach again. Do you think she'd mind if I had some?'

'Of course not. Listen, let me go and make it for you and bring it into the sitting room so you don't smell the eggs if they're going to make you feel bad.'

A short while later Bella carried in a tray and put it down on the low table in front of the sofa where Winnie sat cuddling Trixie. 'Here we are, toast and honey and a cup of weak tea with no milk.'

'Thank you.' Winnie took a bite, enjoying the sweetness on top of the grainy National loaf toast. 'Mmm, delicious.'

Bella had sat down at the other end of the sofa and was watching her closely. 'Winnie, can I ask you something?'

She nodded, taking another bite.

'Is there any possibility that you might be expecting?' Bella bit her bottom lip. 'Only you don't usually react like that to a boiled egg and you look like you've gone up a size or two.' She nodded towards Winnie's chest where the front buttons of her blouse were straining more than they usually did from her slim, willowy figure.

Winnie's cheeks grew warm. 'I hope not! It *is* possible, I suppose . . . but I don't *want* a baby now.'

212

'Have you missed your monthly?'

She shrugged. 'I haven't had a monthly for a while but that doesn't necessarily mean anything with me. My brassiere feels too small now but it's probably just shrunk in the wash.'

'Or you've suddenly grown bigger,' Bella said.

'I don't want to be a mother yet! Or maybe even ever ...' Her voice wobbled. 'I've got a job to do and I don't want to give it up.'

'Whether you want it or not, *if* you and Mac are going to be parents then you've got to go along with it,' Bella said. 'The first thing to do is to find out for sure – you need to make an appointment at your doctor's.'

Winnie nodded. 'All right, but will you come with me?'

'Yes, I'll do anything I can to help you.' Bella reached out and took hold of Winnie's hand. 'Try not to worry.'

Winnie did her best to smile, though she wasn't sure if it came out right because she was scared. What would she do if it turned out that she was expecting? Babies weren't something you could ignore and carry on with your life as before, even before they were born they changed things. Her heart sank at the thought of what a baby would do to her life – worst of all, she would lose her job because of it.

Chapter Forty

'Frankie! You've got a visitor.'

Frankie looked up from where she was checking the equipment in the back of her ambulance to where Sparky stood by the open back doors. 'Who?'

'A friend of yer sister's, so she says.' Sparky indicated with his head to where a young woman dressed in WAAF overalls stood a few steps behind him.

'What – Lizzie?' Frankie jumped out of the ambulance. 'Do you work with her?'

The WAAF nodded and hurried over to Frankie. 'I need to talk to you urgently,' she looked at Sparky, 'and in private.'

Sparky raised his eyebrows. 'It's all right, I'm off.'

'Thanks, Sparky,' Frankie said. 'We'd better go and talk over there if you don't want anyone to overhear us.' She nodded towards the far side of the courtyard, well away from the garages where several of the crew members

214

were watching them while they went about their own work, obviously curious about why a WAAF had turned up at Station 75. Frankie's mind was running through what this could be about. Why would a friend of Lizzie's want to come and talk to her? She'd had no contact from her sister for over a year, not since she'd last seen her at the barrage balloon site where she worked and where Lizzie had made it crystal clear that she wanted nothing to do with Frankie.

'Lizzie's in trouble,' the WAAF said as soon as they were out of earshot.

'What sort of trouble? And who are you?'

'I'm Vera, Lizzie's friend. I work on the site with her and share a room with her at our lodgings. She's . . . She's been seeing some GI and gone and got herself in trouble, in the family way.'

Frankie opened her mouth to say something but was silenced when Vera grabbed her arm, her eyes bright with tears. 'She wouldn't listen to me and went to see someone about getting rid of it and now she's in a bad way.'

Frankie stared at her, taking in what she'd just been told. 'You mean she went to a knitting needle Nora? Bleedin' heck! The fool.'

'I told her not to, but she wouldn't listen. She didn't want to get thrown out of the WAAF.' Vera sighed. 'And now she's in a lot of pain and not looking good.'

'It might be a whole lot worse than that, people die after doin' what she's done. Where is she now?'

'Back at our lodgings. She said she was sick today and

couldn't go to work. I went back to check on her at break time and found her looking bad and didn't know what to do. I remembered she said you worked here. I'm scared she might die, if she doesn't get help. Can you help her, please?' Vera pleaded.

Frankie didn't particularly like Lizzie, but she couldn't ignore the fact that her half-sister was in serious trouble. 'All right, I'll see what I can do but I need to go talk to my boss first, I can't just go off. Wait 'ere, I'll be as quick as I can.'

Hurrying to Station Officer Steele's office, Frankie decided the best thing to do was to tell her the truth – this was too big a thing to make some excuse to ask for time off. What Lizzie had done was illegal and, even worse than that, it could kill her. As the boss listened to what Frankie told her, her face blanched white. 'That's all I know so far. Can I have time off to go and help her? She probably needs to get to 'ospital.'

'The foolish, foolish girl. Abortions are illegal and if it doesn't kill her, she could end up in prison for it. At least her friend's got some common sense to come for help.' Station Officer Steele drummed her fingers on her desk for a few moments and then stood up. 'I'm coming with you, we'll take an ambulance.'

Frankie stared at the older woman, she hadn't expected this. 'What are we goin' to do?'

'Come on, there's no time to stand around, your sister's life may well be hanging in the balance, we can talk on the way.' Station Officer Steele strode out of the door and Frankie hurried after her.

'Right, Vera,' the boss said as Frankie drove them out of Station 75, with the WAAF sitting between them in the front of the ambulance. 'Tell us everything you know: how many months pregnant Lizzie was, when and where she went for the abortion.'

'She'd missed a couple of monthlies before she realised, or at least admitted it to herself what had happened. I know she asked around some of the other girls and heard about a woman who could help . . . for a price. She went to see her yesterday while we were off shift, and was in pain last night and this morning she looked bad, pale and sweaty.'

'Is she bleeding?' the boss asked.

'I'm not sure,' Vera said.

'The danger, apart from developing an infection, is that your friend will haemorrhage and bleed to death. We've got to take her to hospital,' Station Officer Steele said.

'But she'll get in trouble!' Vera said.

Frankie glanced at her sister's friend. 'She already *is* and if she's unlucky she might end up payin' for this with her life.'

They drove along in silence for a few minutes before Station Officer Steele spoke. 'Lizzie isn't the first young woman to do such a foolish thing and she won't be the last. I suggest she tells them she had a fall or something, and it started a miscarriage.'

'You mean lie?' Vera said.

'Yes,' the boss said.

Frankie took her eyes off the road for a few seconds

and looked at her boss who stared directly back at her, her face perfectly composed as if she hadn't just suggested what she had. 'All right, that's what she should do if you think it's best.'

'I do. This isn't the first time I've had to deal with this situation and I hope this one comes off better than the last time.' The older woman sighed. 'It's a sad fact that young women are left to deal with such things while the men get away scot-free. It's no wonder they turn to knitting needle Noras in desperation.'

Frankie knew that Lizzie must be in a bad way because when they went into the room she shared with Vera, her sister didn't complain about her arrival, she just glanced at them, her eyes screwed up with pain as she huddled in a foetal position in the bed.

'Your sister and her boss have come to help you,' Vera said, putting her hand on Lizzie's shoulder. 'I didn't know what else to do, you can't go on like this, you need help.'

Lizzie nodded and started to cry, retching sobs shaking her body. 'I never knew it would be like this.'

'You need to go to hospital, Lizzie.' Frankie gently laid a hand on her sister's shoulder.

'I can't, they'll arrest me,' Lizzie wailed. 'Put me in prison.'

Station Officer Steele went over to her and pulled the covers down to reveal a bright red bloodstain on the bottom sheet that stood out starkly against the white. The boss looked at Frankie and raised her eyebrows – the message on her face quite clear.

'I'll go and get a stretcher,' Frankie said.

Lizzie didn't complain as they gently lifted her on to the stretcher a few minutes later and carried her out to the ambulance.

'I'll ride in the back with her,' the boss said as they loaded her in. 'And on this occasion ignore the usual speed limit, Frankie, get us there as quick as you can.'

The journey to Guy's Hospital passed in a blur as Frankie's mind played out different scenarios of what might happen, the worst being that Lizzie would pay with her life for her desperate visit to the knitting needle Nora. Frankie hadn't developed a good relationship with her in the same way as she had done with her younger sister, Eve, who had been warm and friendly towards her right from when they had first met, unlike Lizzie, who'd been openly hostile, but she desperately hoped that her sister wouldn't pay the ultimate price for her foolish behaviour, as the ripples from it would extend far out into her family and she didn't want to see them hurt like that.

Carrying Lizzie into the casualty department, Frankie was grateful that Station Officer Steele was with them as she swept into action.

'This woman needs immediate attention,' the boss said in a voice that brooked no argument, as they approached the nurse in charge of the reception area. 'Suspected miscarriage and haemorrhaging.'

'This way,' the nurse said, hurrying ahead and opening doors for them.

As Frankie helped to transfer Lizzie onto the examination

219

bed, her sister grabbed hold of her arm and their eyes met, her sister's full of fear. 'Will you stay, please?'

'Patients and staff only allowed in here,' the nurse said. 'But your . . .'

'Sister,' Lizzie said.

'Your sister can stay in the waiting room,' the nurse said kindly.

A surge of pity swelled up in Frankie. 'I'll just be out in the waitin' room.'

Lizzie managed a smile before pain focused her attention again and her face screwed up in agony.

'Right, you need to go now so that we can help her,' the nurse said, ushering them out quickly.

Station Officer Steele put her hand on Frankie's shoulder as they walked back to the waiting area to where Vera stood looking worried. 'She's in their hands now and all we can do is hope. You stay here, and I'll get back to Station 75. Don't worry about work, stay here as long as you need to.'

Frankie nodded. 'Thank you.'

'I'll stay as well,' Vera said. 'The rest of the crew can manage without me.'

'Five minutes and no more,' the staff nurse said quietly as she ushered Frankie and Vera into the women's ward where Lizzie had been taken after having surgery. 'She's lucky to have survived, though she'll never have children of her own now.'

Frankie had been shocked that the surgeons had had to perform a hysterectomy to save her sister's life, as without it she would have bled to death – that visit to the knitting needle Nora had not only nearly killed her but had now deprived her of the chance to ever have her own children. At least she was alive and that was much to be thankful for because it could so easily have gone the other way.

'Hello, Lizzie,' Vera said as they approached the bed where Lizzie lay, pale-faced, her dark hair spread out against the white pillow. 'How are you?'

Lizzie opened her eyes and they filled with tears as she looked at them. 'I've been a bloody fool.' Several tears spilled over and slid down the side of her face.

'Yes, you have been, but you've also been lucky to survive because some don't, you know.' Frankie put her hand on Lizzie's arm.

Lizzie grabbed hold of Frankie's hand and squeezed it tight. 'Thank you for coming to help me, and . . . I'm sorry I've been so horrible to you, you really didn't deserve it.'

Frankie smiled at her. 'Apology accepted. I hope we can perhaps be friends.'

Lizzie nodded. 'What'll happen to me? Will I have to leave the WAAF?'

'Not if you don't want to,' Vera said. 'You aren't in the family way any more, so once you're fit and well again you can come back and help man the balloon again.'

Lizzie smiled. 'I love being in the WAAF, that's why I did . . . ' Her face crumpled, and she started to cry silently.

Frankie took both of her sister's hands in hers. 'What's done is done, you need to look to the future now, you can't change the past. Just focus on getting better and back to keeping that balloon up in the air.'

'Time's up, your sister needs to rest,' the nurse said, coming back into the room. She smiled at them. 'But you are welcome to come back tomorrow at proper visiting hours.'

'Please do.' Lizzie's eyes met Frankie's.

Frankie nodded. 'I'll see you tomorrow then.'

Chapter Forty-one

'You can get yourself dressed now, Mrs McCartney,' Dr Stevenson said as he finished examining Winnie.

She propped herself up on her elbows on the examination couch. 'Well am I, or aren't I?'

Dr Stevenson looked at her over his half-moon glasses. 'All in good time, my dear. Get yourself dressed while I write up your notes.'

Winnie was about to argue with him, but he disappeared around the screen and left her to sort herself out. She was desperate to know if he'd found out that she was expecting a baby; she'd watched his face carefully for any clue as he examined her, but the man was a consummate professional and had given nothing away.

After dressing herself in double-quick time she sat down in the patients' chair and waited for him to stop writing. The room was silent except for the ticking of a clock on the mantelpiece and the scratch of the nib of his fountain pen on paper.

'Well, Mrs McCartney,' Dr Stevenson eventually said, snapping his pen lid on and tucking it into his jacket pocket, 'congratulations are in order, you most certainly are expecting a child.' He glanced down at his notes. 'And since you are unsure of the date of your last monthly cycle I have to go by when your husband was home on leave which makes the baby due some time during the first two weeks of June – I can't be more precise than that at the moment.'

Winnie stared at him, completely lost for words for once, her stomach clenching so tightly she was frightened she was going to be sick. She put her hand over her mouth; she really didn't want this to be happening right now. She didn't want a baby, a voice inside her screamed.

'Mrs McCartney, from the look on your face I would say that this is something of a surprise to you?' He fixed her with his warm brown eyes. 'You are a very healthy young woman and there is no reason that I can see that you shouldn't have a healthy child.'

'We weren't planning on having children until the war was over,' Winnie said. 'I don't . . . '

Dr Stevenson smiled. 'Well, babies don't always come along when planned. I'll give you a letter so that you can sort out an expectant mother's ration book for the extra food that you are now entitled to – the orange juice, cod liver oil, milk and vitamins – they'll all help the baby to grow strong and healthy so do make sure that you take them. If you make an appointment with my secretary for a check-up in a few months' time, I'll see you then. In the meantime, if you have any concerns don't hesitate to come and see me.'

Dazed, Winnie walked out of his office and into the waiting room, where Bella stood up, her face anxious to know the outcome. She gave her friend a small nod before turning to Dr Stevenson's secretary to make an appointment.

It wasn't until they were outside in the street that she looked at Bella properly. 'He said it's due in the first two weeks of June.' Tears stung her eyes. 'But I don't want it, now's not the right time and I don't want what it's going to do to me. I'm going to have to leave Station 75 because of it.' Her tears spilt over and slid down her cheeks.

Bella took hold of both her hands and her kind brown eyes held Winnie's. 'I know this is a shock to you but really it is the most marvellous thing.' She smiled. 'Just think, you and Mac are going to have a child, and I know he'd be thrilled about that, and you will be too once you've had a chance to get used to the idea.'

'Will I?' She sighed. 'As soon as the boss knows about it I'll be out of a job. I was there at the start and I wanted to stay to the end, but now . . .'

'They're the rules. It's a tough job sometimes and not suited for expectant mothers.'

'Rubbish, there's no reason why I shouldn't carry on for as long as I could manage . . .' Winnie paused, a thought blossoming in her mind. 'I'm not going to tell the boss, not until I have to because I can't hide it any more. If I am going to have a baby then I'm not going to let it stop me doing what I love. No one else needs to know about this except you and Connie – she'll need to know because of the extra rations I'll get – but the boss doesn't need to know, or anyone else at Station 75 – that way I can keep on working for as long as I can.'

Bella frowned. 'You can't do that, Winnie. What happens if you hurt yourself or the baby?' She paused. 'Or you put others in danger if you couldn't do something?'

'I'd never do that! I'll be careful and if anything's a bit tricky you can help me, we can get around this.' She squeezed Bella's hands. 'Please, Bella, will you help me? Let me carry on as normal for as long as I can, please. At least if I still have my work it will help me keep going and gradually accept that I'm going to be a mother. If I have to give it all up I don't know what I'd do. I'd probably blame the baby and that wouldn't help me grow to want it.'

'You really feel that bad about it?'

Winnie nodded. 'I feel like I've been invaded, something's taken over my body that I don't want ... I'm scared, Bella, this isn't how it's supposed to be.'

'All right then.' Bella sighed. 'I'll go along with it, but only because I'm worried about you and that baby in there. I know how important working at Station 75 is to you. I'm not happy about you not telling the boss, but I'll keep your secret and a close eye on you as well, but if you go doing anything daft which puts you or the baby in danger, then I will have to say something. Frankie needs to know as well, so she can help me cover for you if necessary.'

'All right, but only Frankie, I can trust her to keep a secret. Thank you, darling Bella, you are the best friend I've ever had, and I promise I won't do anything silly, doing my job for as long as I can means so much to me.' She shrugged. 'I don't know what else I'd do if I didn't have my job to keep me going and busy while Mac's out there somewhere. I know I'll have to give it up before the baby's born but a few months' grace is all I'm asking for.'

Chapter Forty-two

'I think that's enough turnips.' Bella added another on
to the pile that they'd already pulled up at the allotment,
ready to take back to Station 75 for Mrs Connelly to cook
for the crew's midday meal. 'There's just the cabbage
to get now.'

'How many did she want?' Frankie asked.

'Only two today, she's going to cook up the turnip tops
as well as the roots, so we don't need as much.' They each
cut a cabbage which were looking good as they'd been
careful to pick off any caterpillars before they had a chance
to munch their way through the leaves.

Frankie started to gather up the turnips, bunching the
leaves in her hand like a bouquet and giving them a good
shake to knock off the dried soil.

'Wait,' Bella said. 'There's something I need to tell you
before we go back — it's about Winnie.'

Frankie frowned. 'What's the matter? I hope she ain't
done something that's going to upset the boss.'

228

Bella smiled. 'You could say that, she's definitely breaking a rule this time, more like snapping it in two, actually.'

'Go on, what's she's done?'

'Winnie's expecting a baby. She found out yesterday.'

Frankie stared at Bella for a moment, open-mouthed. 'Bleedin' heck!' She sighed. 'That's it, she'll have to leave then. I bet she's not happy about that, she loves her job, but I suppose 'aving a baby will make up for that eventually.'

'I'm not so sure. She's not happy about it, she doesn't want a baby now and if she had to leave Station 75 because of it, well ...' Bella shrugged. 'Our dear friend has decided that she's just not going to tell the boss until she can't hide it any more, so we're going to have to help her, make sure she doesn't do anything to endanger herself or the baby, no heavy lifting, that sort of thing. At least we can help her stay for a few more months.'

'I'll be glad to help her, but she's goin' to have a problem with her uniform – I tailored it to fit her slim figure, there ain't much room for a growin' baby in there.' Frankie paused for a moment. 'There's no reason why I can't alter larger-sized tunics to fit her as she gets bigger but even with doing that there'll be a limit to how long she can hide her condition from the boss.'

'I know, but it's what she wants to do and if we look out for her it will be all right. Station 75 wouldn't be the same without Winnie, so let's keep her here with us for as long as we can ...' Bella smiled. 'It'll be lovely for Winnie to have her and Mac's baby, I think she'll make a good mother.'

'At least she's not goin' to do what my sister did.' Frankie sighed. 'She was a fool and is lucky to still be here.'

'How is she?' Bella said as they started to walk back to Station 75 carrying the vegetables they'd picked.

'All right. I went to see her yesterday and they're going to send her out to a convalescent 'ospital in the country-side to recuperate when she's ready. There shouldn't be any reason why she can't go back to the WAAF once she's fit again.'

'She must have felt desperate, and all because she wanted to stay in her job, like Winnie does,' Bella said.

Frankie nodded. 'Then we just have to help our friend do that for as long as she can, and let's hope the boss is understanding when she does finally find out.'

'Well, the worst she can do is sack her and Winnie has to leave but that's going to happen anyway, sooner or later. Hopefully by then Winnie will be happier about having a baby, or perhaps the war will be over before her secret becomes too big to hide.'

Chapter Forty-three

Frankie was pleased to see that Lizzie was sitting up in her hospital bed with a bit more colour in her cheeks than when she'd last been to visit her.

'Hello, you're looking better,' Frankie said, pulling up a chair beside her sister's bed. 'I brought you these.' She held out a paper bag of mint humbugs which she'd used some of her precious sweet ration to buy.

'Thanks.' Lizzie took them.

'Have you heard any more about moving out to the convalescent hospital?'

'I'm going on Friday, as long as everything's all right.'

Frankie smiled. 'That's good. Has Vera been to see you?'

Lizzie nodded, visibly brightening. 'Yes, her and some of the other girls from the balloon site. Sister had to tell them to keep the noise down, they're a right noisy bunch sometimes. I can't wait to get back to them.'

'I know what you mean, I love being with my friends

at Station 75.' Frankie paused, wondering if she should again broach the subject of telling their mother what had happened. Their relationship was better than it was before Lizzie had had a backstreet abortion, but she still felt as if she were feeling her way with her sister, not sure of how she would take things. 'Have you changed your mind about telling Mother? I'm sure she'd come and see you.'

Lizzie's face went pale. 'No, I'm not telling her, ever. She'd be so disappointed with me. Please don't tell her either.'

'I won't, I promise.' Frankie didn't know her mother well enough to know if what her sister said would be true; she suspected her mother would be worried about Lizzie, but it wasn't her story to tell and if she'd been asked not to say anything then she would stick to that.

'She wouldn't understand, she never would have done such a thing ...' Lizzie frowned. 'It's best she never knows. I'll go to the convalescent hospital, get better and then be back to work, that's all I want to do.' She opened the bag of humbugs and offered it to Frankie. 'Do you want one?'

'All right, thanks.' Frankie took one and popped it in her mouth thinking that her mother might have understood Lizzie's predicament given the chance because she'd made a difficult choice of her own, leaving Frankie as a baby for her grandparents to bring up. Families were complicated things.

'I love these, thanks for bringing them,' Lizzie said, taking one for herself. 'Your boss is kind. Will you thank her for what she did for me?'

'Yes, of course, she's been asking me about you. She's a good boss, though she can be strict, but I like working for her.'

The rest of the visiting time passed with the two of them talking about their work, Frankie telling Lizzie about life at Station 75 and the various characters who worked there, while her sister told her about her balloon team. By the time Frankie left, she felt they had found some common ground between them that didn't just rely on them sharing the same mother. Their love of working at their different jobs as part of the war effort had drawn them a bit closer. There was still a long way to go but it was a good start.

Chapter Forty-four

As the train puffed into West Malling station, Bella was already waiting by the carriage door watching out for her first glimpse of Stefan, her stomach all aflitter at the thought of seeing him again. She'd seen him only last week when they'd gone to the pictures together in London, but it felt like an age since then and when he'd telephoned, inviting her to come and visit her here and see where he lived and worked, she'd jumped at the chance.

He'd promised he'd be there to meet her, and there he was, looking so smart and handsome in his blue RAF uniform. Bella waved to him as her carriage slid past, gradually coming to a stop further along the platform. Stefan ran to her door and had it open from outside before she could do it herself.

'Bella!' He bowed, clicking his heels then holding out his hand to help her down, smiling warmly at her. 'I so happy to see you.'

'Hello, Stefan.' Bella took his hand and moments later was wrapped in his warm embrace, enjoying the feeling of his arms around her and his lips on hers.

Several wolf whistles from soldiers standing by open windows on the stationary train made them laugh when they broke apart, and with his arm around her waist Stefan led her out of the station.

'Your carriage is ready.' He bowed as he opened the door of an open-topped, bright red Morgan sports car, which was parked outside the station.

'Thank you.' Bella climbed into the low seat and he shut the door and went around to the driver's side. 'Is this yours?'

'No, I borrow from Tadeusz, you meet him later.' Stefan handed her a silk scarf. 'You wear this, Tadeusz keep it for women he give a ride to.' He raised his eyebrows and grinned before starting the engine which roared into life.

Bella tied the scarf around her head and settled back in her leather seat as Stefan drove them out of the station and out into the Kent country lanes, the throaty purr of the engine and whistle of the wind making it impossible to hear properly so they didn't talk, but often exchanged glances, Stefan holding on to her hand sometimes. She'd never been in such a fancy car before, one capable of going at a far greater speed than an Austin Seven, but she felt perfectly safe as Stefan drove expertly and not too fast.

She'd thought they'd be heading straight for RAF West Malling where he was stationed so was surprised when Stefan pulled over, parking beside a wood, the world suddenly feeling so quiet when he turned off the engine.

'Come on, I want show you something.' Stefan jumped

out of the car and went around to open her door for her, holding out his hand for her to take.

Out of the car, Bella took the scarf off and shook her hair free, her dark brown curls springing into life. 'What is it?'

'You see.' Stefan put his arm around her waist and led her into the wood where tall beech trees towered above them like a wild cathedral, the trunks a smooth grey while the burnt-orange leaves stood out against the clear blue sky. It was stunningly beautiful. 'I hope you like.'

Bella nodded. 'I love it, it's breathtaking.' She loved autumn and the way the trees put on one last show before winter. She'd written to him in her letters about her walks in the parks and how much she still missed being in the countryside where she'd grown up.

'I'm glad. I see wood from up there,' he nodded to the sky, 'and change of colour and think you would like.'

'Very much, thank you. The parks in London are lovely but nothing beats a wood in the countryside.'

They carried on walking, breathing in the scent of autumn, crunching on the dry dead leaves. Spotting some fallen leaves that had blown into a drift, Bella let go of his hand and started to kick her way through them, enjoying the gentle rustling, then, reaching the end of the pile, turned and went back through it again twice more. 'I love doing this,' she called to Stefan who stood there watching her, a smile on his face. 'Come and join me.'

He laughed and, holding her hand, they kicked through the leaves several times together until Bella was finally satisfied. 'That was fun.'

Stefan pulled her into his arms. 'You extraordinary woman, Bella.' His cornflower-blue eyes held hers. 'You make so happy here.' He put his hand over his heart before reaching into a chest pocket of his tunic and taking something out, holding it out to her. 'I want to give you this.'

Bella looked down at what he was offering her and gasped – it was the Polish version of a pilot's wings, the same as he wore pinned on the front of his tunic, a silver eagle with drooping wings carrying what looked like a wreath. 'I fall in love with you, Bella. I like if you wear my wings, please.'

Tears filled her eyes as she looked into his. 'I love you too, Stefan.' She had never expected to fall in love again, at least not for a long time, if ever, and certainly not with a Polish pilot but Stefan had come into her life and shaken it up: he'd taken her dancing, showed her courtesy and was not afraid to demonstrate how he felt; he'd swept her away from the path that she'd been following since James had died. He'd made her feel so alive and gloriously happy again.

Stefan gently touched her cheek, brushing away a tear that had escaped. 'I so happy we find each other, Bella. Will you wear my wings?'

She smiled at him. 'I'd like that very much, thank you.'

Very gently, he pinned the wings on the front of her dress just below her collarbone, and then kissed her tenderly. 'It looks beautiful, like you.'

The officers' mess fell silent as Bella and Stefan walked in, everyone stopping talking to look at them.

237

'Not often you lot are quiet,' Stefan said. 'Everyone, this is Bella.'

'Welcome to the madhouse, Bella,' someone called.

A tall man, who was older than most of the others, probably in his late twenties, got up from his armchair and came over to them, bowing and clicking his heels, before taking hold of Bella's hand and kissing it. 'I am Tadeusz, very good to meet you. Stefan talks about you very much.'

Bella's cheeks grew warm. 'Pleased to meet you.' She'd heard about Tadeusz too, he was their leader and a very experienced pilot who the men looked up to.

'Please come and sit down, lunch will be served soon.' Tadeusz directed her to sit in the chair he'd just vacated. Stefan perched on one of the arms, putting his hand behind her back to reassure her.

'You're a brave woman coming here for lunch,' one of the British airmen, who was puffing away on a pipe, said. 'You should have taken her out to a restaurant, Stefan.'

'No, it's fine, I'm pleased to see where Stefan works and lives,' Bella said. 'I'm sure it'll be lovely.'

'Stefan says you drive ambulance?' Tadeusz asked.

'Yes, I'm stationed not far from the Tower of London.' Bella was aware that all the men in the mess were listening to her, watching her.

'Is hard job, I—' Tadeusz began but stopped when an orderly appeared and announced that lunch was ready.

'Grub's up, old chaps,' an airman said. 'And lady, of course.'

Sitting at the table with a plate of stew in front of her, Bella faced more questions from the airmen.

'So where did you meet Kaminski then?' a sandy-haired airman with a magnificent moustache asked as he speared a dumpling swimming in his stew. 'He's a lucky fellow to have met you.'

Bella caught Stefan's eye and he winked at her. 'At an incident, Stefan helped my fellow crew member and me to carry casualties to our ambulance.' She smiled at Stefan who sat opposite her. 'He saved us a lot of time.'

'A V1 rocket?' another airman asked from further down the table.

Bella nodded. 'It was a bad one, hit in the middle of the street and caused a lot of damage.'

'We try, but don't get them all,' he said.

'Londoners are grateful for what you're doing,' Bella said. 'I'm sure it's not easy to shoot them down.'

This was an open invitation to the pilots to talk about their exploits facing the doodlebug rockets, and with a great deal of laughter and demonstrations of flying with their hands, Bella watched and listened to them as she ate. She could see the strong camaraderie between them, rather like at Station 75, with different characters making up the whole: there were the loud, boisterous ones who dominated the conversation and a few quieter ones like Stefan. All of them seemed to get on well together and despite their joshing around would support each other through thick and thin, and sometimes life and death, when they were up flying their sorties.

'Are you all right?' Stefan asked, reaching across to touch her hand when they were served their second course of jam roly-poly and custard.

She nodded and picked up her spoon and pointed at the custard. Stefan, who had once told her about his dislike of it, pulled a face and shrugged. 'I try to get used to it.'

'It's bigger than I thought.' Bella touched the side of the Spitfire – she'd only seen them as small planes darting about in the sky in dogfights, never this close before.

'Is best aeroplane,' Stefan said. 'I show you.' He took her hand and guided her around the Spitfire, explaining what part did what, from the pointed nose cone and propellers to the tail, clearly enthralled with his plane. 'You like?'

Bella laughed and nodded. 'Yes, it's very nice.' She caught the eye of the mechanic who was in the middle of servicing Stefan's plane while it was here in the hangar and he grinned back at her.

'It's the best plane, miss,' the mechanic said. 'She's a beauty and no mistake.'

'See?' Stefan laughed. 'We all love Spitfire.'

A loud bell began to ring somewhere outside and Stefan and the mechanic looked at each other and then both dashed over to the hangar door.

'What is it?' Bella hurried over to join them, but her question was answered as she saw pilots dressed in flying jackets, life jackets and heavy boots running out of the mess towards the line of waiting Spitfires standing out on the grass.

'That's Tadeusz.' Stefan pointed to the nearest Spitfire which his friend was climbing into while his ground crew made the final preparations. He put his arm around her as she watched in fascination as the Spitfire's engine roared into life with a burst of exhaust fumes, the propeller spinning around, and then it started to move, taxiing to take off, closely followed by the other planes, going faster and faster down the runway and lifting off as if they were feather light. The air was filled with the throaty growls of their engines which gradually faded as the planes banked to the left and flew away to deal with whatever they were being sent to fight.

Bella suddenly felt sick. This was what Stefan did. She knew he was a pilot, of course, but seeing the others rush off and launch themselves into the air in their Spitfires, no matter how marvellous a machine it was, was terrifying because they weren't going up there for a pleasure flight.

'What happens now?' she asked.

'We wait.' Stefan shrugged. 'There is nothing to do, we wait for them to come back.' The mechanic nodded and went back to his work. 'Come on,' Stefan took her hand, 'we go wait in the mess.'

This time the mess was much quieter, just a few of the pilots remaining, sitting around reading or just listening to the wireless.

'I get us some tea,' Stefan said after directing her to sit in one of the vacant armchairs.

'Is it always like that?' Bella asked the sandy-haired airman she'd spoken to earlier.

He frowned. 'How do you mean?'

'Rushing off like that at the sound of the bell?'

'It's what we do. What do you do when a call comes in for an ambulance?'

'Rush off . . .' Bella paused. 'But we're not going to do battle, in a small aeroplane, that's the difference.'

He smiled at her. 'We're used to it. And it's not always into battle, not really; if we're after doodlebugs, they don't fight back.'

'When will they return?' she asked.

He shrugged. 'When they're done or are running low on fuel. Look, try not to fret over it, we do it mostly because we love it, being up there flying . . . it's the best feeling there is. I'd rather be up there in my Spitfire than driving a tank or ploughing through the waves on a battleship any day.'

Stefan returned with two cups of tea.

'Thank you.' Bella took a sip and spluttered at the unexpected taste. 'What's in here?'

'A tot of brandy, you look like you need it.' Stefan sat down opposite her. 'I think you upset seeing them go out, yes?'

She nodded. 'It scared me, I suppose.'

He reached out and took hold of her hand. 'Is like when you in ambulance in middle of a raid, we do our job.'

'I know. At least my ambulance stays safely on the ground.'

'But squash in by streets and buildings. Up there,' he raised his eyes upwards, 'we have room to move, we are free. I take you flying one day, you go with me? Yes?'

Bella thought for a moment. 'Yes, I would, I'd like to see what it's like up there.'

Waiting on the platform of West Malling station later that afternoon, Bella felt as if she knew a lot more about Stefan

242

now. She'd seen where he worked, met his colleagues, touched his beloved Spitfire, and experienced the worry of the RAF equivalent of a call–out, thankfully counting all the pilots back in again. Stefan's world was different to hers in so many ways, but he shared with her the special bond of fellow crew members and the need to do their duty when required, she understood that completely.

'Thank you for asking me to come here.' Bella squeezed Stefan's hand. 'I've enjoyed myself, and now I can picture where you are and what you do.'

'I think of you at Station 75. I think many, many times each day, Bella. You have my heart.' He raised her hand to his lips and kissed it.

'You have mine too.' Bella touched the wings he'd given her. 'I'm going to wear this every day.'

He intensely blue eyes held hers. 'So part of me with you.'

'I . . . ' Bella began but paused at the whistle of the train approaching, their time together almost up. 'When will I see you again?'

'Soon, I come visit, soon. I promise.' Stefan hugged her tightly and Bella remained in his arms for as long as possible, eking out every precious moment with this wonderful man who had turned her world upside down.

Chapter Forty-five

'Look! What did I tell you?'

Frankie looked up from where she was topping up the water in the radiator of her ambulance, to see Sparky marching through the covered archway to the garages, waving two newspapers in the air.

'Aye aye! Something's upset him.' Paterson stopped cleaning the side of his ambulance and dropped the cleaning rag into the bucket of soapy water.

'I told you they were firing more bleeding rockets at us and they've finally gone and admitted it.' Sparky spread first one and then a second newspaper on the bonnet of his ambulance and the other crew members crowded round to look.

'Blimey, Sparky, you've splashed out on two newspapers today,' Frankie said, looking down at the large photo on the front of the *Daily Mirror* whose headline declared in bold type: *V2 The TRUTH behind latest attack by Nazi secret weapon*, and at the bottom of the page was a diagram of the new weapon.

'Well they both showed different things and I wanted to know everything, so I had to get both,' Sparky explained, his breath pluming in the cold November air.

'Read it out to us then,' Paterson said. 'We can't all read it at once, you've had a bee in your bonnet about this so educate us all so we know what's what.' He caught Frankie's eye and winked at her, and she smiled back, knowing that he would have heard plenty about these flying gas pipes from Sparky in the past few weeks because once Sparky got an idea into his head he didn't like to let go, especially if it was about something like this when people were being kept in the dark about what was happening.

Sparky cleared his throat and began to read: '"Now that Mr Churchill has broken the government's long silence . . ."' He stopped for a moment. 'It's been bleedin' weeks, the first one was back in September, so I heard, and only now do they decide to be honest.'

'We all know that, Sparky,' Paterson said. 'The government only tell us what they want us to know and when. Just get on with it and read the paper out, will you.'

'Just stating a fact,' Sparky said, and then began to read again from the paper.

Everyone listened intently as they heard how these new long-range rockets, dropped on them from sixty to seventy miles up in the air, travelled faster than sound so that there could be no siren warning or time to take shelter, and how they were designed to penetrate deeper before exploding than the doodlebugs.

When Sparky had finished, Frankie went back to her job, trying hard to focus on the task again, but it was hard to forget what she'd just heard about the sinister new weapons because just when you thought the war might be heading towards the end something else came along to make it a whole lot worse. After D–Day it had been the doodlebugs, and now these V2s, which were even worse.

'Are you all right?' Bella asked, quietly. 'Sparky's caused quite a stir with his newspapers.' She nodded to where most of the crew were still crowded round looking at the photos and diagrams and reading out sections of the articles themselves.

Frankie sighed. 'I'm fine, just sad that we've now got these horrible things being fired at us. Those poor little children killed by a V2 while they were at a birthday party . . . ' She'd wanted to cry when Sparky had read out the bit about the children dying as they sat at the table watching the burning candles on the cake. 'It's not right that they should have been killed like that, it's not fair.'

Bella put her hand on Frankie's arm. 'I know, but war's not fair, you and I have seen enough doing this job to know that. These new rockets have just upped the game, coming with no warning or chance to get away. Let's hope our troops soon capture more of the launch sites and they stop.'

Frankie leaned closer to her friend and whispered, 'I hope so, I can't help wondering if we should persuade Winnie to leave London until it's safe again.'

Bella looked over to where Winnie was talking to Sparky, clearly enjoying sparring with him. 'Do you think she would go if we asked her?'

'No, not really. That woman will stay at Station 75 as long as she possibly can – nothing will shift her from here except when she has no alternative but to go.'

Chapter Forty-six

Winnie scraped the last of the apple crumble and custard out of her bowl, ate it and then sat back in her chair feeling quite content. 'That was absolutely delicious, Mrs Connelly, thank you.' She smiled at the older woman who sat at the far end of the table next to Station Officer Steele.

'Well, clean plates are always a good sign.' Mrs Connelly surveyed the empty crockery that littered the large table in the common room around which the crew sat to eat their midday meal.

'You always do us proud, Mrs Connelly.' Station Officer Steele smiled at her.

'It's much better than having to bring sandwiches to work like we used to have to do,' Sparky added. 'There's only so many fish paste sandwiches a man can stand.'

The crews' laughter filled the room but was brought to an abrupt halt by the sound of the telephone ringing in the boss's office. Without saying a word, Station Officer

Steele got up and hurried off to answer it, while everyone strained to hear what was going on, passing glances between each other as they waited.

Winnie got up from the table and went to stand near the open door of the office and one glance from the boss told her all she needed to know: it was a call-out. She waited until the older woman put down the telephone receiver. 'Who do you want to go out?'

'They've requested three ambulances, it's out of our area, down in Deptford. I'll explain more in a moment.' She paused for a moment. 'I think it's best if you, Rose, Frankie, Bella, Sparky and Paterson take this one, it could be tricky.'

Winnie nodded. 'I'll rally the troops then.'

A few minutes later they were all gathered in the office.

'I can't tell you much, I'm afraid, only that it's out of our area at New Cross in Deptford. Whatever it is must be bad to send crews from here, and no doubt other stations out of the usual catchment area have been called in as well,' Station Officer Steele said.

'Is it a V2 rocket?' Winnie asked.

The boss shrugged. 'Probably, there's been no air-raid warning so it's not from bombers. As it's out of our area you're going to need to check the map before you go.' She nodded to the large street map of London that was pinned on her office wall.

'I roughly know where to go.' Sparky went over to look at the map and check the route. 'I can lead the way.'

'Excellent. I know I can rely on all of you to do a good job.' She smiled at them. 'Right, drivers, go and get your ambulances ready while I quickly write up the chits, and good luck.'

Winnie was glad that Sparky knew the way as they drove south across Tower Bridge and out of Station 75's usual area. His work as a taxi driver before the war had proven invaluable so many times over the years, especially when they'd been sent out of their usual patch.

'It feels odd going in this direction,' Rose said, holding on to Trixie who was sitting on her lap.

'I know, but whatever it is, it's serious.' Winnie had dealt with many such calls and always they brought with them a mixture of worry about what they were going to, but also a sense of being glad that she could pitch in and help people who desperately needed it when times were tough.

When they reached New Cross, the devastation that met them seemed at odds with the fine, late-November Saturday afternoon, a day when people would normally be going about their business, shopping and enjoying their weekend. Winnie parked the ambulance where a policeman directed her to, pulling up behind Sparky, and they quickly got out, grabbed stretchers and their bags from the back of the ambulance.

'What's happened?' she asked, approaching the policeman who was waving more ambulances to park in the row behind them.

'One of them V2s hit Woolworth's . . . ' He paused, his face pale. 'It was packed with Saturday shoppers, it's completely collapsed. Be careful how you go, there's broken glass all across the road.'

Winnie nodded at him and turned to look at Sparky, Paterson, Frankie and Bella who'd all come over to listen to what he said. 'Right, let's do what we can then.'

Making their way towards the collapsed building, Winnie thought that this had to be one of the worst incidents she'd been to. The air was still filled with grit and dust, the smell of brick plaster irritating her nose, while her feet crunched over broken glass and rubble which lay ankle-deep across the road. Cars that had been nearby had been blown apart into pieces of jagged metal, and telegraph poles had been thrown like matchsticks by the blast and lay across rooftops. But worst of all was the sight of what remained of people thrown haphazardly on the ground, some of whom had been covered with sheets of corrugated iron until they could be dealt with, from under which blood seeped out, pooling and congealing in the dust and broken glass.

'Sylvia was in there!' The loud, anguished voice made Winnie look over to where two ambulance crew stood, supporting another colleague who was sobbing hard and shouting out between heaving breaths. 'She didn't deserve this.'

One of the crew saw Winnie looking. 'One of our crew mates had gone to Woolworth's on her dinner break, she 'eard they'd got some saucepans in and she was getting married next month . . . ' Her voice wavered.

'I'm so sorry,' Winnie said, knowing from the look of the huge crater where the shop had once stood, now piled high with debris, that there was little chance that their friend would be found alive. They clearly were a close-knit crew, just as they were at Station 75, and her stomach knotted at the thought of something like this happening to her dear friends. Tears smarted in her eyes as she pictured the scene of a busy Saturday in the shop, with people queueing up to buy precious saucepans which were so rarely available these days. There would have been mothers with their children, innocent people just going about their everyday lives and then ...

'Come on.' Frankie tugged at Winnie's arm. 'We can't do anything for their friend but there're plenty of injured that need our help.'

Winnie nodded, sniffing back her tears; she wasn't usually so affected while she was on the job, but these days her emotions felt like they were on a knife edge. She tucked her arm into Frankie's, glad of her friend's steady presence, and went with her over towards where Rose and Bella were already busy tending to some injured people lying on the ground.

'You all right?' Frankie said.

'Yes, just being a bit silly, you know ...' She shrugged.

'Look, Winnie, if you want to go and wait in the ambulance, we'd all understand, we could gather up the casualties and you could just drive them to hospital if that's easier. Being ... you know ... might make you more sensitive to all this.' Frankie indicated with her head the devastation around them, where moans of pain and shouts from people digging through the rubble filled the air. 'It ain't easy dealing with this.'

'I can do it!' Winnie took a deep breath. 'Sorry to snap at you. Thank you for the offer, but no,' she squared her shoulders, 'I'm here to do my job and just because I am ... ' she raised her eyebrows, 'it doesn't mean I can't do what I'm here for any more.'

Frankie smiled at her. 'Fine, but just say if you do need a bit of help, all right?'

She squeezed her friend's arm. 'I'll be fine, come on let's get to work.'

Chapter Forty-seven

Frankie woke with a start and was just in time to see a shadow slip through the open door of the women's rest room, closing it quietly behind her. She put out her hand to feel the mattress beside hers where Winnie had been lying but it was empty, the blanket still warm from her body. Everyone else seemed to be asleep, their even breathing showing no indication that they had been disturbed by Winnie's exit, and she must have taken Trixie with her as the little dog always slept at the end of her bed when they were on duty.

She lay there for a few moments pondering what to do. She'd found Winnie splashing her face with cold water in the changing room a couple of hours after they'd got back from the Woolworth's V2 incident, clearly trying to cover up the fact that she'd been crying. Frankie had tried to talk to her then but Winnie had shrugged her off and tried to pretend that nothing was wrong; she hadn't believed her and now, with her getting up in the middle of the night and going off, perhaps something was wrong with her. Or she might have just gone to the lavatory and be back soon. Frankie decided to wait a few minutes and if Winnie didn't come back then she would go and find her and see what was wrong.

She guessed at least five minutes had passed and Winnie still hadn't come back, so Frankie quietly peeled back her blanket and tiptoed over to the door, grateful for the crack of light showing underneath it to guide her way, then she slipped out of the room as quietly as she could, blinking her eyes in the unaccustomed light of the common room. It was empty, apart from the figure of Sparky who was fast asleep on the sofa, snoring gently. Moving slowly so as not to disturb him, she peeped in the window of the door of the office, and could see Station Officer Steele at her desk, where she was resting her head on her arms and appeared to be asleep as well.

Next, she tried the women's changing room but again there was no sign of Winnie. She must have gone outside, either up on the flat roof, which was a favourite spot for crew members to go for a bit of peace and quiet when they needed to think, or out at the garages – either option would be chilly on a November night. Frankie grabbed her greatcoat from the hook and put it on, along with her scarf and hat, then made her way as quietly as she could up the stairs to the roof.

Stepping out of the door, the sight of the beautifully clear, starlit night arching millions of miles high above London was breathtaking. One of the benefits of the blackout was that the celestial sky was now clearly visible above the city, something that she only used to see when they went hopping down in Kent every year, otherwise she'd never have known that there were so many stars up there.

Her arrival on the roof was greeted by the pattering of paws as Trixie hurried across to greet her, jumping her front legs up on Frankie's trousers, her tail wagging happily. 'Hello, Trix, where's your mistress then?'

'Over here,' Winnie's voice called from behind the chimney stack which poked up through the roof and made a comfortable place to sit against.

Frankie went over and sat down beside her friend who was sitting with her knees up, leaning her elbows on them, looking up at the stars. 'Couldn't you sleep?'

'No.'

Frankie waited for her to say something else, but unusually she stayed silent after her single-word answer. Something was definitely up with her then. 'Why not? Are you worried about Mac?'

Winnie stroked Trixie who had settled herself down on her mistress's lap. 'No more than usual.'

'What, then?' Again, Frankie waited for an answer, but none was forthcoming. 'For God's sake, Winnie, what's got into you? I know you've been cryin' earlier and now you are getting up in the middle of the night and coming up here to sit out in the cold.' At least her friend had had the sense to put on her greatcoat as well.

Winnie sighed. 'I can't get the sight of those little children out of my mind. They'd gone to Woolworth's to do some shopping with their mothers, they didn't deserve to die like that . . . ' Her voice cracked. 'It's so bloody rotten and unfair.'

Frankie put her arm through Winnie's, knowing just how she felt. Seeing small children pulled out from the rubble of Woolworth's had been hard to bear, their lifeless bodies a stark reminder of the horror and wastefulness of war. There'd been no warning, no chance to get to safety, one moment they were perhaps spending their sweet ration, and the next the V2 had exploded and their lives snuffed out in an instant. 'It was bad, but we know that nothing is fair as far as war is concerned, there ain't no discrimination between who should die and who should live, especially with them blasted rockets. Anyone can die or be hurt by them.'

'I know, but there was even a little baby killed in its pram . . . ' Winnie began to cry.

That must really have hit home with Winnie expecting a baby of her own, Frankie thought. Perhaps it was time for her to get out of London in case she and her unborn child were unlucky enough to come into the path of a V2 rocket, but would her stubbornness and determination to remain at Station 75 stop her from considering it? Perhaps she needed somebody else to suggest she should.

Frankie took a deep breath and braced herself for her friend's response. 'Winnie, do you think it might be a good idea if you left London? None of us know when or where the next V2 will land. If you don't want to do it for yourself then at least consider it for your baby. Mac would probably want you to.' The silence that followed

257

seemed worse than if Winnie had shouted at her. 'What do you think?'

Winnie turned to her. 'What do I think? I'm surprised at you even asking me to think about it, to be honest, Frankie. I'm not leaving my job. Not for the risk of a V2 landing on me because if it does then I'm a goner and there's nothing I can do about it. And please don't bring Mac into this, he's not here and I am.'

'I 'ad to ask, you understand that. I didn't think you would leave though. What does Mac think? Is he happy for you to stay working 'ere in London?'

Winnie shrugged. 'I wouldn't know, because I haven't told him about the baby. That way he can't tell me what to do – not that I'd necessarily do what he wanted anyway!'

'You haven't told him! But he should know.'

'And he will, when I'm ready to tell him. He'd only worry, and I want him to focus on looking after himself rather than be thinking about me.'

Frankie sighed. 'You always do go about things your own way, so this ain't nothing new.'

Winnie patted Frankie's arm. 'I appreciate your concern but honestly I'm all right, just very sad about what happened today, and I'd rather be working here than anywhere else. What else would I do with myself, Frankie? I love being at Station 75 and with the way our troops are going now it can only be a matter of time before they reach Berlin and hopefully the war will be done. I want to stay here doing my bit for as long as I can until either my secret is out and the boss sacks me or the war is over and Station 75 closes.'

'I understand.' Frankie leaned her head on Winnie's shoulder, looking up at the sky. 'Do you think Mac and Alastair can see the same stars as us?'

'Yes, the stars are the same where they are and, who knows, they might be looking up too.'

'When the moon is up I always look at it and think it's shinin' down on Alastair too,' Frankie said. 'It helps.'

'I know what you mean.' Winnie sighed. 'One day I hope they'll both be home and we can look up at the moon with them standing beside us.'

Chapter Forty-eight

Bella opened the Queensberry All-Services Club programme that Stefan had bought and could hardly believe who was appearing here tonight, the twelfth of December – The American Band of the AEF, conducted by Major Glen Miller. When Stefan had said he had a surprise for her she never expected something like this.

'You like?' Stefan smiled, his blue eyes twinkling.

'I love it!' Bella grabbed hold of his hand and leaned over to kiss him. 'Thank you, I can't believe I'm about to see Glenn Miller and his band playing live. I've listened to them so often on the wireless but to actually see them . . . '

Stefan kissed her hand. 'I thought you like to come and see tonight.'

'You were right, this is the most wonderful surprise and I . . . ' She paused as the musicians started to file onto the stage and take up their positions. The audience fell silent watching them, probably feeling as much in awe as she did. And when Glenn Miller joined them a few moments later she turned to Stefan and mouthed, 'This is marvellous,' before returning her attention to the stage.

Listening to Glenn Miller speaking, his soft American voice sounding so different to her ear accustomed to English accents, and the band beginning to play, Bella felt goose pimples rise up on her arms. She squeezed Stefan's hand, holding on to it for the rest of the show. Seeing the musicians playing, and hearing the music coming live, directly from their instruments, songs that she'd heard many times before on the wireless, it seemed to have a greater depth, especially the trumpets, trombones and saxophones who blasted out their notes with such toe-tapping vibrancy it made her want to get up and dance. Sadly she couldn't, as the audience were seated because this performance was being recorded for broadcasting. She had to content herself with jiggling her feet around to the music, all the while keeping her eyes steadfastly fixed on the stage and drinking in every moment.

Time seemed to pass so quickly and after the final song had been played, Glenn Miller signed off, closing the show and telling the audience both here and listening over the wireless to 'keep an eye on the papers and an ear on the radio for the time and place' for the next performance. 'Until we meet again, then, it's good luck and goodbye.'

Thinking that was it, Bella was delighted when the band went on to play another concert just for the audience in the club; another half an hour of spine-tingling music, ending on the famous 'Tuxedo Junction', which had the audience clapping loudly in appreciation.

'That was one of the best things I've ever seen!' Bella said, clapping so hard that her hands were tingling. 'Thank you, Stefan, for bringing me, I'll never forget tonight.'

He bowed his head. 'Is my great pleasure, Bella. We stay for the dance, yes?'

She nodded. 'Definitely.' Hal Kent's band were on next, so the programme said, and she wasn't going to turn down a chance to dance with Stefan as she absolutely adored it now – her days of having two left feet were far behind her. He had come into her life and literally swept her off her feet, and she loved it – and him.

Chapter Forty-nine

'Cocoa's ready.' Frankie put the tray of steaming mugs that she'd just filled with the hot, chocolatey drink on the table and glanced up at the clock on the wall of Station 75's common room. 'We'd better get a move on if we want to be up there in time.'

'Here's your coat, hat and scarf.' Bella handed her the clothes, having fetched them from the ladies' changing room.

'Thanks.' Frankie put on her coat, wrapping her scarf tightly around her neck and pulling on her green knitted wool beret, dressing up warmly like Bella, Winnie and Rose already had. They were all going up on the flat roof of Station 75 to see in the New Year.

'Thanks for making the cocoa, Frankie.' Winnie took a mug. 'Come on then, ladies, time waits for no man . . . Or woman, we don't want to miss it.'

Grabbing their own mugs, they followed Winnie up

onto the roof where the waning moon, just a day past full, shone its cold light down on the London rooftops, making the frosty night seem all the crisper and colder. The shadowy greyness wasn't light enough to show it, but Frankie knew that their breaths would be pluming in the chill air and she was glad of the warmth of the mug that seeped through the wool of her gloves, keeping her hands warm.

'How long to go now?' Bella asked.

Winnie flicked on her small torch for a few seconds to look at her watch. 'Just a couple of minutes. Then we'll be in 1945, imagine that.'

'Do you remember when we first did this?' Frankie said. 'It was the first New Year's after I joined Station 75, we came up here to see in 1941, and we've done it a few more times since.'

'Never thought that first time that we'd still be here doing this now,' Bella said. 'This war's gone on far longer than any of us expected and it's not over yet. Do you think . . .'

Winnie checked her watch again. 'It's nearly time, about thirty seconds to go.'

They fell silent, waiting for the seconds to tick round and the old year to pass into history and the new year to begin.

'Ten, nine.' Winnie flicked on her torch again and began to count down, the rest of them joining in with her. 'Eight, seven, six, five, four, three, two, one. Happy New Year!'

Other faint cries bringing in the new year came from the surrounding streets where people were out in pubs celebrating, but there was no ringing of church bells as there used to be.

'A toast then, in best Station 75 cocoa, to 1945.' Winnie held up her mug and the rest of them clinked their mugs against hers and each other's before taking a sip.

'What will 1945 bring us, do you think?' Bella wondered. 'The end of the war?'

'I hope so,' Frankie said. 'We're nearer now than we've ever been. I hope this time next year we'll be at peace.' And that Alastair would be with her again, she added silently.

'I hope so too, you know I have a good reason to want it.' Winnie paused for a moment. 'Rose, I think it's time I told you something, we work closely together and I should tell you.'

'You're not leaving, are you?' Rose asked.

Winnie shook her head and put her hand on the young woman's arm. 'Not if I can help it, not for a while until I absolutely have to.' She lowered her voice. 'You see, the thing is, I'm expecting a baby.'

'A baby!' Rose said, her voice coming out in a squeak of surprise.

'Shhh! Yes, but it's a secret, only you, Frankie and Bella know about it here at work and that's the way it's got to stay. If the boss finds out then I'll have to leave and I don't want to – I love my job and intend to stay for as long as I can.'

'For as long as you can hide it, you mean,' Frankie said. 'There's going to come a time when even the biggest size tunic won't disguise it.'

'I know, but I'll stay for as long as I can until my secret's out. I hope I can depend on you to keep it for me, Rose.'

'Of course you can.' Rose smiled, her face shadowy in the moonlight. 'I'm glad you told me, it feels like an honour to be in on the secret.'

'An honour and a worry,' Bella said. 'We're all trying to help Winnie as much as she'll allow us to, but without giving the game away.'

'I'm perfectly capable of doing my job at the moment but don't worry, I'll let you know if I can't.' Winnie laughed. 'Right, enough about that, what do you all hope for in 1945 – and not just for the war to be over, that goes without saying. Frankie, what's your wish?'

Frankie didn't need to think before she answered. 'Alastair and Stanley to be 'ome with me.'

'Rose, what about you?' Winnie asked.

'To see my parents again.'

Frankie put her arm around Rose. 'And we all hope that for you, too.'

'Absolutely,' Winnie added. 'Your turn, Bella, what would you like to happen this year?'

'For my brother to come home safely and if, and when, the war is over, for us all to remain friends and keep in touch.'

'Of course we will, you ain't going to see the back of us just because the war ends. We've been through too much together to just go off on our separate ways and never see or hear from each other again,' Frankie said. 'It seems odd to think that if . . . *when* the war ends that Station 75 won't be needed any more. Our jobs here will come to an end . . .'

'Don't!' Winnie said. 'War is a terrible thing but being here, working with you three is the best thing about it.'

'Whatever happens, let's always be friends and keep in touch, promise,' Bella said.

'Promise,' they chorused as one.

'Another toast then.' Winnie held up her mug. 'To always being friends, no matter where we are or what we do.'

They all chinked their mugs together. 'To always being friends.'

And as Frankie took a sip of her cocoa she mentally promised herself that whatever happened in her life, whichever direction it took, she would always make sure that this promise held because these three young women had played such an important role in her life, being there for her when things were tough, and sharing the good times, and that was what true friendship was – it was precious and needed to be held on to.

Chapter Fifty

'Let's pencil in a stirrup pump practice for Thursday afternoon then, shall we? Providing, of course, there are no incidents . . . ' Station Officer Steele paused and looked at Winnie who clearly hadn't listened to a word she'd said. The young woman was staring at the large street map of London which was pinned on her office wall. In fact, she doubted that Winnie had been fully paying attention for any of their meeting. 'What do you think, Winnie, is that a good idea?'

At the sound of her name Winnie looked at her, her grey eyes wide with surprise. 'Ummm . . . '

'I was saying that I think we should have a stirrup pump practice on Thursday afternoon.'

Winnie nodded. 'Yes, good idea.'

As she wrote it down on the calendar, she wondered what was the matter with Winnie. There was something about her that was different, she had a feeling that there'd been a change – what, she didn't know, but it was clearly affecting the young woman's ability to focus on the job and that concerned her.

'Right, are you going to tell me what's wrong?'

'Nothing's wrong.' Winnie's peachy complexion grew pinker.

'Come on, Winnie, I'm no fool, I can see that something's bothering you, you're not paying attention and you seem to be . . . off with the fairies. As my Deputy Officer I need you to be focused and attentive. Is there something I can help you with?'

Winnie looked uncomfortable, twisting her hands in her lap. 'Not unless you can bring Mac home. I'm worried about him, that's all.'

'I know you are, and I wish I could bring him and all the men safely home again and the war was over, but I can't.' She shrugged. 'You can always come and talk to me about it. I understand how worried you are, but you still need to be able to focus on work when you're here, we have to leave our personal worries at the door when we arrive. I know it's not always easy, but remember we have an ambulance station to run and people rely on us.'

'I know, I'm sorry,' Winnie said. 'I'll try harder.'

She reached out and patted Winnie's arm. 'Thank you, and that's all we needed to talk about for now. Go and make yourself a cup of tea.'

Winnie stood up quickly, clearly keen to get away. 'Would you like a cup as well?'

'No, thank you.' She watched as the young woman went out to the common room. She wasn't sure that Winnie had been completely honest with her about what was worrying her. Was Winnie's mother causing her problems again? She'd had difficulties with her in the past and it was possible that she was having issues with her again. Her instinct told her that there was more to Winnie's inattention than her worries about Mac and over the years she had learned to trust it. She'd be keeping a close eye on Winnie from now on.

Chapter Fifty-one

One of the lovely things about having Rose live with her at Matlock Street, Frankie thought, as she laid the table, was that the two of them could cook their meals together – sometimes one would cook and the other wash up, but other times, like today, they both worked together on the meal.

After they'd got home from their shift this morning they'd prepared a stew and left it to cook for a few hours while they did other things, and now it was ready, a delicious aroma filling the kitchen.

'The dumplings are cooked,' Rose said, taking the lid off the saucepan and turning off the gas. 'Are you ready to eat?'

'Definitely. I'll get the plates.'

They'd just sat down to eat, and Frankie was enjoying the taste of Rose's delicious herby dumplings, when they heard the front door open, and the unmistakable sound of Ivy's high heels tip-tapping down the hallway towards them. She instantly tensed and from the look on Rose's face she felt the same way.

Ivy opened the kitchen door and when she saw the two of them looking at her, she stopped for a moment, clearly surprised to see them there, but quickly recovered herself. 'What you lookin' at?'

Frankie considered what to say for a moment: should she comment on the fact that Ivy was obviously returning home after a night out on the tiles? She was dressed up to the nines, but even perfect make-up couldn't disguise the bags under her eyes and her hair was out of its usual primped style. She decided it was best to ignore Ivy's baiting comment. 'Hello, Ivy.'

Ivy rolled her eyes and tottered over to the kettle, putting it on to boil, the smell of perfume, cigarettes and beer oozing out of her.

Frankie did her best to carry on eating, although the meal they'd so carefully prepared and which had tasted so delicious just moments ago was now like sawdust in her mouth. Rose kept her head down and concentrated on her plate and eating.

She couldn't help wondering where Ivy had been, who she'd been with, though she could probably answer that question – no doubt with Micky Chandler. She'd just assumed that Ivy was upstairs still in bed when they'd got home this morning, but obviously she hadn't been. What would her grandfather have thought? Frankie knew the answer to that: he'd have been disgusted.

It seemed to take an age for the kettle to boil and for

Ivy to make herself a cup of tea, her presence in the room casting a shadow over them despite her not saying a single word and studiously ignoring both her and Rose. When at last Ivy left the kitchen and clumped up the stairs to her room, slamming the bedroom door shut behind her, Frankie let out a sigh of relief, causing Rose to look at her and smile.

'I thought she'd never go,' Rose whispered.

'Me too, she looked a bit rough, so we probably won't see 'er for a while, she'll be sleepin' off whatever she's been up to.'

'Where do you think she's been?' Rose asked.

Frankie shrugged. 'Probably with that spiv, Chandler, I suppose. I'm just hopin' she might take up with him full-time, marry him and move out of here.' She sighed. 'Right, I'm not goin' to let her put me off my food. Tuck in before it gets cold, your herby dumplings really are the best, mine always come out so tough.'

Chapter Fifty-two

'Some things never change,' Frankie said, folding the tunic fabric to make a tuck and securing it with a pin.

'What do you mean?' Winnie looked at her friend who was kneeling on the floor in front of her.

'You never keep still for long when I'm tryin' to do any alterations on your clothes.' Frankie raised her eyebrows. 'Please, just stand still for a couple of minutes so I can get the tunic pinned properly. I've got to do a good job if it's going to accommodate your growing stomach and yet not look like it from the outside.'

Winnie smoothed the front of the larger-sized tunic over her belly which had a definite swell to it now. She was five months pregnant and although her willowy figure was definitely changing, it was only at the front – from the back she looked as she always did. 'Do you think anyone will notice I've gone up a tunic size?'

'No, you'll be able to get away with it for a while longer,' Bella said. She was standing on guard by the door of the women's rest room, ready to stop anyone from coming in and catching them red-handed. They'd waited until Station Officer Steele had gone out to a meeting and most of the other crew members were either out doing voluntary work, classes, or taking an afternoon break in the common room. 'You're lucky that it's wintertime so you can get away with wearing a tunic all the time; if it was summertime you'd have a much harder job of hiding your condition, or you'd end up overheating because you daren't take off your tunic.'

'Perhaps the war will be over by the time I get too big to hide it any more,' Winnie said, hopefully. 'The Allies are making good progress, so it can't be long before they reach Germany, then Hitler will have to surrender and it will be all over and this little one,' she laid a hand on her stomach, 'will be born in a world at peace.'

Frankie looked at Bella who shook her head and shrugged. 'I wouldn't go getting your hopes up too much, Winnie. Let's just concentrate on keepin' you here at Station 75 for as long as we can, the rest of the war's out of our hands.'

'Well it would be nice if it was born in peacetime, wouldn't it?' Winnie said as Frankie turned her around so that she could work on the back of the tunic.

'Of course it would,' Frankie said. 'But we've been waitin' years for this war to be over so who knows when it will finally come true.' She stepped back to check where she had just pinned to make sure the darts were level with each other. Satisfied, she turned Winnie back to face her. 'Have you told Mac yet?'

Winnie's creamy skin flushed pink. 'Not yet.'

'Winnie!' Frankie and Bella chorused together.

'I thought you'd have written and told him by now,' Bella said.

Winnie put her hands on her hips. 'I haven't because I know what he'd say, and I don't want to do it.'

Bella sighed. 'You are too stubborn for your own good sometimes, Winnie.'

Winnie's grey eyes filled with tears. 'Don't badger me about it please, Bella. Don't you think I worry about if I'm doing the right thing or not? But I couldn't bear to not be working here, I've been here since the beginning and I want to stay for as long as I can.'

Frankie put her arm around Winnie's shoulders, her friend's once stiff-upper-lip attitude had softened dramatically since she'd become pregnant and she was more prone to tearfulness these days. 'But what about the V2s?'

Winnie shrugged. 'If one's got my name on it then so be it, it will be over before I know it.'

'And what about the baby?' Bella probed.

Winnie folded her arms firmly across her chest which emphasised her rounded belly under the tunic. 'Please, just leave it. I must stay, because what else would I do?'

Bella left her post by the door and came over and put her arms around her friend. 'I'm sorry, Winnie, I'm just worried about you, that's all.'

Winnie wiped the tears from her eyes. 'You two are the best friends I've ever had, and I appreciate what you're both doing for me, covering up my secret. I couldn't do it without you, you know.'

Frankie smiled at her. 'Right, take that tunic off so I can sew the alterations before the boss gets back, and then you can start wearin' it later and no one will be the wiser what's going on underneath.'

'So I don't have to stand still any longer?' Winnie smiled and began to undo the brass buttons on the front of the tunic. 'I never usually have trouble keeping still, it's only when someone tells me I've got to.'

Bella rolled her eyes. 'You and your inability to do as you're told, I hope that your baby doesn't take after you in that way.'

Winnie laughed. 'So, do I, but I'm sure it will be as delightful as its darling father.'

Chapter Fifty-three

Bella shook the drops off her umbrella before going in the front door of Connie's house, glad to be out of the miserable February rain. She'd just done a shift volunteering at the Red Cross POW parcel packing centre and planned to spend the rest of the day working on a new story.

She'd just shrugged off her coat and hung it on the carved coat stand when the door of the sitting room opened and Trixie shot out, closely followed by Winnie.

'Hello, Trix.' She bent down and stroked the little dog's head, whose tail was wagging in a golden blur of joy.

'You've got a visitor.' Winnie smiled. 'Stefan's here. I've given him some tea while he waited.'

Bella's heart skipped at the thought of seeing Stefan. She wasn't expecting him but time off from his job could be erratic, so perhaps he'd been given some unexpected leave for a few hours. 'Thanks, how long has he been waiting?'

'About half an hour.' Winnie bent down and scooped

Trixie up into her arms. 'I'm going upstairs for a bit, we'll leave you two lovebirds in peace.' She wriggled her eyebrows and headed for the stairs.

Bella smoothed down her hair before going in to the sitting room, her stomach doing its usual flip at the sight of him. 'Stefan, I didn't know you were coming, I'm sorry I wasn't here.' She went across to him and, as always, he stood up when she entered the room. He bowed, clicking his heels before opening his arms to embrace her.

Bella hugged him back and then loosened her arms and looked up at him. He smiled at her but it didn't reach his eyes, and she instantly knew something was wrong. 'Are you all right?'

He shook his head and sighed. 'Is not good. You heard on wireless about Yalta and what they do to Poland?' His voice cracked, tears filling his eyes, making their blueness even more striking.

'Let's sit down.' Bella pulled him down to sit beside her on the sofa. 'I heard the news, yes. I'm so sorry, I know that's what you didn't want to happen.' She gripped both his hands in hers.

The Prime Minister, along with President Roosevelt, had met with Stalin and agreed that eastern Poland should be given to Russia and the control of the rest of the country handed over to a provisional Soviet-style Communist government, crushing the dream of a free Poland that so many Poles like Stefan held dear. She knew that dream had kept him going, especially after he'd heard the dreadful news that his parents had been killed in the Warsaw uprising last year, the news filtering out via the Red Cross. He had lost his family and now his country.

'Never!' Tears spilled over and trickled down his cheeks. 'All this time we fight for Poland to be free and this . . .' He hung his head.

Bella moved closer and put her arms around him, pulling him towards her and gently stroking his back as he wept. It seemed odd to see a man cry, but she'd learned that Polish men were not ashamed to show when they felt something, and this betrayal of Poland's freedom that servicemen like Stefan had fought so long and hard for, many of them dying in the process, was devastating for them.

'Here, let me.' She gently wiped away the tears with her handkerchief when Stefan sat up and looked at her.

'Thank you, I wanted to see you.' He reached out and took her hand and kissed it. 'To be with you.'

'I wish I could make it better for you, I know how much you love Poland. Perhaps there is something you can do about it when you go home after the war.'

His shoulders slumped. 'I have no home to go back to, I cannot return to Poland if it is under Stalin's watch. Many of my fellow Poles think the same.'

'What will you do? Where would you go?'

He shrugged. 'I stay in England, join English RAF if I can.'

'I'd love you to stay here.'

'You would?'

She nodded. 'If you can't go back to Poland then you staying here makes me happy.' They hadn't talked about the future, about what would happen when he went back to Poland after the war. Bella had just been enjoying the time they had and not dared look too far ahead. For once in her life where Stefan was concerned she hadn't worried about the future, just revelled in the delight of being with him and swept away by the unexpected joys he'd brought into her life. 'If you stay here then at least I will still be able to see you.'

Stefan smiled – this time it reached his eyes. 'Yes, that is very good thing.'

Chapter Fifty-four

Breakfast times at Station 75 were usually cheery affairs, unless it had been a sleep-deprived night punctuated with call-outs or air raids. Fortunately last night had been a quiet one and everyone was on good form this morning having had a reasonable night's sleep. Now, with just an hour and a half of the shift left to go before they could all go home, there was a hum of chatter as people had their breakfast.

Frankie took a mouthful of porridge, enjoying its comforting warmth on this cold March morning. Her grandad always used to say porridge stuck to your insides and not only warmed you up, but filled you up and kept you going all morning. She thought of him whenever she had a bowl of it, and loved the way it gave her physical warmth and strength and also provided that emotional link to her grandfather; it was food for the body and soul.

'What have you got planned for today?' Bella asked, as she scraped a thin layer of margarine on her toast.

282

'The usual: a bit of shopping and housework, and hoping the postman will bring a letter from Alastair.' Frankie smiled. 'How about you?'

'I'm packing POW parcels this afternoon, and I want to—' Bella stopped talking as the telephone in Station Officer Steele's office began to ring, its shrill sound making all the crew fall silent in an instant.

The boss, who'd been helping herself to some toast from the pile, abandoned her plate and hurried into her office and snatched up the receiver. Going by the little she said into it, something they'd seen and heard countless times over the years, Frankie knew it was a call-out. Winnie, who was sitting opposite her, caught her eye and was clearly thinking the same thing.

The atmosphere subtly changed as the crew waited on tenterhooks to see who would be sent out to attend; call-outs at this time in a shift were never popular as the chances were that they would overrun into the next shift – once the crew had been sent out, it was their responsibility to stay until the job was done, no matter if it was past their usual finishing time. Nobody wanted to have to go now.

Station Officer Steele appeared in the doorway of her office. 'Sparky, Paterson, Winnie, Rose, Bella and Frankie, this job's for you.' She didn't elaborate but went back inside her office to write out the necessary chits.

Frankie looked at Winnie who shrugged, grabbed the piece of toast she'd just spread with a thin layer of jam and got up from the table. 'Come on, you lot, we need to go.'

'Bleedin' heck!' Sparky downed the remains of his tea

in a couple of gulps and followed. 'Must be a big one to send all of us.'

'If you want to drive, I'll get our chit,' Bella said.

Frankie nodded and headed for the door, following behind Winnie and Sparky, with Trixie following close behind.

'Where to?' Frankie said a few minutes later when Bella climbed into the ambulance.

'Hughes Mansions, Vallance Road in Stepney.'

Frankie's hand froze on the gearstick for a moment at the word 'Stepney'. Any incident they were sent to in her home area always sent an icy shiver down her spine, because a rocket or bomb falling a few seconds earlier or later could so easily have landed on Matlock Street.

'Do you know it?'

She nodded, putting the ambulance in gear and following behind Winnie, with Sparky at the front of the convoy, out through the arched passageway onto the Minories. 'It's an estate with three separate blocks of flats. If a rocket's hit one there'll be a lot of casualties, especially at this time of the day with people still at home before going out to work. No wonder they've sent three ambulances from here and it's not even in our normal patch, so you know what that tells us . . .'

They fell into silence as they drove along. Frankie had attended enough V2 rocket incidents now to know the destruction that the weapons brought. Instead she focused her thoughts on her driving, preferring to deal with what she was doing rather than dwell on what they were going to.

Arriving at Vallance Road, Frankie parked the ambulance at the side of the street, pulling in behind Winnie and Rose. Over to their right was the remains of what had once been the three blocks that made up the Hughes Mansions housing estate. The middle one was almost completely gone, with just the far end still standing; the rest of it had crumbled into a huge pile of debris, while the two remaining blocks had been severely damaged by the blast, windows and doors blown in, which now stood like black empty eye sockets staring out. Frankie felt sick. How many people had been in the middle block, eating their breakfast, like they had been back at Station 75, getting ready to go out to work? They wouldn't have stood a chance.

'Do you think anyone's alive in there?' Bella asked.

Frankie shrugged. 'Perhaps. Let's 'ope so.'

Outside, with stretchers ready, they hurried over to wait for more injured to be freed – the ones who had already been dug out were being attended to by ambulance crews that had arrived earlier. The firemen who were working to free those still trapped were being hampered by distraught people clambering about on the piles of rubble, frenziedly looking for their relatives and friends.

'Get off there!' bellowed the chief fireman who'd just arrived.

'My family's in there!' a woman screamed back at him. 'I'm only tryin' to 'elp.'

'Your weight is crushin' down on anyone trapped in there, so get off now!'

His message got through to some of them, but others had to be led away from the rubble still protesting. The chief quickly organised the setting up of rope barriers to stop any more members of the public coming in to dig.

'You can't blame 'em wanting to do something,' Frankie said, looking at the despair and helplessness on the faces of those who'd been evicted from the site and now stood huddled in groups watching and waiting.

Bella tucked her arm through Frankie's. 'I know, but the firemen and rescue services know what they're talking about and how to do it safely.'

It was a grim sight watching and waiting; far more people were being pulled out dead than were being found alive and the ambulance crews helped carry them straight to waiting mortuary vans rather than their ambulances. Frankie and Bella had just delivered one unfortunate victim to a van when Rose came hurrying over to them, her face pale.

'Frankie, you need to come.' Rose grabbed hold of her arm and pulled her over to where Winnie stood beside a stretcher bearing another recovered body.

'What's the matter? What's—' Frankie began but stopped as they drew near and she saw the face of the dead woman, instantly recognising it despite the covering of grey dust. It was Ivy.

It was as if she had been drenched in a pail of freezing cold water. She began to shake as she stared at the icy-blue eyes that looked sightlessly up at the sky, eyes that had so many times in the past fixed their steely glare on her but would now never do that again. She kneeled by Ivy's body and gently closed the older woman's eyelids, shutting off the blank stare.

'I'm so sorry,' Bella said, kneeling beside her and putting her arm around Frankie's shoulders.

Frankie nodded and turned to her friend, and then looked up at Winnie and Rose who were looking sympathetically at her. 'What was she doing 'ere? If she'd have been at home in Matlock Street, then she'd still be alive.'

'Mind your backs!' Two rescue workers carrying a stretcher bearing another dead body came over to them and placed it down next to Ivy. 'Can you see to it that he's taken to the mortuary van?' one of them asked.

'Of course,' Winnie said.

'Oh my God, it's Micky Chandler.' Frankie stared at the dead man's face.

'We found 'im not far from her.' The rescue service man nodded at Ivy. 'Must have been in the same flat when the rocket hit. You know her as well?'

Frankie nodded.

'Well, write out the label for both, will you? That'll help with identifying all the victims.' He touched the brim of his steel helmet and headed back to the rubble for more survivors or, more likely, bodies.

'I'll write them.' Bella fished in her bag and took out the labels that they used to identify the casualties they took to hospital, clearly writing Ivy's and Micky Chandler's names on them.

'She must have stayed the night with 'im.' Frankie knew that her step-grandmother stayed out all night sometimes, but she had had no idea where she was. She'd said that she wanted to enjoy herself because you never knew what

287

was around the corner for you in wartime, but ironically doing just that had led her here and into the path of the V2. To Frankie's surprise, her eyes filled with tears and she began to cry.

'Here, take this.' Winnie handed her a clean, neatly ironed handkerchief and gently pulled Frankie to her feet and wrapped her arms around her.

'I don't know why I'm crying.' Frankie's voice came out croaky. 'We didn't get on, we 'ardly spoke and I . . . didn't like her but I never would 'ave wanted this to happen to her. She should 'ave had years of life left to live, but look at her.'

'I know, those bloody rockets!' Winnie said.

'You're in shock.' Bella gently rubbed Frankie's back. 'You might not have had a good relationship with Ivy, but she lived in the same house as you, she was married to your grandad and part of your family. You had a connection with her and a history, and because of the person you are, Frankie, it's only natural that you are feeling the way you are.'

Winnie put her hands on Frankie's shoulders and looked at her. 'You need to go back to Station 75 and the boss can send out another crew. Will you take Frankie back, Bella?'

'No! I need to stay 'ere in case there's casualties that need to get to hospital,' Frankie protested.

'I've never done this before but I'm going to pull rank on you, Frankie, and as Deputy Station Officer, I'm ordering you back to Station 75. There are enough ambulance crews here to cope, and most of the work is carrying bodies to the mortuary van anyway.' She nodded towards

Sparky and Paterson, who were carrying another recently recovered body to the waiting van.

'Come on.' Bella put her arm through Frankie's. 'You're in no fit state to be here.'

Frankie looked down at Ivy. 'What about her?'

'Don't worry, Rose and I will see her safely into the mortuary van, you just need to go back to Station 75 and then it will soon be time to go home.'

'I'll take you home and stay with you,' Bella said.

'And Rose and I will be along as soon as we can,' Winnie added.

Frankie nodded. 'Thank you.' She suddenly felt exhausted, her emotions strung out taut, and having her dear friends around her was what she needed.

'Cooee! Only me,' Josie's voice called from the hall, making Frankie jump. She and Bella hadn't been home very long, just time enough to boil the kettle and brew tea, and were now sitting at the table with cups of tea in front of them.

Bella stood up. 'Do you want me to tell her not to come in?'

Frankie shook her head. 'Tell her to come in.' She'd be glad to see her friend, she thought, as Bella went to meet her in the hall. Josie's innate radar for knowing when something was up in Matlock Street had worked again and if she knew about what had happened then she could help to spread the news to the rest of the inhabitants of the street.

Cradling her cup of tea in her hands, the warmth of the cup helping to heat up her cold fingers, she could hear a

289

whispered conversation going on out in the hall, no doubt Bella telling Josie what had happened.

'Oh, ducks!' Josie came hurrying into the kitchen a few moments later and pulled Frankie to her feet, wrapping her meaty arms around her and hugging her tightly. 'I'm so sorry. I know you and Ivy didn't see eye to eye but for this to happen to her ain't right.'

'If she'd been here, like she should 'ave been, she'd still be alive,' Frankie said.

Josie loosened her arms enough to step back so that she could look Frankie in the eye. 'It ain't no good thinking about ifs – she was there because that's where she wanted to be, out enjoying herself, but it's a pity it put her in the path of a V2 rocket ...' She shrugged. 'Ivy weren't an easy woman to live with, but no one would 'ave wanted that ending for her.'

Frankie's eyes filled with tears. 'I didn't like her, and I often wished she'd move out of here, but I never wanted her dead.'

'Course you didn't, ducks. You ain't got nothing to feel bad about; you were patient, kind and long-suffering, you put up with Ivy's contrary ways for far longer than most people could 'ave done. She lived her life the way she wanted to and died doing it. Right, get that tea down you. Is there any left in the pot, Bella?' Josie guided Frankie back into her seat at the table and pulled out a chair and sat down next to her.

'Do you want a spoonful of sugar, for the shock?' Bella asked, pouring a cup of tea out of the brown earthen-ware teapot.

Josie nodded. 'I'd better, thanks, ducks. I never expected this to 'appen to Ivy.'

'At least she wouldn't have known anything about it,' Bella said. 'It would have been quick.'

'I'm glad my kiddies ain't here. I miss them every moment of the day but rather that than the risk of one of them blasted V2s dropping on them.' Josie took a sip of tea. 'And your Stanley as well.'

Frankie nodded. As hard as it had been to make the decision to evacuate him to the countryside back in the autumn of 1940, she'd never regretted sending him there for his safety and now she and Stanley were the only ones left of her family that had been living here at the start of the war.

'Let's hope we don't get many more of these rockets aimed at us,' Bella said. 'At least with the Allies now capturing the launch sites there's less opportunity for them to fire them.'

Chapter Fifty-five

Winnie and Rose had arrived at Frankie's house, and they were all tucking into some Spam sandwiches that Bella had made for them when there was a loud knocking on the front door.

Frankie started to get up, but Winnie put a hand on her arm to stop her. 'You stay there, I'll go, you need some peace and quiet.'

She didn't protest and carried on eating a sandwich, listening when Winnie answered the door. She could hear a man's deep voice but not clearly enough to hear what he said. A few moments later Winnie appeared in the kitchen doorway accompanied by three policemen.

'Sergeant Jeffries!' Frankie instantly recognised the oldest of the three, who'd been a colleague and good friend of her grandad's.

'Miss Franklin.' His face looked strained. 'I'm sorry to have to do this 'cos of your grandad, but we're here because of black-market goings-on in this house. I'm going to 'ave to ask you to come down to the station with me, and Ivy, if she's 'ere, or we'll go and pick her up at work.'

Frankie stared at him for a few seconds but before she could say anything Winnie leapt to her defence.

'If you think Miss Franklin has anything to do with the black market you are very much mistaken.'

'Our very reliable sources tell us that black-market goods are available from this house.' Sergeant Jeffries' neck had turned red from embarrassment. 'It's best to come quietly.'

Frankie felt sick. Had Ivy been deeper involved with the black market than just a bit of extra butter and bacon? 'I don't know anything about it, it ain't nothing to do with me and if you want to ask Ivy you can't now cos she's dead.'

Sergeant Jeffries looked shocked. 'Dead? How?'

'She was killed in a V2 hit on Hughes Mansions this morning. Looks like she was at Micky Chandler's flat with him. He was killed too,' Frankie explained.

The policeman nodded. 'I'm sorry to hear that in more ways than one. Your grandad wouldn't 'ave been happy her knockin' about with Chandler. He was mixed up in the black-market business, right up to his ears.' He paused. 'The fact remains that black-market activities have been happening in this house and with Ivy gone it's just you here, you're responsible.'

'But I ain't! It ain't nothing to do with me, honestly,' Frankie protested, her heart thudding hard. What had Ivy done? She might be dead but she'd gone and left a mess and she was being dragged into it.

'Frankie has nothing to do with any black marketing,' Rose said, her pale cheeks flushing. 'I should know.'

Sergeant Jeffries turned his attention to Rose, looking down at her sitting at the table from his lofty height. 'And who might you be?'

'My name's Rose and I lodge here with Frankie. If there was any black marketing goings-on I would have seen it. And I haven't, not while we're here.'

Frankie sighed and put her head in her hands, leaning her elbows on the table. 'But we ain't here all the time, are we? We work shifts, twenty-four hours on, twenty-four off. We don't know what Ivy gets up ... got up to while we were at work, did we?' She looked up at the older policeman. 'If she was up to no good, then she did it when we weren't here. I honestly didn't have anything to do with it, I didn't know anything about it. I wouldn't have anything to do with that dirty dealing, I'm working for the war effort.'

'Frankie has put herself in danger countless times out in raids,' Winnie said, her hands on her hips. 'Would someone who did that get involved with black-market goods? Besides, her grandfather was a policeman like you!'

Sergeant Jeffries looked uncomfortable. 'We'll need to search the house for evidence, start—' He stopped as a loud hammering began on the front door. 'Are you expecting anyone?'

Frankie shook her head.

'Get it, see who it is,' he instructed.

'I'll go.' Rose got up from the table and as she went out into the hall he nodded at his constables who positioned

294

themselves either side of the kitchen door out of sight of the front door but where they could listen.

Frankie couldn't hear what was being said but when Rose returned to the kitchen a few moments later, she looked worried.

'It's a man, he says he's a friend of Micky Chandler and has come to collect some things Micky left here,' Rose said.

Frankie glanced at Sergeant Jeffries who beckoned his constables over and spoke to them in a low voice. 'Go out the back door, one wait there, the other go round the back alleyway and round to the front door and both of you be ready.' They quickly went off. Turning to Rose he said, 'Tell him to come in, the rest of you act normally, I'll be in the scullery.'

With surprising speed for a man of his height and build, Sergeant Jeffries hurried into the scullery which led off from the kitchen, where he could listen to what was going on but not be seen.

'Who are you and what do you want?' Frankie asked when Rose led the man into the kitchen. He had the same look as Micky had had, smart suit and shiny, slicked-back hair, and a sense of cockiness about him. He wasn't a bit put out by them all staring at him.

'All you need to know, darlin', is I'm a friend of Micky's, you could say business partner, and I've come to get the stuff he left 'ere since he can't any more.' He smiled, the thin moustache on his top lip wrinkling like a furry cat-erpillar, while his crooked, nicotine-stained teeth looked more like a snarl than a smile. 'He was sadly killed this morning in a V2 attack.'

'I know, I saw his body there,' she said. 'And Ivy's.'

The man looked surprised for a moment, but quickly recovered himself. 'Like I said, I've come to get 'is stuff; he won't be needing it any more and as we're business partners it now belongs to me.'

Frankie frowned. 'Well there ain't nothing here for you to get.'

'Well that's where you're wrong, cos I 'elped bring it in myself. Ivy has been 'elping us out, kept it in her room, so I just need to go upstairs and get it and then I'll be on my way.'

Frankie folded her arms, her stomach twisting at the thought of what Ivy had been up to. It looked like the woman had stooped to even lower depths than Frankie had thought. Buying a bit of black-market butter was one thing, but to be involved with harbouring such goods was a far greater crime. 'And just what sort of things are you talkin' about?'

'Nothing for you to worry about, darlin'. Ivy was 'appy to keep them here for us, that's all you need to know, and now she's gone I've come to take it away. Me van's outside ready.'

Frankie sensed Winnie bristling beside her and reached out and put her hand on her friend's arm. She didn't want her bursting out with something to try and stop him because she knew enough about policing that it would be best for Micky's business partner to be caught red-handed with whatever Ivy had been keeping upstairs, especially as she'd been implicated in the whole nasty business and needed to prove her innocence.

'All right then, you go up and get it, we need to finish our sandwiches.' She picked up her Spam sandwich and took a bite, nodding for the others to follow suit, which they did, although they all looked uncomfortable as they ate.

'Right you are.' He touched the brim of his hat and with a last snarly-looking smile went out of the room, clumped up the wooden staircase and went into Ivy's room which was at the front of the house.

Sergeant Jeffries appeared in the scullery doorway, a look of disgust on his face. 'Ivy was up to her neck in it then,' he whispered. 'I'll nip out the front door and wait with the constable and be there to catch 'im on the way out. You lot stay in here.' Again, with surprising speed and lightness of foot, he went out into the street ready to catch Micky's friend red-handed.

'I wanted to smack that spiv's smarmy face!' Winnie hissed.

Frankie smiled at her friend. 'You and me both. Let's just hope they catch him red-handed.'

'Shouldn't we do something?' Rose whispered.

They could hear Micky's friend moving around in Ivy's room, it sounded as if he were dragging boxes across the floor.

'No, we need to stay here for the moment until he comes down, but be ready to catch him in case he bolts back out this way when he sees Sergeant Jeffries outside.'

Frankie and Rose positioned themselves just inside the kitchen door on one side, ready to pounce on him if he came that way, while Winnie and Bella stood ready on the other. They heard him lumbering down the stairs, whistling a tuneless song between his teeth, clearly very pleased with himself, but his whistling stopped abruptly when he opened the front door and saw the looming bulk of Sergeant Jeffries. Like a rabbit faced with a waiting fox, he turned tail and ran back towards the kitchen, but they were ready. As he came through the door Frankie stuck out her leg and he tripped, the box he was carrying flew through the air and there was the sound of breaking glass as it crashed to the floor, closely followed by the pungent smell of whisky. Sprawled on the floor, Micky's friend didn't have a chance to struggle up as Bella and Rose fell on him, pinning him down.

'You stay right where you are!' Winnie said, kneeling on one of his arms and twisting the other back behind him so that he lay there like a stranded fish.

Sergeant Jeffries and the constable who'd been positioned outside the back door hurried into the kitchen and swiftly locked the man's wrists into handcuffs.

'Came here to offer condolences for Ivy's death, did yer?' Sergeant Jeffries said. He made a show of sniffing the whisky fumes. 'Looks like quite a black-market haul you've got there.'

'It ain't mine!' Micky's friend blurted out as he was hauled to his feet, a bruise beginning to bloom on his face where he'd hit the floor. 'I was just collectin' some friend's belongings, that's all. It was Ivy's, she's been looking after it for us, I mean him.'

'You can tell me all about it down the station,' Sergeant Jeffries said. 'Take him away,' he ordered his two constables.

'With pleasure, Sarge,' one of the constables said as they marched the man out.

'What about that?' Frankie pointed to the box from which whisky was now leaking onto the tiled floor.

'It's evidence, just put some old newspaper around it to soak it up for now. I need to 'ave a look in Ivy's room.'

He, along with Frankie, Rose, Winnie and Bella, went into Ivy's room. 'Looks like quite a stash!' Sergeant Jeffries said. There were boxes piled up against one wall, under her bed, and on top of her wardrobe as well.

'Is it all whisky?' Frankie asked.

'Some, by the look of it.' Sergeant Jeffries pulled a box out from under the bed and opened the top to reveal tins of meat, fruit and cocoa. Another had packets of nylons and make-up. 'They had quite a racket going on 'ere and the perfect hidin' place – who'd have thought the widow of a policeman would be storing it in her bedroom?'

Seeing all this stuff snuffed out any last feeling of remorse that Frankie had for the way Ivy's life had panned out: the death of her husband and then her own in a V2 attack. The woman had had no scruples and Frankie would not miss her one tiny bit. She was furious that she'd been dragged into this mess by association when she'd had nothing to do with it, hadn't known anything about it. If she had, she'd have thrown Ivy out.

'I really didn't know anything about this, Sergeant Jeffries, honestly I didn't,' Frankie said. 'Ivy must 'ave taken advantage of my shift work to bring it here when I wasn't in.'

'Are you still going to take Frankie to the police station?' Winnie asked, one hand on her hip.

'No, it's clear you knew nothing about this.' Sergeant Jeffries laid a hand on Frankie's shoulder. 'I'm sorry if I upset you, it didn't feel right coming 'ere and accusing you of being involved, I was just following orders . . . but there's no doubt that Ivy was part of it.' He looked around the room and sighed. 'Your grandad would 'ave been horrified at what she'd got herself involved with, she'd now be facing a prison sentence. Perhaps it's just as well she died this morning.'

Frankie nodded. It was bad enough now but how much worse would it have been if Ivy had still been alive and brought the wrath of the law down on herself and number 25 Matlock Street? She shouldn't think about the what ifs because Ivy was gone and after this final horrible mess, the woman wouldn't be casting a shadow over Frankie's life any more, and for that she was grateful.

Chapter Fifty-six

Station Officer Violet Steele was enjoying the warmth of the April sunshine as she strolled down towards the Tower of London. It was a delight to be outside with a cloudless blue sky soaring above the city, and now that the terrible V2 rockets had stopped and the Allies were in Germany, it could only be a matter of weeks before Hitler was captured, and the war would finally be over. After more than five long years the idea of peace once more seemed simply incredible. Of course, it meant her life would change again, and she had to admit she would sorely miss her job at Station 75, and especially the crew members who worked there. They had made this awful time so much more bearable and she felt honoured to have served with them.

Approaching the dry moat where the allotments were, she could see that Frankie, Winnie and Bella were busy at work, their tunics off and shirtsleeves rolled up in the warm April sunshine. Bella and Frankie were hoeing between the rows of vegetables, while Winnie knelt, doing the finer weeding between plants. Trixie spotted her before the young women and rushed over to greet her with a yelp of delight, her golden plume of a tail wagging joyfully. Bending down to stroke the little dog, she thought that she would miss this delightful creature as much as any of the crew.

'Come on, Trixie,' she said. 'Let's see how things are growing.'

Trixie's rush to greet her had alerted the young women to her presence and their reaction was odd – they were like rabbits that had just spotted a fox approaching, making them scurry this way and that. A guilty-looking Bella darted forward to meet her, while Winnie scrambled to her feet, aided by Frankie, and hurried over towards where the pile of discarded tunics lay, but in her haste she tripped over a rake, sending her sprawling down onto the ground with a cry.

'Winnie!' shouted Frankie running over to help her friend, closely followed by Bella who'd turned and run back.

Violet stood rooted to the spot, stunned at what she'd just seen and which Winnie had been in such a hurry to hide – from the definite swell of the young woman's belly straining at the front of her shirt, there was no doubt about it, she was expecting a child, and from the look of it, she only had a few months left to go before it was due. Her instinct had told her there was something up with Winnie, but she never expected this. A surge of disappointment and anger that Winnie had hidden it and defied the rules swept through her, but she hastily pushed it aside for the moment and hurried over to where Bella and Frankie were now crouched by their friend.

'I'm all right.' Winnie struggled to sit up, her rounded belly making it more difficult than usual.

'Don't get up yet,' Violet Steele said. 'Are you in any pain?'

'I think I've just bruised my side where I hit the ground.' Winnie rubbed her hip, but then her face suddenly went white as she put her hand on her belly. 'It's not moving! I can't feel it moving any more, it's been so active today until now. Oh God, have I hurt it?' She started to cry.

Bella put her arm around her. 'I'm sure it's all right, just a bit shocked, that's all.'

'I think we'd better make sure,' Violet Steele said. 'Frankie, go and get an ambulance, bring it down as close as you can. Hurry.' She mouthed the last word so that Winnie didn't hear.

'I'll be right back.' Frankie ran off towards Station 75.

'Do you think I've hurt it?' Winnie croaked. 'I never meant to.'

'Of course you didn't, but I think we should take you to hospital just to be sure, and luckily we have ambulances at our disposal to take you there.' She smiled as she put her hand on Winnie's shoulder. 'All you need to do for now is keep calm. Frankie won't be long.'

'I don't need to go in an ambulance ... ' Winnie went to get up.

'Stay where you are. You're going in an ambulance

303

whether you like it or not, and that's an order!' She met Bella's eyes who nodded her agreement.

Winnie sighed and sat back down, not arguing for once, her hands cradled around her stomach, while Trixie leaned against her, giving her mistress comfort.

Lying on a stretcher gave the back of an ambulance a whole new perspective, Winnie thought, trying hard to distract herself from her fear for her unborn baby as Frankie closed the back doors, shutting her and Station Officer Steele inside. Bella had taken Trixie to sit on her lap in the front of the cab after the boss had insisted that she would ride in the back so that she could keep an eye on her. If Winnie hadn't been so worried about her baby she might have protested, wanting to put off the moment when she'd be given her marching orders and no longer be a crew member at Station 75. The boss hadn't said a word about discovering her secret, but she knew it was only a matter of time before she did and now, trapped in the back of the ambulance with her, it felt like her world was about to crumble, the job she loved gone and her baby . . .

'Are you warm enough?' Station Officer Steele fussed with the edge of the blanket spread over Winnie, as the ambulance's engine started and they began to move, making the vehicle rock gently.

'Yes . . . Are you going to sack me?' The words were out of her mouth before her brain had time to stop them.

The boss arched her eyebrows, her brown eyes warm behind her owlish spectacles. 'Don't worry about that now, let's just get you to hospital.'

'I was going to tell you eventually,' Winnie said. 'It's just I didn't want to leave my job. If I'd told you, then I knew I'd have to go, and I really didn't want to, working at Station 75 has been the best thing I've ever done ... I didn't like deceiving you, but I wanted to keep my job. And ...' Her eyes filled with tears, as the words poured out of her. 'I didn't really want this baby, or how it would change my life ... but now it might be ... I might have ...' Guilt for not wanting her baby had whacked her hard in the chest when she'd realised it had stopped moving, that she might have harmed it and it could die. Be dead already. That guilt had been closely followed by a rush of longing as she had finally realised just how much she wanted this baby, her feelings for it had silently crept up on her and grown, growing inside her like her child. But now it might be too late ...

Station Officer Steele paced up and down the waiting room of the casualty department of the London Hospital, oblivious to the stares she was attracting from others waiting there.

'Any news?' Frankie asked as she and Bella came hurrying in after moving the ambulance to somewhere they could leave it after they'd dropped Winnie off.

She shook her head. 'Nothing.'

'Please don't sack her,' Bella said. 'Winnie loves her job and we can help her do anything she finds difficult. We can go out on calls instead of her, we can work through our breaks to do her jobs.'

'She ain't done no harm,' Frankie added. 'She ought to be commended for carrying on when she didn't 'ave to.'

She held up her hand to silence them. 'I commend your loyalty, and I presume you both have known about Winnie's condition for some time and have probably helped her to hide it, but the fact is she *should* have told me. What she did is against the rules.'

'The rules won't matter any more if the baby's ...' Bella's brown eyes filled with tears.

Frankie put her arm through her friend's. 'Don't think that, we've got to keep hoping it's all right.'

'I hope it is too.' Station Officer Steele sighed. 'You know I would hate to lose Winnie from Station 75, but the fact is, a pregnant crew member is not permitted. I ...' She paused as the doctor who had been seeing Winnie came out from the treatment rooms and, spotting them, walked towards them.

'Here he comes.' Bella grabbed hold of Station Officer Steele's arm with her free hand and the three of them stood there, united, waiting for news.

Approaching them, the doctor's face broke into a smile. 'I'm glad to tell you that everything appears to be fine. Mrs McCartney's baby is moving again and has a good strong heartbeat. I suspect it had just been having a doze, despite its mother's gymnastics, it's well cushioned in there, but as a precaution I'm prescribing rest for twenty-four hours and if there's any bleeding or pain she should come back straight away.'

'I'm very glad to hear that, and I will make sure that she rests.' Station Officer Steele smiled at him. 'Thank you.'

'Here comes Winnie,' Frankie said, rushing forward to meet her friend who was being led out by the nurse looking a great deal more relaxed than she had when they'd brought her in.

'Right, let's get you home, so you can rest,' Violet said. 'Bella, will you go and bring the ambulance round to the door and we'll meet you there.'

Going over to Winnie she linked her arm through the young woman's. 'I'm very glad everything is all right.'

Winnie looked at her and smiled, placing her hand on her stomach. 'So am I. I want my baby born safely. That's the most important thing now.'

Lying on a stretcher in the back of the ambulance once more, again at Station Officer Steele's insistence, Winnie felt a huge sense of relief that her baby wasn't harmed. It was back to its normal squigglyness and none the worse for her tumble – unlike herself with her hip blooming into a large purple bruise. She gasped as what must be an elbow passed across the inside of her belly, the oddest of sensations but most welcome.

'I'm very glad that everything is all right.' Station Officer Steele was leaning against the stretcher frame opposite her to keep herself steady as they drove along. 'You must be very relieved.'

Winnie nodded. 'I am, but it took a shock like this to make me realise that I do want this baby, very much. I will do everything I can to protect it and keep it safe.'

'Even leave Station 75?' The boss raised her eyebrows.

'Even that.' Winnie sighed. 'It's all right, you don't need to sack me, I'll go quietly, obey the rules.'

Station Officer Steele began to laugh.

'What's so funny?'

'I never thought I'd hear you say that . . .' The older woman paused. 'I must admit you shocked and disappointed me this morning. I didn't know whether to be angry or sad that you hid your condition from me; you've put not only your own life at risk going out on calls but also the life of your unborn child. I can't think what Mac was doing, letting you stay working here. He knows what it's like and with the doodlebugs and then the V2s targeting London, it's been hellish at times.'

Winnie bit her bottom lip. 'Mac doesn't know I'm expecting. I haven't told him because I knew he'd tell me to leave.'

Station Officer Steele stared at her for a few moments. 'You haven't told your husband that he's going to be a father? I can't believe you'd do that, he has every right to know.'

Winnie looked away from the boss's gaze. 'I know, but it's only because I wanted to keep working at Station 75. And I have been extra careful . . . until this morning, and it was only because I was in such a rush.'

'Who *have* you told besides Frankie and Bella?'

'Rose knows and my godmother, Connie, but they promised not to say anything.'

'So, you haven't told your parents either?'

'No, definitely not.'

The boss considered for a few moments. 'I know how much working at Station 75 means to you and understand why you want to stay. The war will be over soon and you've played a huge role at Station 75 so it would be a shame to have to go so close to the end.' She paused. 'I shouldn't do this as it's going against all regulations but . . . I'm prepared to let you stay, as things are quiet and there isn't the same danger as before, but it's only on these conditions, and these are strictly unbendable and non-negotiable. If you aren't prepared to stick to them exactly then I'll have no option but to ask you to leave.'

Winnie nodded, biting her bottom lip to stem the tears that were threatening.

'Firstly, you are to tell Mac that he is to be a father and explain why you haven't done it before; and secondly, I think you should tell your parents. I appreciate that you haven't always seen eye to eye with them, especially your mother, but I think with Mac being away you might need their support.'

Winnie couldn't help pulling a face. Telling Mac she agreed with, but telling her parents would be like opening up a can of worms, they would want to interfere and that was exactly why she hadn't told them already. 'But I've got Connie!'

'Even so, I think it's a good idea. You can never be sure how things will go, and you may be glad of their help . . . and it is their grandchild you are expecting, don't forget that.' The boss waited for a moment to let that sink in before continuing. 'Lastly, if you are to stay at Station 75 then you must only do the lightest of duties: no call-outs, no cleaning ambulances, understand? If you can't agree to *all* of those then you can leave now.'

Winnie sighed. There was no way out of this, it was either do exactly as Station Officer Steele said or go now, leave Station 75 and the job she loved for ever. There was no way of wriggling out of any of the conditions, especially the one that irked the most.

'All right then, yes, I promise I'll do what you ask. Even tell my parents, though what sort of maelstrom that will unleash I dread to think, but if that's what I've got to do to stay at Station 75 . . . then I will.' Winnie stopped as a dam of tears burst and she began to cry, taking the neatly ironed handkerchief the boss handed her to wipe her eyes. 'Thank you, I appreciate you bending the rules for me.'

'A bit more than bending in this case, more like snapping them in half.' The boss smiled warmly at her. 'I think in this case it's worth it.'

'I can't believe you're doing this for me.'

The boss laughed. 'You've told me enough times that rules are there to be broken. I'm sticking my neck out for you, though, just don't let me down.'

'I won't, I promise.'

'Good.' Station Officer Steele patted her arm. 'I'm glad you've seen sense. You can start with that first condition right away. After we get you home you can write to Mac and let him know and make sure you rest for twenty-four hours as the doctor ordered. You haven't got any other surprises for me, have you?'

'No.' Winnie rested her hand on her belly. 'This one's big enough, there aren't any more, I promise you.'

Chapter Fifty-seven

Bella was in the library of Connie's house, working on a story, when the insistent ringing of the front doorbell pulled her out of her imaginary world. Sighing, she put down her pen and went to answer it, hoping that whoever was there wouldn't ring again in case they woke up Winnie who'd gone upstairs for an afternoon nap, her advancing pregnancy making her more tired; on days when she wasn't on duty at Station 75, she usually disappeared off to her room for a sleep. Connie was out working at the Red Cross relatives' parcel packing centre so unless it was someone who wanted to see her, Bella thought, whoever it was would be disappointed.

Before Bella got to the library door leading out to the hallway, the doorbell rang again, whoever was there pressing down on it three times as if in irritation that their first ring had gone unanswered – their impatience made her cross. Stepping out into the hallway where she could see a figure shadowed through the glass panes of the front door, Bella's stomach suddenly sank. Unless she was very much mistaken the visitor was Cynthia Churchill, Winnie's mother and the last person that her friend, or she, wanted to see. Bella hadn't forgotten how the stuck-up woman had treated her in this very hallway, telling her that, being a former housemaid, she wasn't suitable for her son, James, or the sort of person who was socially acceptable. The memory stoked the flame of anger that was burning inside her and as Bella approached the door she was in no mood to put up with any of Cynthia Churchill's nonsense.

Taking a deep breath and steeling herself for battle, she opened the door.

A look of displeasure settled on the older woman's face; she'd clearly been expecting Winnie or Connie. 'I've come to see my daughter.' She went to step inside, but Bella swiftly moved in front of her, blocking her entrance, and closed the door towards her, narrowing the gap so that she couldn't get in.

'She's not here,' Bella lied. 'She's had to go into work.'

'Then I'll just have to wait for her then.' Again, the woman stepped forwards, trying to intimidate Bella so that she'd let her in, the smell of her Chanel No. 5 perfume irritating Bella's nose.

Bella held out her hand to stop her. 'There's no point, she's on a twenty-four-hour shift, so won't be back till tomorrow. You could always go and see her, it's down in the East End, you should be all right there if you're careful.' Bella played on the fact that Cynthia Churchill was such a snob that she'd never venture to the East End of

312

London, preferring to stick to the wealthier areas around the West End.

'No, I haven't time to go all the way down there, I have a train back to Oxford to catch.' Winnie's mother paused, her immaculately powdered forehead creasing in a frown. 'You can give her a message for me: tell my daughter that I've arranged for her to have the baby in a maternity home in Oxford where she will receive the best care.'

'Is that what Winnie wants?' Bella asked, knowing full well that her friend would hate the idea and was planning on having the baby here in London. It was typical of Cynthia Churchill to try and take over and ignore anything that Winnie wanted, steamrollering her beliefs and decisions over her daughter's. Bella knew that her friend would refuse to do as her mother wanted, but it would still annoy Winnie that her mother was trying to push things onto her when she should be keeping as calm as she could. After all the battles that Winnie had had with her mother, the woman still tried to dominate her – would she never accept that Winnie would only do what she herself wanted?

'It's the best place. I only want the best for my daughter and grandchild,' Cynthia Churchill said, smoothly.

'But it might not be what *I* think is best for *me*!' Winnie's voice called out across the hall.

Bella turned around in surprise as her friend strode across the black and white tiled floor of the hall towards them, dressed in her blue silk dressing gown, her blonde hair tousled from sleep. 'Winnie, did the doorbell wake you?'

With Bella's attention on Winnie, Cynthia took the

opportunity to slip inside like an unwanted door-to-door salesman, making Trixie, who was close by her mistress's side, growl, baring her teeth.

'It's all right, Trix.' Winnie patted the little dog's head. 'What do you want, Mother?'

'That is not the way I expect to be greeted by my daughter, Margot!' Cynthia snapped. 'I've come to speak to you about the arrangements I've made for your confinement.' Her eyes rested briefly on Winnie's rounded belly which was accentuated by the shimmering smooth silk. 'Perhaps your . . . friend here could go and make us some tea while we talk.'

'No. Bella's going nowhere. What you have to say you can say now and be quick because I need to go back to sleep.' Winnie folded her arms.

Bella had to bite on her bottom lip to stop herself from smiling at the look on the older woman's face. She wasn't happy, but had the sense to pick up on Winnie's hostile mood which was coming off her in waves – *she* wasn't happy at being woken up by her mother's arrival.

'Let's go into the drawing room and sit down, shall we?' Cynthia started to move across the hall.

'No need, I have already decided where I'm going to have my baby,' Winnie said. 'Right here in London where I live.'

Cynthia's eyes narrowed. 'I'm your mother, Margot. I really do know best about these things. The maternity home I've booked you into in Oxford is excellent, comes highly recommended. Then you can come and stay with your father and me. We'll hire a nanny to look after the baby.'

'Absolutely not!' Winnie's face reddened with anger. 'I'm going to look after my child, I'm not going to palm it off on a nanny like you did to us. And I will be living here till Mac comes home and we can get a home of our own together.'

'Well, really!' Cynthia sniffed. 'I don't know what your father is going to say about this.'

'I don't suppose Father's really bothered about where I have my baby, or live. He was never very interested in any of his own children when we were small, and not that much now either. You didn't interfere with Harry and Meredith when they had their son.'

'Well they live a long way away, and not so easy to help.' Cynthia smoothed her carefully styled hair.

'More like Harry would have told you to mind your own business if you did. He and Meredith knew what they wanted and so do I. Now, if you'll excuse me, I need to get some sleep. Goodbye, Mother.' Not waiting for a reply, Winnie turned around and winked at Bella before going back upstairs.

'Shall I show you out?' Bella asked.

Cynthia glared at her. 'No, I know the way.'

'"No thank you", I think you mean,' Bella couldn't help herself from saying, looking the older woman directly in her cold, pale-blue eyes. 'I was brought up to have good manners.'

Cynthia's face flushed and without saying another word she hurried across the hall and out the front door, slamming it loudly behind her and making the panes of glass in it shake.

'Bravo, Bella!' Winnie called from the dogleg corner of the stairs where she stood peering down at her.

Bella went to the foot of the stairs. 'I'm sorry she woke you up.'

'It's not your fault. You know, I'm rather glad she came and I've had my say. It's been long overdue. It's about time she finally accepted that I know my own mind. I thought something like this might happen after the boss made me write and tell them I was expecting.' She sighed. 'That's precisely why I didn't want to tell them before or I'd have had months of being told to do this and that. The idea of my child being brought up by a nanny instead of me is horrible. It made my blood boil.'

'I think she got the message you didn't want that. You were fearsome, Winnie.'

Her friend laughed. 'I've never been so rude to her before . . . I rather enjoyed it.'

'So, you're not going to the best place in Oxford to have your baby, then?' Bella asked, fighting to keep a smile off her face. 'Not even tempted just a little bit?'

'What do you think?'

Bella laughed. 'Absolutely not!'

Winnie nodded. 'Exactly.' She put her hand on her swollen belly. 'This baby is going to be born here in London where I live. The maternity hospitals here are perfectly fine and my mother won't be on hand to interfere.' She suddenly frowned. 'I've never known you tell a lie before, Bella, telling her I was at work. I heard you when I was coming downstairs.'

'Needs must, as they say. I didn't want her coming in

316

to wait. I thought if I pretended you were at work and not back until tomorrow that would stop her waiting for you. It was a bit of a gamble in case she decided to go to Station 75 but playing up the East End location did the trick — she didn't like that.'

'I nearly burst out laughing when you said that, but I thought it was best to face her or she'd only have come back another time.'

Bella glanced at her watch. 'You'd better go and get some sleep. Remember we're meeting Frankie and Rose at the pictures tonight, you don't want to be falling asleep during the film.'

'I'm bound to if I don't have a proper nap. Thank you again for fending her off, you're like my gallant knight against the terrible dragon.'

Bella stood up and bowed. 'At your service, my lady. Now go and get some sleep.'

Chapter Fifty-eight

'Hurry along now, the film's about to start,' the woman in the ticket office said as she handed out the tickets. Frankie, Rose and Rose's American cousin, John, hurried inside to meet Winnie and Bella who were already there waiting for them as arranged.

'Sorry, the bus was late,' Frankie said. 'I hope you don't mind some company. This is Rose's cousin John, he's in London on a forty-eight-hour pass. I invited him to join us.'

'Glad to meet you,' John said, shaking first Bella's and then Winnie's hand. 'I hope you don't mind me tagging along with you guys.'

'Not at all,' Winnie said. 'We've heard lots about you from Rose, so it's lovely to meet you. Have you been to the Eagle Club yet?'

'Come on, you can talk about that later,' Frankie said. 'We'd better go in or they'll start without us.'

Inside the picture house auditorium the lights had

already gone down and the beam from the projector shone out through the darkness, dancing with thick cigarette smoke, onto the screen at the front.

'There's five seats 'ere.' The usherette shone her torch at the end of a row halfway down and they quickly sat, aware that the Pathé newsreel was about to start.

Frankie always liked the newsreels; she, like many people who came to the pictures, was glad to see what was going on in the war both at home and in distant lands. Hearing about it on the wireless or reading in the newspaper wasn't nearly as good as actually seeing it on film where you could take in the tiny details that were overlooked in print, or the spoken news on the BBC. And then after that there would be the film. Today's was *The Keys of the Kingdom*, starring Gregory Peck, which sounded like it should be very entertaining and a world away from wartime London.

As the familiar Pathé News opening title began she settled back in her seat and watched the image of British troops marching along a dusty track somewhere in Germany with a tank moving in the background. Then the scene switched to a camp, one of the concentration camps that she'd read about in the newspaper. She sensed Rose, who was sitting beside her, suddenly stiffen and reached out and grabbed her friend's hand as shocking images played out before them. Stick-thin people dressed in what looked like striped pyjamas, their heads shaven, eyes huge in their gaunt faces, cheekbones jutting out, shuffled around or sat on the ground, too weak to move. Even worse were the images of piles of corpses, many of them naked, their pale bodies emaciated, bones jutting out under their skin.

She heard Rose gasp and glanced at her and could see the light from the screen reflected in the tears running down her cheeks. She wasn't the only one crying, others were doing it but more loudly. The atmosphere of the auditorium had changed as everyone stared at the incomprehensible cruelty before them. Frankie felt sick, but couldn't tear her eyes away from the screen – these people had been treated worse than animals, starved, humiliated, left where they'd dropped dead. How could people treat others so horrifically? What sort of person could do this to another? Silent tears rolled down Frankie's cheeks.

'Do it to them . . . bastards!' a man's voice shouted out.

'Kill the bastard Nazis!' another called out.

Their sentiment was echoed by others, who shouted their thoughts at the screen, wanting to vent the feelings the images were arousing in them.

As the Pathé News reel came to an end, Rose got up. 'I need to get out.'

Frankie grabbed hold of her hand and together they stumbled out towards the doorway. She was glad to leave too as she couldn't sit and watch some flighty Hollywood film after seeing what had happened to those poor people in that camp in real life.

'You not staying for the main picture?' the usherette asked as they came out blinking into the light.

Frankie shook her head. 'No, not after watching the newsreel.'

'You ain't the only one; it's caused quite a stir. I've

never known people shout out and swear at a film like that before, though the Germans deserve it. Nasty devils, thank God they never invaded us. I . . . ' The usherette paused as the doors to the auditorium swung open and Winnie, Bella and John came out. 'Ain't you staying either?'

Winnie shook her head. 'Not in the mood for a jolly Hollywood film any more.' She put her arm through Rose's. 'Come on. Let's go and have some tea.'

'Do you mind if we get something stronger than that?' John asked. He looked pale and upset. 'There must be a pub around here somewhere.'

'Just down the road,' Frankie said. 'We can go there.'

Settled at a table by the window a few minutes later, with stiffer drinks than tea in front of them, Frankie looked at her friends. The good humour of just a short while ago had gone, replaced by shock and deep sadness at the knowledge of the terrible atrocities that had been going on in the camp. Rose looked especially pale and hadn't said a word since they'd left the auditorium; she just sat staring at the glass of brandy that John had bought for each of them, saying that they needed something strong. Frankie knew she must be thinking about her parents, grandparents and other family members who'd stayed behind in Austria, and wondering at their fate. The thought that your family might have ended up in one of those camps, been one of those starved people, or worse in a pile of emaciated corpses, would be hideous.

Frankie took a mouthful of her own brandy. She wasn't keen on the taste but the heat it gave felt welcome after the chilling images they'd just seen. 'Have a sip, Rose, it will warm you up.' She pushed Rose's glass closer to her, encouraging her to drink some.

Rose looked at her and took a sip, then coughed, her blue eyes watering as the fiery liquid went down. 'It's strong.'

'You need it.' John took a sip of his own drink. 'After seeing what those ... bastards ... Excuse me, ladies, but I think they deserve that description ... have done. Why would you do that to another human being?'

'Because of stupid beliefs, bigotry and twisted thinking,' Winnie said. 'The cruelty and inhumanity the Nazis have dealt out in the name of their ideals is horrific.'

'It shows that we were right to fight Hitler if that's what he's capable of inflicting on people,' Frankie said. 'I hope they make those who were in charge pay for it.'

'I'm sure they will, it's all there in black and white for the world to see, they can't hide what they did.' Bella sighed.

Frankie took another sip of her brandy, thinking about the haunted faces of the prisoners who had been filmed, what was their story, where had they come from and where would they go now?

'At least now our soldiers are there they can start to look after the people, help them get better and strong again,' Bella said.

'And then what?' Frankie asked. 'What'll happen to them next? They need to find their families again and go home – if they still have one to go to after all the fighting.'

Winnie sighed. 'We thought we had it tough with all the bombing, eh?'

Frankie shook her head. 'We're lucky, we've always been free, not like those poor people.'

'Do you think my parents are in there?' Rose suddenly said.

Frankie looked at the others whose faces betrayed their thoughts for a moment before each of them covered them up with a neutral expression. They must have thought like her: if they had been sent there or to another camp like it, then they might not have survived.

'I hope not.' Frankie put her arm around Rose's shoulders. 'They might still be in Austria.'

'The Red Cross will do everything it can to find people,' Bella said, reaching across the table and taking hold of Rose's hand. 'You need to keep hoping they will find them safe and sound and you can be reunited with them.'

Frankie caught John's eye from where he sat on the other side of Rose. She could see from his expression that he didn't look hopeful that Rose's family would have survived but he forced himself to smile at his cousin. 'It won't be long before you hear from them again. It's only a matter of time before the war will be over and then families can get in touch again.'

Rose nodded and did her best to smile.

Frankie hoped so much that when news did eventually come for her friend it would be good, and she could be reunited with her parents. There was nothing any of them could do to help find them, except keep waiting and hoping.

Chapter Fifty-nine

Station Officer Violet Steele stared at the words typed onto the paper. She'd known that it had been only a matter of time before this came, but seeing it written in black ink still felt like a hammer blow. Station 75 was to close in just two weeks' time, on the tenth of May 1945, its job done. Other ambulance stations across London had already closed since the capture of the enemy's rocket sites, and their turn was coming. Emotion caught in her throat and she took several deep breaths to steady herself. It would be the end of an era, one that had pushed her and her crew members to the limit, had cost some of them their lives and injured others, but through the adversity had come great friendship and loyalty and she wouldn't have missed it for the world.

Pulling out her handkerchief she wiped away the tears that were blurring her eyes. She was inordinately proud of all they'd achieved since they'd first arrived here in the autumn of 1939, little knowing what they would face in the coming months and years, going out when bombs rained down during the Blitz and more recently dealing with the destruction from the doodlebugs and V2s. It was going to be hard to not be involved with all the wonderful crew any more, sharing in their ups and downs, watching them grow in confidence and ability. Her time serving as Station Officer had been one of the greatest achievements of her life, something that she was incredibly proud of and honoured to have done.

The future stretched out in front of her, as it would for all her crew. They had all longed for peace to return and for the fighting and killing to be over, but she suspected that many of them, like her, would desperately miss the work and the close comradeship of their colleagues. Would they go back to the lives they'd had before the war? Could they? Not just because that lifestyle didn't exist any more, more probably because they'd changed and didn't want to live that life again.

Telling the crew wasn't going to be easy, she needed time to take in the news and prepare herself first. She wanted to see the station working as it normally did for one last time before she announced the news that it would soon be over, because once that was revealed, and everyone knew that a definite end was in sight, then it would subtly change Station 75. Time would be running out and with it the crew would be looking ahead to their lives and no longer be completely focused on the station.

She folded the letter and put it back in its envelope, then tucked it inside her tunic pocket before leaving her office.

She headed to the kitchen first where Mrs Connelly and Hooky were busy preparing the midday meal.

'Good morning, Mrs Connelly,' she said. 'Is everything in hand?'

'Aye, the stew's cooking and we're just waiting for the vegetables from the allotment.' Mrs Connelly's fingers were expertly rubbing margarine into flour to make the Welsh cakes she'd planned for today. 'I sent Winnie and Frankie down there to pick some sprouting broccoli and pull up a few turnips to go with it.' She turned to Hooky who'd been mixing eggs and milk together. 'Are they ready?'

'Yes, shall I add these?' Hooky picked up the pan from the scales where sugar, nutmeg and chopped dried apple had been weighed out.

Mrs Connelly checked the appearance of the flour and margarine which her fingers had turned into a breadcrumb-like consistency. 'Aye, tip them in.'

Hooky was much happier in the kitchen than when she'd been working on the ambulances, Station Officer Steele thought, watching her helping Mrs Connelly. She worked hard preparing the meals and clearing up after the crew had finished. It wasn't an easy job, but the young woman had, after a brief shaky start, embraced the role and made a success of it.

'Well, I look forward to having a Welsh cake later,' she said.

Leaving the kitchen, she went over to the common room window, to her usual lookout post, a place where she'd stood so many times before, watching the crew at work down below in the courtyard as they tended their ambulances, making sure they were prepared to go out to an incident at a moment's notice. From her vantage point she could see how battered and scarred the ambulances were, most of them with pits in their roof and bodywork from flying shrapnel and falling debris when they were out in the middle of a raid.

A sudden image of Winnie's ambulance on the day that she'd narrowly missed being crushed by a falling wall flashed into her mind. The young woman had returned with her ambulance covered in a layer of pinkish-grey dust, and it was pitted with dents from falling rubble. It had been filthy both inside and out, she recalled, as the back doors had been open, and the inside had caught the full force of the cloud of pulverised bricks and mortar. She'd torn Winnie off a strip for taking such a risk, knowing full well that she'd have probably done the same herself.

A cheerful whistling from below brought her attention back to the present. Sparky walked in through the arch-way, a newspaper tucked under his arm. She watched as he proceeded to spread it out on the bonnet of his and Paterson's ambulance as he always did, and read out the latest headlines to the working crew. She smiled. He was like some ancient oracle who spread the news, along with a good dollop of his own opinion. Sparky had played a central role at Station 75, his encyclopaedic knowledge of London coming from his previous work as a taxi driver had been invaluable, along with his sheer force of nature and no-nonsense attitude.

One of the greatest things about working at Station 75 had been the eclectic mix of people who'd come to work here from such different backgrounds and jobs: debutantes mixing with East End factory girls, what they did before and who they'd been didn't matter; everyone worked together and had gelled into a strong team. The war had brought a lot of bad things but good had come out of it too. The mixing of different aspects of society here had been one of them and she hoped it would have a long-lasting effect for all the crew, changing opinions and discriminations.

Bella's laugh rang out below, something Sparky said had amused her as she brushed out the inside of her ambulance cab. Watching as she parried some comment back at Sparky, Station Officer Steele thought that out of all the crew, Bella had made the most remarkable transformation during her time here. The former housemaid, who'd been bombed out on the first night of the Blitz and who she'd given a temporary home to, had, with a bit of pushing and nurturing, blossomed into a confident young woman whose writing talent she hoped would carry her forward into an interesting and fulfilling career.

Leaving her lookout post, she went down to the courtyard. Her arrival was quickly spotted by Sparky who beckoned her over to come and look at today's front page of the *Daily Herald* with its headline *Berlin Encircled: Break-in From West*.

'See, boss, they're nearly there. Old Hitler must be quakin' in his boots, just wait till the Allies get hold of him and make him pay for all he's done,' Sparky said.

'I'd like to be a fly on the wall when they break in and catch 'im.'

'They'll make him swing,' Paterson called from where he was up a ladder washing the roof of his and Sparky's ambulance.

She nodded. 'That man has got a lot to answer for, that's for sure. I'm just going down the allotment, would you mind going up to the common room, so you can answer the telephone if it rings, Sparky? I don't think we're likely to get any call-outs, but just in case.' Their workload of incidents had dropped off dramatically since the capture of the V2 rocket sites, and there hadn't been any fired at London or anywhere else in southern England since late March, when the last one had hit Hughes Mansion in Stepney.

'Right you are, boss.' Sparky gathered up his newspaper and headed upstairs.

Walking towards the Tower of London, she thought how beautiful it looked with its mellow, sandy-coloured stone glowing warmly in the late April sunshine. It was a miracle that it had survived the bombing when so many other areas had been devastated, centuries-old buildings destroyed and the landscape of the city irrevocably altered. It had also become important to the crew of Station 75 through their allotment in the dry moat, which had provided a good source of vegetables for their diet, especially since they'd switched to twenty-four-hour shifts and Mrs Connelly had arrived to cater for them using produce they'd grown here.

As she drew closer she could see Winnie and Frankie

cutting the flowering heads off the sprouting broccoli for Mrs Connelly. Her arrival didn't go unnoticed as Trixie spotted her and let out a bark of recognition and came hurrying over to her, her tail a golden blur.

'Hello, Trixie.' She bent down to stroke the little dog's head. She would miss her as much as any of the crew, Trixie having so easily wormed her way into her affections.

'Have you come to help?' Winnie called to her, with one hand on her hip, her protruding stomach peeping out of her open tunic which no longer fastened at the front.

'We've nearly got enough.' Frankie put a handful of broccoli into the basket on the ground. 'We just need to pull up some turnips.'

'I'll get them for you.' She went over to the row of healthy-looking turnips and started to pull some up, reminding her of helping her mother in the garden at home when she was a child. 'There's a good crop.'

'So there should be, after all the care and attention they've had,' Winnie said. 'This place has been a gold-mine for the station – our meals would have been a lot less appetising if we didn't have it. What will happen to it after the war's over? It can't go on much longer, can it?'

Station Officer Steele looked over at her deputy and shook her head. 'Sparky's headline today is "Berlin encircled", so there's no escape for Hitler. It's only a matter of time, weeks even, before the end.' She sighed, focusing her eyes on the turnips in her hand, gently rubbing them together to wipe off the sticky London clay soil. 'How many turnips did Mrs Connelly want?'

'A dozen,' Frankie said. 'It always goes down well, she says.'

They worked in silence for a while, the young women picking the broccoli while she pulled up enough turnips and arranged them in two bunches, tying them with string to make them easier to carry back.

'Right, I'm going to stand by the river for a bit. I've left Sparky in charge in case there is a call-out, but you can take over if you want, Winnie.' She left them and made her way down to the wall on the bank of the Thames and leaned her arms on it, watching a tugboat ploughing its way downstream against the incoming tide. She loved it down here and had often come to spend some time just watching the toing and froing and enjoying the openness across the river and the fresher air carried in from the Thames estuary further downstream.

'What's the matter?' Winnie came to stand beside her, putting one elbow on the wall and looking at her, while Trixie jumped her front paws up on her leg to greet her again.

She patted the little dog's head. 'Shouldn't you be taking the veg back to Station 75 with Frankie?'

'She wouldn't let me carry them even if I did, she can manage perfectly well on her own. I thought I'd better come and talk to you, find out what's wrong.'

'Nothing's wrong ...' she began but stopped at the sight of Winnie shaking her head at her.

'I think there is, you don't look right.' Winnie frowned. 'Has our turn come?'

Station Officer Steele nodded. The two of them had

talked about the closure of other ambulance stations and had debated when the end would come for Station 75. 'I got a letter this morning.' She took it out of her tunic pocket and handed it to Winnie to read.

'The tenth of May? But that's only two weeks away!' Winnie's eyes were suddenly bright with tears.

She put a hand on the young woman's arm. 'I know.'

'But the war's not over yet, the Germans might still come back and bomb us and they'll need ambulances then. Can't we delay it?'

'I don't think so, they're closing stations gradually so if anything did happen, there'd still be ambulances available.' She shrugged. 'We knew it was coming, Winnie, it was only a question of when.'

'Have you told anyone yet?'

'No, I needed to come down here to think for a bit first, but I will this afternoon so that people can start to prepare for what comes next.'

Winnie nodded. 'Do you want me to leave you in peace?'

'No.' She smiled at her. 'Stay with me, let's enjoy the sunshine here together for a while.'

Station Officer Steele looked around at the crew assembled in the common room, all eager to know why she'd asked them to come here. She glanced at Winnie who'd positioned herself next to her, providing support as she was about to announce the death knell of Station 75. Winnie nodded at her and gave her an encouraging smile.

She took a deep breath and began. 'This morning I

received a letter from our regional superintendent informing me that Station 75 is to close on the tenth of May. In recognition of your work, you will each receive a travel pass which you can use to go anywhere in the country, perhaps take a holiday if you choose.'

Silence followed her announcement for a few moments as each crew member took in the words and registered what it would mean for them personally. Then the room erupted into talking as everyone had an opinion and thoughts on the closure. She let them talk; this news, however much they knew it would eventually come, was still a shock and they needed time to absorb and discuss what would happen.

After a few minutes, when the talking showed no sign of abating, Winnie tapped on her cup with her teaspoon to attract everyone's attention and gradually the room fell silent once more.

'What's going to happen to this place?' Sparky said.

'I have no idea – it may return to its previous use as accommodation for chauffeurs and their families and garaging for the cars, or there may no longer be a requirement for them, things may have changed.' The crescent of grand terraced houses opposite Station 75 who'd used these buildings to house their staff before the war had had to manage without chauffeurs since 1939, and perhaps would never return to their pre-war needs. 'All I know is that officially the station will cease to be operational from the tenth of May and all of us will be released from our work as part of the London Auxiliary Ambulance Service and will be free to resume our former jobs.' Her eyes met Bella's who, like everybody else, was watching her intently. 'Or may pursue new careers.'

'Like motherhood, eh, Winnie!' Sparky said, making everyone laugh.

'Indeed,' Station Officer Steele said. 'And if Winnie is as good a mother as she has been an ambulance driver then she will do an amazing job.' She looked at Winnie whose cheeks blushed prettily. 'In the meantime, we will continue to keep up the high standard that we have always maintained throughout the war and I encourage you all to also look ahead and consider what comes next for you.' She paused for a moment. 'It has been the greatest pleasure to work with you all and I am immensely proud of all that we have achieved together in extraordinarily challenging times.'

Sparky started to clap, and the rest of the crew rapidly joined in, adding their appreciation wholeheartedly. Swallowing back the lump in her throat she smiled at them all, doing her best to commit this moment to her memory to treasure for the rest of her life.

Chapter Sixty

Frankie had known that it would only be a matter of time before Station 75, like some other ambulance stations had already done, closed its doors for the last time and she would be out of a job. The thought made a hard knot form in her stomach, and it wasn't just because she'd have to find new work, it was the loss of all she'd held dear working here; not just being with her friends but actually doing the job itself.

She looked around at the courtyard where others like her were taking their break, sitting out in the sunshine, talking, laughing, some reading or just quietly soaking up the warmth of the day. She remembered how she'd felt on that first morning here, walking in under the archway, so thrilled at joining the Ambulance Service, having learned to drive – something girls like her from the East End didn't usually do. She'd been so excited and was determined to do her utmost to do her job well, and she had. It hadn't always been easy, and she'd had to face some difficult things – seeing innocent people injured and killed, going out while bombs were raining down, but despite all that she'd loved it and the thought of going back to the job she'd had before, sewing clothes at Cohen's factory, felt bleak in comparison. She didn't want to go, she wanted to do more, to do something . . .

'You all right, Frankie?' Bella's voice brought her attention back to the present. 'Only you're sitting there looking like you've got the weight of the world on your shoulders.'

She smiled at her friend and nodded. 'Just thinkin' about this place closing. We knew it was coming but . . . ' She shrugged. 'Hearing that it is, it was still a shock.'

'I know, but we're not needed any more, our job is done so it's time for us all to move on and get back to normal life again, whatever that is – it's been such a long time since the war started. I like the idea of taking a holiday first though. Maybe we could all go somewhere together, me, you, Winnie and Rose.'

'I'd like that, we'll speak to the others about it. But what will you do about a job? You won't go back to what you were before, will you?' Frankie asked.

'Definitely not! My days of clearing up after people who have more money than sense are well and truly over. I want to write for a living and I'm determined to do it.'

Frankie smiled at her friend. 'Well, you're already off to a good start and I 'ave no doubt that you will make a successful career as a writer.'

'What about you?'

Frankie shrugged. 'I'm married so my situation's not

336

quite the same. It depends where Alastair is working when he comes 'ome, I suppose.'

Bella frowned. 'But it might be some time before he's demobbed from the army. What will you do in the meantime?'

'I'm not sure. Stanley will be 'ome again, and I'll need to look after him.' Frankie was aware she was avoiding answering Bella's question properly but didn't want to voice her fears. 'How about a cup of tea? I'll go and make us one.'

'Oh yes, please.' Bella smiled at her. 'Thank you.'

Going up the stairs to the common room, Frankie couldn't get Bella's question out of her mind. She had the desire to do more, for this not to be the end for her. Passing by Station Officer Steele's office she glanced in and saw that the older woman was busy at her desk, working her way through a pile of paper as she so often had to do, keeping the records of the ambulance station up to date. She hesitated for a moment and the boss must have sensed her presence as she looked up and saw her.

'Frankie. Is everything all right?'

She was the second person to ask her that in a matter of minutes – was her mental turmoil written all over her face? Talk to her, a voice in her mind said. Ask her advice. 'Do you 'ave a moment?'

'Of course, come in, and close the door behind you if you like.' She indicated for Frankie to sit down in the chair beside her desk. 'Is there something I can help you with?'

Frankie looked down at her hands for a moment before returning her gaze to the boss, whose brown eyes were warm behind her horn-rimmed glasses. 'I don't know what to do after this place closes. The thought of returnin' to work sewing clothes again just . . .' She shrugged, spreading her hands wide. 'After working 'ere it would seem so . . . boring and tame and pointless and . . . I just don't want to do it . . . I want to do more, something worthwhile like we did 'ere. Going back would feel like I'm taking backward steps in my life, so I don't know what to do.'

The boss looked at her steadily, taking a few moments before she replied. 'Your circumstances have changed significantly though since you first came here: you're a married woman now and your future is tied to Alastair's.'

'I know, but he's still in the army and may be for some time yet. He's even hinted in his letters that he may carry on longer while there's still work to be done. I don't know when he'll come 'ome and we can begin life as a proper married couple. It might be months, or much longer. I don't want to sit around waitin' and doing the job I did before . . . I can't 'elp thinking there must be something I can do, I want to help people like I've been doing here.'

Station Officer Steele nodded. 'I understand. There *is* something you might like to consider, only it would mean going abroad and facing some very challenging situations, quite different to the ones you've had to face in this job. Have you heard of UNRRA?' Frankie shook her head. 'It's the United Nations Relief and Rehabilitation Administration, hence UNRRA for short. They're look- ing for volunteers to work in the camps housing the thousands of displaced persons who were incarcerated in Nazi camps, or shipped from their homelands by the enemy to work in their factories as slave workers. They need people to help look after them and return these victims of war back to their homes, or to new ones. Could you do that?'

Frankie recalled the images that she'd seen on the Pathé newsreel at the pictures – taken at Belsen concentration camp after it was liberated by the Allies – and how the stick-thin people had stared at the camera, their eyes huge in their emaciated faces. There'd been so many of them, far from their homes and families, ripped away from all they had known before the war and badly treated in the camps. The images had haunted her; she'd felt so angry and helpless at their situation. Perhaps volunteering for UNRRA was a good idea, she'd be doing something worthwhile, she'd be helping people who desperately needed help, but it would mean going abroad for who knew how long, and there was Stanley to think about, and Alastair.

'I need to think about it, but I do like the sound of it. Would my experience as an ambulance driver be useful, do you think?'

'Absolutely, and your voluntary work at the day nursery: some of the displaced persons are children, many of them are probably orphans now, they'll need looking after. Think about it and I'll find out some more information for you.' The boss reached out and patted Frankie's arm. 'I do understand how you feel about wanting to do more and this may well be ideal for you. Who knows, perhaps Alastair may want to volunteer for UNRRA as well when he's demobbed?'

'Thank you, I appreciate that. You won't say anything to anyone about this, will you?'

'No, of course not.'

Frankie stood up. 'I was on my way to make some tea; would you like a cup?'

'That would be lovely, thank you.'

As Frankie left the boss's office she felt a spark of hope; perhaps she could do something more, something worthwhile . . . She had a lot to think about.

Chapter Sixty-one

'Is the boss going to give us the day off, then?' Sparky asked, sitting down on the arm of the sofa next to Winnie.

She shrugged. 'I don't know any more than you. She just asked me to gather everyone into the common room as they arrived at the start of their shift.'

'Well, since today's been declared a national holiday, she might. I hope so. If—' He stopped as Station Officer Steele came out of her office and surveyed the crew members waiting for her, their chatter immediately falling silent as everyone wanted to hear what she had to say.

'I'm sure I don't have to tell you that today has been declared VE Day – Victory in Europe Day – the day that we have long hoped for is finally here. I . . .' She paused as the crew broke out into loud cheering and clapping. 'And I know that it has been officially designated a holiday but I'm afraid it's not one for us . . .' Again, she paused, as this time people groaned. 'We need to be here on duty as ambulances may still be needed today, perhaps not for injuries caused by bombing but with the number of people celebrating there could be accidents and we need to be prepared as always. But I'm sure we can have some celebrations of our own after the ambulances have been prepared in the usual way.'

'How are we going to celebrate?' Sparky asked.

'Well, I'm sure that between us we can come up with some good ideas.' The boss looked at her deputy. 'I thought you could oversee organising celebrations, Winnie, so if any of you have any ideas that are practical and sensible, bearing in mind that we are still very much on duty and could be called out to an incident at any time, then speak to my deputy about it.' And without waiting to hear any suggestions, the boss went back into her office.

'Over to you then.' Sparky nudged Winnie's arm.

She got up and stood where the boss had been just moments before and looked at the assembled crew. 'All right, so it's bad luck that we're still having to be on duty today, but I hope we can still enjoy ourselves. So, does anyone have any sensible ideas?'

'Get some beer from the local pub,' someone shouted from the back.

Winnie laughed. 'Sensible ideas, I said. You know it's strictly forbidden to drink alcohol while we're on duty, even today.'

'We could have a dance,' Taylor called out. 'We could take the gramophone and some records down to the courtyard – we'd have plenty of room down there.'

'Good idea,' Winnie said. 'What else?'

'Have a sing-song?' Sparky suggested.

'Yes, as long as you lead it,' Paterson said.

'I'll put you in charge of that then, Sparky, shall I?' Winnie raised her eyebrows questioningly at him, knowing that he would do a good job as he had a fine voice and had often led the crew in singing before.

He nodded. 'I'll ask the boss if she'll play the piano for us.'

'How about some decorations?' Frankie said. 'We could make some.'

'Yes, no celebration would be complete without some sort of finery, we'll have to see what we can do. Let's make this a day to remember. I know thousands of people will be celebrating in the middle of the city, there were plenty of them already there last night . . .'

'Yes, look here!' Sparky pointed to the front page of today's *Daily Mirror* newspaper with its picture of some WRENs sitting on top of the lions in Trafalgar Square, waving Union flags. He'd splashed out on two newspapers today: his usual *Daily Herald* and this one. 'It'll be heaving with people today and all around that area as well.'

'Well, we'll do our best to enjoy ourselves here,' Winnie said, 'but before we do we need to get the ambulances ready, so let's get to it, everyone.'

'Shhhh!' Winnie hissed as the clock on the wall reached three o'clock and the announcer on the wireless introduced the Prime Minister. The chatter in the common room immediately stopped as everyone listened to the familiar voice.

343

'Yesterday morning, at 2:41 a.m. ... signed the act of unconditional surrender of all German land, sea and air forces in Europe ... Victory in Europe Day ... let us not forget for a moment the toils and efforts that lie ahead ... Japan ... remains unsubdued ... '

At the end of Churchill's speech there was a moment of silence before the room erupted into clapping and cheering.

'I don't know about you, but I needed to hear it from Churchill himself to finally believe it,' Station Officer Steele said, leaning close to Winnie so that she could be heard in the noise.

Winnie nodded. 'I know what you mean.' She smiled at the boss. 'But it's true, they've surrendered – we're at peace with them again.'

'But not the bleedin' Japs!' Sparky said.

'Not for much longer, I hope,' Winnie said. 'But let's not dwell on that just now. We should be celebrating this victory, we've waited long enough for it, so let's enjoy it.'

'How about that sing-song now?' Paterson called out. 'To get the celebrations going.'

'All right, if you'll provide the music, boss?' Sparky stood up.

Station Officer Steele smiled. 'I'd be delighted to accompany you – what shall it be to start with?'

'How about good old "Knees Up, Mother Brown"?' Sparky suggested. 'It never fails to get people in the mood.'

Winnie watched as the pair of them went over to the other side of the common room where the piano stood and prepared to entertain the crew as they'd done so many times before over the years. The top of the upright piano had been decorated with bunting which they'd made from newspaper and string, with more of it draped around the walls of the common room, and stuck up on the beam running across the centre of the ceiling were large letters cut out of newspaper spelling out the word 'VICTORY'.

As Station Officer Steele began to play the piano, other crew members abandoned their conversations and hurried over to gather round, ready to join in.

'Come on, Winnie.' Bella stood up from where she'd been sitting next to Winnie on the sofa and held out her hand to her. 'You don't want to miss Sparky's singing, it might be the last time we hear him.'

The piping sounds of the clarinet introduction to Benny Goodman's 'Wang Wang Blues' filled the courtyard and Bella began to dance with Sparky, joining other crew members filling their impromptu dance floor. Station Officer Steele was partnering Paterson, while Winnie and Rose were doing their best with a baby bump making usual dance positions difficult. Everyone was enjoying themselves, the happy, vibrant, toe-tapping tune bringing out energetic dancing.

'You're quite the twinkletoes these days,' Sparky said, twirling Bella round. 'I thought you always said you 'ad two left feet?'

'I did, but Stefan taught me how to dance. He's very good and I just followed him and got the hang of it. I love it now.'

'I suppose he'll be going back to Poland now the war is over.'

Bella shook her head. 'He's not going back, his family have been killed and as Poland's going to be under Stalin's watch, it won't be the free country he's been fighting for.'

'Can't say I blame him, I wouldn't want to live under Stalin's thumb.' Sparky twirled them around again so that he was facing the archway leading out of Station 75. 'Aye, aye, talk of the devil.'

Bella frowned. 'What you mean?'

Sparky spun her around in response so that she was now looking the way he'd just been, and coming in under the archway was Stefan. He spotted her and headed straight for them.

'You can take over here, you've done a good job improving Bella's dancing.' Sparky handed Bella over to Stefan who bowed his head and quickly took the older man's place.

'What are you doing here? I thought you'd be celebrating at West Malling?' Bella asked as they danced together, seamlessly fitting in with each other, his hand moulding to her waist and her hand resting on the shoulder of his air force blue tunic. She smiled. 'It's very good to see you, the loveliest surprise.'

'We have been, but I wanted to celebrate with you too. I have two hours then I must go back.' He smiled, his eyes holding hers. 'Is good they have surrendered at last.' He paused, a shadow passing over his face. 'I wish it was a different end for my country though.'

Bella touched his face. 'I know.'

He took hold of her hand and kissed it. 'We should enjoy now, is not VE Day every day.'

'Oy! Don't just stand there in the middle of the dance floor, looking all lovey dovey at each other, you're meant to be dancing,' Sparky shouted at them. He was now partnering Pip in an energetic dance.

Paterson, who was leading Station Officer Steele around their impromptu dance floor, winked at Bella as they passed by.

Bella hadn't realised that they'd ground to a halt and, grinning at Stefan, put her hand back on his shoulder, and, his hand on her waist, they began to dance again, losing themselves in the joy of the music and being together.

Later, after the gramophone records had been changed many times as the crew of Station 75 enjoyed the dancing, letting their hair down as much as they could while still being on duty, the music was stopped for a short while so that everyone could get some refreshment, an urn of tea and some carrot buns having been organised by Mrs Connelly.

'Bella, I would like talk to you. Can we go somewhere quiet?' Stefan asked after he drained his teacup, his face serious.

Now the war was over had he changed his mind about going back to Poland? He loved his country so much, perhaps he was willing to live with the new regime there after all. The thought settled in her stomach like a heavy stone: the idea of not seeing him again, or being with him, was too much to comprehend. 'Yes, what do you want to talk to me about?'

'Not tell you here.'

'All right, we could take a walk down to the river, but I'll need to ask the boss first.'

Station Officer Steele was happy for Bella to leave the station for half an hour and as they walked down past the Tower of London she wondered what Stefan wanted to talk about.

Stefan waited until they reached the wall overlooking the river, where the tide was in, lapping up to the edge. He looked out across the river for a moment and then turned to her, taking both of her hands in his and meeting her eyes. 'Bella, I want ask you if you will marry me, be my wife?'

She stared at him for a few moments, the dread of him saying he was going back to Poland evaporating and her heart lightening.

He suddenly looked worried. 'You not like that I ask?'

She shook her head. 'I'm surprised. I never expected you to ask me that.'

'You know I fall in love with you.' Stefan gently touched her cheek. 'I would like spend my life with you.'

'And I love you, Stefan, so very much . . .' She paused and smiled at him, because she didn't need to think about what to say as her heart and head were shouting out the answer in unison. 'Yes, yes, I would love nothing more than to marry you!'

Tears filled Stefan's eyes. 'I promise with all my heart I always look after you, Bella. You make me so happy.' He threw his arms around her and hugged her tightly.

Bella leaned against his chest, her heart full.

Chapter Sixty-three

Frankie looked out across the London rooftops. It was dark now, but the city's darkness had undergone a miraculous change: after more than five years of blackout, tonight the city was aglow with light. Lights shone out from windows and doorways now freed of their blackout restrictions, bonfires were burning and the beam of searchlights that had been used to pick out enemy bombers overhead now shone upwards in a huge V for Victory shape. It was as if London had come out of hiding and was celebrating the victory in Europe with an outpouring of light after so many years of darkness.

Sitting on the flat roof of Station 75, Frankie could hear laughter and music coming from the courtyard below where their impromptu dance floor was still alive with dancing, the crew determined to enjoy themselves on this momentous day, making up for not being able to join in the celebrations that they'd heard were going on in the centre of London around Trafalgar Square and Buckingham Palace. She'd joined in for a while but had felt the need for some quiet time on her own.

She leaned back against the chimney stack and closed her eyes, thinking about how her life had changed since the start of the war. She'd lost her grandad – the hole he'd left in her life still felt huge and she would never stop missing him; his loss made today bittersweet. She was glad the war was over but couldn't forget what it had cost her. She doubted she was the only one who must be feeling this way: although there were thousands out celebrating, there must be many at home mourning those they had lost in the bombing or who'd been killed on active service and who would never come home again.

Family lives had also been disrupted in other ways, like the children being evacuated. Sending Stanley away for his safety had been hard and she'd missed him growing up. Her family life had changed irrevocably because of the war. She sighed. It hadn't been *all* bad though, because she'd come to work here, and she'd met Alastair. The thought of him made her smile. She wondered what he was doing now, was he celebrating too?

And what next, what did the future hold for her now that the war against the Nazis was over and the end of Station 75 coming in just two days' time? She still hadn't decided about what she was going to do next. Station Officer Steele had been as good as her word and found out more information about volunteering for UNRRA and it looked like a good possibility. There was one problem against her joining – though 'problem' was the wrong word because it wasn't truly an issue as it was something that she'd been longing for, for years, ever since her grandad had evacuated him to the safety of the country-side – now the war was over it was finally safe for Stanley to come home. She'd been waiting for that and had held on to 25 Matlock Street so that he'd have his home to return to. She'd put up with Ivy and her difficult ways to be able to do that and all that would be worth it when he returned, now in perhaps just a few days' time, as soon as he could leave. Making a home for Stanley took prece-dence over volunteering for UNRRA. If she couldn't do that perhaps there was something else she could do to help here in London – maybe the Red Cross needed volunteers, she could talk to Connie about it.

'Frankie!'

Rose's voice made her jump and she opened her eyes to see her friend looking down at her with a concerned expression on her face.

'Are you all right?'

She nodded. 'Just needed a bit of quiet time, it's quite lively down there. Come and sit down if you want, it's a good view out there tonight.' She waved at the light show going on across London. 'It seems so strange to see the city lit up again after years of darkness.'

Rose sat down next to her and leaned back against the chimney stack. 'It's symbolic, coming out of the darkness into the light. I like it.' They sat quietly side by side look-ing out over the rooftops for a few minutes before Rose spoke again. 'I'm going to miss working here very much. I can't quite believe this station will cease to exist in two days' time, can you? And it must be even worse for you because you've been here much longer than me.'

Frankie shrugged. 'We knew it was comin' and for the best reasons: that the war is nearly over, no *is over*. Better that than it dragging on for longer and us still working 'ere.' She turned to Rose and smiled. 'I will miss it though, very much.'

'I've been thinking about where I could get another job. I'll need to do something until I hear about my parents, until I know where my future lies.'

Frankie put her arm through Rose's. She hadn't talked much lately about her parents and what might have happened to them. Frankie suspected that she was terrified that they might have ended up in one of the concentration camps, and she desperately hoped this wasn't the case, but if they had perished in one of those terrible places then Rose was an orphan and her future lay elsewhere than back with her family in Austria.

'Whatever 'appens you've always got a home with me, whether that's at Matlock Street where we are now or somewhere else if I have to move when Alastair finally comes home from the army. You're like family to me now, Rose.'

Rose put her head on Frankie's shoulder. 'Thank you, Frankie. I appreciate that very much. I don't know where I will be until I hear news of my parents and only then can I decide what to do. I'm . . . I'm frightened that they were taken to a camp.'

Frankie took hold of Rose's hand. 'I would be too, but they may not have been taken to one, there's no telling until you 'ear from them or find out otherwise. I hope that they are alive and well and are just waitin' to send a letter to you.'

Rose sighed. 'It is my dream.' She sighed. 'But until I hear what has happened I must find work to earn my living so I will search for a new job on the eleventh of May. What about you, what do you want to do?'

'Firstly, I'll make a home for Stanley, and then I'm going to see if I can 'elp people somehow, perhaps volunteer for the Red Cross here in London. The one thing I am certain of is that I don't want to go back to doin' what I did before the war. I've changed so much and sewing clothes in a factory again would feel ...' She shrugged. 'Feel like I've gone backwards, and I would hate it and want to be out there doin' more.'

Rose nodded. 'The war has changed so many people's lives, for good and bad. If it hadn't started I would probably still be living in Austria, or maybe in America if my parents had finally got permission to emigrate there, but I would never have had the experience of living in England and meeting you and working here ...' She threw her arm wide to encompass the whole of Station 75.

'My gran always used to say every cloud has a silver lining. Station 75 is yours.'

Chapter Sixty-four

Station Officer Steele surveyed Station 75's crew arranged before her in front of the open garage doors, some sitting on chairs at the front, others standing in a row behind, all of them smart in their Ambulance Service uniforms.

'Yes, that will do very nicely.' She smiled at the photographer who'd been sent from headquarters to take the group photo today – recording for posterity the last day of Ambulance Station 75 – and went over to join her crew, sitting down on the empty chair in the middle of the front row between Winnie and Sparky. Trixie, who'd been sitting on Winnie's lap, jumped down and sat in front of her, looking towards the photographer.

'Here, girl, come here!' The photographer patted his legs, calling to Trixie, who ignored him and stayed where she was. He tutted and marched over and went to pick her up.

'Trixie stays where she is,' Station Officer Steele said. 'I want her in the photograph.'

He frowned. 'But none of the other ambulance stations had a dog in their photo, or even at the station come to that.'

'Well this one *does*! Trixie has been an important part of our crew and deserves to be in the photograph as much as anyone else. She has saved lives.' The rest of the crew clapped and cheered, making her smile. 'So, when you're ready then.'

'Very well, if it's what you want.' The photographer shrugged and returned to where he had his camera and tripod set up.

'Right, everyone, let this be a good one to remember Station 75 by,' she called out. 'Everyone facing the front, no funny faces, everyone smiling please, I don't want to look at the photograph in years to come and be annoyed because someone's sticking out their tongue.' Everyone laughed.

'On the count of three, smile please,' the photographer shouted. 'One, two, three.' He pressed the shutter. 'One more for luck, one, two, three ... Right, thank you very much.'

'Thank you, I hope you got some good ones, I look forward to seeing them.' She stood up and turned to address the crew. 'Right, thank you very much, everyone, you'll all be sent a copy to keep and I hope that when you look back at it in the future you'll have good memories of your time at Station 75. Our celebratory meal is at midday so until then if we can all carry on with our assigned jobs to finish the clearing up and packing away.'

'What's going to happen to everything?' Sparky said.

'Useful equipment will be taken to be used by the regular ambulance service and I'm not sure what will happen to anything else, but nothing will be thrown away or wasted. There's been a war on, don't you know, things are still very much in short supply!' Everyone laughed. 'And as for this place,' she looked around at the garages, then the rooms above them overlooking the courtyard which had played such a huge role in her life, 'perhaps they'll go back to what they were used for before, who knows.'

'What, for chauffeurs for people who are too lazy to drive themselves?' Paterson said. 'They've managed without them for all this time, perhaps they won't want them again.'

'Or get anyone who wants to be a servant again!' Sparky said. 'I hope the war's changed all that for the better.'

Station Officer Steele shrugged. 'Well it has certainly broken down some barriers and things won't go back to the way they were before.' She glanced at Bella who was sitting on the front row listening, and who nodded and smiled back at her – she was definitely someone who would not be going back to her role as a servant. Her life had taken a new direction and allowed her talents to shine out, which she hoped would carry on. 'Right, let's get to work so we can be finished by the time Mrs Connelly has our meal ready.'

Mrs Connelly's farewell to Station 75 was a triumph. Everyone had donated what they could, and she had prepared a meal of rabbit pie with vegetables from the allotment and baked a cake from the precious donated sugar and butter rations. With plates now cleared and everyone relaxed after their meal, Station Officer Steele stood up and tapped on her teacup with a spoon to get their attention.

'Mrs Connelly, you have once more done us proud and we all owe you a great deal of thanks for providing us with such hearty meals to keep us going, and today's has been a final triumph. Thank you for all you have done for us, and Hooky who has most ably assisted you.' She began to clap, and the rest of the crew quickly joined in, cheering, some of them banging on the table with their hands as well. She waited until the noise died down before going on. 'And to the rest of my most excellent crew, I thank you from the bottom of my heart for your service here. It has been the greatest privilege of my life to serve alongside you for five and a half years. It hasn't always been easy and we have faced some difficult and trying times, we have lost crew members . . . ' She paused for a few moments, remembering the two Jones sisters who had been killed when their ambulance had received a direct hit from a bomb while they were out on call. 'We have been injured and tested to the maximum, but we did it and have come through to the end and I wouldn't have missed it for the world.' She looked round at her crew who were listening intently to her words, some looking directly at her, others staring at the table, their eyes looking suspiciously bright. It was going to feel very strange not to have these people in her life as they had been for so many years now, she would miss them desperately. 'And I am immensely proud to have served alongside such splendid people, and I hope that we will keep in touch.'

As the room erupted into applause and cheering she sat down, glad to have finished before the aching in her throat grew even worse and she would betray the emotion building up inside her.

Winnie stood up and waved both her hands to bring the crew back under control again, waiting until they were silent and looking at her. 'Station Officer Steele, I know I speak on behalf of all the crew here when I say how glad we are to have served under your leadership. You have been the best of bosses and even at times when perhaps we didn't always see eye to eye,' she raised her eyebrows, gaining a laugh from her audience, 'we have always sorted things out and put the running of Station 75 and the casualties that we've helped first ...'

''ear! 'ear!' shouted Sparky.

'So, thank you for all your guidance, wisdom and friendship to us all, Station 75 wouldn't be the place it is without you.' This was followed by more cheering and clapping. 'Now please raise your cups of tea and join me in a toast.' Winnie picked up her own cup and held it aloft. 'To Station Officer Steele, a champion amongst us!'

As the crew members echoed Winnie's words Violet Steele couldn't stop her eyes from filling with tears and she had to wipe them away with her handkerchief as she smiled at the crew. 'Thank you. Thank you, all.'

Goodbyes had been said, along with promises to keep in touch, and now Station Officer Steele was the last one left at Station 75. She stood in the middle of the common room and looked around her. All personal items had been taken home by their owners: the books, jigsaw puzzles, the knitting and sewing; boxes full of equipment were piled up ready to be collected and taken to London County Council ambulance stations, leaving just the furniture, the battered old armchairs and sofa and the table around which the crew had sat for so many meals and discussions. She'd never seen it looking so empty and abandoned. Always there'd been crew here, either her shift or the others, Station 75 had always been alive with people and the energy they brought to the place, the laughter and arguments that they'd brought with them, but now all of that was gone, had passed and would never come again.

She sat down in the overstuffed armchair and closed her eyes. She knew she should go but she was loath to leave, wanting to hang on to the threads of what had been her life for so long. Just a few more minutes and then she'd go and start the next phase of her life, one that wasn't ruled by wartime and the responsibility of sending people out while bombs were raining down. Her life from now on would take on a more measured, stable routine – she'd be returning to her teaching post at the grammar school, trying to infuse her pupils with a love of history and English, although she feared it would feel very tame after this.

'I thought I might find you still here.' Winnie's voice made her jump, just as a wet nose touched her hand. She opened her eyes and saw Trixie looking up at her, wagging her tail rapidly from side to side as her mistress came and sat down on the sofa opposite her. 'Are you all right, boss?'

She nodded, stroking Trixie's butter-soft ears. 'Just taking a few moments to soak it all up, you know, so I can remember it . . . .' She looked around the room and sighed. 'But it feels so different already with everybody gone and not coming back. It's as if the old place knows . . .' She tried to laugh but it came out in a rather strange hiccup instead. 'Hark at me, as if a building has feelings.'

'Who knows, but it does feel very different in here, so quiet and still with everybody gone, I— Ouch!' Winnie rubbed her swollen stomach. 'This one's very lively today, that must have been an elbow jabbing at me.'

'You'll be able to concentrate on getting ready to have the baby now,' Station Officer Steele said. 'You will let me know when you've had it, won't you?'

'Of course, and actually I was rather hoping that you would be his or her godmother.'

She stared at Winnie, quite taken aback by the request, but then she smiled at her. 'I would be delighted to, thank you very much for asking me.'

'Thank you! I thought the baby would need someone sensible to look out for it. You know I'm not always the most level-headed of people, and you've prodded me back into line on more than one occasion.' She grinned. 'And there's every chance I will need that again while I'm struggling to be a decent mother, my own hasn't set the best example and I'm determined to do better. I'm not going to leave the care of my child to a paid servant.'

Station Officer Steele leaned forward and put a hand on Winnie's arm. 'You will make a splendid mother, Winnie, I have no doubt about that, but I'm very happy to help you in any way I can. Your baby is very lucky to have you and Mac as its parents.'

Winnie's eyes shone with tears and she nodded. 'Thank you, don't mind me, I'm so prone to crying these days, Connie tells me it's because of the baby.'

'Right, it's time to go.' Violet Steele stood and put out her hand to help Winnie up. 'I'm glad you came back, it's making leaving that bit easier. I'll just get my bag from my office and then I'm ready.'

A few minutes later they were standing outside in the courtyard where the garage doors stood locked, with the ambulances and cars inside ready to be taken away to wherever they would be used next.

'Well this is it. Goodbye, Station 75, it's been a pleasure ...' Station Officer Steele's voice wavered, and she was grateful that Winnie tucked her arm through hers; then with Trixie trotting by her side they walked out under the archway towards the road for a final time. Stopping by the pavement they both turned and looked back for a few moments before turning left and walking off together towards the rest of their lives.

Chapter Sixty-five

Frankie stood by the kitchen sink nursing a cup of tea in her hands while she stared out through the window at the back garden, the beautiful sunshine outside contrasting with the odd sense of loss that she'd woken up with which had settled heavily in the pit of her stomach. For the first time in over four and a half years she didn't have a job to go to, she wasn't needed at Station 75 any more. It had closed and all that had been part of it was now gone for ever. Her close friendships with Winnie, Bella and Rose would carry on, but it wouldn't be the same as when they'd spent their days working together.

She gave herself a mental shake, of course she'd miss working at Station 75, but it was more important that the war was over, something they'd all longed for during the long years of hardship. The fighting had stopped, at least in Europe, and people would be coming home again — that was what mattered — and it had already started:

Josie's children had arrived home yesterday, her friend so delighted to have them home again. Stanley was due back any day now as well, and Alastair would come home when the army finally decided they'd done with his services. Life never stayed the same, it was always changing, and she should grasp this new change wholeheartedly, peace was priceless.

In the meantime, Frankie thought, drinking the last of her tea, she needed to occupy herself. She could start by digging over the part of the vegetable bed where she planned to plant the potatoes.

Outside, she took a spade from the shed and got to work, thrusting the spade into the soil and stamping down on it before levering it up with a clod of soil and turning it over, then repeating the process again and again.

Stopping to catch her breath a few minutes later, she went over to the hen coop where the girls had been watching her, squawking loudly at her, making it clear that they wanted to come out and help her as they'd done many times before, delighting in scraping around looking for worms and grubs that she unearthed.

'Come on then.' She opened the chicken-run door and they shot out, running over to where she was digging and starting to scrape in the earth, their feet rapidly working. Whenever one of them found a worm, it would swallow it down quickly before the others could steal it. They were completely focused on what they were doing, making happy 'tuk-tuk' noises when they struck lucky.

Frankie watched them for a few moments, smiling at their antics, and then began to dig again, this time having to take care that the hens didn't get in the way as they attentively watched every turn of the spade, one of them even jumping onto it, balancing on the blade to improve her chances against the other hens, as Frankie turned over the soil.

'Their eggs will be a rich yellow after eating all them worms,' a deep voice called across the garden.

Frankie spun round and dropped her spade at the sight of who was standing on the back doorstep. 'Stanley!' She rushed over to him, throwing her arms around him and squeezing him tight.

'Welcome home!' she said, stepping back to look up at him, marvelling at how tall he was now. She still wasn't used to the transformation from small boy to tall young man that he'd undergone since he'd been evacuated back in 1940. 'It's good to see you. You should've let me know you were coming back today, I'd 'ave come to meet you at the station.'

Stanley grinned. 'Thought I'd surprise you.'

'Well it's the best of surprises.' Frankie tucked her arm through his. 'Come on, I'll go and make a cup of tea and we can have a good catch-up.'

Sitting outside on the back doorstep in the warm sunshine a short while later with their steaming cups of tea, Frankie smiled at Stanley. 'It's 'ard to believe it's over, ain't it? No more bombing, no more air raids, V rockets. It's finally safe for people to come 'ome again. You know, when Grandad 'ad you evacuated back in 1940 I never thought it would take this long for you to come 'ome again.'

'Nor me.' Stanley took a sip of his tea. 'But I'm glad he sent me.'

Frankie nodded. 'It was the right thing to do, knowing you was safe was important.' She sighed. 'It's just you and me left now Grandad and Ivy are gone.'

They sat in silence for a few moments, Frankie thinking of her grandad and wishing he was still here to see Stanley finally come home.

'Rose will be pleased to meet you when she gets back from shopping. She's moved into what was Ivy's room so your old room is ready for you. Have you thought what you want to do next? Where you're going to look for a job? I've been thinkin' perhaps you could do something like you've been doing and get a job in one of the parks looking after them. Or you might want to do something completely different, there's a lot more choice 'ere than in the countryside.'

Stanley took a sip of his tea and then looked at her, his blue eyes troubled. 'The thing is, I don't want to come back here to live. I'm really sorry, but I want to stay in the countryside. I love it there and doing my job . . . It's what I want to do.' He shrugged. 'I'm planning on going back in a few days.'

Frankie stared at him, not wanting to take in what he'd just said, an icy coldness drenching the happiness that his arrival home had brought. She struggled to speak for a few moments. 'Since when?'

'When I came back for your wedding I felt . . . so out of place here, like it wasn't my home any more. The streets and buildings closed me in, I ain't used to that any more.

366

I like the space and the green, to hear birds singing and fresh air. And I love working in the garden and I don't want to swap it for city life. I didn't know that till I came back here. I always thought I'd come home here after the war, but I've changed since I left here. I'm sorry, I know you must be disappointed.'

She nodded, swallowing against the lump that had formed in her throat. She'd never thought this would happen, a Stepney boy turning into someone who preferred to stay living in the countryside rather than return to his home in the streets where he'd been born and spent the first ten years of his life. Ever since he'd been evacuated she'd been imagining him coming home again one day when there was finally peace; all through the years of bombing, losing Grandad and putting up with Ivy, always it had been with a view to Stanley coming home. But now that dream had suddenly been popped like a balloon; he didn't want to come home. She could stop him, of course, make him stay as she was his guardian now that Grandad was gone . . . but that would be like caging a wild animal and as much as she wanted him to be here, she wouldn't do anything to make him unhappy. There'd been enough of that in the world, life was precious and should be enjoyed.

'Say something,' Stanley blurted out. 'Are you angry? You look shocked.'

'I am shocked. I never expected this to 'appen. Why did you come back? You could have just told me in a letter.'

'I couldn't tell you like that, it wouldn't have been right and you could stop me if you want to, I suppose.' His eyes were anxious.

'I could . . . but I ain't going to. If you really feel that you want to stay there and have somewhere to live and a job, and most importantly if that makes you happy, then that's what you should do.'

He flung his arm around her shoulder. 'Thank you. I've been really scared about telling you.'

She leaned her head against his. 'I'm glad you did come here to tell me, it would 'ave been worse finding out in a letter.' She sighed. 'Both our lives are going to be different to how we imagined they would be at the start of the war. If you're not coming back here to live, then I might not be here for much longer either.'

'Where are you going?' Stanley asked.

'If you don't need me here then I'm going to volunteer to join UNRRA.'

'What's that?'

'It stands for the United Nations Relief and Rehabilitation Administration, UNRRA for short. They work in the camps housing the thousands of displaced persons who were imprisoned by the Nazis or shipped from their homelands and made to work as slaves. They look after them and help them return to their homes or go to new ones. You must have heard about what happened in the camps?'

Stanley nodded. 'I read about it in the paper. It was horrible, how could they treat people like that?'

Frankie shrugged. 'I don't know, but that's why we had to fight them. And I want to go and help now Station 75's closed, and as you're not coming back here.'

'It won't be an easy job.'

'I know, but I want to do something, Stanley. After working in the ambulance service I don't want to go back to sewing clothes in a factory until Alastair comes home. I want to do something useful.'

'What if I had been coming back, you'd have stayed here then?'

'Yes, but I'd have found something else to do helping people.'

His eyes met hers. 'So, me staying living in the countryside ain't all bad then?'

'No. I want you to be happy and if that's what makes you happy, then that's the right thing to do, and if you don't need me here then I can go and volunteer for UNRRA.' She smiled at him. 'I want you to know that when this is all over, when I come home from being away and Alastair's demobbed, you'll always have a home with us if you want it. It might not be here in Matlock Street because where we'll live will depend on where he gets a job, but wherever it is you will always be welcome, Stanley.'

He nodded. 'Thank you.'

She stood up and held out her hand to him. 'Come on, while you're here you can give me a hand with the garden, you know a lot more about gardening than I do.'

Chapter Sixty-six

Bella stared out of the train window at the passing countryside, enjoying being able to see miles off into the distance after the confined views of London and drinking in the subtly different shades of green painted across the hedgerows, woods and fields. The Norfolk landscape was beautiful, glistening, green and fresh-looking, spring clearly in full swing, stretching out under a perfect duck-egg blue sky dappled with small puffs of cloud. As they passed by a field where Land Girls were hoeing, the young women stopped work and waved at the train – Bella waved back.

'Who are you waving at?' Winnie asked, looking up from the letter she was writing to Mac.

'Some Land Girls,' Bella said. 'They're still working. I doubt they'll be demobbed for a while yet, unlike us.'

Frankie looked up from the drawing she was doing. 'Even though the war's over there ain't no change in people needing to be fed.'

'Or rationing either,' Winnie added. 'It's going to take a while for the country to get back to normal.'

'We're well off compared with many, at least we've still got our homes and country.' Frankie tapped her pencil on her sketchbook. 'Unlike those poor souls who've been in the concentration camps, how many of them don't have a home to go to any more?'

'But they'll get help,' Bella said. 'After what they've been through they won't be turned out with nowhere to go.' She smiled at Frankie who had seemed serious and troubled about something lately. She planned on having a quiet talk with her friend while they were away to see what the matter was – perhaps she was worried about Alastair.

They fell into silence again, Winnie went back to her letter-writing and Frankie to her drawing while Bella returned to watching out of the window, the air blowing in feeling refreshing. It would have been lovely if Rose could have been here too, but she'd decided to stay at home in case any news arrived about her parents, and that was quite understandable.

'Can you smell it?' Bella leapt to her feet and stood by the open window sniffing the air. 'It's changed, it's got the scent of the sea.'

'With a dash of coal smoke added,' Winnie said. 'You've been like a cat on a hot tin roof since we left Norwich, Bella. We're supposed to be on holiday and relaxing.'

Bella turned to her friend and smiled. 'I'm excited about seeing the sea, I've only been to the seaside once before.'

371

'Me as well.' Frankie stood up and joined Bella by the window. 'I loved it.'

They stayed by the window, craning their necks for the first sight of the sea, and as the train began to gently descend through some woods and bend around the side of a hill, they were rewarded with the first sight of blue glinting off to the horizon.

'Look!' Bella pointed to the sea glittering with diamonds in the sunshine.

Winnie got up and joined them at the window. 'It looks beautiful. We're going to have the most marvellous holiday together.' She put her arms around Frankie and Bella's shoulders as they stood looking out as the train rolled along the track towards their destination.

'We've got a sea view!' Bella rushed across the room and pulled up the sash window letting in the scent and sound of the sea. She and Frankie were sharing a room in the hotel they'd booked right on the seafront, while Winnie had opted for the room next door – she wasn't sleeping so well now as the baby often kept her awake at night and she didn't want to disturb the others.

Frankie came over and stood beside her. 'We'll be able to 'ear the sea in the night.'

'And wake up to the sight of it in the mornings.' Bella smiled at Frankie, linking her arm through hers. 'This is just what we needed, a holiday by the sea, in the sunshine and fresh air, don't you think?'

Frankie nodded but didn't say anything, just stared out of the window, her face not giving anything away.

Bella looked at her for a few moments before returning her gaze to the sea. There was definitely something up with Frankie, she thought, she wasn't usually so quiet or serious-looking, whatever was on her mind was clearly weighing her down. When you were worried about something it did that to you.

She, on the other hand, was fit to burst with happiness and was planning to tell her friends about her and Stefan's engagement while they were here after hugging it to herself since he'd asked her. If it hadn't been for Stefan having to return to West Malling soon after he'd asked her, they'd have announced it at Station 75 on VE Day, but going back there on her own after saying goodbye to him, she'd decided to keep it to herself for a while, there'd been so much going on, first with VE Day, then the closing of Station 75. She'd just wanted to savour the excitement and happiness, let it sink in before she shared their news.

'Knock, knock,' Winnie said, coming in the open door. 'You've got a sea view as well. Isn't it splendid? I've tried out my bed and can see the sea from it so should be quite happy lying there awake watching it in the moonlight.' She came and stood the other side of Bella.

'Perhaps the sea air will tire you out more, so you get more sleep,' Bella suggested.

Winnie put her hand on her large belly. 'It's not me that's keeping me awake, it's this one who prefers to sleep all day and dance all night!'

'It won't be for much longer,' Frankie said. 'After we get back from here, you'll only have a couple of weeks before it's due and then it'll be keeping you awake in a whole different way.'

Winnie laughed. 'Then I should make the most of it being safely tucked away inside here.' She stroked her stomach. 'Who's for a paddle? I'm dying to get down on that golden sand and cool off my hot feet.'

Chapter Sixty-seven

Another wave swashed up the golden sand and then washed back again until it collided with the next incoming wave. Winnie stood mesmerised, her bare feet sinking slightly into the saturated sand, watching the play of the sea coming in, rolling back, the wave edges decorated with a frothy lace of bubbles. She sighed happily – being here was complete bliss and a world away from her life in London and the work of Station 75.

She began walking again, enjoying the sensation of splashing her feet through the water and the touch of firm sand under the soles of her feet while spring sunshine warmed her back. They'd been here in Sheringham on the north Norfolk coast for several days now, and had fallen into a gentle routine of walks, talking, laughing and with plenty of time to just potter around doing what they each enjoyed. For Bella that was reading beside the sea, sitting up on the high bank of stones on the shoreline overlooking the sand, where Winnie could see her now, buried in her book, while Frankie was off somewhere around the town sketching whatever took her fancy. She'd done a fine drawing of the town from the top of the high cliffs to the east yesterday. But for Winnie, her favourite pastime had become paddling in the shallows when the tide went out far enough to reveal the golden sands. The sea was still cool, it made her gasp when she first went in, and it was far too cold for her to swim, as much for the temperature shock as the worry that it might cause her to go into early labour, so she'd contented herself with paddling, which was quite delightful once she'd got over the initial surprise of the cold water.

Others were making the most of the fine day: some mothers and their young children had ventured down onto the sand and the youngsters were busy constructing a sandcastle, chattering happily with each other as they worked. She paused for a moment, watching them, before carrying on paddling again, thinking that was something that she was determined to do with her child. She rested her hand on her stomach, feeling its solidness, knowing that inside was her and Mac's child, and that both of them would do whatever they could to ensure it was well looked after and loved. She'd never been to the beach with her parents, of course it was impossible where they'd lived in India so far from the sea, but she very much doubted that, even if they'd lived right beside it, her mother would have brought her and her brothers down to the beach to enjoy themselves like those mothers had.

Her mother's lack of hands-on care when she'd been a

child didn't stop her from interfering and trying to push Winnie into doing what she wanted even now. Despite her making it crystal clear to her mother that she would not be having her baby at the maternity home in Oxford, being ruder to her than she'd ever been before, the woman still hadn't given up. She'd switched tactics, telephoning Connie and trying to persuade her via her godmother. Fortunately, Connie was having none of it and hadn't tried to make Winnie change her mind, merely laughing at Cynthia Churchill's persistence like an irritating wasp around a picnic. Winnie sighed: at least her mother wasn't pestering her directly any more and for that she was grateful. It wouldn't be long now until the baby was born and then her mother's argument for the Oxford maternity home would be irrelevant, although knowing her she would find something else to interfere with. She hoped she would never dare try the nanny suggestion again.

Feeling herself becoming annoyed with the situation, she turned and looked out to sea, focusing on the horizon and taking some slow, calming breaths – she was on holiday and should relax and enjoy the moment. She had better things to think about, like Mac coming home. She didn't know yet when that would be as he was still in Germany as far as she knew, but with the war being over it could only be a matter of time before he'd be recalled to Britain and hopefully be demobbed and they could start their life together as a married couple with a child. Whether he would be home before it was born was anybody's guess.

A larger wave splashed the hem of her dress, the cold

water reaching higher up to her knees and shocking her dry skin, pulling her attention back to the moment. The tide was creeping up the beach and she waded across to the shallower water where the waves gently washed over the sand. It wouldn't be long before the waves were licking at the shingle bank at the back of the beach and the children's sandcastle would be flooded and returned to the sea; she should concentrate on now rather than worry about what was to come.

Chapter Sixty-eight

Frankie walked along the seafront carrying warm news-paper parcels of fish and chips in her arms to where Bella and Winnie were waiting for her; the delicious smell wafting up was making her mouth water. She was hungry after spending the day walking along the cliff tops towards Weybourne, doing some drawings as she went, spending time on her own, lost in her art and giving herself time to relax and recuperate ready for what lay ahead.

Since they'd arrived on holiday she'd spent a lot of time thinking about her future and the decision she had to make. She finally had her answer and it was time to share it with her friends after keeping it to herself for so long, although how they would take it she wasn't sure. Bella knew that there was something on her mind, she'd asked her more than once if she was all right, gently probing to see what was dis-tracting her, but she hadn't told her anything, not wanting anyone to influence her decision one way or another.

The fish and chips were as delicious as they smelt, the added salt and tangy vinegar enhanced their taste, and eating them outside in the fresh sea air added an extra delight as well.

'These are good.' Bella picked up a fat chip between her finger and thumb and blew on it to cool it down before popping it in her mouth.

'And the fish is so fresh,' Winnie added, breaking off a piece of crispy batter from her portion.

Frankie smiled at her friends, both of whom looked relaxed and happy, their faces lightly tanned from spending so much time outside since they'd arrived, the weather having been good all week with gentle spring sunshine warming the air after the chill of winter. They'd spent time together and apart, each doing their own thing, and it was proving a perfect mix for their holiday. Now, eating their meal sitting on the bank of stones watching the sea gradually creep up towards them as the high tide reached its peak, Frankie was so glad that they'd come here, together this last time as a band of three, before their lives took them off in different directions. Now that Station 75 had closed, that connection of working with each other had been broken and it was unlikely that they would ever be together in the same way as they had been, day after day, throughout the war, and she would miss their companionship so much.

'I've got somethin' to tell you,' she blurted out, unable to wait until they'd all finished their fish and chips as she'd planned to do.

Winnie nudged her arm. 'At last, we've been wondering when you were going to spill the beans.'

Frankie stared at her two friends. 'What? Who told you?'

Bella touched her arm. 'Nobody's said a word, but we know you well enough to see that you've been worried about something, and no doubt have been working it out while you've been off drawing?' She raised her eyebrows questioningly. 'We presumed it might have something to do with Alastair and when he comes home, but now that Stanley's going to stay in the countryside your plans might have changed.'

Frankie smiled at her friends. 'I should have known I couldn't hide anythin' from you two.' She paused for a moment and looked out to sea where some of the small fishing boats had just been launched, the fishermen going out to check their crab pots. 'You're right, I 'ave been thinking about the future and what I want to do next. I didn't want to go back to what I did before and I don't know when Alastair will come 'ome, so, in the meantime, I want to do more, something that will 'elp people like we've been doing working at Station 75.' She paused and took a breath before continuing. 'I've decided to volunteer for UNRRA to help with the displaced persons coming out of the camps.'

Winnie frowned. 'UNRRA?'

'The United Nations Relief and Rehabilitation Administration. I've read about it in the newspaper,' Bella said. 'But you'll be sent abroad.'

Frankie nodded. 'Possibly to Germany, there are so many people there who need 'elp.'

'What about Alastair? If you go, he'll come home and you won't be here,' Winnie asked.

'From what he's said in his letters he might want to join UNRRA too, especially if I'm there. It won't be for ever and I just feel the need to do somethin' more with the experience I've got from working at Station 75.'

'Well, I think it's a very brave and noble thing to do,' Bella said. 'When will you go?'

'As soon as I can. I'll apply, then there's some trainin' and then I'll be shipped out to where I'm needed. Station Officer Steele helped me find out about it, she thought it was a good idea.'

Winnie raised her eyebrows. 'I'm sure she did, and I rather think she's right. If it weren't for this one,' she rested her hand on her stomach, 'I think I'd volunteer myself. They will be very lucky to have you, Frankie, and I'm sure you will be a great asset to them. You could go, Bella.'

Bella looked startled for a moment but recovered herself quickly. 'No, it's not for me! I'm not sure I could cope with the work, and I have other plans . . . my writing, I need to keep that going.' As she dropped her eyes and took her time to select a chip from the open newspaper parcel lying on her lap, Frankie's eyes met Winnie's and the pair of them exchanged a silent message, Winnie shrugging at their friend's odd reaction. Frankie got the feeling that there was something that Bella wasn't telling them, but what it was she didn't know.

'Before I go, I'm going to go and see my mother in Suffolk. I'd like to spend a bit of time with her,' Frankie said.

Winnie let out a loud sigh. 'You know, it's a good thing that the war in Europe is over now but it's got its downside too: it's going to be hard not being with you two the way we have been for so long. I'm used to seeing you every day and I love being with you, but that's all over now.' Her grey eyes filled with tears. 'When this holiday's over, and we go back to London, everything's changed and it'll never be the same again.'

Frankie put her arm around Winnie and Bella did the same. 'You're right, everything 'as changed, it won't be the same as it was when we were all working together at Station 75, but we'll *always* be friends, that won't ever change. Even if we can't see each other so much, we can write and meet up when we can.'

'We'll be there for each other when we need help,' Bella said. 'Life moves on, nothing stays the same for ever, but our friendship won't alter. After all we've been through we're cemented together, and distance is not going to change that.'

Winnie nodded, sniffing back her tears. 'Thank you, I'm just being silly, I get rather emotional these days! Getting to know you both has been the best thing about the war for me.'

'What about Mac?' Frankie asked.

'Oh, he's not so bad either.' Winnie laughed.

Frankie looked up at the seagulls which were flying back and forth above them, their beady eyes on the chips lying in their laps. 'We'd better finish our chips, or those birds will drop in and do it for us.' Tucking in again to the delicious food, she felt lighter than she had for a long time, her decision made, her friends told and her future on a steady path again, and importantly, one where she would be doing something worthwhile.

Chapter Sixty-nine

Bella sat in the window seat of her and Frankie's room looking out at the inky black sea over which arched a sky pin-pricked with thousands of stars. It was beautiful; calm and peaceful with the gentle shushing of waves breaking on the beach. She'd got into the habit of sitting here when she woke up during the night, looking out at the vastness of sea and sky while she thought about the future.

Movement from across the darkened room startled her. 'Bella, are you all right?' Frankie sat up in bed. 'Are you ill?'

'I'm fine, I just woke up and couldn't get back to sleep so I thought I'd look out at the sea for a bit. Go back to sleep.'

Frankie slipped out of bed and came over to the window and laid a hand on her shoulder. 'Don't you think it's about time you talked about what's worrying you?'

'There's nothing worrying me ...' Bella laughed. 'Quite the opposite, in fact. Stefan asked me to marry him.'

'And what did you tell 'im?' Frankie sat down next to her.

'Yes, of course!'

Frankie threw her arm around Bella's shoulders and hugged her. 'That's marvellous, I'm so pleased for you, Bella.'

'He asked me on VE Day, I've been keeping it a secret since then.'

'Why?'

Bella shrugged. 'I just wanted to hold it to myself for a bit. There's been so much going on and I felt I needed to keep it close and enjoy it for a bit, you know what it's like once news like this gets out.'

Frankie laughed. 'Station 75 crew love a wedding. I don't think I'd 'ave been able to keep it a secret when Alastair asked me, and Winnie definitely wouldn't.' She paused for a moment. 'You ain't regretting saying yes, are you?'

'Absolutely not, I didn't hesitate when he asked me, my heart and head were both in agreement for once. Stefan has completely bowled me away. I'd never have believed someone could have that effect on me until I met him. I loved James, I really did, but with Stefan it's different, more passionate, perhaps because of his Polish ways.' She shrugged. 'Whatever it is, I don't doubt that it's the right thing to do. Now he's staying in England there's no problem of going to live in a foreign country where I don't speak the language or know the customs, and he supports my writing wholeheartedly. He's perfect, Frankie.'

'You make a lovely couple, I'm really pleased for you. You need to tell Winnie, she'll be delighted.'

'Who's going to be delighted?' Winnie's voice asked.

Bella hadn't heard their bedroom door open. 'I've got something to tell you. Stefan asked me to marry him. I—'

'That's marvellous, congratulations.' Winnie hurried across the room. 'When did this happen? Why didn't you tell us?'

'He asked me on VE night, but I've been keeping it to myself,' Bella explained.

'Blimey, I'd never have been able to do that.' Bella and Frankie both laughed. 'What's so funny?'

'We know!' Frankie said.

'It's wonderful news, when are you going to get mar— Ouff!' Winnie suddenly bent over, clutching her swollen belly.

'Are you all right?'

Winnie shook her head. 'I woke up with these pains in my stomach and it's getting worse. I think this baby's ready to be born.'

Chapter Seventy

Winnie grabbed hold of the back of the chair and leaned against it as a pain in her pelvis and belly gripped her in its vicelike claws again. She closed her eyes, moaning as she focused all her energy on riding out the wave until it subsided again. She never knew it was going to be like this, she thought as the pain slowly diminished and she could spare some of her mind to focus on something else until it began all over again. Coming out of her pain-induced trance, she was aware of hands on her back, gently rubbing, trying to soothe her, where Frankie and Bella stood either side of her doing their best to support her.

'How much longer is this going on for?' she asked, looking across at the midwife who'd been sent for and was busy preparing the bed in her hotel room for the baby's delivery. 'It hurts.'

The midwife, a woman of similar age to Station Officer Steele, and who had the same no-nonsense look about her, looked at Winnie and smiled. 'Of course it hurts, what did you expect?'

'Not this!' she snapped. 'I didn't think it would hurt this much and if I'd known it would have put me right off having one.' She'd seen women in labour before while she worked at Station 75 but had never fully appreciated what they were going through, how the pain felt so all-encompassing, as if your body was taking on a mind of its own, and she was helpless to do anything about it.

'Giving birth is hard work, Mrs McCartney, it's not called labour for nothing.' The midwife smoothed out the clean sheet she'd just put on the bed over a layer of brown paper.

'It's Winnie, please, Winnie. I keep wondering who you're talking to when you say Mrs McCartney.'

'Right, Winnie, I need you to lie down on the bed so I can examine you and see how long it's likely to be before this baby's born. If your friends would like to leave the room.'

'No!' Winnie grabbed at Frankie and Bella's hands. 'I need them to stay with me.' She looked at her friends who were both looking worried, but nodded their agreement. 'Them being with me helps.'

'Very well, onto the bed please, Winnie, so I can see what's going on.'

Winnie did as she was told, and climbed onto the bed, the paper laid out beneath the clean sheet crackling underneath her.

'Not long to go now,' the midwife said after she'd examined her. 'You're almost fully dilated and then the baby can start to come out.'

'Thank—' Another wave of pain started to build, and she had to focus her attention on riding through it once again, vaguely aware of Frankie and Bella either side of the bed holding on to her hands.

'Blimey, Winnie!' Frankie said, pulling her hand free of Winnie's and shaking it when the pain subsided again. 'I ain't going to have any feeling left in my hands if you carry on at this rate.'

'Me neither,' Bella said, rubbing her own hand. 'You've got a tight grip, you know, Winnie.'

'Well it bloody hurts!' Winnie snapped. 'I've had enough and want it to stop.'

Frankie and Bella looked at each other and smiled.

'What's so funny?' Winnie said. 'I've never been in such pain in my life.'

'Well there's only one way to make it stop and that's to get the baby born,' Frankie said. 'You ain't the sort of person to give up when things get tough, Winnie. You've been through some tricky situations in the Blitz. What about when that building came down and your ambulance almost got crushed?'

'You were an ambulance driver?' the midwife asked.

'We all were, we worked at Station 75 in London.' Winnie frowned. Driving an ambulance was one thing but giving birth was a totally different challenge; but Frankie was right, there was no way out of it, she had to get on with it, no matter how much it hurt. 'Oh no . . . here it comes again.' She winced as the pain began to build yet again and reached out for her friends who gallantly took hold of her hands and held on as she squeezed them.

Winnie didn't know how much time had passed, it was a hazy world of pain with intermittent bursts of relief which got shorter and shorter as the agony built up, her body seeming to know what to do to push the baby out.

'The head's there,' the midwife said, as a burning pain burst between her legs. 'Don't push, you need to pant now.'

Winnie did as she was told and as she panted looked at her two friends whose eyes were fixed on her and who strangely were panting alongside her.

'That's it,' the midwife said. 'On the next contraction you need to push gently.'

The next few minutes passed in a blur of pain and pushing which miraculously stopped the moment the baby slithered out of her, and a sense of euphoria flooded through her. She'd done it and the pain was gone.

'Congratulations, Winnie, you've got a little girl,' the midwife said as her daughter whimpered and began to cry.

'Oh, Winnie, that's wonderful.' Bella bent down and kissed her cheek. 'You did it.'

'Well done!' Frankie said. 'I knew you could do it.'

Winnie pulled a face. 'I didn't have a choice, did I? But it's over, thank goodness.' She smiled at her friends as they watched the midwife efficiently cutting the cord and then wrapping the baby in a clean towel before she handed her daughter to her.

Looking down into the face of her child, tears filled Winnie's eyes. 'She looks like Mac, don't you think?' She stroked the baby's face which was downy soft. 'She's got his dark hair.'

'She's beautiful.' Frankie sat down on the bed next to her and put her finger in the baby's palm and she immediately gripped her fingers tightly around her. 'She's got her mother's strong grip.'

'What are you going to call her?' Bella asked sitting on the other side of her.

'Daisy Constance. That's what Mac and I want: Daisy after the beautiful little flower and Constance after Connie.' Her daughter's eyes were fixed on her face and she smiled at her. It had only been a matter of minutes since she'd been born but already Winnie felt a fierce and protective love for her child, she would do everything she could to look after her well and bring her up knowing that she was loved and cared for by her mother.

'Feeling better now?' the midwife asked.

Winnie nodded. 'Yes, much.' She looked down at her daughter who had drifted off to sleep, the weight of her in her arms feeling the most natural thing in the world. 'It was worth it in the end.'

Chapter Seventy-one

As the bus came to a stop outside the row of village shops Frankie looked out of the window expecting to see her mother waiting there to meet her, but to her surprise it was her sister Lizzie. The last time she'd seen her had been in the hospital last autumn after her backstreet abortion had gone badly wrong, and she had heard nothing from her since. So why was she here now? Grabbing her suitcase, Frankie mentally braced herself as she got off the bus, expecting Lizzie to be her usual prickly and unwelcoming self.

'Hello.' Lizzie held out her hand to take Frankie's case.

'Hello, Lizzie. It's all right, I can manage, thank you. I wasn't expecting you to come and meet me.'

'I asked Mother if she'd mind if I did.' Lizzie's cheeks flushed, and she looked around at locals who'd got off the bus and now stood chatting outside the shop and within earshot of them. 'Let's go.'

Frankie nodded and they fell into step heading away from the shop and the chance of being overheard. 'I didn't know you'd be 'ere. Have you been demobbed?'

'No, and I'm not going to be. I'm going to stay on in the WAAF, I like it.' Lizzie looked around her, checking no one was close by. 'I wanted the chance to talk to you about what happened, and to thank you for what you did. I probably wouldn't be here now if you hadn't helped me like you did.' She sighed. 'And God knows I didn't deserve your help after the way I treated you.'

Frankie stopped walking and put a hand on Lizzie's arm, making her halt. 'Did you expect me to ignore you? I'd never 'ave done that.'

'You're a better person than me, and I need to say sorry for being such a cow to you. I was jealous, plain and simple jealous, I hated the idea of Mother having another daughter older than me ... and the way Eve took to you ... it made my blood boil.' Lizzie looked down at the ground for a moment before looking up and meeting Frankie's eyes. 'I'm not like that any more, I promise.'

'Well there ain't no denying that you were an unwelcoming cow, as you put it, but the past is the past and I hope we can move on from that. You had nothin' to be jealous of, in fact you were the lucky one because you grew up with our mother, I didn't. I was told she'd died and I missed out on 'aving her in my life all those years.'

Lizzie nodded. 'Thank you. It must have been a shock to find out she was still alive?'

'It was, and I was very angry about being lied to for so long and her leaving me, making me grow up thinkin' I was an orphan. I know she had her reasons, thinking it was for the best, and she regrets it now.' Frankie shrugged. 'But I'm glad I've 'ad the chance to find her again.' They started walking again, leaving the village behind and heading out to the farm.

'They don't know the truth about what happened to me,' Lizzie blurted out. 'I told them I had a fall and it caused damage, so I had to have the hysterectomy. I don't want them to know about what I did. You won't tell them, will you? Please don't, they'd be so angry and never forgive me.'

Frankie slipped her arm through her sister's. 'It's not my story to tell. I promise I won't ever say a word about it.'

'Thank you.' Lizzie's voice was thick with tears. 'I still feel bad about it and I always will, but I can't turn the clock back. At least if I stay in the WAAF I can have a job I enjoy, it keeps me busy.'

'I think you're doing the right thing. After serving in the war it's hard to go back to normal life and the jobs we had before. I've got plans myself.'

'What are you going to do?' Lizzie asked.

But before Frankie could answer a shout of delight reached them as their sister, Eve, came rushing around the corner on her bicycle and called out at the sight of them, waving madly.

'I couldn't wait any longer!' Eve said breathlessly as she brought her bicycle to a halt beside them and leapt off, wrapping her arms around Frankie and squeezing her tight. 'It's so good to see you. I couldn't believe it when Mother said Lizzie wanted to come and meet you.

394

I thought you might need rescuing.' She frowned. 'Is everything all right?'

Frankie and Lizzie looked at each other, nodded and smiled. 'Yes, everything's just fine.'

It was a beautiful evening, a blue sky gently streaked with fine threads of cloud arching overhead, with the sweet smell of drying hay filling the air as swallows darted to and fro hawking for insects while Frankie and her mother walked around the edge of the field. Frankie would be returning to London in the morning, her few days staying with her Suffolk family having passed so quickly.

'I'm glad you came to stay,' her mother said, linking her arm through Frankie's. 'You're always welcome here any time, you know that, don't you?'

She nodded. 'Thank you, I've enjoyed being 'ere and even helping with the haymaking.' She held up her hands which had a few blisters on them from handling her pitchfork to turn the hay over so that it dried evenly in its rows across the field. 'There ain't a lot of haymaking going on in Stepney, it was a whole new experience for me.'

'You did a good job. Are you looking forward to joining UNRRA next week?'

'Yes, it'll be a month before they send me out to Germany, though. There's the training to do first, lectures and practical exercises.'

'Are you sure about wanting to go?' her mother asked. 'It's not going to be easy.'

Frankie stopped and looked across the field where some rabbits were out around the edges, their powder-puff white tails bobbing as they hopped around. 'I know it will be hard, but those people need help and I need to do something more than working back at the clothes factory till Alastair comes home.' She smiled at her mother. 'Helping them will help me as well. I'm not quite sure yet what I'll be doing, they know I was an ambulance driver but whether they will get me to drive or not I'm not sure, but whatever I'm asked to do I intend to do it well.'

'I'm sure you will. And I understand about wanting to do something more, you've had years of doing an important job so to go back to where you were before would be hard. You and Lizzie have been changed by the war and your lives are taking a different path to what they would have done if it had never happened.' She sighed. 'After the Great War women had to return to their normal lives after doing so much for the war effort and so many of them found it hard.'

Frankie looked at her mother. 'Did you?'

'Yes, sometimes. Working as a VAD, then going out to France, was a world away from the place and life I'd grown up with, but then I met your father and had you and, well, you know the rest of the story. I've never forgotten that feeling of having a job that stretched and pushed me far out of all I was familiar with and took me to places I've never thought I'd go . . . ' She shrugged. 'I am happy with what I have here, but a little part of me wonders what I would be doing now if I hadn't come back . . . So now young women, like you and Lizzie . . . I understand your need to go on doing more. You proved that you can, that you are more than capable and should use that rather than retreating to the narrow confines of previous lives.'

'Thank you, I'm glad you understand, though not everyone does – lots of people think women should go back to running a home like they did before. Especially men.'

'What does Alastair think?'

'That it's a good idea. He's going to do the same when he's demobbed, they need doctors as well.'

'I'm very proud of you, you know.' Her mother put her hand on Frankie's arm. 'And your father would have been too.'

Chapter Seventy-two

Winnie gently tucked the blanket around Daisy who had dropped off at the end of her feed, her tummy satisfyingly full, and stood back and admired her little daughter. Since she'd been born nearly four weeks ago, she couldn't get enough of her, spending hours just looking at her, loving her rosebud mouth that sucked in her sleep, her soft downy skin and silky hair, marvelling that she and Mac had brought her into the world. Winnie completely adored her. Trixie clearly thought along the same lines too, and was utterly devoted to the baby, and now lay, as she always did, beside Daisy's cot as she slept.

A yawn crept up on Winnie and with it a longing for some much needed sleep of her own. The lack of sleep was the one thing she found hard, though she should be used to it after working shifts at Station 75, especially during those terrible days when the Blitz was at its peak and getting enough rest was impossible. She glanced at the clock on the chest of drawers. It was a little after six o'clock in the morning, and since she'd been up two other times in the night feeding Daisy, Winnie decided to climb back in bed and get what sleep she could before her daughter woke up again.

The sound of Daisy stirring filtered down into Winnie's dream, pulling her out of her sleep. She took a few moments to gather herself before she opened her eyes, aware that Daisy would get louder and more insistent very quickly if she was hungry again, filling her lungs and making a lot of noise for someone so small. But Daisy didn't get louder. Instantly alert, Winnie sat up and gasped at the sight of her daughter being gently cradled in the arms of Mac.

'Good morning, sleeping beauty.' Mac carried Daisy over to the bed and sat down on the edge of it, leaning over to kiss her.

'How? I mean, when?' Winnie blustered, her head still fuzzy with sleep and the shock of seeing Mac here.

'I arrived about half an hour ago and came in here to find you both fast asleep. I didn't want to wake you, so I've been sitting there,' he nodded towards the chair by Daisy's cot where Winnie sat and fed her. 'She's beautiful, Winnie, just like her mother.' He smiled at her, his eyes bright with tears. 'I can hardly believe we've got a daughter.' He stroked the baby's cheek with one finger, the little girl looking up at him with her wide blue eyes.

'She's real enough and just wait until you hear her yell.'

Mac laughed. 'Likes to make herself heard, just like you! I'm going to have to stand up for myself with two of you in my family.'

'I'm sure you'll manage very well.' Winnie laid her head on his shoulder and the pair of them sat watching their daughter together with Trixie lying close by. It felt as if they were in a perfect bubble of happiness.

'I couldn't wait to come home and see her after I got your letter to say she'd been born. Even before she was born, knowing we were having a child . . . I kept thinking about it, wondering what it was, imagining all the things we could do as he or she got older. It made me really happy to know we were having a baby.'

'I'm sorry I didn't tell you straight away when I found out I was expecting,' Winnie said. 'I thought it was the best thing to do for you and for me.'

Mac moved slightly so that their eyes met. 'I was cross you didn't – you should have. I had every right to know.' He sighed. 'But knowing and loving you, Winnie . . . I soon got over it. You had your reasons and there was nothing I could have done to help you from where I was.' He smiled at her. 'I was thrilled to know we were going to have a child together. It was the best news . . . when it finally came!'

'It's going to be wonderful watching her grow up together.' Winnie snuggled against him again. 'We can start to make plans, you can apply for teaching jobs . . .'

Mac took hold of her hand. 'I'm not back for good yet, Winnie. I only have a seventy-two-hour pass. We're going for more training to be deployed again.'

'Where? The war's o—' She stopped, looking at him. The war wasn't completely over, there was still fighting in the Far East. 'Are they sending you out to pick up soldiers injured by the Japanese now?'

400

Mac nodded. 'It looks like it, but we need training for jungle conditions.'

She put her hand over her mouth, fighting back tears. 'Haven't you done enough?'

Mac shrugged. 'I don't want to go, Winnie, especially now with Daisy here, but I have to. It won't be straight away because of the training, we'll need to be ready, and then it'll take a while to get there.' He gently touched her cheek. 'I know it's not what you wanted to hear, but let's not let it spoil now, I've got two nights here with you both and for that I am grateful. I get to be with my wife and to meet my daughter, what more could a fellow want, eh?'

Chapter Seventy-three

Bella stared at her reflection in the dressing table mirror. She couldn't quite believe it was her, dressed in Station Officer Steele's wedding dress, her hair and make-up done. She was ready to go and marry Stefan.

'Is anything wrong?' Frankie asked, standing beside her, their eyes meeting in their reflections.

She shook her head and smiled at her friend. 'No, I'm just not used to seeing myself dressed up like this and . . .' Bella shrugged. 'I can't quite believe I'm getting married in half an hour.'

'You're not having second thoughts, are you?' Winnie asked from where she sat on the other side of the room, discreetly feeding baby Daisy.

Bella turned around. 'Not at all, I'm nervous . . . excited!'

'I was nervous too, couldn't believe how anxious it made me feel,' Winnie said.

'What!' Frankie said. 'That ain't like you, Winnie.'

Winnie laughed. 'I know, but Trixie sorted me out, didn't you, Trix.' She leaned down and patted the little dog's head, who sat close by her feet, protecting both her mistress and the baby who she was utterly devoted to. 'I sat and cuddled her for a bit and it made me feel a lot better. You could do that as well, Bella. A cuddle from Trixie works wonders.'

'You'd better not, we'll end up with golden hairs on your dress,' Frankie said. 'I'll give you a hug instead.' She put her arms around Bella and gently hugged her, taking care with the lace wedding dress.

Bella hugged her back, glad that her dearest friends were here with her.

Frankie stepped back, putting her hands on Bella's shoulders. 'Better?'

She nodded. 'Everything's changing, it takes some getting used to after us all being together for so long. I'm excited about being married to Stefan, but sad that my life working at Station 75 with you two is over. Winnie's got baby Daisy and you're off with UNRRA soon, Frankie.'

Frankie's blue eyes met hers. 'Nothing stays the same for ever, Bella. Time moves on and we have to as well. What we had at Station 75 will never leave us, we'll always have each other, that's right, ain't it, Winnie?'

'Absolutely.' Winnie stood up, putting Daisy over her shoulder, and came over to them. 'This is just another chapter in our stories, and you know all about stories, Bella, ours will still be woven in together as much as we can make them. We may not work together and see each other every day any more but we will always keep in touch and meet up as often as we can.'

Bella nodded, not daring to speak for fear that she might cry and make the precious mascara that Winnie had so painstakingly applied run down her cheeks.

Frankie put her arms around both of them and hugged them to her, taking care not to squash baby Daisy, who had fallen asleep on her mother's shoulder oblivious to everything apart from her milky dreams.

The bedroom door opened and Rose came in, dressed in her pre-war silk bridesmaid dress – the same one she'd worn for Frankie's wedding. 'Your mother's just arrived, Bella. She . . . ' She frowned at the sight of them. 'Is everything all right?'

Bella looked at Winnie and Frankie, the two of them smiling at her. They would always be an important part of her life and whichever way their individual stories took them, being friends together would be a constant and that thought snuggled around her like a warm blanket on a cold winter's day. She smiled at Rose. 'Yes, everything's fine and I think we're ready to go.'

Winnie stood up as the opening bars of the wedding march suddenly boomed out through the church. She threw a glance at Daisy's pram which she'd parked next to her at the far end of the front pew beside the wall, checking that her daughter was still asleep; she should be as she'd had a good feed and with any luck would sleep it off for an hour or two. Thankfully the music hadn't disturbed her, so she turned and looked past Connie who stood beside her to see Bella, and her mother – who was giving her away as her brother was still in the army and couldn't be here – followed by her bridesmaids, Frankie and Rose, coming down the aisle. Bella looked radiant, the lace wedding dress fitting her slim figure beautifully after Frankie had worked her magic yet again altering it to fit another bride. That dress had been worn by both her and Frankie at their weddings and now it was Bella's turn to marry in it, the three of them grateful for their former boss's generosity in loaning them the wedding dress that she never got to wear because her own fiancé had been killed in the Great War.

Standing waiting for her in the front pew of the groom's side was Stefan and his best man, both looking smart in their air force uniforms. He turned to look at Bella before she reached him and the look of love he gave her brought tears to Winnie's eyes. There was no doubt that he loved her friend very much and knowing Bella as she did, the feeling was mutual. She was happy that after all that had happened to her, the heartache that she'd suffered after James had died, she'd found love again, and with a good man who was worthy of her.

Listening as the parson led Bella and Stefan through their vows, Winnie was taken back to her own wedding day here with Mac. They'd stood in the same places, she'd worn the same dress, made the same promises, been watched by many of the same people who were here today. It was a day she would always treasure, the memory held dear in her heart, and she wished that Mac could have been here with her today as well, but the army still had first claim on him. The war in Europe was over but the one still raging against the Japanese was far from done, and although Mac's unit had been withdrawn from Germany not long after VE Day, they were now in training for a different deployment. The thought caught in her throat and she swallowed hard to dampen it down before it could spoil what was happening now. There was nothing she could do about when or where he'd be sent, but with any luck he'd have some embarkation leave before he left. At least he'd been home since his return from Germany and seen Daisy, whom he'd been enthralled with, and had delighted in his new role as a father. She looked forward to the day when they could all finally be together as a family with the war completely over and the army no longer being in charge of Mac's life. The plan then was for them to go and live in Gloucestershire, not far from Mac's mother, and for him to return to teaching while she looked after Daisy, and she was very happy with that; being with her husband and caring for their daughter was what she wanted to do.

Chapter Seventy-four

'Get ready, here they come!' Violet Steele left her look-out post by the church doors and hurried over to join the guard of honour who were waiting on the steps of St George's church. On one side stood former crew members from Station 75, and on the other Polish and English RAF friends of Stefan's. She'd rounded them up and bustled them out of the church while Bella and Stefan were in the vestry signing the register, and now they stood waiting, ready to form a guard of honour, holding their RAF or Ambulance Service steel helmets high to form an archway.

When Bella and Stefan appeared in the doorway everyone let out a mighty cheer, surprising the bride and groom who beamed with happiness.

'Hurry up, me arm's going to drop off in a minute,' Sparky called out, making everyone laugh.

The newly-weds ducked their heads and obliged,

walking underneath the archway that was a fitting tribute to their work in the Ambulance Service and the RAF, their friends from both services honouring them as they began their married life together.

'They make a lovely couple,' Connie said as she came to stand beside Violet Steele while Bella and Stefan were being photographed on the steps of the church by some of his colleagues. 'I'm so glad that Bella found love again.'

'So am I, he's a good man and will be a good husband to her.' She smiled at Connie. 'I think James would have been happy for her.'

Connie nodded. 'I'm sure he would. I always hoped that he and Bella would marry but . . . ' She shrugged. 'Fate had other plans.'

Violet Steele put her hand on Connie's arm. 'Life's a strange thing, there are no guarantees, so we have to make the most of every day and enjoy what we can.'

They fell into silence for a few moments, watching the bride and groom, with the bridesmaids looking beautiful in their dresses and smiling happily at the camera. To look at Rose, you'd never know what she had been through, and was still going through, Violet Steele thought. The poor girl was still waiting to hear about the fate of her parents under the brutal Nazi regime. Information was slowly filtering out and it was only a matter of time before she would know one way or the other what had happened to them, and until she did she must feel as if she was in limbo, not able to move on, and always hoping that she would be reunited with them.

'Winnie told me that you're planning on going back to Devon,' Connie said.

'That's right, I've got my old teaching job back and start in September.' She smiled. 'I'll be trying to inspire my pupils with a love of history and English once more. It will be rather a drastic change from running a wartime ambulance station.'

'You won't have Winnie to keep on track any more. You were very good at dealing with her. I know she doesn't always agree with rules and regulations and found her own schooldays rather difficult because of that.'

Violet laughed. 'Oh, she bucked against the rules a lot to start with, though, interestingly, giving her responsibility was the best thing to settle her errant ways. We did have a few differences of opinion, but I loved having her as part of my crew and I'm very fond of her.' She looked across to where Winnie was gently jiggling Daisy's pram, the picture of a contented mother.

'And she you. I think she made a wise choice making you one of Daisy's godmothers.'

'I'm delighted to be. I can still be part of Winnie's life and it will be a delight to watch her little girl grow up.' Daisy's christening a few weeks ago had been a great joy to her, joining Frankie and Bella as they made their promises to look out for the little girl, the three of them joined in a precious thing whose origins began at Station 75 when Mac arrived to join the crew.

'How much longer are you in London for?' Connie asked.

'Just a couple of weeks, and then I'm moving down to Devon in the middle of August. I'm going to be living with my sister and two nieces.' She smiled. 'I'm very much looking forward to being with them. And of course, I'll do my best to see Winnie and Daisy as often as I can, and I hope that they'll come and see me in Devon too. I'll be living not far from a lovely beach, it's perfect for building sandcastles.'

Chapter Seventy-five

'This is it!' Bella's brown eyes were bright with tears. 'I don't know when I'll see you again. You will write, won't you?'

Frankie nodded. 'I promise, I will. I won't be gone for ever and as soon as I come back we'll meet up, all of us.' She glanced at Winnie who stood beside her with baby Daisy in her arms, the little girl wide-awake and looking at them with her big blue eyes which were so much like her father's.

'Go on, your new husband's waiting to whisk you away on honeymoon,' Winnie said.

Bella looked over to where Stefan was waiting, talking to some of his Polish airman friends, and as if sensing his new wife's gaze on him, he turned to look at her and smiled.

Frankie put her arms around Bella and hugged her tightly. 'Be happy, my friend. It won't matter where any of us are, we'll always be there for each other, our friendship will never falter.'

Bella nodded and the two of them stood in silence hugging each other for a few moments before they stepped apart.

'Look after yourself out there, Frankie. You won't have me and Winnie to keep an eye on you,' Bella said.

'I will, don't worry.' Frankie gave her friend a gentle push. 'Off you go then, Stefan's waiting.'

Bella smiled. 'I'm going.' She gently kissed baby Daisy's cheek and carefully hugged Winnie, taking care not to crush her friend's daughter. 'Goodbye then.'

Winnie linked her free arm through Frankie's as they watched their friend go down the front steps of Connie's house and join her husband, where they were showered with confetti from other wedding guests standing round near the taxi that was ready to take them to the station. 'We're all going to miss you, you know.'

'And I'll miss you, too, but we'll all be busy – you've got Daisy to look after and Bella's got her new married life and her writing, and I'm sure there'll be plenty to keep me occupied. It's the right thing for me to do now.' Frankie waved as Bella and Stefan's taxi pulled away, the pair of them waving out of the back window until the taxi reached the end of the street and turned out of sight. 'I'd better go and get changed, I'm due to report in an hour's time.'

Upstairs in Bella's bedroom, Frankie changed out of her bridesmaid's dress and into her new UNRRA uniform. It still felt odd to be wearing it after years of the

Ambulance Service uniform, this one looking more like an ATS one: khaki shirt, tunic, skirt and tie, a beret and brown shoes, with the arch-shaped red badge and white-stitched letters spelling out U.N.R.R.A. sewn on the top of her sleeve. She looked at herself in the mirror, tucking stray auburn hairs into the bun she'd put her hair into. She looked different, ready to take on a new role, do something completely out of her experience. Going to work in the displaced persons' camps was going to test her, she knew, but it felt like the right thing to be doing. Joining the Ambulance Service had taught her so much and she'd changed in many ways from the person she was on that first day when she'd walked through the archway into Station 75. She'd seen and done things that she could never have imagined, and she had survived and grown stronger because of them and now she was ready for the next chapter of her story.

Adjusting her beret, she smiled at her reflection and then turned and picked up her suitcase which she'd brought here ready this morning. Going down into the hall below she met Station Officer Steele, or rather Violet as the older woman had instructed them all to call her now that she was no longer their boss.

'Are you ready for the off?' Violet asked.

Frankie nodded. 'I'm all packed, trained and inoculated against various diseases, so I'm as ready as I'll ever be. A bit nervous, I must admit, but no second thoughts, this is what I should be doing.'

Violet put her hand on Frankie's arm. 'I think you're doing the right thing, and I'm very proud of you. I hope you'll write to me when you have time, I'd very much like to hear how you are getting on.'

'I will. I've got lots of people to write to, but I think I'll need that connection with the outside to help me deal with the job and it will be a pleasure to get letters back from you all. Everyone's going to be busy getting on with their new lives. My only worry is Rose, I feel bad leaving her. My neighbour, Josie, has promised to look out for her while she waits to hear about her parents.'

Rose was staying on living at number 25 Matlock Street, and now had a job working in an office in the city. Her plans for the future depended on the fate of her parents, with the hope that they were alive and that they could be reunited either here in England or perhaps Austria, but until confirmation came that they'd survived, Rose didn't know in which direction her future lay and in the meantime would stay here.

'I'll be keeping in touch with her as well and keeping a watch out wherever I'm sent in case they're there, and I know that Connie's doing her best to help her try and find out any news through the Red Cross. Winnie's still here in London till Mac comes home, and Bella, of course, will keep in touch, too.

She won't be alone, Frankie, all of us will keep an eye on her for you.'

She nodded. 'Thank you. And you'll be going back to teaching, are you looking forward to it?'

'I am.' Violet smiled. 'I feel like I'm returning with a renewed enthusiasm. I miss my work at Station 75 and all of you crew, but it was a huge responsibility and it will be nice to only have to worry about lessons rather than sending people out under falling bombs. And living with my sister and nieces is going to be rather lovely.'

'Frankie! There you are, I was beginning to think you'd sneaked off without saying goodbye.' Winnie came out of the sitting room, with Daisy on her shoulder.

'I wouldn't do that, or I'd never hear the end of it.' Frankie looked at Violet who winked back at her. 'But I do have to go now. I mustn't be late or I'll miss the transport out.'

'Good luck, Frankie.' Violet kissed her cheek. 'Take care of yourself.'

'I will.'

'Come on, we'll walk you to the door.' Winnie put her arm through Frankie's and they set off across the black and white tiled hall towards the front door but stopped halfway across when Rose came hurrying out of the sitting room.

'Frankie, are you going now?' Rose looked close to tears.

Frankie opened her arms and the younger girl hurried into them. 'I'm going to miss you.'

She hugged her tightly. 'And I'll miss you too, but I'll be back.'

'Come and wave her off with us,' Winnie said.

Standing on the doorstep of Connie's house, with the July sunshine shining down on the white stonework of the street, Frankie looked at her friends: Winnie with baby Daisy, Rose and Violet, all of them very dear to her, and for a few seconds she almost felt like changing her mind, not going and just staying here in London so that they could still be part of her life, but that wouldn't be right in the end. Sometimes you had to push yourself, even when you felt scared about doing something new. She'd done it before when she joined the Ambulance Service and now she was ready to do that again, with UNRRA. It would take her to places she'd never been and to see sights that would shock and humble her, but she, Frankie Munro, was ready.

She smiled at her friends. 'Goodbye then. Write to me and I promise I'll write back, tell you what I'm doing.'

'Not so fast, you haven't given me a hug goodbye.' Winnie quickly gave baby Daisy to Violet and threw her arms around Frankie, squeezing her tightly. 'Goodbye, dear friend and fellow conspirator of Station 75.' When she stepped back, Winnie's grey eyes were bright with tears. 'Right, off you go now ...' Her voice wavered. 'Just you make sure you come back and see us just as soon as you can.'

'I promise I will.' Frankie picked up her suitcase and with a final glance at her friends she walked down the steps and set off to the end of the street. Aware that they were still watching her she stopped and turned around and waved to them, smiling as they waved back, and then she walked away towards her future, so grateful that she'd made that step of leaving the comfort of sewing uniforms back in the first year of the war to fulfil her dream of becoming an ambulance driver. It had been the best thing she'd ever done, bringing her good friends, a loving husband and whole new world ahead of her.

Letter from Rosie

Dear Reader,

I hope you've enjoyed this book and finding out what happens to Winnie, Frankie and Bella as their time at Station 75 comes to an end.

It's hard to say goodbye to them having spent three years living with them in my head, thinking about what will happen to them and writing their story. I've loved getting to know them and seeing their lives unfold as they were faced with different challenges both in their personal and their working lives. I'm going to miss them very much.

Working out how to end the story for them was tricky, especially for Frankie as I felt she needed to do something more and not just go back to wait for Alastair to come home, so when I discovered the work of UNRRA I knew that it was the perfect thing for her to do. I imagine her working for them for several years and Alastair joining her to offer his medical expertise once he's demobbed from the army. When they return home again, perhaps they'll . . . I leave that for you to decide.

As for Bella, I imagine her going on to be a successful writer and living very happily with Stefan who continues his role in the Royal Air Force.

Winnie will be an excellent mother but involving herself in her community as she is never one to not be busy, while Mac will return to his teaching having never been sent out to the Far East as the war finished before he'd completed the training.

With Rose, I couldn't decide on her fate, realistically knowing that so many people perished in the Holocaust and yet knowing some did survive. I hope that Rose's parents might be some of the fortunate ones that lived to be reunited with their family.

Beyond that I'm undecided how the girls' lives would pan out. I'd love to know what ideas you have on how their futures might go.

Thank you so much for reading and loving the East End Angels series, it has been such a delight to hear from readers who have enjoyed getting to know Winnie, Frankie and Bella. One of the best things about writing these books has been sharing it with you all.

I love hearing from readers — it's one of the greatest joys of being a writer, so please do get in touch via my Facebook page — Rosie Hendry Books, Twitter @hendry_rosie or my website www.rosiehendry.com, where you can sign up for my newsletter and get all the latest news about my writing life and books.

If you have the time and would like to share your thoughts about this book, do please leave a review, I read *and appreciate each one and it's wonderful to hear what you think of the story.*

Watch out for Station 75 reappearing briefly again in my new series, as the main character, Thea, is an old friend of Station Officer Steele and I have plans for her to go and see her pal at some point, and I'm sure I won't be able to resist Winnie, Frankie and Bella putting in an appearance there either!

With warmest wishes,
Rosie

ACKNOWLEDGEMENTS

Every time I write the acknowledgements at the end of a book it gives me time to pause and think back over the journey of the book, how it started and what went into it as it grew. Although I work out the story and write the words many other people help me along the way and without them it wouldn't all come together into this book. I am grateful to each and every one of them for their help and support.

My fantastic editor, Maddie West, is a constant source of calm support and advice, who gently pushes me to bring out the best in the story, seeing things that I can't because I'm too close to it.

Felicity Trew, my brilliantly supportive and encouraging agent, is such a star and having her watching over me and holding my hand is a great privilege.

The team at Sphere are tremendous at producing a beautiful book and sending it out into the world – thank you to Tamsyn Berryman, Liz Hatherall, Bekki Guyatt, Clara Diaz, Sophia Walker and Brionee Fenlon.

No historical novel can be written without research and I owe a great deal of thanks to the Imperial War Museum for access to their brilliant archives and to Norfolk Library Service for supplying many books.

Huge thanks to Clare Marchant for so generously sharing her experience of childbirth with me and for patiently answering my questions – I hope I got it right in Winnie's birth scene – you were the inspiration behind it.

Thank you to Shirley Blair for her help with researching freelance writers selling their stories to *The People's Friend* magazine during the 1940s – it gave me the knowledge I needed for Bella's writing career to blossom.

Writing can be a lonely business sitting working on your own most of the time so my dear friends in the Norfolk & Suffolk RNA chapter, Clare, Heidi-Jo, Jenni, Pam *et al* and in the Strictly Saga group are a great source of fun, laughter and advice. I'm so lucky to have you all in my life – thank you all.

Thank you to all the readers and bloggers who have shared and loved Winnie, Frankie and Bella's journey along with me. It has been a delight to share it with you.

Finally, thank you, as always, to David for his love and unwavering support.